Praise

Tangle was a fabulous book. Through battles and plot twists, I kept wanting to read more. And a warning to all future readers: this book is very hard to put down.

—**Gavin Montgomery**, age 10

Brock Eastman's writing reflects his personality: full of life, full of truth, and most likely to hold your attention to the very last moment.

— **Donita K. Paul**, Author, The DragonKeeper Chronicles and Realm Walkers Series

The Quest for Truth series is an entertaining fusion of archaeological mystery and space adventure. It's *Indiana Jones* meets *Star Wars*—but with family values and spiritual truth as its warp core. The first three volumes kept me reading . . . sometimes far past my bedtime! *Tangle* is a satisfying addition to the sequence.

—**Jeremiah W. Montgomery,** Author, The Dark Harvest Trilogy

Wow! *Tangle* has left me wanting more. As a father and bookstore manager, I'm glad that there still is good, clean kids' fiction. I highly recommend The Quest for Truth series.

—**Chris McCormick**, Manager, LifeWay Christian Stores

Read this before your friends do. Full of twists, this action-packed installment in The Quest for Truth is sure to be your favorite.

—**Jerel Law**, Author, Son of Angels Series

Just when I thought The Quest for Truth couldn't get more exciting, along came *Tangle!* Book 4 is the best yet, with mysteries unfolding in ways my children and I never imagined. Above all, I love hearing my kids' excitement about the Wikk family's spiritual discoveries. Brock Eastman has outdone himself once again!

—**Ann Hibbard**, Senior Editor, Home Educating Family Association

TANGLE

THE QUEST FOR TRUTH

TANGLE

THE FOURTH ADVENTURE IN
THE QUEST FOR TRUTH

BROCK EASTMAN

P U B L I S H I N G

P.O. BOX 817 • PHILLIPSBURG • NEW JERSEY 08865-0817

ISBN: 978-1-59638-248-0 (pbk)
ISBN: 978-1-62995-213-0 (ePub)
ISBN: 978-1-62995-214-7 (Mobi)

Printed in the United States of America

Library of Congress Control Number: 2015946124

To my Elsie Mae:

Your smile could light up the darkest place.
Your beautiful eyes melt my heart.
Your sweet kisses and hugs bring me happiness.
Your graceful dance delights.

You are certainly a princess of our King.
I'm blessed to call you mine.
I love you.

And, yes, I will cuddle you a bit longer.

Contents

Acknowledgments

A few well-deserved thanks.

Ashley, my love, we did it again: another book complete. Thanks for putting up with my crazy, sporadic writing habits. Thanks for letting me chase after this dream. I hope you enjoy the character bearing your name; she's getting a spotlight in this book.

Kinley, you've grown up so much, and you're always telling me that you're growing bigger every day, while I'm growing littler. I sure wish it worked that way. It was exciting to celebrate with you as you chose to ask Jesus into your heart. Mommy and Daddy are so excited for you and the journey ahead. I'm excited to see how God uses your desire to be a leader for Him.

Elsie Mae, Mommy and Daddy have found that you're an entertainer. You love to dance, act, and sing. Whatever God has in store for you, I pray you'll always use your talents for Him. I love how you start your nightly prayer, "Dear God," but it sounds like *Gawd*. And, yes, I shall always ask you, "Why are you so cute?"

Waverly, my little laughter bug, you are a delight to hold and to tickle, always watching the world around you and always excited to see me. As you run to me and I scoop you up, you giggle wildly. If ever I need a smile, I simply need to look at you.

Declan Grey, we may still be very outnumbered (four girls), but you're going to be such a great daddy and husband someday because of it. I'm excited about the adventure of growing you into a man of God.

Mom and Dad, thanks for your continued support of my writing. Thanks for always being willing to drop everything and come to see us in Colorado if we need you. We love you and miss you.

Ty, Tiff, Autumn, Maddie, Hadley, and Beckett Knapp, thanks for your love and encouragement. And thank you, Sis, for letting me use your name for one of the characters.

Mom and Dad Mullen, thank you for your encouragement—and for your visits to Colorado.

Andrew and Emily, it's nice to have family in Colorado. We're so excited that you made the move here.

My family—grandparents, aunts, uncles, and cousins—thank you for all your support and encouragement along the way. I know we don't get to see you as often as we would like, but it's a comfort to know that you're praying for my family.

Cherith F., thanks again for your willingness to support the series. Your design and marketing has helped to get TQ4T into more hands.

Laura S., all your comments and notes on the manuscript really helped to bring the story to life. Your insight and attention to detail tightened the plot and flow of the story. Our readers have you to thank.

Bryce and Melissa C., your continued support and direction for the series is an encouragement to me. Thank you.

Amanda M., thank you for your patience and guidance through the editing of *Tangle*. Wow, this one was the hardest by far. There were a few times I wasn't sure it was ever going to get done. Thank you for pushing me forward.

Aaron G., as always, thank you for bringing the manuscript across the finish line. And thanks for always providing me with the artwork and illustrations when I misplace them. They are a great help to me as I write.

To the amazing team at P&R—Ian T., Jan P., Kim M., Charles C., Sam C.—thank you for your support and work on TQ4T. I know you all are doing so much behind the scenes to get these books into the hands of readers. Thank you.

Chris T., thank you again for the amazing cover design. The template you created for The Quest for Truth is just perfect, and it's proven true as it's been applied to each of the books.

Brandon D., your artwork always inspires me. I look at these covers again and again in awe of the wonderful talent God gave you. Thank you for working on this series and bringing your quality, creativity, and expertise to each cover.

Johnny B. and Marty D., you both brought Tangle's visual glossary to life with your illustrations.

#Questers: Katelyn W., Sierra B., Alyse P., Rachel F., Josh D., Matthew (TheStiletto) T., Rebecca R. L., Benjamin P., Rebecca P., Luke M., thanks to each of you for your support and research. The documentation you all have created and are continuing to create has been such an amazing help to me as I write. How awesome it's been for me to shoot out an e-mail with a question and to have you get the answers back to me within minutes. You are an amazing crew, and I am thankful for each of you and the time and attention you have put into the series. One more book to go!

To our Creator, I couldn't have done any of this without You. I look back in awe at the life You've given me and the path You've set before me. I am thankful for every moment You give and for the wonderful people You have surrounded me with. I'm thankful for Your grace that covered even a sinner like me. Thank You.

4.0

Prologue

The winter wind swept flurries around the man as he trudged through the knee-high snow. The forest thinned, and a plain covered in heavy drifts of snow lay before him. A wall of blue steam rose from a lava river at the far edge, turning the snow closest to it into slush. It cloaked the entrance to the secret valley: a door hiding answers that the man hoped would finally end his search.

He paused before taking his next step—a step that would expose him to any onlooker. He could have sent his soldiers, but he knew that uncovering this secret would take more than brute strength and powerful weapons. Research had made it clear that the only way to learn this secret was from the people who held it—the Gläubigen. Many times before, they had escaped when threatened, taking with them the information he sought. He'd seen the ruins of their past settlements. Only he and a few other top officials knew of the remnant of these people, now living just beyond the blue curtain of cloud. And if the Gläubigen truly had the knowledge he sought, the man didn't trust any of his comrades to return and share the answer to his lifelong quest. Although they were united by a single goal, their alliance was a fragile one. He still wasn't

17

sure that their loyalties went further than discovering the secret for themselves.

This was the moment. He had with him only a few essentials that a traveler might have, but none of his regular comforts or any markings that might reveal his true identity. The outfit itself was secondhand, as the bite of chill wind on his skin reminded him.

A handful of razor-thin electronic components were sewn into the lining of his outer jacket. With these pieces, he would build a communication transponder to send and receive simple messages in an ancient code called Morse. These transmissions would be picked up and sent by a discreet beacon circling the planet high above. There was to be strict communication silence until he called for extraction, except for a brief update every six months—or news if his men discovered a clue of dire significance. Until then, he would remain a resident in his new home.

He was ready for a long mission. Secretly he welcomed the break from the rigorous searching and exploring that had yet to yield anything significant. If something was discovered while he was gone, his men had orders to break silence and retrieve him immediately.

He looked toward the sky one last time, at dark gray clouds laden with snow. He'd better get in before the next blizzard struck. He stepped into the open and started across the plain, dragging his feet as if weary from days in the cold forest. He could hear the waterfall ahead and the sizzle of water and lava below. He fell to the ground by the edge of the chasm and let out a desperate moan.

The wind howled in response and dusted him with new snow. A fleeting thought crossed his mind that his men had gotten the location wrong.

He moaned again, his voice echoing around him. Then it came: the creaking of a pulley. Two wooden poles broke through the steam and rested on solid stone a dozen feet away. *The end of a bridge?* He heard hooves galloping toward him. Two riders armed with bows leaped from their horses and approached. Three more men stepped out of the steam.

The man fought back a victorious smile and groaned. A blue hand grasped his shoulder and lifted him to his knees.

"Feng, is he alive?" a soldier asked.

"Yes. But we must get him in before the blizzard hits."

The foot soldiers came forward and lifted him on their shoulders, then hurried back toward the bridge and across it. The two horsemen followed. The moment they were all across, a horn blew and the bridge began to rise.

He was in. His mission could officially begin.

Archeos
Security
Brief

Case 07.06.20.15

Funding by

Archeos Personnel

Elliot Wikk

Laura Wikk

Oliver Wikk

Tiff Wikk

Mason Wikk

Austin Wikk

MISSING

★ THE ARCHEOS ALLIANCE

Archeos Personnel

Rand McGregor

Jenn McGregor

Ashley McGregor

Rich Hixby

Phillip Skalker

MISSING

THE ARCHEOS ALLIANCE

Suspects

Phelan O'Farrell

Recently linked to Corsairs

Last seen with Wikk children
on Jahr des Eises

Captain Vedrick

Stalking Wikks and McGregors
over last year

Potential connections to the
Übel society

Red Cloak

Identified in recently
obtained security footage

Constant proximity to Wikks
and McGregors

Awaken

Mrs. Wikk leaned over Mason, a cold wet cloth in her hand. She slid it across his forehead. What a wonderful dream. He was with his mom.

"Mason," she said, a tear rolling down her cheek. She brushed back his bangs. "My sweet son, you're finally awake."

His breath caught. He wasn't dreaming? "Mom? Is it—really you?"

"It is." She looked away. "Elliot, come quick," she said, her voice laden with urgency.

Mason's dad came into view.

"Dad?" Mason started to push himself up but fell back.

"Son, just rest. You've been out for several hours. You need to recover," Mr. Wikk said. His dad's eyes glistened. Mason couldn't recall the last time he'd seen his dad cry. "You were stunned multiple times."

Mason's mom's cheeks flushed with anger at the words.

Mason had thought for the briefest of moments that perhaps everything that had happened—the Übel, the Corsairs—had all been nothing more than a bad nightmare and that he was finally waking up.

Instead, it was true. All the past days' events had happened. Mason shivered, and his mom tucked his covers beneath his chin.

"Where is everyone?" he asked.

"Your brothers and sister escaped," his mom said.

"We're on the *Skull*," his dad added.

Mason's memory was foggy, his thoughts jumbled. He recalled the large room of the cathedral and the invasion of the soldiers. They'd attacked; he'd tried to rescue Obbin. Now he was a prisoner of the "darkness," as Sister Dorothy had described the Übel.

At least he was with his parents. He had so much to ask and tell them.

"What about Obbin?"

"He's in another cabin down the corridor. Most of his family is here," Mason's dad said. "Nice people."

"They told us about your visit," his mom said.

A sense of guilt flooded Mason as he remembered the valley. Austin and his arrival and departure had attracted the Übel's attention to Obbin's home.

The intercom buzzed. "Minus three hours until destination." The intercom beeped and went silent.

Mason's eyes slid shut. He forced them back open, fighting a sudden onslaught of sleepiness. "Where are they taking us?"

"A place called the Valley of Shadows," his mom explained. "The king of the Blauwe Mensen insists that there should have been twelve crosses at the location and that we will need all of them for the quest."

Crosses? Truth? Memories were surfacing. The Valley of Shadows sounded oddly familiar.

"Vedrik still won't admit that he followed us there, kidnapped Hixby and Skalker, and stole the crosses right from under our noses," Mason's dad said.

"Maybe he didn't," said Mason's mom. "I don't think Hixby and Skalker were seeking the place of our origin. They might have sold the crosses' locations to someone else."

Mason's dad shook his head. "I'm telling you, those two were solid, Laura. They weren't treasure hunters."

"I never trusted them," she said. "Not after they forced their way into our expedition."

"*Forced* is a strong word," Mason's dad said. "Though you're right: they did invite themselves."

Mason tried to keep his eyes open as his parents debated. His eyelids were heavy, but he didn't want to sleep; he wanted to analyze the clues with his parents and learn about their past week with the Übel.

"So there are more crosses at this valley?" he asked.

"The king insists that there are twelve hidden crosses," his mom said. "Our original map only showed seven. We attempted to access four of them, but in the end only reached two."

"The king had some books, *The Chronicles of Terra Originem,* that mentioned the valley," his dad added.

"I've heard of those," Mason said. "Obbin's brother Rylin took the books so he could trade them."

His mom smiled. "The missing prince has the missing books."

Mason imagined that the Blauwe Mensen were worried about Rylin. He was only slightly older than Obbin.

"And we found some paintings with a hidden map of the valley," Mason added. "We were copying it onto an e-papyrus."

"Did you see how many chambers might have contained crosses?" his dad asked.

Mason frowned. "We hadn't gotten that far. We didn't have the e-journal, and we were trying to find information in books that we'd recovered from the libraries on Evad and Jahr des Eises."

His mom patted his shoulder. "That's okay. This information will help get back some of the king's credibility with Zebra Xavier."

"Why?" Mason asked.

"An Übel tactical team was sent back to the Cobalt Gorge, but they were unable to find the books in the library. Vedrik accused the king of setting a trap for his men." Mason's dad smiled. "The Übel finally got some of their own medicine."

"What do you mean?" asked Mason.

"Two Übel soldiers on the mission were captured by the Blauwe Mensen. The Übel also lost one of their shuttles," his dad said. "This time the Blauwe Mensen were ready when the Übel arrived. It sounds like it was a pretty fierce fight."

Mason was glad the Blauwe Mensen had fought back with some success. Outgunned and out-teched, they still had plenty of courage.

"If there were twelve crosses, that would leave five in the valley," Mason's mom said.

"*If* Vedrik extracted crosses from all the marked chambers and found the one we started to remove," Mason's dad said. "But we don't know if the crosses were still in each location. They could have been removed prior to our expedition."

"And if Vedrik isn't admitting how many he has, then we don't know how many remain," Mason said.

"Assuming that he has any at all," Mason's mom said.

"The Archeos extraction team saw the *Vulture* swoop in and attempt to extract at least four crosses before our men were evacuated," his dad said.

"We don't know if the *Vulture* belongs to the Übel," Mason's mom said. "We've been with the Übel for a week now, and not once have we even heard them mention the *Vulture.*"

"That doesn't mean it's not running another mission else-where," Mr. Wikk said.

"Fair point. But I don't see why Vedrik wouldn't admit to having the crosses if he actually did have them," his mom said.

"He could be holding back to use this to his advantage."

"He's been awfully straightforward with us on the expeditions."

Mr. Wikk took his wife's hand. "You may be right. The captain is on a short leash. Zebra Xavier has warned him that he doesn't have time for lies that cause delays."

"Captain Vedrik seems like a puppy compared to a wolf like Zebra Xavier," his mom said.

Mason's dad laughed. "Now you're just teasing me."

Mrs. Wikk squeezed her husband's hand. "We've got to keep smiling, don't we?"

Mason's dad put his free arm around his wife and kissed her forehead. "Yes, we do."

It was nice to see his parents in good spirits, and Mason was interested to hear what their interactions with the captain had been like. Vedrik was indeed as cruel as he'd been when Mason had run into him on Evad and Enaid. How much more evil must Zebra Xavier be, if a man like Vedrik was a puppy compared to him? Mason knew his mom was exaggerating, but it sounded like Zebra Xavier unsettled Vedrik, and Mason was sure that Vedrik wasn't easily intimidated.

Again Mason's eyes began to slide shut; his spurt of adrenaline was waning. He asked another question to keep himself awake. "So we're headed to the valley without the books, even though Vedrik doesn't trust the king?"

"Zebra Xavier overrode Vedrik's decision," his dad said.

"And we've been piecing together other materials and artifacts that were recovered," his mom explained. "We believe we have created a nearly complete map."

"So we're going to explore the Valley of Shadows?" asked Mason.

"That's the last we were told," Mason's mom said.

"Vedrik trusts us less every day," Mason's dad said, ruffling Mason's hair. "We haven't exactly been good allies."

Mason surged with pride. His parents had been fighting against the darkness also. They'd just used different tactics.

"We couldn't sabotage them too badly, or we risked losing you," his mom said. "We only needed to stall them long enough to ensure that the four of you had the information you needed to continue the search."

"What about when they destroyed the basin on Evad?" Mason asked.

His mom turned away.

"Son, that was the *scariest* moment of our lives," Mason's dad admitted. He placed a sturdy hand on his wife's shoulder as a sob escaped her lips. "Vedrik used it as a warning to us to make sure we started helping. We expect that he knew you were safe but wanted us to believe otherwise to show what he was capable of."

It was hard for Mason to hear his mom cry. He reached out and took her hand. "I love you, Mom. I'm glad I'm with you."

Mrs. Wikk smiled at him and wiped a tear from her eye.

"We're glad we found you," Mr. Wikk said. "We'll get your sister and brothers back soon—don't you worry."

Mason smiled. "I know." He yawned as he started to lose the fight with sleep. "How will Oliver and Tiffany and Austin find . . ."

Everything went dark; Mason couldn't stay awake any longer.

4.2

Rescue

The red numbers ticked down: nine minutes now until they'd exit hyper flight. The flashing red numbers were like a gate holding Oliver back from rescuing Ashley. The zero seemed an eternity away.

Austin's footsteps echoed in the corridor as he returned from his mission to locate exploration suits that might withstand the corrosive atmosphere of their destination. "I found some suits with a high MCRR."

"MCRR?" asked Tiffany.

"Maximum Corrosion Resistance Rating," Austin explained. "I read it on the label. The suits don't look especially flexible."

"Can you get one ready? I want to get going as soon as we land," Oliver said.

"We can't let corrosive gases get into the *Phoen*—the *Eagle*," Tiffany said. "You'll need to put the ATC in place."

"ATC?" asked Austin.

"Atmospheric Transfer Chamber," Tiffany said. "I thought I'd use an acronym too."

"Nice, sis," Austin said. "Can you show me how to work the chamber?"

"You have just eight minutes, so hurry," Oliver warned.

The two were already jogging out of the bridge.

Oliver took the e-journal from Tiffany's seat and tapped the screen. He typed in *McGregor*. A series of files came up, and he clicked on a picture of Ashley and her parents, Rand and Jenn. He stared at the girl he'd known nearly all his life and experienced many adventures with.

He'd felt different somehow when he'd seen her alone in the cell on the *Black Ranger*. The same feeling had rallied to the surface when he'd heard her voice on the distress call. She was in danger, and he wanted to rescue her.

A glowing orange planet, Ledram, dwarfed their destination: the small, hazy green moon of Cixot, a moon known for its highly corrosive atmosphere. Ledram was uninhabitable and posed a serious threat to any nearby spaceships. According to information in the NavCom, large, unpredictable explosions from its molten lava surface launched daily barrages of flaming rocks and plasma into space. These were capable of taking out the largest of spaceships.

When Tiffany had read the information aloud earlier, it had shaken the three Wikks. They were already stressed about Ashley's situation, but now they knew they were competing against an explosive neighboring planet. Still, the three were united in their resolve to rescue Ashley.

The countdown read seven minutes.

Oliver and Tiffany had tried to determine if the *Eagle*'s exterior would hold up on the moon. It was the sort of thing Mason could have figured out in no time. The computers on the *Eagle* had estimated a 60 percent chance that the *Eagle*'s exterior would hold up, *if* the ship were on the planet for less than three hours.

A boulder seemed to be rolling around in Oliver's stomach. It grew worse when Oliver thought about Ashley sitting alone in an escape capsule. *How long has she been there? Is the exterior of the pod holding up? Is it beginning to deteriorate? Is it too late?* Oliver took a deep breath and cast the ideas aside. The only solution was to get to Ashley quickly.

Oliver jogged down the corridor and stopped on the landing atop the stairs. The ATC covered the smaller of the two hatches.

Austin stood on a hover ladder, a Magnilox in his hand. "The top latch won't lock."

"I'll get it. You two get situated on the bridge. Five minutes." Oliver took three stairs at a time as his siblings raced past him.

He climbed the ladder and waved the Magnilox over the latch. It didn't budge. He lifted his foot and kicked it. The hinge shifted. He kicked the latch again, and it moved over the hook. He waved the Magnilox and heard the latch click into place. A loose latch could weaken the seal and allow the oxygen-rich air of the *Eagle* to escape or the dangerous air of Cixot to get in.

Two minutes remained as Oliver made his way to the bridge and took the pilot's seat. "Everyone ready?"

"Yes," his siblings said in unison.

Tiffany had reclaimed the e-journal. Oliver blushed. Had he closed the picture of Ashley? If he hadn't, what would his sister think? Ashley and Tiffany were best friends, inseparable at Bewaldeter.

Oliver shook off the concern. He had to focus on the landing and the rescue, not on his sister's opinion of him.

He ran his fingers across the screen, checking and rechecking. Everything from a systems perspective looked fine. He hoped this would be another smooth landing.

The *Eagle* dropped out of hyper flight. The straps of Oliver's harness dug into his chest. He and his siblings had done this so many times in the past few days, yet Oliver still had a bit of anxiety at the controls when landing.

The titanium heat shields slid out of sight, revealing two globes floating in the pure blackness of space: Cixot and Ledram.

"Impact alert!" the computer's voice echoed overhead.

Oliver saw it, a huge twisted heap of burned metal. He twisted the controls and the *Eagle* spun right. Then he pressed forward, diving the ship.

"Impact alert!" the computer repeated.

Oliver shifted left as a long metal boom sliced toward them. There was a screech across the top of the bridge.

"Impact!" the computer said. Then nothing.

Oliver exhaled a breath he'd held since the first alert.

Tiffany was searching the NavCom. "No major damage reported."

"That was close," Austin said. "What *was* it?"

"Looked like a space platform of some sort," Oliver said.

"Or it was a thermal harvesting station," Tiffany said. "The Federation once tried to harvest the heat from Ledram to produce power. The projectiles destroyed all the stations within a month."

"Yikes," Austin said. "And we'll be within range for how long?"

"As long as it takes to rescue Ashley," Oliver said.

"Right," Austin said.

They were all quiet for a moment. They knew what they had to do, no matter the risks.

"Tiffany, still no contact with the escape pod?" Oliver asked urgently.

"No, but it'll be easier when we're closer," Tiffany said. "The landing may have damaged the receivers on the pod, making long-range communication impossible."

"Do we have the exact location of the pod?" Oliver asked.

"Yes. The coordinates are locked in the NavCom. We just can't pick up a com signal," Tiffany explained.

Oliver took a breath. "Any . . . any signs of life?" The question seemed cold, and he avoided looking toward his sister. He didn't mean it emotionlessly.

She looked at him, her eyes glassy. "I can't tell." This was hard for her too. "The location beacon doesn't deliver any sort of information on the passengers . . ." Her voice cut out.

"I just wish we could communicate with her," Oliver said.

"I might be able to tap into the escape pod systems now that we're out of hyper flight," Austin suggested.

"Really?" asked Tiffany hopefully.

Austin shrugged. "Yeah, why not? I've overridden a few systems in the past."

Oliver and Tiffany both eyed their brother curiously.

"Nothing illegal," he assured them.

Oliver remembered how the temperatures in his room had fluctuated to extremes the last time he'd been on break from the Academy. Austin and Mason had wanted Oliver to take them camping near the chasm behind their house. He'd said no—until his room had become unbearable to sleep in and he'd decided he might as well. Coincidentally, the next day the temperature controls in his room had worked again.

Oliver sighed. "Austin, go ahead and do what you can do. Tiff, you two swap spots so he can work on it while we land." Austin glowed at taking the copilot's seat.

"Prepare for atmospheric entry. Visibility will likely be low; I'll be using the information our scanners provide." The screens before him buzzed with data.

Sweeping tendrils of green haze swirled, looking ready to entangle the *Eagle* and crush it.

"High atmospheric toxicity levels," Tiffany said.

The *Eagle* cruised toward the outer edge of the moon's atmosphere. Oliver took a look at Ledram, which was glowing orange off to their left side. He saw flashes of yellow and orange on the surface and hoped they weren't projectile-launching explosions.

"Escape pod signal located," Austin said.

"Can you crack in?" Tiffany asked.

"Not yet," Austin replied.

Oliver gripped the controls. "I'm putting the shields back over the windows as a precaution."

"Good idea," Tiffany said. "Windshield material might not withstand the toxicity."

The silver shields slid into place and locked with a click. Oliver concentrated on the consoles showing a graphically simulated display of the world before him. The video feed was useless in the thick green clouds.

"Ten seconds until entry," Oliver said.

The ship bucked as the countdown struck zero. Several storage compartments flew open, spilling their contents.

"Whoa!" Tiffany said. "Is everything okay?"

It wasn't. The ship rocked side to side, then dropped quickly, only to lift back up, pressing the three Wikks hard into their seats. Oliver held tight to the controls, but the sudden jerks made it difficult. It was like riding waves in a boat.

The *Eagle*'s altitude had started at 180,000 feet from the moon's surface, but now they were dropping a thousand feet per second—far too fast.

Oliver adjusted the thrusters to slow the descent. Still they dropped.

"What's wrong?" asked Austin.

A warning flashed across the screen, and the computerized voice spoke, "Surface Impact. One minute fifteen seconds until impact with planet surface."

Either the gas makeup of the atmosphere wasn't allowing the engines to create enough lift, or else the gravity of the moon was too powerful. None of the information they'd read about Cixot had warned of this.

The ship spun onto its back.

"Oliver!" yelled Tiffany. "You've got to slow our descent!"

Oliver twisted the controls, righting the ship. "I'm trying! I can't get any lift."

The red countdown to impact showed fifty-nine seconds. They were still dropping a thousand feet a second.

The *Eagle* shook violently. A deafening roar echoed in the bridge.

"Approaching terminal speed," the computer warned. "Ship structural integrity failure threshold reached."

"The ship's going to rip apart!" shouted Austin.

An outline of the ship flashed red. What could Oliver do?

"Oliver!" Tiffany cried out.

"I'm trying." The *Eagle* shook so fiercely that Oliver couldn't hold on to the controls or even retake them.

"Forty-five seconds until impact with planet surface," the computer warned.

"We've got to eject," Austin cried.

"Then we'll be stranded too," Oliver said.

"That, or we're dead!" Austin yelled.

Oliver's hand moved toward an icon labeled *Emergency Ejection.*

What would happen if he touched it? Would they blast out individually? Without spacesuits, they would suffocate in seconds. Would the bridge seal off like a capsule? Many ships were built that way, but the *Eagle* seemed to be older than the ones Oliver knew. He didn't know what would happen.

Oliver's breaths were quick and labored.

Suddenly, the ship blasted upward. The movement was so sudden and powerful that the safety harness dug painfully into his legs. A ripping noise resounded outside the *Eagle*. Fear surged over Oliver; his chest tightened.

He saw his sister flying upward. She'd come out of her seat. There was nothing he could do to save her.

This was it. The *Eagle* was ripping apart around them.

"Rescuer . . ."

4.3

Alive Again

A soft light glowed overhead, bathing him in white.

"Mom?" he called out softly.

"I'm here." A comforting face appeared over him. "Your friend came to check on you."

A bright blue face with green spiky hair appeared beside his mom's. "Hi, Mason. I'm Branz, in case you don't remember."

"I remember." Mason pushed himself up on his elbows. The Blauwe Mensen prince wore brown leather pants and an open vest of the same material. "How's Obbin?"

"He's awake. Dad's practically holding him down in his bed. He doesn't want to rest anymore. He wants to find you and take on the Übel." Branz let out an uncomfortable laugh.

"That sounds about right."

"I can't blame him. I want to take them on too. But I've seen our situation, and he hasn't yet."

Mason thought of the men he had faced on Evad. They weren't all that intimidating. Hadn't the Blauwe Mensen captured several of the Übel soldiers, with only spears as weapons? Maybe there was some hope.

"Mom, can I see Obbin?" Mason asked.

His mom sighed. "You can, but don't push yourself. You're not fully recovered yet."

Mason pressed himself up into a sitting position. He felt woozy and had a dull headache. "Where's Dad?"

"He was summoned to meet with Zebra Xavier. I was allowed to stay because of your condition," his mom explained.

Mason slid his legs over the edge of the bed. They felt numb, shaky. He put weight on them. His mom stood on one side, Branz on the other.

"Take your time, honey," she said.

Mason took a deep breath. He felt twinges of pain across the surface of his body, but not internally. He wore only a pair of gray pants. Bandages covered spots all across his bare skin.

"What are all these?" he asked.

His mom scowled, her anger evident. "Burns. Those are where you were hit with stun shots."

"Obbin has at least as many," Branz added. "The soldiers were ruthless, like their captain."

Branz meant Vedrik. Mason stood for a few seconds before he became wobbly and had to sit back down.

His mom smiled at him. "It's okay, Mason. It might take a little longer. You've only been awake a few times."

"Laura Wikk, report to Expedition Command Chamber," a voice ordered over a speaker in the room.

Mason's mom sighed. "Branz, can you help Mason if he needs anything? I'm not sure how long this will take. Mason, if you can stand again, you can visit Obbin with Branz's help."

Mrs. Wikk leaned over and kissed Mason's forehead. He blushed but didn't protest.

"Branz, what happened when the Übel invaded?" Mason asked after the cabin door closed tight.

Branz sat on the side of the bed by Mason's feet. "Our soldiers had just returned from the forest," he started.

They'd been coming back from a showdown with Oliver because of the twins' escape, right before the *Phoenix* took off.

"My oldest brother, Voltran, told of the fight with your brother. He said Obbin had been kidnapped. The council debated heading to the nearby town to capture a spacecraft, but because of the onset of the freeze and the dangers of being discovered, the idea was dismissed. Voltran was convinced he could capture a spacecraft and said Mr. Thule could help him fly it, but my father and the council agreed it was too dangerous."

"What did you think would happen to Obbin?" Mason asked.

"We weren't sure. My parents were worried. Voltran said you were going to sell Obbin as a spectacle; then he disappeared to his chambers. Mr. Thule seemed agitated all day. I tried several times to ask him if he knew how to fly a spaceship."

Branz glanced at the door. "I'd discovered something deep in Cavern Haven, the place where our people go when there's danger."

Mason was aware of Cavern Haven; his brother and Obbin had met the council there. He also knew what was hidden there, but he didn't let on to it. The prince was showing that he trusted Mason.

"I found the ship my ancestors arrived in, the *Ontdekking*."

"How'd you find it?" Mason asked.

"While my two younger brothers preferred exploring the *dangers* outside our gorge, I wanted to unlock the secrets within. I'd found a book of our history and read about our arrival here. When I asked my father about it, he quickly hushed me and told me not to ask anyone about it again. Of course, this made me realize that the ship probably still existed, so I simply began thinking of where it might be hidden."

Mason was impressed with Branz's investigative spirit.

"There was nowhere in the open gorge large enough to hide it, so I began my search in Cavern Haven. When I surveyed the cavern, I realized that most of its columns were uniform in size, but the council building butted up against a column fifty times the size of the others. I get that a strong structure should protect our leaders, but that was overdoing it. I spent the next two weeks exploring every inch of the council building and finally discovered a painting with a hidden door behind it. After that it was pretty easy."

"You told no one?" Mason asked.

"No one. I figured that if I told my dad, I'd be in trouble," Branz said. "I was only going to mention it if Mr. Thule could indeed help us fly it. But before I had a chance to speak to him, the soldiers struck in the night. They destroyed a central portion of the palace and neutralized the palace guards. They knew where my family slept, and within minutes they'd captured almost all of us. Rylin wasn't in his room, though. He'd told me he was going to his and Obbin's fort outside the gorge. I'd told him it wasn't the time to leave—we'd already lost one of our brothers—but he was sad and frustrated that Obbin had left without him. Of all my brothers, they were the closest." Branz seemed choked up as he spoke about the two missing princes. "And Voltran wasn't in his room either. Perhaps he escaped through one of the secret passages."

Mason spoke up. "Oliver learned that he led a group of soldiers to a nearby town to capture a ship."

"That's what he wanted to do all along," Branz said, nodding. "He'll never find us now. I always knew space was vast from the star charts my father kept, but being among the Übel and attending the meetings in the Expedition Command Chamber has showed me there's more than I imagined. The Federation is huge."

Mason nodded. "Yet the planet we search for doesn't appear to be inside its borders."

"True," Branz agreed. "Anyway, my entire family was taken, as well as my father's most trusted guard, Feng. We left on a ship called the *Raven*."

"When we returned to Jahr des Eises to take your brother home, there were ships fighting just off the planet," Mason said.

"Yes, we heard about that later. The Übel left men to explore and pillage the palace. They'd been given exact instructions on what to take and where to go. The traitor Thule had been cataloging all he had discovered about us. They cleaned out our artifacts and library in a day, but when they left they ran into space pirates. They were outnumbered and outgunned, and several of their shuttles and fighters were destroyed." Branz looked sad. "Who knows how many of our artifacts and books were lost."

"I visited your library. They took a lot, but not everything." This didn't come across as a comfort, the way Mason had hoped.

"We've seen some of what they took. My dad has been sifting through it," Branz said.

"Branz, will you help me stand, please? I want to see Obbin."

The prince took his arm, and Mason took to his feet. He counted down from sixty. His legs felt good; his breathing was steady. "I'm ready."

4.4

Buoyant

"Structural integrity failure threshold stabilized," the computer said.

"Is everyone okay?" asked Oliver.

"Tiffany?" Austin asked.

Tiffany was kneeling next to Austin's chair, her hands locked in a viselike grip on the chair's armrest. Austin unstrapped himself and helped his sister into the copilot's chair.

"Are you okay?" asked Oliver.

She touched her knee and winced, then held up her left elbow. "Bruised and scraped, maybe. I don't think anything's broken."

"Why were you out of your seat?" asked Austin.

"Para-Orbs," Tiffany said, her voice quivering. "Emergency floats. I deployed them."

"You saved us again," Oliver said.

Tiffany looked at her hands. "I don't know how I thought of it. I just realized out of nowhere how I could help."

"It was Helper," Austin said with confidence. "He helped you think of it."

Tiffany nodded.

"Thank you, Helper," Austin said.

"You slowed our descent," Oliver said. "We're going to make it."

Oliver looked at the console. The outline of the ship was green, with the exception of a yellow highlight on one of the tail fins.

"What was wrong?" asked Austin.

"I think the gaseous atmosphere must have made it impossible for the *Eagle*'s engines and wings to create lift," Tiffany explained. "We were like a rock in the water until the floats gave us buoyancy."

"Now we just have to wait until we land," Oliver said, "which will be a while."

"How will we get back off the moon?" asked Austin.

"I'm not sure," Tiffany said. "But we're alive."

"We're also going to have to hike farther now, because I can't fly to the coordinates of the escape pod," Oliver said.

"Can't you use the engines to push us through the sky?" Austin asked.

"That could damage the floats," Tiffany said. "The good news is that the exterior coating on the *Eagle* seems to be holding up. There aren't any breaches as of yet," Tiffany said.

"But will the floats hold up?" Austin asked. "They can't be made of very thick material."

"That's a good question," Tiffany said.

"Why don't we ask Rescuer to protect us?" Austin suggested. "Obbin did that once."

Tiffany nodded, than bowed her head.

"Rescuer, please keep us safe," Austin said. "Let us land safely and find Ashley, then get off this moon. Thank you."

A few minutes later, Oliver was busily looking over the screens before him as Austin tried to communicate with the escape pod.

"I can't seem to get through," Austin said, and Tiffany's heart sank. "I've connected to the mainframe, and I'm sending messages to the pod's display, but there's been no response yet."

"Did you try an audio message?" Oliver asked. Tiffany could hear the concern in his voice.

"I wasn't able to get control of that," Austin said.

"Any chance the screen is damaged and the message you're sending isn't being displayed?" asked Tiffany desperately.

To her relief, Austin nodded. "It's possible."

Oliver sighed. "Why don't we finish getting the ATC in place? I'll gear up once we're closer to touchdown."

Tiffany sensed that this "get to work" action was a way for her brother to get his mind off Ashley's well-being. She'd found an image of Ashley open on the screen of the e-journal when she'd returned to the bridge. She was curious why Oliver had looked it up, but she wasn't going to say anything to her brother about it right now.

She reached into her pack and pulled out the e-journal. Then she gasped. She pulled out a small, crinkled note, turning it so that Oliver could see it. "Oliver! We never did this!"

"What is it?" asked Austin.

"A note from Dad," Tiffany said. "He wanted us to read the entry in the e-journal on the Valley of Shadows, but we never did look it up. It was Dad's one request of me, and I didn't do it," she added dismally.

"It was as much my responsibility as yours," Oliver admitted. "Don't beat yourself up about it. You can read it now."

"All right," she said. "Let me know if you need me. After I read it, I want to look for information on Eochair and mark the coordinates for YelNik Eisle. I should have done it much sooner."

"Tiffany, it's not all on you. We should have made sure you had time to read through Dad and Mom's notes and research. Deciphering clues and gathering knowledge is as important to our quest as anything else we've done," Oliver said. "From now on, your priority is reading. Austin and I will handle the rest."

"So I'll go with you to the escape pod?" asked Austin.

Oliver paused. "Buddy, I'd appreciate your company . . ."

"But?" Austin asked.

"If something happens to me, you'll need to get yourself and Tiffany off this moon."

The notion that something could cause Oliver not to return should have caused Tiffany to protest the mission. But dangers to their lives had become ever-present.

"I won't let you down," Austin said.

A few days ago, Austin would have put up a fight at being told to remain in the ship, but now mutual respect had developed between the brothers. Tiffany could tell that Oliver and Austin had drawn closer. In fact, each of them, herself included, had found their roles, learned about each other, and decided to follow Rescuer, Creator, and Helper. They were, on all fronts, unified.

Austin stood at the NavCom, tapping information into his mTalk. "Are these the current readings from the atmosphere of Cixot?"

"Yep, should be," Tiffany said.

"Great. I've got what I need, Oliver."

"Do you need my help?" Tiffany asked. "If you need me, don't hesitate—"

"Sis, we got this," Austin said. Oliver smiled and ruffled his brother's hair, and the two left.

They certainly weren't blaming her for missing the clues. Tiffany was glad for their unusually high spirits in light of their crash landing on a toxic moon, kidnapped parents and brother, pursuit by space pirates and sinister soldiers, and quest to seek a planet no one had ever returned to.

Was this the peace she had heard Obbin mention to Mason when they were in the narrow tunnels headed to the Cathedral of the Star? If so, she was thankful she had it, and she was excited about what else Rescuer might bring.

Finally she had the two things she needed: time and the e-journal. Maybe the fact that they were slowly floating down to the surface of Cixot was part of a plan—a plan to let them take a breath. A smile crossed her face. *Was that the sort of thing Creator would do?*

First, she located the sketch of the paintings from the castle and the message that had been hidden in them. She read the clue quietly to herself. "Within the depths, we do leave the keys to passage safe and free. We hope in time the Truth will reign freely, when man again sees the way. Until the time when darkness is unveiled for what it is, we shall protect the path. We pray only that redemption again is clear to the masses, for so long it has been overlooked as something valueless."

The map Austin had copied from the paintings was expansive. Tiffany recalled the sketch O'Farrell had had in the book on his coffee table; it had been smaller and less detailed. She transferred Austin's copy and the text of the message to one of the NavCom's screens so she could look at them while reading the e-journal.

Opening the e-journal, Tiffany typed in *Valley of Shadows*. There were several entries, but the one she was most interested in was from the first day her parents had visited the valley:

January 29, 1600. Captain Vedrik and his men seem to be lurking near our dig sites all the time. This expedition to the Valley of Shadows is no different. Vedrik already offered us a "substantial salary" to join his group. This was nothing more than a bribe. Elliot and I mentioned it to a key donor of our expeditions, who explained that the captain has undesirable connections to an unscrupulous organization. He asked us to provide hourly updates so he could provide support if things turned dangerous. The remoteness of the site, along with Vedrik's continued interference, has made higher security essential, so an Archeos security detail has been assigned to the expedition.

We assume Vedrik and his men are working with the locals to their advantage. Today, shortly after we landed the *Turning Leaf* on Cao, a band of Saharvics approached the ship and demanded that we leave. They claimed ownership over the valley since they had settled in the caverns on the eastern ridge.

Elliot provided an Archeological Grant of Access issued by the Federation's research board. It permits us to explore any tunnel or chamber in the valley. The Saharvics are occupiers with no ancestral link to the settlers. They have no official claim. The Saharvics backed down but said that they'd be back after reviewing the document for authenticity. We informed the closest federal outpost about the confrontation, but it is our understanding that the federal contingent is not reliable. Vedrik may have bribed them as well.

Tiffany recalled the Archeos ship her parents had used prior to the *Phoenix*. The *Turning Leaf* was a larger ship that could carry a lot more equipment and passengers, though it was not as sleek or new as the *Phoenix*. In fact, more than once their flights on the *Turning Leaf* had been delayed while new parts were brought in for repairs.

Who was the "key donor"? Was it Mr. O'Farrell? Tiffany's mom hadn't mentioned him by name, likely to keep his identity secret from any who read the expedition notes and updates she produced. Had O'Farrell planned to use the *Black Ranger* to rescue Tiffany's parents if Vedrik got too close? He'd used the ship for a rescue on Re Lyt. Would he have revealed his relationship with the Corsairs at that moment? Her parents' capture had caused Mr. O'Farrell to take desperate measures and imprison the McGregors by force. Even if the situation had been different, he likely would have come for Tiffany and her brothers as well.

Tiffany tried to refocus her attention on the reading. She couldn't let these questions distract her.

Archeos has started employing stun towers and electrified mesh barrier fences as deterrents against saboteurs and other interference from outside organizations. We know little about these groups, but their meddling is increasing with every clue and artifact that leads closer to Ursprung. The increase confirms that perhaps we are on the right path.

Why have other groups desired the information for themselves instead of sharing it with others? Archeos for one is known for producing accurate, accessible reports on its discoveries.

Unfortunately our defensive precautions will protect only the encampment around the ship. The Valley of Shadows is far too large for a secure perimeter. Instead, each team in the expedition will be assigned a squad of armed security escorts.

Tiffany hadn't known about the danger posed to her parents or the great lengths Archeos had taken to protect them. Surely that confirmed that Archeos could be trusted. Then again, had Archeos been involved with the expedition at Dabnis Castle? She couldn't recall any mention of security escorts or defensive perimeters. As far as she knew from the e-journal, the expedition had been just her parents and the McGregors. But they had used the *Phoenix*, which meant O'Farrell had known of the expedition. The Übel had also known, because Vedrik had known about the book her parents had recovered.

Perhaps Tiffany's parents had kept their expedition hush-hush to stop Vedrik from finding out about it. Or had they gone rogue and not told Archeos?

Tiffany continued to the next day's entry.

January 30, 1600. We set out for the valley before sunrise to beat the heat of this desert planet. Elliot and I made up one party, along with our escorts; Rand and Jenn McGregor were in another; Rich Hixby and Phillip Skalker were in the last. Each party was assigned one chamber to make for. Exploring the entire catacombs would take years and a multitude of teams, neither of which we have at our disposal. The catacombs are believed to consist of nearly a hundred miles of tunnels and underground rivers, a subterranean network of canals and roads used by a prior civilization to survive in the extreme desert climate. The Saharvics live in underground chambers and tunnels during the day. Most of the tunnels are interconnected, except where cave-ins have occurred, which kept us on heightened alert for an ambush.

As Elliot and I neared our selected point of entry into the catacombs, the first rays of the sun started to peek through the tall stone spires that rim the valley like sharp teeth. From the valley's base to the top of its highest spire is a difference of eight thousand feet. The lowest known catacomb is another two thousand feet below ground.

Tiffany stopped to pull up some pictures. The images were breathtaking. The spires weren't just solid stone; they appeared to be translucent in areas, which caused them to sparkle as they defused the sunlight. She hoped that someday her parents would take her to see the place.

Once we entered the catacombs, I activated the mapping application on the journal (access map VOS-Map2). Our goal is to sync the information from the three teams and create a more accurate map. We'll not be able to mark every tunnel or canal this time around, but it's a start.

The recent discovery of a hand-drawn map at Ad Nama Castle on Tenrohwas one of the catalysts for this expedition (access map VOS-Map1). The map was found in a burned-out spaceship outside the castle walls. Whoever had been exploring the castle had either been attacked or had crashed.

The map we recovered had had at least two owners. The original maker had outlined a series of tunnels and chambers across the parchment. Seven dodecagonal chambers were marked with red crosses.

"Dodecagonal?" Tiffany asked aloud. She checked the e-journal: a *dodecagon* was a twelve-sided polygon. Twelve seemed to be an important number. There were twelve pillars, twelve rubies, twelve planks, twelve stones to activate the doors, and probably many other sets of twelve that she didn't remember.

None of the other chambers on the map of the valley were this shape or were marked with crosses. Next to each cross was the word *Schlüssel*, which means *key*. This made our next destination clear.

The second owner had scribbled dozens of notes across the map, updating where tunnels had collapsed and adding arrows that likely signify the direction of water flow in the canals. (The arrows were key to determining the routes our teams would take in and out of the catacombs. According to the markings, no team would be able to exit the same way it had entered.) It appears that the map's second owner had found the map in Tenroh, visited the Valley of Shadows in Cao, and then returned to Tenroh, although we don't know why, since we found no other artifacts in the burned-out ship.

The second catalyst for this expedition was a yellow sphere, found in a chamber beneath the library in Ad Nama Castle that contained coordinates for the planet Cao. The chamber appeared untouched, which led us to believe that the prior explorer had obtained the coordinates for the valley in another way. We believe that the valley was originally settled by the Gläubigen, so it is possible that the map had been recovered at another settlement.

Tiffany's mom had mentioned the Gläubigen before. Perhaps searching for items related to them would allow her to connect the dots more quickly—then again, it could also result in thousands of notations. Tiffany made a note to research more about them.

Based on the markup, three of the tunnels leading to chambers appear to be collapsed, leaving just four cross-marked chambers accessible. Our plan is to explore the accessible chambers first, then return with an excavation crew to dig out the tunnels marked impassable if we determine the Schlüssel to be assets to our mission.

The hand-drawn map was scanned into the e-journal to use as our guide and was subsequently updated with a series of radar, thermal, and sonar overlays, which gave us a composite and extensive map to the tunnels. Our real-time tracking will add even more detail and accuracy.

We began our expedition by following a narrow two-mile path with a five-hundred-foot elevation gain that ended at a round chamber. To our disappointment, the room was empty, likely looted long ago by treasure hunters or Saharvics.

A second tunnel branched off the chamber. We followed it for three miles and a thousand feet of elevation gain before it split into five new paths. So far the map was accurate, which gave us hope that we would reach our target chamber. According to the map, we were to take the center tunnel of the five.

After about a half mile, the tunnel turned into a long, winding staircase. We'd started at the base of one side of the valley's wall and were now climbing up within it. We'd ascended nearly 2,500 feet. I began to consider that our target might be in one of the spires.

At the top of the staircase, we came to a stone porch that had stairs leading into a canal running perpendicular to the staircase. The original settlers to the valley had created a network of canals to supply water to different parts of their city. We had brought two rafts, and the escorts were happy to know we would not be going against the current.

Before we started down the canal, I noticed an inscription and two faded symbols etched into the wall. The first symbol was an arrow pointing upstream; the second was an oval that came to a point on one end. The opposite side was hardly visible. The legible portion of the inscription read *Access Craft*. Perhaps there are watercraft housed in a room farther up, to allow for travel down the canal. As we had an assigned destination, we decided not to investigate. We took several images (see VOS-138 and VOS-139) and marked the location on the map (VOS-Map2) so we could explore the area later.

Tiffany looked at the map that had been created. It was smaller, but with the new information it was up to date.

Seeing the orange line that marked her parents' path made her feel as though she were closer to them somehow, although they were a thousand light years away. Each detail of Tiffany's mom's thoughts and notes was precious to her.

4.5

Brother to Brother

ustin tapped the screen on the Atmospheric Transfer Chamber. He set the external pressure and atmospheric makeup so the ATC would properly transition Oliver's body from the pressurized interior environment of the *Eagle* to the atmosphere of Cixot.

He had to admit that he was nervous. He checked and double-checked the numbers he'd gotten from the NavCom.

Oliver was getting the heavy spacesuit ready. It too had a separate set of controls that had to be calibrated before use. Oliver asked Austin for the Cixot numbers as he set the suit's calibration.

Austin looked at his older brother admiringly. There was something incredible about his brother's willingness to sacrifice himself without hesitation for someone else. Had this come from his year at the Academy, or had it always been in him? Was it something that occurred when a boy became a man?

Oliver had always been a leader and a go-getter. Once, when Oliver was fourteen, Tiffany twelve, and the twins eight, their parents had been delayed on an expedition. The kids had come from Bewaldeter on their scheduled transport, but no one had been there to take them home from the spaceport. Oliver had taken it on himself to take care of them. He'd spoken to the owner of Rent-A-Craft and convinced her to rent him a deluxe sky scooter. He flew his sister and brothers home, then got them all inside before night fell. He even assisted Tiffany in cooking an actual meal, not an instant one. Oliver had never showed any fear, so Austin and Mason hadn't felt a reason to be scared that their parents weren't there. They'd just followed their brother's instructions.

Austin still regretted being difficult at the beginning of the quest. Yes, he'd realized his mistakes and apologized, but he should have known that his brother and sister had his best interests at heart; they always had.

Now he was preparing Oliver for another mission, and his older brother trusted him to handle tasks to complete it. It was an honor to have his brother's approval, and it encouraged him.

"Austin, I think I'm nearly ready," Oliver said. "Would you double-check my work?"

Austin joined his brother. He read the entries Oliver had made and checked them against the data on his mTalk. Then he did it a second time.

"All looks good," Austin said. "Oliver?"

"Yes, Austin?" Oliver tightened a strap on the suit.

"I just want to thank you," Austin said. "Thanks for leading us through this. Thanks for always being there for me. I know I haven't always made it easy, but you've helped me and taught me."

Oliver chuckled. "I'm coming back, bud. No need for an 'if you die' speech."

"That's not what I meant. I know you're coming back."

"You don't have to thank me. This is what family is for. We're meant to take care of each other." Oliver placed his hand on Austin's shoulder. "And I'm sorry if I've ever been too harsh. I care so much for you, Tiffany, and Mason, and I take it as my full responsibility to get us all through this." He turned toward the bridge. "If anything happened to any one of you, I'd never stop blaming myself. I love each of you."

Austin smiled. "I love you. And I know that Tiffany and Mason do too."

"I know," Oliver said and side-hugged his brother.

"When we get through this, I hope we can spend more time together," Austin said. "I mean, I guess you won't be going back to the Academy for a while."

Oliver laughed. "Why not? Once we find Ursprung, we can return home."

"You think so?" Austin asked. "I sort of figure if we make it to this place, we'll be stuck there, or there'll be so much to explore that we'll spend a very long time there."

"Either way, I don't think we'll be returning to life as usual."

"Will you help me get stronger? And teach me hand-to-hand combat techniques and evasion maneuvers?"

Oliver grunted. "Of course. I'll build you an obstacle course. We can spar."

"Cool!" Austin said.

"Now, let's get this finished up so I can rescue Ashley," Oliver said.

4.6

Strange Warning

Tiffany pulled herself from thoughts of her parents and continued to read the e-journal. In it her mother described the expedition's steep descent by raft to a wide pool a thousand feet lower in the tunnels. After seven hours of exploration, they had neared their destination, but they'd still had to climb up a long flight of stairs before reaching a short tunnel that led to a metal door.

Elliot and I surveyed the path ahead. We'd been looking all along for potential hazards or booby traps but had yet to see any signs of danger or difficulty. Now before us was a change in our path. The floor was inlaid with three rows of a dozen flat white stones. Each stone was marked with a symbol.

Tiffany immediately thought of the Roman numerals from Evad.

I recalled the expedition of Ad Nama Castle on Tenroh. We had found a circular chamber beneath the castle's library. The floor of the room had twelve sections, coming to a point in the middle where the polished yellow globe with the coordinates for Cao sat. Each of the sections had been marked with similar symbols. I pulled up the images, and we examined the path ahead. Using the twelve symbols, we identified a path through the stones to the door.

One of our escorts volunteered to go first, but Elliot insisted it was his duty. He carefully stepped from stone to stone on the path we'd identified and arrived at the door.

When the rest of us reached the door, we discovered that it didn't have a handle. Forcing entry could collapse the chamber on the other side, possibly destroying any artifacts.

A set of twelve white stones in the shape of a cross matched the symbol on the map to confirm the location. When I touched the stones, they lit up. Surprised, one of our escorts stepped onto a stone that hadn't been part of our path to the door. The results were immediate. The stone beneath him broke away, and he fell, but not before Elliot grabbed his arm. Elliot and another escort pulled him to safety.

In the chaos, we missed the door's opening. A blast of light filled the staircase, overwhelming our flashlights. The door opened into a tall, narrow chamber glowing with the warm orange light of the setting sun that came through differently shaped windows of translucent crystal. The coolness of the room suggested that the warmth could not penetrate the stone. In the center of the room a tall wooden cross towered thirty feet into the air, its crossbeam running perpendicular three-quarters of the way up. It was serene in contrast to our escort's near injury seconds before. The wooden structure exactly matched the symbol marked on the map.

Our escorts spread out within the room and identified a second door, which would be our exit path.

Elliot and I catalogued the chamber with pictures (see files VOS-141 through VOS-150).

Tiffany pulled up the images and flicked through them. The cross dominated the empty room. Unfortunately, her parents were rarely in the images, as they were meant for documentation. In one image, her dad's hand could just be seen as he pointed to a small marking burned into the wood. It was the letter *V*. Did it stand for *Veritas Nachfolger*?

Tiffany took a deep breath. She couldn't get distracted with theories. She had to finish this entry before they landed. Plus, she still needed to look up *Eochair* and *YelNik Eisle*.

We examined the rest of the room and discovered only a shelf built into the wall. It held three items: a bag of twelve rubies, a silver disc three inches in diameter, and a map labeled *Washed Stones*. We will need to analyze each of these items separately to determine their relation to the cross.

The cross stood alone in the empty chamber. The orange light had turned to a deep red. Something about the scene stirred my heart.

Though the exit door appeared to be large enough to fit the cross through, the cross was too large for Elliot and me to remove ourselves. The extraction team will have to come with their equipment once they have finished their work on Tenroh. We decided to set up camp in the chamber as the day drew to an end and the warm light was quickly fading.

I attempted to contact the other two search parties but was only able to get ahold of the McGregors. They'd not reached their chamber; although the map had shown the path clear, a collapse had forced them to turn back midway through their journey. They reported that the collapse appeared to be recent. Saharvics may have been responsible. The McGregors had identified a path that would take them to the fourth and final unblocked chamber. They had not heard from Hixby and Skalker either.

Our escorts set up camp, positioning themselves at each of the two doors, while we stayed at the foot of the cross. One escort will remain on watch at all times, should the Saharvics or Captain Vedrik's men come. The disappearance of the other two archeologists has heightened the security team's concerns.

Elliot and I looked over the three items we discovered. We've found several rubies during our expeditions but have yet to determine their significance. The silver disc has an indentation on one side and two ports on the bottom. Neither of the ports resembles any type we've seen before, but it's evident that they are designed to allow the disc to attach to something. We believe the disc to be some sort of data storage or key. Archeos cyber engineers will have to determine a way to access and retrieve the information on our return. The third item, the map, shows an unfamiliar location. I have scanned it with the e-journal and started a search for a match. However, it could take a long time to search using the e-journal. We'll begin again aboard the *Turning Leaf*, where we have access to faster processing and a wider archive of maps.

The entry ended. Tiffany was excited about her parents' discovery, but where were the crosses now? Were they still in the Valley of Shadows? Her parents hadn't mentioned the crosses to her. Of course, in the last year they'd not mentioned Vedrik, the *Phoenix*, or whether or not they were still working for Archeos. She was still unclear on that last point.

The rubies must have been a link to Dabnis Castle and Evad. Rubies had been the keys to unlocking the chamber on Yth Orod.

Tiffany was curious about the silver disc. Had her parents been able to unlock the information it contained? Did Archeos have it now, or was it on the *Phoenix*? She hoped that further reading would reveal the answer.

As for the map, she recognized its title. She and Austin had found a map of the Washed Stones in the observatory on Yth Orod. Unfortunately, the map was on the *Phoenix*; they'd not scanned it yet. Tiffany searched for the map her parents had scanned and transferred it to the NavCom so she could look at it as soon as she finished reading the entries.

"How's it coming, Tiffany?" Austin asked over the mTalk's speaker.

She leaned forward and tapped the mTalk. "Fine. Just reading about the Valley of Shadows."

"How are the exterior and the Para-Orbs holding up?"

Tiffany glanced at the screen. "Everything looks good."

"When will you be done reading?"

"I still have two more items to look up."

Oliver's voice came over the speaker. "You're supposed to be a fast reader."

"Ha ha," she said. "I'm doing the best I can." She knew her brother was trying to relieve her stress. "I'll pick it up."

"All right. See you in a bit." Oliver signed off.

She plunged back into her reading. In the next day's entry, her parents packed up the artifacts they'd found on the shelf and checked in with the McGregors, who were nearing the fourth chamber. Tiffany's mom gave them the symbols to identify the path of white stones outside the door. No one had heard anything from Skalker and Hixby.

When the team left without the cross, they discovered a ramp leading down to a barge on a waterway and decided to try to move it after all.

Tiffany hadn't seen a cross among the cargo in the *Phoenix* or heard Mr. O'Farrell mention it. In fact, when she'd done a search for crosses on Evad, why had this one not come up? Perhaps it was because she hadn't been searching for crosses specifically, just for a symbol of truth.

She read on.

We lifted the cross from its base and lowered it to the floor of the chamber. That's when we saw a dodecagon and a silver circle carved into the underside of the vertical beam of the cross. On the top of the vertical beam, twelve rubies had been inlaid into the wood. They were impossible to see if you stared at the cross from any direction except above.

I suggested that the cross was wired to be used as a key, perhaps to unlock some system on Ursprung or at the Washed Stones. Elliot touched the silver disc to the circle inset in the bottom of the cross, but nothing happened. There were no connection points to latch with the ports on the disc.

The expedition moved the cross down the ramp and into the barge, where it fit nicely. As Tiffany read on, they traveled behind the barge until the canal ended in a wide pool, with a grated exit that the water disappeared through.

As we approached the final section of the tunnel, a man stepped out of the shadows. He wore a long brown tunic with a hooded cape that shadowed his face. The escort commander ordered us to drop the cross, and the security detail moved between the stranger and us.

The man warned us to leave the valley and take nothing with us. Then he backed away and disappeared into the wall. The commander ordered two escorts forward, but the man had sealed himself behind a door. At the security commander's orders, we abandoned the cross and headed for the exit. When we reached it, the tunnel collapsed behind us, sealing the cross in. We couldn't leave the tunnel due to the high temperatures outside. Our commander called for immediate extraction.

The sand rover arrived a few minutes later. After the doors were sealed, our escorts informed us that Hixby and Skalker have been confirmed missing. There has been no contact with them or their escorts since they entered the catacombs. The McGregors had reached their destination and were on their way back as well. The fourth chamber had contained a cross like the one we had discovered (access notes VOS-1-16-1699-McGregor). They'd left the cross behind but discovered artifacts similar to the ones we'd found.

Once the McGregors boarded the ship, we departed the planet. After the warning from the stranger and the disappearance of Hixby and Skalker, our security team was taking no chances. Half the security detail remained behind to search for the missing archeologists, awaiting a second contingent of security personnel from Archeos that would join them. We have no choice but to wait for them to remove the rest of the artifacts themselves, if they aren't already too late.

The team then compared the artifacts they had found. Both had found a silver disc with ports. The two maps they'd discovered had a key difference: while one of the circles on the Wikks' map was marked with a *V*, a different circle on the McGregors' map was marked with a *VIII*. The team concluded that the "Washed Stones" were islands in a body of water.

As they examined the images of the crosses more closely, they discovered the symbol *V* carved into the Wikks' cross, while the McGregors' cross had *VIII* carved into it.

Finally, the McGregors had found three cross-shaped pendants on chains instead of a sack of rubies. The pendants matched the crosses that had been labeled as *Schlüssel* and the white stones at the entrances.

Tiffany thought about the pendant necklaces she and her brothers had been given and first used on Evad. Those were indeed keys. Were these the same? The white stone formations at the doors were similar to stone sets on Evad that had lit up when touched. It was clear that rubies and cross pendants were commonly used for accessing locked areas of the Gläubigen. Were the crosses, rubies, and necklaces to be used at the next destination, YelNik Eisle? Was that where the Washed Stones were? Was this why her dad had told her to read this entry?

When he'd left the note, Tiffany and her brothers had already explored Evad. They had used the cross pendants and the rubies. The Roman numerals and rubies had been discovered in Dabnis Castle, along with a circular chamber like the one on Tenroh. It was clear that the Valley of Shadows was connected, but what part of this did Tiffany's dad want her to know? That the crosses were keys? Or had he wanted her to see the map of the Washed Stones?

She glanced at the map, still on the screen. It wasn't detailed. Her mom had written that the map would be analyzed to discover its planetary location. Maybe that was what her dad wanted them to do. He had known that his kids had the e-journal with the maps, but he hadn't been sure they would make it to Enaid and reach the chamber with the mural. Perhaps he had simply been trying to help them get to the location of the Washed Stones. It would be an opportunity for the whole family to rendezvous.

That was it. Tiffany smiled, confident she'd reasoned it out.

She closed the e-journal as Austin's voice came across the mTalk. "Tiffany, we need you in the cargo bay. Oliver is ready to go."

"On my way," she said.

"Could you check on the status of the *Eagle*'s exterior first, please?"

"Sure," she said.

Tiffany tapped the NavCom and checked the status of the ship. She analyzed the elemental makeup of the atmosphere, thinking back to what she had learned in chemistry at Bewaldeter. The elemental combination of the atmosphere wasn't corrosive. It was poisonous, yes, but not so dangerously corrosive that it could deteriorate even a basic durable material. The information she'd read about the moon had been wrong. Now that they were in the atmosphere, she could see the truth through the sampling that the *Eagle*'s system showed.

4.7

Swinging Escape

The black clothes that the Übel had lent Mason hung off him oddly. They looked like exercise clothing. He'd also been given a pair of black sandals, a water bottle, and an e-papyrus and stylus with the Übel skull logo imprinted on them. It was like he'd gained membership into the Übel's club, yet he wanted nothing to do with their dark society. Still, he'd keep the e-papyrus; he was happy to have something to write on again. Before he'd been captured, he and Tiffany had been sharing the e-journal.

The thought of his sister brought a frown to his face. Mason missed her; he missed his brothers. Sure, it was good to be with his parents, but he'd spent more time with his siblings over the last few years. They'd been to school at Bewaldeter, while their parents trekked across the universe exploring. He didn't resent his parents for their way of life, but it had caused him to rely on his siblings.

An announcement overhead interrupted his thoughts. "Captain Vedrik, report to Expedition Command Chamber immediately. Captain Vedrik, report to Expedition Command Chamber immediately."

Branz was at Mason's side. Mason might have mistaken him for Obbin, if not for his deeper voice and slightly taller height. A thin yellow light bar ran along the center of the black walls, giving just enough light to see the next few steps ahead. There were no guards to be seen. If this place was like the prison level on the *Black Ranger*, there was no concern about prisoners escaping their confinement.

Branz stopped and rapped his knuckles on a door. The hatch shifted open, and Queen Dotty's warm smile greeted them. "Welcome, Mason." She opened the hatch the rest of the way. "It's nice to see you again."

Mason looked down at his sandals. He felt bad about his escape from the gorge. What if it had triggered everything resulting in their capture?

It probably had.

"It's good to see you again as well," Mason said.

Obbin stood on top of a bed, wearing a pair of baggy black shorts with ragged ends. Clearly the shorts had started life as a pair of pants like the ones Mason was wearing, but Obbin had ripped off the fabric below each knee.

"Mason!" he called and jumped down.

"Son, be caref . . ." his mom started.

But it was hopeless to try to stop Obbin. The prince embraced Mason with all his might, causing him to twinge; several of Mason's bandages pressed painfully into his burns.

"It's about time you came to see me! My parents won't let me out."

Mason looked around. The two princesses sat together. One was stitching something, and the other was writing on the Übel-branded e-papyrus. The king was not present. "Your highness, is the king with the Supreme Commander?"

"Yes, he went with your father to the Expedition Command Chamber," Queen Dotty said.

Mason blushed. "Your majesty, I'm sorry for leaving the gorge."

"Mason, an apology is not necessary. Obbin can make his own choices; he decided to go with you. Besides that, you forced Thule to reveal his true colors before we revealed even more to him or allowed him into our inner chambers. Everything is in the time of Creator."

So his and Austin's arrival and escape had triggered the attack. Thule had been working for the Übel as a spy all along.

"It seems it was time for us to leave the comforts of our home and, like our ancestors, explore the universe around us," the queen said.

Obbin yanked on Mason's arm. "Let's go," he said, working to get around Branz while pulling Mason with him.

Mason looked at the queen. She said nothing of Obbin's rudeness.

"Mom?" Branz asked.

"There's not much keeping him here," the queen said. "But you stay with them. These two aren't on the dark soldiers' good list."

Obbin blew past Branz and down the dimly lit corridor. Mason and Branz exchanged looks; clearly Branz felt the same way about Obbin as Mason felt about his own troublemaking younger brother—even if Austin was only thirteen minutes younger than Mason.

"My brother was going on and on about your family—how you get to go on amazing adventures, how your parents encourage adventure while our family is prisoner to the gorge," Branz said.

"Oh, really?" Mason asked. "We actually spend most of our time at a boarding school."

He thought of the past days' adventures. Obbin had been with them nearly from the beginning. Though he'd been in the shadows on Evad, he'd perhaps had a more exciting adventure as he did the work of Brother Sam.

Windowless black double doors blocked the next section of the ship, but Obbin pressed on them and they swung open.

A swarm of noises overwhelmed Mason's ears. He, Obbin, and Branz stood at the beginning of a walkway that stretched across a large landing bay. They had a perfect view of dozens of Übel ships: fighters like the one that had chased them that first night, troop shuttles, sky scooters, and other assorted craft. Men moved weapons and supplies among them, and sparks flew.

It was clear that the Übel were rearming after their recent battle and preparing for another assault. Mason wished he knew more about their destination, the Valley of Shadows. He remembered the map they'd uncovered, but his mind was foggy as to the riddle.

His parents had been to the valley before. His mom had mentioned the place. As soon as he got back to his parents' cabin, he would ask. But first he wanted to explore with Obbin and Branz.

It appeared he had been wrong; they weren't on a prison level at all. In fact, it seemed they had pretty free access to the ship. Maybe the clothing and e-papyrus had been some sort of welcome gift. Maybe he shouldn't have accepted them. Had he agreed to join the Übel?

He shook the thought from his head. No, it certainly didn't mean that. His allegiance was to Creator, to the Veritas Nachfolger.

There were no ladders or stairs attached to the walkway, and Obbin appeared to be scouring the bay for a way down. Branz simply said, "Don't get any ideas."

They walked across the gangway and through another double door. This time the area beyond the doors was swarming with guards. Two guards stood at each of the three clear lift tubes. This was a nexus for traveling to different levels of the ship.

Maybe they didn't have unrestricted access after all. Odd as it was, Mason was relieved to be a prisoner. It meant he wasn't one of the Übel.

As soon as the boys came through the door, one of the guards put up his hand and motioned them to turn around. Obbin hesitated, but the guard tapped the trigger of his weapon. Sparks surged across the tips at the end of the gun in warning.

Branz pulled Obbin and Mason back through the door.

"Branz, we could take them," Obbin said.

"Ha," Branz scoffed. "It's time to look around, brother. We're not in the gorge anymore. These aren't soldiers serving our father."

Obbin leaned over the railing. "If only I could get down there. Then I could do something."

Branz grabbed Obbin, spinning him around. "You don't get it, do you? You've done enough already," he shouted. "Our family is hostage on this ship. We've been separated from our people, our home. Rylin is missing. Voltran was left behind." He grunted and released his brother. "You've caused nothing but trouble."

Mason saw the shock on Obbin's face. He was surprised at the direct blame Branz had laid on him. Branz had seemed even-tempered a half-hour ago. Of course, Mason knew that an exchange between brothers could be more heated than one with a friend or stranger.

Obbin scowled and brushed the spot where Branz had grabbed him. Then he turned from his brother and looked out over the bay. His knuckles were light blue as he gripped the railing in frustration.

"Maybe we'd better leave him alone for a little while," Mason suggested.

Branz nodded and started to walk away. "My brother and I aren't alike," he explained. "Obbin and Rylin have more in common. I'm more like my brother Voltran, or at least like how he was."

"Was?" Mason asked.

"Voltran liked to research and learn, much like I do. His research was purely for the fun of discovery."

Mason smiled. He could relate to that.

"But then *he* came."

"Mr. Thule?"

Branz nodded. "Something changed then. Voltran will be the king of the Blauwe Mensen one day. He began to have an idea that he could expand the kingdom." Branz sighed as he looked down at the spacecraft below. "I am almost 100 percent sure that Mr. Thule planted the idea in his brain that he could conquer a greater kingdom or, at the least, learn from the outside world and bring new technologies into our kingdom."

Mason looked at the boy in front of him. Branz had been torn from his home and everything he knew, thrown into the middle of a battle between two sides, just like Mason had.

"We all knew that we had come to our home on a starship. Voltran didn't know about the ship in Cavern Haven, but he always hoped to obtain space-flight technology from the people in the city of Brighton and lead an expedition into space before he had to take over rule of the gorge." Branz sighed. "Voltran was going to leave the gorge whether or not you came. He just needed a reason."

"Why did you two grow apart?"

"He became obsessed, and at times cruel, I guess is how I would describe it. He no longer spent time with the family but commandeered a room in the castle and made it his laboratory."

"Was Mr. Thule helping him?"

Branz shrugged. "Probably. Either way, Voltran didn't need me anymore. We no longer discussed what we were learning." Branz's eyes narrowed. "And he became secretive. He spoke only to his select inner circle. They called themselves the *Slimme Degenen*."

"What does that mean?" asked Mason.

Branz laughed. "Smart ones."

Mason thought about Oliver's return from the Academy and those first few days of the adventure. He'd had a "better than everyone else" attitude too.

"Ooouhoooh!"

Mason and Branz spun around. Obbin was flying through the air, holding on to a thick black cable.

4.8

Exploding Gas

"It seems the computer was overestimating the dangers of the corrosive gases in the atmosphere," Tiffany said. "Honestly, I'm not sure you even need that suit."

"Really? Then why did we sink?" said Austin.

"The atmosphere is dense, poisonous, and volatile but not highly corrosive," Tiffany said.

"Why would the computer say otherwise?" asked Oliver.

"I have a theory, and it's not good," Tiffany said with a frown. "Remember the molten projectiles from Ledram?"

"Yeah," the boys said.

"Well, occasionally the foggy gases have cleared enough for the exterior cameras to get a view of the terrain. It's charred."

"So . . . ?" Austin asked.

"So if a molten projectile passes into the moon's atmosphere, the entire sky becomes a flaming ball of explosive gas," Oliver said. "Am I right?"

Tiffany nodded.

"And that's what would destroy the *Eagle*," said Austin. "That's what would corrode our exterior."

"More likely melt it or flat-out incinerate us," Oliver said.

Tiffany and Austin stared at him. He gave an apologetic smile.

"The toxic gases come from the remains of smoldering projectiles," Tiffany said.

Austin stared at Tiffany. "How often?"

Tiffany's ponytail bounced as she shook her head. "Can't be sure, but I'd say it's been a while, hence the heavy buildup of gases and thick atmosphere."

"Either way, I've got to get to Ashley. Do I need the suit?" Oliver asked.

"Perhaps not that one, but you'll want some sort of suit and breathing mask," Tiffany said.

"An Oxyverter?" asked Oliver.

"No, those are only good for *extracting* oxygen. Cixot's atmosphere doesn't contain any," she said.

"Right." Oliver thought about Ashley in the escape pod. What if it had been damaged? Did she have oxygen to breathe?

"I think I saw some O-tanks and masks," Austin said, heading for the console to look up their location.

"Be sure to take extras for Ashley," Tiffany said.

"Found them," Austin called. "They're toward the back of the bay. There are a couple of light terrain suits as well. I'll get them."

"Oliver," Tiffany started, "be careful, and hurry. If something erupts from Ledram and comes toward Cixot, we'll have less than twenty minutes before it crosses into the thick cloud of gas and . . ."

"Boom. I know."

"It's too bad you can't use a scooter," Austin said as he returned with two tanks attached to helmets. He handed them to Oliver, then disappeared into the stacks of crates and equipment to find the suits.

"How far away are we?" Oliver asked.

"Five miles," Tiffany said. "Although the atmosphere is dense, the gravity isn't much, so you'll be able to travel quickly."

Austin returned, and Oliver suited up. Austin put the second tank, mask, and suit into a pack that Oliver tossed over his shoulders.

Tiffany stood ready at the controls to the ATC. "Wait. Shouldn't we say a prayer? Remember when Obbin said one for Mason?"

"I think that's a great idea," said Austin.

"Creator, please watch over Oliver as he searches for Ashley. Keep him safe and return them back to the *Eagle* quickly," Tiffany prayed.

"You should take this too," Austin said, holding up a Zinger.

Oliver slipped the weapon's strap across his shoulder and chest.

The three exchanged glances as Austin pulled open the hatch to the ATC. A snake's hiss escaped.

Oliver stepped in, and the hatch closed. Tiffany tapped the keypad as jets of air streamed from vents. She spoke into the intercom. "Is your mask working? Are you getting enough oxygen?"

Oliver nodded.

"All right, starting compression and atmospheric transfer."

Austin and Tiffany watched Oliver through the small, round window. Oliver felt a bit lightheaded and upped his oxygen supply. Finally, a green light beamed overhead, and the hatch behind him opened.

He waved goodbye and stepped out. The earth crunched beneath his boot, and a flurry of ash swept up around him. Dust continued to swirl with each step. A loud clank sounded behind him, and the hatch to the *Eagle* closed. At least his sister and brother were safe inside.

Oliver lifted his mTalk. "See if you can cloak the *Eagle*. I'll let you know when I return."

"We don't have the cloaking device Brother Sam gave us," Austin said.

"Perhaps it's built in on the *Eagle*. I doubt the Veritas would leave their ship without one," Oliver said.

"I'll look for it. Same passcode as last time," Austin said, and the communications link closed.

It was just Oliver and his mission now. He looked at his mTalk. Two timers were going. One was counting up, tracking how long he'd been away from the *Eagle*; the other counted down, showing approximately how much of his oxygen supply remained based on his usage. Both were important. An arrow on the small mTalk screen pointed him in the direction of the pod, and a counter showed the distance remaining.

An ashen plume darkened the path behind, though it was quickly lost in the thick green gas cloud. Each step continued to kick up more soot, a reminder of what could happen should Ledram erupt.

Oliver hastened his pace to avoid the soot cloud masking his path ahead. One positive was that he was practically leaping; his body weight was not affected by the dense atmosphere like the *Eagle* had been. At this pace, he'd reach the escape pod in no time.

4.9

Over the Edge

Obbin was a blue streak swinging down from the walkway, holding a large black cable between his legs. Red gas poured from the end of the hose as he zipped through the air away from them, then swung back toward the walkway.

Mason and Branz leaned over the rails to see Obbin pass below them. He let go and rolled across the floor of the hangar, popping to his feet in perfect form. Oddly enough, no one seemed to notice or hear the prince's battle cry. They were all far too preoccupied with their own tasks to take note of a small boy invading the bay, even if he was blue.

Obbin looked around in disappointed surprise. "OOOOOOO-AHHHHHH!" he called again, throwing his hands into the air.

Mason looked toward the nearest group of soldiers. They were still concentrating on fitting weapons to a star fighter. Why did Obbin want to get their attention? If he was trying to sabotage the Übel, he'd be better off doing it covertly.

Branz grunted. "We'd better get him back before someone actually notices or, worse, he hurts himself."

"There's no ladder."

Branz pointed. The cable hung next to the walkway. "We'll go the same way he did."

Mason hesitated for a split second. He'd done crazier things in the last few days. This didn't frighten him, but it was still a long way down.

Branz climbed atop the rail and slid down the cable. Mason followed at a slower pace. He clearly didn't have the practice that the princes did.

At the bottom, neither of them saw Obbin. During their descent, he'd slipped off.

Branz pointed. "You go that way, and I'll go this way."

Mason didn't like this idea. Whenever his family had split up, trouble of some sort had followed. Regardless of what Obbin thought, the Blauwe Mensen were certainly adventurous, and perhaps reckless.

Branz dashed off and disappeared behind a black, long-nosed star bomber.

Mason sighed. He was on his own, sneaking around in the Übel's arsenal. Plus, he was on the Übel's bad list, which he figured meant that a serious punishment would be doled out if he were caught where he shouldn't be. If Obbin did do anything, Mason would be accused of being an accomplice.

Mason didn't run; he crept. Over the past few days, he'd watched how Oliver had moved. Now Mason applied what he'd observed. He kept his back pressed against a collection of large silver canisters labeled *fuel*.

Footsteps echoed toward him, and he squeezed between two of the canisters so quickly that he didn't realize how tight the space was until it was too late. He took a deep breath as two Übel soldiers walked past, one pushing a hover-cart laden with Kraken Torpedoes.

He could hardly wait until they were past to free himself from the narrow confines of the fuel tanks. He wiped his brow and stepped out.

A series of large bangs rang out from Branz's direction. Mason froze. No shouts followed the commotion, so probably no one had been caught. It was best to continue searching.

Mason slipped around the canisters and came upon six bat-winged star fighters similar to the ones that had chased them that first night on Tragiws. He gasped. Obbin sat in the pilot's seat of one of the craft. The canopy was still open, and he was securing a harness over his shoulder.

"Obbin! What are you doing?" Mason called in a muffled shout.

Obbin either ignored him or didn't hear. Mason slipped to the ship and started up a set of floating boarding steps. But Obbin wasn't having any of Mason's interference. The canopy lowered and shut with a hiss, locking Mason out.

Obbin looked at Mason and gave a resolute nod. His expression seemed to say, "I'm sacrificing myself for the rest of you. Be brave."

Mason pounded on the canopy, "Obbin, don't. You can't."

Obbin pointed a finger ahead and motioned as if he were shooting.

"Obbin! You can't! You don't understand what you're doing!"

It wasn't that Mason thought Obbin was about to die, though that was possible. A hole in the wall of the *Skull* would suck everyone and everything in the bay out into the vacuum of space. Everyone in the bay would die, and the heavily armored cruiser would come apart at the seams. Only Obbin would survive in the safety of the fighter's cockpit.

The fighter started to shake. A soft rumble reverberated from the vectored thruster as the engines started. Mason stepped down a few stairs. The ship began to rise.

Mason waved his arms. "No, no, no!"

Too late. Obbin twisted the controls, and the ship turned. Mason leaped off the stairs and landed with a hard thunk on the bay floor. His elbow ached, but he pushed himself up as the tail of the fighter swung directly over him.

Mason had to stop Obbin. He pushed himself up and ran to the front of the ship, waving his arms and screaming. Obbin paid no attention. The three launchers on the wing closest to Mason began to glow orange.

Was he going to fire the weapons? This was crazy.

Mason needed to find Branz. He ran in the direction the older prince had gone.

There was a loud clatter. Mason looked back. Several canisters were rolling across the floor. Two were spewing thick white gas. The star fighter's tail wings had smashed into the collection, puncturing the pair.

"Branz! Branz, where are you?" Mason shouted. He no longer worried that a soldier would hear him. He hoped they would help him stop the prince from blowing up the entire ship.

Bjoooo! Bjoooo!

Kaboom! Kapow!

The floor began to shake. Mason spun around as an orange fireball erupted toward the ceiling of the hangar.

Mason gasped and held his breath, looking toward the explosion. The room went dark. An instant later, the entire bay was bathed in flashing red lights.

Bjoooo! Bjoooo! Bjoooo!

Boom! Pow! Pow!

"Alert! Alert! Level 2 fire in Hangar Alpha. Level 2 fire in Hangar Alpha. Fire suppression teams report to Hangar Alpha!" an automated announcement warned, then repeated.

Mason thought about going back. Perhaps Obbin would realize what he'd done and Mason could get the prince out before the Übel brought him down by deadly force.

No, it wasn't to be. The ship lifted higher in the hangar, a series of bright green flashes zipping from the launchers. Obbin wasn't done yet, and he probably believed he was winning his fight. Did he believe he was immune to the Übel's anger? Did he think he was invincible? Did he not realize that he'd harm his family as much as the soldiers?

Bjoooo! Bjoooo! Bjoooo! Bjoooo!

Rapid-fire shots rained against the far wall of the hangar. The floor of the *Skull* shook violently. The alert message changed mid-announcement.

"Alert! Ship structural integrity at 30 percent in Hangar Alpha. Structural engineering team report to Hangar Alpha! Alert! Level 4 fire in Hangar Alpha! Fire suppression teams report to Hangar Alpha! Alert!"

Mason jumped at the sudden approach of several soldiers. The Übel dashed right past him toward the hovering fighter. Up ahead, two men aimed a large, black-barreled weapon at the fighter.

They were going to shoot Obbin down!

"Stop!" screamed Mason. He started toward the soldiers, fearless of any consequences. He wanted Obbin stopped, not killed.

A continuous green streak of light zipped up toward the Übel fighter, and the fighter dropped to the hangar floor with a thunderous crash.

Mason's heart sank. It was too late. He couldn't save his friend.

Someone was behind him. More soldiers? Mason turned and raised his arms in the air.

No, it was Branz, waving for his attention.

"Quick, Mason! We can't help him. We need to get out of here. If we get caught, they'll think we were part of this."

"What if he's hurt?

"We can't do anything for him! Are you a doctor?"

Mason shook his head and looked back at the crash site. Soldiers were swarming across it.

Branz grabbed Mason's shoulder. "I'm serious. My brother has caused enough trouble. We can't get dragged down in this."

Mason understood. "But how can we get out of here?"

"The same way we came." Branz looked toward the cable. "We climb."

The boys ran to the cable. Übel soldiers, engineers, and firefighters ran past them without a second look, focused on their own tasks.

Mason started up the cable hand over hand. Halfway up, his arms began to burn. Branz was right behind him.

"Keep going. You can do it. Just don't look down," Branz said.

Of course, as soon as Branz said that, Mason naturally looked below. Obbin was climbing out of the wrecked ship on his own accord, hands raised. Übel soldiers surrounded him. There was no way he could escape this time. Even if he did, the Übel knew exactly who he was: Obbin, prince of destruction.

A soldier pushed Obbin to the ground and bound his hands behind his back. Then he pulled Obbin to his feet and heaved him over his shoulder.

As Mason grabbed the top rail of the walkway, a strong hand grasped his forearm and pulled him up. His dad's stern expression and booming voice greeted him. "Mason, what happened?"

4.10

Destruction

Austin had found the application to cloak the *Eagle* easily enough. Invisibility gave Tiffany some comfort, though she couldn't imagine anyone else wanting to come to this toxic moon. Austin had left to take a shower and change, so Tiffany went to check out the cabin that would have been hers on the *Phoenix*. The inside was drab: no pink walls, just cold gray metal. Two sets of four bunks lined the longer walls, and a porthole looked out onto the green, cloud-covered landscape.

Tiffany confirmed that two of the other cabins were the same. But the cabin that would have been Oliver's was locked. Tiffany tried the keypad next to it but couldn't get the hatch to open. It required a code. What might be behind the door? What would the Veritas Nachfolger lock up?

Tiffany wandered back to the bridge and took her seat before the NavCom. She opened the e-journal and found January 31, 1600. She swept down the entry until it ended, then touched February 1, 1600.

The image that appeared at the top of the entry surprised her. It was rare for her mom to embed an image, but there it was: a wide-angled picture of a valley with several spires surrounding it, four of which were crumbled and blackened. A large ship hovered over a half-crumbled spire with cables lifting something out of it. A cross! The caption read, "Valley of Shadows, February 1, 1600."

Tiffany began to read the entry.

Austin let warm water run over his face and down his body. He wasn't interested in washing as much as in relaxing in the steam. The shower rinsed away the stress of the last week as the water swirled down the drain. Still, Austin couldn't get rid of the loneliness he felt.

Sure, Austin fought with his twin brother, but he couldn't remember a time before this adventure that they'd ever been apart for more than a day. They were nearly inseparable, and not knowing where Mason was or how he was doing brought an almost physical pain to Austin's gut.

He pressed his forehead against the wall and banged his fist. Why hadn't he fought back? Why hadn't he tried to save his brother somehow? Even if he'd been captured, he still would have been with his brother and maybe even with his parents.

What if Mason were being held alone in a cell? He couldn't bear the thought. His brother was claustrophobic; a cell would be like a death sentence, causing him all sort of mental anguish.

The glass of the shower was fogged over. Austin used his finger to etch a cross. From what he'd learned, this symbol represented Rescuer's single, selfless act to provide true freedom.

The cross fogged over again, and Austin turned off the water and grabbed a towel. He bowed his head to pray for both Mason and Oliver. There in solitude he felt the peace that he was beginning to recognize that only belief in Rescuer could provide.

"Rescuer, I ask you to keep Oliver safe. Watch over him and help him find Ashley quickly, and when he does, I ask her to be okay and unharmed. I ask you to bring them back to us safely and quickly. Rescuer, help us find a way off this planet. Help me to think of something; help me to realize what I'm missing." Austin paused and brushed his wet bangs from his eyes. He choked back a sadness that had begun to well up in him over thoughts of his twin. "Rescuer, be with Mason. I know I haven't always treated him as I should, but please let me find him again. I won't take him for granted anymore. Rescuer, be with him wherever he is; Helper, give him peace and hope. Keep him safe and let him be with my parents, not alone." The thoughts and words were flowing from his lips. "And bring my family back together. I want to see my parents again." An ache formed in Austin's chest as he thought of his mom and dad. He'd been away from them longer than this while at school, but that was part of the way of life they'd chosen. This was different; it had been forced on them. "Creator, give me the strength to overcome the soldiers and defeat them." The final words strengthened his resolve, encouraged him, and gave him a clear mission.

Austin dried off and dressed. He and Tiffany had work to do.

February 1, 1600. On route to the Archeos headquarters for debriefing, we received the above image and a message. A large ship has attacked the valley, and all but two of the remaining security escorts have been captured. The two that escaped took the image.

Radio static that the escorts picked up identified the shuttle as the *Vulture*. We believe it belongs to Vedrik but can't confirm at this time.

The Saharvics ambushed the security team in the dead of night. Shortly after, the *Vulture* arrived and destroyed the tops of several of the spires over chambers marked *Schlüssel* on the map.

We're unsure if Vedrik knows of all seven chambers, or just the four our teams were heading for. As far as we know, he did not have a copy of the map (see files VOS-Map2). If he is responsible for the continued absence of Hixby and Skalker, then it is likely that Vedrik now has a copy of the map.

The extraction team had the coordinates to the seven chambers that had been marked on the map, and we updated them with the coordinates where we'd last left the cross we'd attempted to remove. We assume that the Saharvics have relayed the map's location to Vedrik and that he now has control of all seven crosses, if each was still in its respective chamber upon our arrival.

Tiffany's parents had underestimated Vedrik. If the Übel had seven crosses in their possession, how could Tiffany and her brothers possibly get them back? And, based on the description of the crosses, how could all of them fit in the *Eagle*?

She tapped the link, and the map to the valley's catacombs opened. It showed the original map with the handwritten notes and markups, but also her parents' newly created overlays. She pored over it, examining how the tunnels connected to the chambers.

Tiffany looked up at Austin's version of the map, which was still glowing on the NavCom; she sent her parents' version to the screen as well. After a few taps and a bit of stretching and skewing, Tiffany had integrated both. The new map wasn't perfect, but it was close.

There were hundreds of rooms and chambers. There were also five additional dodecagonal chambers to the west side of the known map. These were the ones she cared about; crosses were likely within them.

She rethought her conclusion about her dad's message. Had he intended that Tiffany and her brothers go to the valley to retrieve the additional crosses?

No, that couldn't be it. Her dad didn't have the copy of the map created by Austin. He most likely hadn't known about the additional crosses when he'd left the note in the chamber on Evad. Of course, the king of the Blauwe Mensen likely knew about the twelve and might have told her dad about them after he was taken prisoner.

Tiffany switched to the map of the Washed Stones that her mom had scanned, and she searched for the application that would analyze the image and attempt to place it. She wasn't on the *Phoenix* and didn't have access to the maps in the Archeos archives, so she'd be limited to the maps within the *Eagle*'s navigation system. She wasn't sure how long it would take to get a match, so she switched back to the map of the Valley of Shadows' catacombs.

The five additional chambers stood out to her. Were some of the keys still available? Brother Samuel had said that the crosses were needed, along with the Eochair. Perhaps that meant that they should go to the valley first and head for YelNik Eisle after.

It wasn't a decision she could make alone, so she continued to the next entry in the e-journal. She wanted to see if there were any more updates on the Valley of Shadows.

Austin's hair was still damp as he checked out the galley. The cryostore was not stocked with the same things as the

Phoenix's was. Austin sighed. He picked out yogurt and blueberries for Tiffany, then took out a hydroponic lemon-apple fruit juice and a chicken alfredo Insta-Meal.

He popped the lid off the chicken alfredo. Steam poured from the food as a thermal heating core heated the precooked food in a nanosecond. Austin's stomach grumbled at the savory smell.

He found Tiffany with her eyes glued to the screen of the e-journal. "Hey, sis."

Nothing.

"Hello?" Austin asked. "Tiffany!"

Tiffany jerked. "What's wrong?"

"Nothing. You were just really into your research," Austin said. "Any word from Oliver?"

"Not yet."

"I brought you some food," Austin said.

"Thanks, Austin." Tiffany looked at the e-journal again. "We may need to change our destination from YelNik Eisle to Cao. There are potentially five more crosses in the valley. It seems Dad wanted us to go there, and Brother Sam said we would need the crosses." She showed Austin a map.

"I drew that," Austin said. "Or . . . one like that."

"You sketched a map from the Blauwe Mensen paintings," Tiffany said. "This one is a combination of yours and our parents'."

"You said there were five crosses?" Austin asked between bites of food.

"You see these five chambers here?"

Austin nodded.

"I think those are the crosses that Brother Sam said we would need."

"How can we get them out?"

"I think Brother Sam will be waiting for us there. He said he'd meet up with us, and I think this is where he wanted us to go."

"I thought he said YelNik Eisle was our destination."

"He did, after we asked about the planet image on the mural. But he said we needed the Eochair and crosses first."

"Okay, now I'm following."

"I was just reading about what happened after Mom and Dad left the valley. They flagged the entry so it wouldn't upload to Archeos."

February 2, 1600. We just received an encrypted message from Phelan O'Farrell, one of the many benefactors who support our work. He has offered us the use of a private ship, the *Phoenix*, as well as its sister ship for the McGregors, the *Griffin*.

He plans to meet us at Archeos headquarters tomorrow. We'll have to go with him to rendezvous with the two ships, which are still being outfitted. He asks that we keep the offer secret for now.

After the incident with Hixby and Skalker, and given Vedrik's continued pursuit of us, Elliott believes we should accept the offer and keep it private as requested.

"Vedrik had attacked the expedition, which I think is why Mr. O'Farrell offered them the ships," Tiffany said. "Mom and I spoke that day. She told me they were embarking on a series of short missions, several of which would take them to previously visited sites, such as Yl Revaw. But she said they'd still be at Bewaldeter in April for my performance."

"Why did she mention Yl Revaw?"

"I was paraphrasing," Tiffany said. "I scanned the destinations they visited between February and April. They went to Yl Revaw on March 4. It's a forest planet they'd already visited at least a half dozen times before. In fact, we went once when you and Mason were just five, though I doubt you really remember."

Austin shook his head, mouth full of chicken alfredo.

"The trees aren't anywhere near the size of the ones on Jahr des Eises, so the Federation doesn't harvest the lumber there. The forest is mostly uninhabited. The planet has a few scattered outposts, but nothing significant." Tiffany smiled. "We camped in this moss-covered clearing next to a stream and waterfall."

"Wait, I remember this," Austin said. "Everwood Ridge, right? Mason and I went swimming. There were those big playful animals swimming in the river with us. They were flipping in the water?"

"Otters, yes. The two of you nearly flew out of the water when the first one swam past you," Tiffany said with a laugh.

"I did not," Austin argued. "That was Mason."

"No, I am fairly certain it was both of you," she said.

Austin grunted and took a drink of hydroponic lemon-apple juice.

"Anyhow." Tiffany turned the e-journal to show Austin an image. "The settlement consists primarily of stone buildings, the majority of which are nothing more than foundations."

"So this place is like every other dig site we've been to," Austin said, thinking of the ruins on Evad.

"No, and yes. There was an underground building that our parents couldn't access," Tiffany said. "They tried removing the door and digging in from other angles, but with no success. The chamber was built of thick stones and plates of metal alloy that blocked any efforts to analyze the chamber or to drill into it successfully. In the end, they had to abandon the dig and move on."

"Come on, they must have had explosives powerful enough to get through," Austin said.

"They didn't want to destroy whatever the chamber was protecting. Our parents were patient. They went back several more times with possible keys. They were unable to get in, but I believe we have the key," Tiffany said. "Next to the chamber door was a—"

"And the door was a dodecagon."

"A what?"

"A twelve-sided shape."

"Got it. We didn't cover those at Bewaldeter," Austin admitted with a smirk. "I get why the cross indent is important. We have those keys from Evad."

Tiffany gasped. "No, we don't! We left them on the *Phoenix!*"

Austin reached under the collar of his shirt and pulled on the cord holding his cross-shaped pendant. "I'm still wearing mine." He saw the relief wash over her. "But why is the shape of the room important?"

"The Valley of Shadows contained crosses that were labeled as keys. The chambers that held them were built as twelve-sided rooms or—"

"—Dodec-thingies," Austin finished.

"I have a gut feeling that the Eochair is in the locked chamber."

"Why?" asked Austin.

"Brother Sam said the mural had the clues. I checked the images of the mural. The *Ark* landed on YelNik Eisle, and there's a wooded planet after that."

"Jahr des Eises?" Austin said.

"No, Yl Revaw. The planet came before the image that I think was supposed to be of Enaid," Tiffany said. "Just after it in the timeline was a globe similar to Cao."

"So you think that the keys are on Cao in the Valley of the Shadows and that the Eochair is on another planet—on Yl Revaw?" Austin asked.

"Yes, none of the other locations Mom and Dad visited between February and April match like Yl Revaw does. And Cao and Yl Revaw are in the linear path between YelNik Eisle and what I believe is Enaid."

"But you haven't verified that Yl Revaw or Cao are the planets painted on the mural," Austin said.

"Not yet. I need to check the NavCom to confirm that," Tiffany said.

"Great. I need to figure out how we can take off from Cixot."
Though the situation seemed dire, Austin had a hopeful feeling.
He wondered if this was because of his new trust in Creator,
Rescuer, and Helper.

4.11

Escape Pod

A newly created rut gouged deep into the earth. The escape pod's beacon pulsed on the small screen of Oliver's mTalk. Ashley was somewhere just ahead, cloaked by the thick green cloud.

After a dozen more steps, the silhouette of the pod became visible. Soon he could see the gray, diamond-shaped pod.

Oliver dashed forward, pressing his gloved hands against the exterior. Concerned with what he might find, he had to muster the courage to knock.

There was no response back from the pod, but it was no less than Oliver had expected. The angular exterior was thick for protection and unlikely to allow any sound to be heard within. Further, Ashley was unlikely to open the door for fear that the atmosphere was toxic.

He had to make visual contact. Oliver moved around and peered in through one of the two portholes at the front of the pod. His heart sank.

Ashley was lying face down on the floor. Her head was away from him, so he couldn't see her eyes.

Was she alive? Oliver pounded his fist against the porthole. Still nothing.

Oliver tapped his mTalk. "Tiffany or Austin, are either of you there?"

"Oliver, it's me."

"Aus, I need you to try communicating with the escape pod again. I'm not seeing any movement inside," Oliver said, concern rising in his voice.

"Is she there?" Austin asked.

"Yes," Oliver replied. "But hurry—she's on the ground."

"Will do," Austin said.

Oliver moved around the side of the pod until he located the hatch. A crimson panel of light pulsed next to the door. Oliver reached to touch it. He hesitated. What if the hatch opened and all the oxygen escaped from the pod? Though the atmosphere wasn't corrosive, it wasn't breathable either, and he wasn't sure how many breaths it would take to cause asphyxiation.

"We're trying to connect to the pod again," Austin said.

Oliver moved back to the porthole and peered through. A console on the wall inside lit up and text appeared, but Oliver couldn't read what it said. Austin was sending the message, but if Ashley was asleep—or, worse, dying—a lit screen wasn't going to do anything.

"Did she do anything?" Austin asked.

"No. I'm going in."

Oliver moved back to the glowing panel. He took a breath and touched it. A gasp of air released near the hatch, and the panel changed shades from red to a cautionary orange. A series of words flashed across it: *Exterior atmospheric gases in opposition to pod interior. Use portable atmospheric transfer bubble.*

Oliver lifted his mTalk. "There's a transfer chamber like the ATC on the *Eagle*."

"Be careful," warned Tiffany.

Oliver tapped the screen on the escape pod. A small hatch opened to the right of the door.

Inside he found a folded square of silver material. He pulled a cord, and the material formed into a bubble. Its door was zipped shut, and a warning label read, *See panel for sealing instructions.*

New instructions appeared on the panel. Oliver followed them and pressed the edge of the fabric against the pod. It melded to the exterior instantaneously. He worked quickly. Given Ashley's unknown condition and the possibility that an explosive projectile would obliterate him and his siblings, he had little time.

Oliver pressed the orange strip against the pod until he'd made a complete circle. Once the plasma seal was in place, he unzipped the door. Another zippered door was in front of him. A sign read, *Open once plasma seal is secure.* It was, so he unzipped the door and found the hatch directly behind it. To the right of the fabric door was a silver vent with a purple button labeled, *Atmospheric exchange. Seal bubble access, then press to activate.* He zipped the door he'd entered through and returned to the purple button. Gases swept into the bubble and inflated it further. The purple button glowed green, and the hatch hissed again, popping a few inches open. A surge of relief swept over him. This was it. Oliver gripped the door and swung it open.

Ashley lay still. Oliver kneeled beside her and shook her shoulders. "Ashley?"

To his relief, she stirred and groaned. She shifted to her side and slowly lifted her head. Her eyes opened, and she blinked several times.

Oliver took the second mask and put it over her face, then began the flow of oxygen. The air inside the pod had become stale. Ashley was in the early stages of asphyxiation.

He waited nervously. Then her eyes opened again, wider. "Oliver?"

He nodded, tears pooling in his eyes. Hearing her voice and knowing that she was alive brought great joy. If they'd waited any longer, they might have been too late. "You're going to be okay," he told her. "Austin, Tiffany, she's okay."

"Yeah!" Tiffany screamed. "Ashley, I'm so glad we found you."

"Me too," Austin added.

He knew his sister and brother were smiling with happiness. He was glad they hadn't seen her in this state.

"Ashley, how are you?" Tiffany asked.

Ashley sat up. "I'm okay. You guys saved me."

It was strange that the air supply had faltered so soon. Why hadn't she gone for an oxygen tank? There usually were some on board the escape pod. "Will you guys be leaving soon?" Tiffany asked.

"We will." Oliver wasn't ready to tell Ashley what lurked just outside. The thick atmosphere of Cixot was a danger that they still weren't sure they could escape.

"We should get back to the *Eagle*, where you'll be safe," said Oliver. "That mask and tank are for you, and here is an extra suit." He pulled it from the pack. "I'm going to look for an extra O-tank that I can swap out for mine. I should have enough, but I might as well have a full supply."

"You won't find any," Ashley said. "The supply cabinet is empty. I think the Corsairs wanted to ensure that any prisoner who used an escape pod would be stuck inside."

Oliver grunted. That made sense. He walked over to the control panel for the escape pod, and his heart sank. The air filtration system was functioning at 15 percent. It was designed to make any survivors unconscious, but not to kill them. The Corsairs were crueler than he'd thought.

"We need to go," Oliver said.

Ashley slipped the suit over her clothes, and Oliver helped to get the O-tank and mask in place.

"Wait! My pack." Ashley pointed just behind Oliver.

Oliver picked up a tattered, avocado-colored backpack. Bewaldeter's patch was stitched on the front flap.

"Those were easier days," he said, pointing to the emblem.

She smiled. "True. To think they were just a few weeks ago."

"Ready?" Oliver asked.

"Lead the way," Ashley said.

"Tiffany and Austin, we're coming back," Oliver said. "Focus on our takeoff." He was trying to remain vague about the liftoff so as not to panic Ashley. She'd been through enough without having to stress over the fact that the *Eagle* appeared to be trapped on Cixot. He hoped Austin would get his meaning.

"Will do. Tiff and I will be ready," Austin said.

Oliver and Ashley stepped into the bubble and unzipped the flap to the outside. The thick green atmosphere obscured their view. Oliver checked his mTalk to get a bearing on the *Eagle*. "This way."

Oliver bounced forward, Ashley right behind him.

They started up a charred ridge, following the path of the gouge dug out by the crashing escape pod.

They'd made it only fifty feet when Oliver froze. A dark silhouette had caught his attention. He pulled Ashley to the ground.

He slipped his Zinger from his back and aimed at the threat. Who else was here?

4.12

Cabin Arrest

Back in their cabin, Mason sat across from his dad. "We only wanted to stop him. You have to believe me."

"Mason . . . I do. I just hope the Übel do as well," Mr. Wikk said. "They don't trust any of us, son, and our value seems to be running out. Honestly, I'm not sure how much more they'll tolerate. Now that they've captured direct ancestors of the Gläubigen, we're really falling down the pyramid of importance."

"You mean the Blauwe Mensen?"

"Yes."

"Who are the Gläubigen?"

"The original people who departed Ursprung. All the settlements and clues appear to have come from them," Mr. Wikk said. "We can learn quite a bit from the Blauwe Mensen. I just hope the king doesn't give too much information to the Übel."

It surprised Mason that the king was giving *any* information. Hadn't they sworn some sort of oath of protection? Wasn't it the king's job to protect the secrets above all? Then again, the oath had been to protect the gorge's secrecy, and that secret was out now.

"I haven't had a lot of time to talk to you since you woke up. I'm glad you're here and safe."

"We wanted to rescue you. We were so close on Evad. You were there; we were there. We just ran out of time," Mason explained.

"We knew the four of you would work together. You're a great team, and your strengths complement each other," Mr. Wikk said.

The door opened, and Mrs. Wikk came in. She looked worried. "He wants to see him."

Mason looked from his mom to his dad. "Who? Vedrik?"

"Zebra Xavier."

"When?" asked Mr. Wikk.

"Now," she said. "These arrived on a cargo pod." She held out a change of clothes to Mason: khaki cargo pants, a long-sleeved blue shirt, and a khaki vest. The clothes were his size and matched his parents'. These were exploration clothes.

"Have you seen my pack? Or the cross necklace I had?" Mason asked.

"No. The Übel confiscated your things and haven't returned them," she said.

Mason's heart sank. Many things in that pack were important to him and to the quest. Now they were in the hands of his enemies.

Mr. Wikk sighed and got to his feet. "Go and change. We can't keep him waiting."

Mrs. Wikk shook her head. "We aren't going. They've sent escorts."

"I'm not letting him interrogate my son," Mr. Wikk said.

"Dad, I'm fine. I've been chased by star-fighters, attacked by vines and black catlike creatures, and nearly blown up. He can't scare me."

"You've had to grow up more than you should have," Mr. Wikk said. "I'm sorry."

"Dad, it's not your or Mom's fault. I know who did this," Mason said.

His parents smiled.

"Not only do you sound older, you even look older," his dad said.

Mason stepped into the private lavatory to change. He looked at himself in the mirror. His mouth dropped open as he held up his arm. *A bicep?* He looked at his other arm. *Matching biceps?* They weren't comparable to Oliver's yet, but they were still more than he'd had not all that long ago. His hair was unruly and his skin more tanned than usual for this time of year. Burns still marred his body, as did scrapes from other injuries of the days past.

What his dad had said resonated in his mind. Sure, he'd grown physically, but he'd grown in other ways too.

There was a tap on the door.

"The escorts are growing impatient."

"Coming." Mason slipped on his shirt and tossed some water on his face.

As he walked for the door, his mom grabbed him into a hug and kissed his forehead. "Be brave, son. I love you."

Two escorts waited outside. One carried a pistol like Vedrik's and one held a StingerXN.

"This way," one of the soldiers said. Mason looked at the name stitched on his uniform. *Rutledge.* The other guard was Currie.

They marched to the Blauwe Mensen's cabin and stopped. Rutledge pounded on the door until it opened.

"Yes?" It was the queen.

"Prince Branz is required to meet with Zebra Xavier," Rutledge said.

"Why?" she asked. "Zebra Xavier has spoken with him many times already."

"This is not a request, it's a command, your highness," the soldier said disrespectfully. "Now!"

"Mother, it's fine," Branz said, stepping out of the cabin. He raised his eyes in an annoyed way, but at his mother or the summons, Mason wasn't sure. His outfit was similar to

Mason's, though he wore an orange shirt that was striking against his bright blue skin.

Currie stood between Mason and Branz, ensuring that they could not speak as they walked. Mason watched Branz curiously; the prince was writing on something. The soldiers paid no attention.

They didn't take the catwalk over the hangar. Mason knew why. He wished he could have seen the destruction Obbin had caused. The alerts had stopped shortly after his dad escorted him back to their cabin. But Mason doubted that the fires were out or the damage repaired. Perhaps the alerts didn't broadcast in their area. After all, that could be dangerous information. Prisoners might hear an alert and make a break for it in the chaos.

They arrived at a bank of three clear tubes that pierced the floor and ceiling. Rutledge stepped forward and touched a screen floating next to one of them. A silver capsule large enough for a half-dozen people zipped into view. A soft chime rang, and the doors opened.

Branz gave Mason a quick sideways glance with a half-smile before tackling him to the ground without warning. Mason's elbows burned.

"Read it," Branz said.

Currie yanked the prince from Mason. "What are you trying to pull?" He held Branz under the arm and shoved him into the now-open lift. "We'll take this one."

Rutledge nodded and tapped the floating kiosk screen. He and Mason waited for the next elevator. Mason now held a piece of paper in his clenched hand. The attack had simply been a diversion.

Mason gasped as Vedrik stepped out of the tube to the left. The captain stared down at him. "Enjoying your stay?" he asked snidely.

Mason's face tightened. No words crossed his lips.

"You might as well try. You're not going anywhere for a long time." The captain laughed and headed off. Two soldiers followed. Mason recognized them from Evad: Cruz and Bargoz.

Rutledge shoved Mason into the elevator. "Show some respect next time. You should be honored that he took the time to speak to you." He typed out a code on the screen inside the capsule, then pressed his hand to it. His hand glowed red, then green.

"Granted," a gravelly voice confirmed on the speaker. Without a second's pause, the lift shot upward.

The elevator stopped, and Mason stepped into a softly lit corridor. The walls were wood paneled, and potted plants sat at five-foot intervals. The corridor had an oddly cozy feel to it, especially compared to the starkness of the rest of the *Skull*. There was no sign of Branz.

Rutledge shoved Mason into a room with a round table and two padded leather chairs. "Sit!" he commanded. "I'll see if Zebra Xavier is ready for you."

The door shut and locked with a click. Mason unclenched his fist and unfolded the paper. In hastily scribbled handwriting it read, "Tell no lies. Speak not of Truth."

Tell no lies? Speak not of Truth? The capital *T* told Mason that this was the Truth Brother Sam had spoken of. Yet lying was wrong, so Branz was encouraging him not to do that either. These men seemed to know too much. Mason couldn't risk getting caught in a lie.

The handle to the door began to turn, so Mason tucked the note into his pants. "Zebra Xavier is ready," Rutledge said as he entered. "Come with me."

Rutledge led Mason to two wooden doors at the end of the corridor. He knocked.

"Come in."

Chills ran along Mason's spine. The voice had a sickening familiarity. The door opened, and he gasped when he saw Zebra

Xavier sitting behind a wide desk. He could hardly believe it, yet he felt he should have known all along.

4.13

Shadow Shapes

Austin knew from Oliver's tone that his brother was concerned about how to get the *Eagle* off Cixot. He wanted to have a solution to put Oliver's fears at rest the moment he and Ashley arrived. He sat in the pilot's seat at the NavCom, while Tiffany sat in the copilot seat, searching for additional features the *Eagle* might have that would help them to get off the planet. She had found a promising note about something called a *plasma pod governor* and was checking on it.

Based on the system's calculations, the *Eagle* would need an unusually large amount of thrust to lift vertically off the planet. The engines on the *Eagle* were not capable of creating this amount of thrust with their current power supply. They needed either a miracle to get off Cixot or a way to increase the power, and it wasn't as though they had an extra generator or engine lying around.

A dozen dark shapes shifted in the thick green clouds. Oliver and Ashley lay in the soot.

"Stay still. Don't say anything," Oliver whispered.

His Zinger was ready, but he was far too outnumbered to take out all of them. Firing would only draw attention to him and Ashley. He hoped the figures would pass by without seeing them.

Footfalls crunched the ash that covered the ground as the intruders approached. A moment later, the outlines of tricorne hats came into view. Dozens of lights blinked across the figures. Their glowing silver swords were out and ready for a fight. *Corsairs.* Oliver felt the hair on the back of his neck rise. They'd tracked the escape pod. Causing escaped prisoners to lose consciousness from asphyxiation made them easier to recapture.

"Peterson, Pierpont, Sanders, take the right flank. Sheppard, Powers, Hawkins, left. Santoyo and Pierce, you're with me," ordered a commanding voice with a thick accent. "Everyone, set to stun. Her life is more valuable than yours to the Supreme Admiral."

So they didn't know that Oliver and his brother and sister had landed on the planet. That gave him the advantage of surprise. Still, there were at least nine of them.

Six silhouettes moved away from the group. The remaining three continued directly toward Oliver. He could see that several were armed with the electrified silver swords he'd encountered on the *Black Ranger.* He might just have a chance to take out these three with the Zinger. Their weapons were only good at close range.

"Pilot Mayo, come in," the voice ordered.

Oliver couldn't hear the response.

"We're approaching the target. Wings up in ten minutes. Out."

The three Corsairs were headed straight for Oliver and Ashley. He should never have followed the rut. The soldiers were sure to step on them if they didn't see them first.

The idea of an extra generator stuck in Austin's mind. Would it be possible to redistribute the power from the auxiliary generators to boost the power to the vectored thrusters? If he were able to do that, would the thrusters be able to handle the additional power? Would they produce more thrust? Or would they burn out? He wasn't sure.

He told Tiffany his idea, finishing, "We'll briefly lose the NavCom and some flight systems, maybe the primary lights as well."

His sister looked at him, eyebrows raised. "Are you sure that's safe?"

Austin shrugged. "Staying here isn't any safer. We're running out of time and have no other options."

"Can I help?"

"It may take me a bit to figure out what we need to do."

"I'll go with you just in case you need me," she said.

Austin was fairly certain that Tiffany was going in case he shocked himself, or worse.

"I read about the plasma pod governor," Tiffany said. "Each plasma pod has a governor installed to control the amount of energy they are capable of releasing. This ensures that the cables don't burn up with surges of energy and also regulates a smooth burn from the engines."

"Plasma pods—we don't want to mess with those," Austin said. "We'd need special gear for that."

"Actually, the governors can be switched off from a control panel on each of the generators."

"That would be better than rerouting the energy from the auxiliary generators."

Tiffany shook her head. "Not necessarily. An uncontrolled surge of power could destroy the cables and cause the engines to misfire."

Austin knew what she *wasn't* saying. The engines could explode and send them crashing down to the moon's surface in a fiery ball.

"Then why allow them to be turned off at all?" asked Austin.

"The surge is an uncommon result, but possible."

"Okay, we'll try the auxiliary cable first."

Oliver motioned for Ashley to stay down. He rolled to the side and slid backward on his stomach.

He waited as he aimed the Zinger.

The soldiers were only a dozen feet from Ashley. Since the thick green fog made sight difficult and the Corsairs weren't expecting to find Ashley outside the pod, they had the advantage of surprise.

"What do we have here?" the leader suddenly said with a laugh. "Out of your pod, aye?" The man moved forward, the other two Corsairs flanking him.

The soldiers' attention was on Ashley. Oliver popped to his feet and fired the Zinger at the soldier on the left of the leader. The two zips of blue from the Zinger hit their mark, but the man didn't drop. Oliver let the Zinger fall against his body, held to him by its strap.

In less than half a second, Oliver reached the Corsair. With his right hand he reached for the man's sword, and with his left curled into a fist he socked the man below the right eye. The impact with the semi-metal face stung Oliver's knuckles.

Oliver swept his Zinger up and fired at the Corsair leader, but he'd already ducked. The shots struck the third man. He slumped to the ground, dropping his glowing silver sword with an explosion of sparks. Oliver turned the Zinger on the

Corsair he'd socked and fired again. This time the man dropped to the ground.

A purple shot zipped past Oliver. He dove to the ground, then lifted the Zinger and fired a volley of shots in the direction of the commander.

The Corsair was skilled and quick. He jumped, dove, and somersaulted, then fired a series of shots at Oliver from his stun pistol. The Corsair held a sword in his other hand, ready for action.

A silhouette crossed before Oliver and struck the Corsair in the side, dropping him to the ground. Oliver jumped to his feet and rushed on the two figures now wrestling back and forth.

It was Ashley. She had the Corsair on his—no, *her*—back. The soldier's tricorne hat lay to the side. Long black hair fell from her head. The Corsair shoved her knee up and sent Ashley backward, gasping. Oliver fired the Zinger at the Corsair commander, rendering her unconscious.

Ashley reached for the discarded sword, and Oliver pulled her to her feet. He was impressed.

"Put down the weapon," yelled a newly approaching Corsair.

Some of the other soldiers had returned. Oliver knew he barely had a moment. He twisted and fired two shots at the nearest shadows. The soldier dropped to the ground, but a spray of purple streaks flew at him and Ashley from the left and right. Oliver slid left, dove right, and jumped up to his feet to fire, but several incoming shots peppered him. Though he wore a spacesuit, his vision went black as he fell to the ground.

Austin held a Magnilox in his hand as he disconnected the gray supply cable from the auxiliary generator. The power cable came in from the reactor housed under the corridor that connected the bridge to the rest of the ship; Austin's task was to connect this cable into one of the primary generators. It wouldn't be easy, but the concept was simple. Jump ports existed on each generator to be used in instances when the generators were unresponsive.

Tiffany shone the light from her mTalk so Austin could see. The power had been shut off. Only the oxygen filters were still running off the auxiliary power supply.

Austin slipped the Magnilox back into his inventor's pouch and pulled out his Lazerzip. He first sliced the plug at the end of the cable, then pried it off. Then he carefully split the sides of the cable enclosure. He peeled back the lining, revealing five clear wires. He untwisted the strand of wires and connected two to each of the jump ports and the remaining one to a black grounding plug.

"Are you sure that's right?" she asked.

"These power channels aren't current specific. They apply the correct current as needed," Austin said. "The key will be to re-enclose them safely."

"How do you know that?"

"Advanced Engineering and Mechanics class," Austin said.

He removed a roll of insulation and began carefully wrapping it around each of the three new connections. He was careful to completely cover the wires. He ended with a fourth layer of insulation.

Austin bit his lip and admired his work. Was it enough? Was it hooked up correctly? Would his work result in their escaping the planet or crashing to their deaths?

"Tiffany, I think we're ready," Austin said.

She nodded and walked to the panel that would turn all the ship's power back on.

"Ready?" asked Tiffany.

Austin nodded. "Ready."

4.14

The Suit

Mr. Thule's face and thinning hair were all too familiar, although his bright blue skin and hair had paled since they'd met in the gorge. When Mason had last seen him in the Blauwe Mensen's amphitheater, he'd thought it would be the last time they'd ever see each other, but here he was. He still wore a freshly pressed suit, but now a shiny silver skull pin gleamed against the gray fabric. A second skull pinned his black tie in place.

So this was Zebra Xavier, the man whom even Vedrik feared.

"Well, Mason, it seems our paths have crossed again," Zebra Xavier said.

Mason wasn't scared. In fact, he felt an odd relief. He'd spoken to this man before. "Our paths didn't cross. You attacked and kidnapped us."

Zebra Xavier smiled. "No, no, I rescued you. Your parents missed their children." His voice carried a sickeningly fake sorrow. "We never intended for your family to be separated. That was Captain Vedrik's failure."

"Then he's failed twice," Mason said.

"Oh, more times than that." Zebra Xavier scowled. "Yet he is still useful to me . . . at least for the moment."

Mason considered the implications of this. His dad had said that their family's value was waning in Zebra Xavier's eyes. Even his own men were disposable to him.

"Mason, I brought you here for a reason. You were in the mural room. You saw the history of mankind on the wall and the star map painted across the ceiling." Zebra Xavier rubbed his chin. "I've had a team deciphering the clues from the moment we left. Your parents are part of that team. I want to invite you to join us."

"I'm not part of your team, and neither are my parents," Mason countered.

Zebra Xavier smiled. "Then why have they continued to provide me valuable insight?"

Mason's fists tightened into balls. His parents weren't on Zebra Xavier's team. "Perhaps you've misinterpreted their actions."

Zebra Xavier shook his head. "Perhaps, but it's unlikely." The man stared at Mason for a moment. "I wish to bring you up to speed."

"Do I have a choice?" Mason asked.

"Not really." Zebra Xavier flicked his wrist, and two holographic images glowed to life, floating in midair. One was of the mural from the Cathedral of the Star. Directly below was an image of the star map from the ceiling in the same location. The blue-green planet where the *Ark* had landed was flashing on both images. Zebra Xavier reached out and touched the image of the planet on the mural holograph. It turned into a globe and began to rotate. Zebra Xavier grasped the globe and set the holograph to float beside the other two images, where it continued to rotate.

"After cross-referencing the mural of the history of mankind with the star map on the ceiling, we know where to go next— YelNik Eisle. And, thanks to King Dlanod, we know that we need the keys from the Valley of Shadows. Unfortunately, Captain Vedrik failed to secure all the keys when he was there before."

Mason shifted uncomfortably. He'd searched for the Valley of Shadows while Austin sketched the map from the Blauwe Mensen paintings. He'd not found anything substantial. He tried to remember the quote from the paintings that Tiffany had read aloud as she entered it into the e-journal, but he hadn't committed it to memory. It seemed important.

Zebra Xavier made a fist with one hand, and the images vanished. He leaned back in his chair, his hands clasped. "During my nine years in the gorge, I collected a lot of information, much of which is still being scanned from my handwritten journals so that I can access it on my e-journal." His fingers went to the tablet device on the desk, and he tapped them across the cover. "But none of the information I gathered was as important as what the king knew. I expected it would take more time to fully earn his trust."

Mason grunted. "Nine years is a long time to be patient."

Zebra Xavier's eyebrows rose. "Indeed it is. I'm a patient man." He took a drink from a silver goblet on his desk. "When I came to the gorge, it was the closest we'd ever come in centuries to a group of people who might hold the answers we sought. I wasn't about to risk losing the answer now that we'd come so close. But when you and your brother appeared, I knew that things were moving far more quickly outside the gorge."

"You knew all along who we were?" Mason asked.

Zebra Xavier shook his head. "Only after I searched through your mTalks and the supplies that the Blauwe Mensen guards confiscated. We'd been tracking your parents before I went on my mission to the gorge. I even knew of your birth. Twins—a viable genetic anomaly indeed." Something about how Zebra Xavier said this gave Mason the chills. "The fact that you weren't with your parents told me that Vedrik had failed again."

Mason tried to recall their conversations. He'd been suspicious of Mr. Thule from the beginning, but there hadn't been any clue that he was part of the Übel. In Mason's opinion, Zebra Xavier's patience made him even more dangerous, like a spider waiting in its web for a bug to make a life-ending mistake. Was that why Zebra Xavier was tolerating Mason's resistance?

Zebra Xavier continued, "Once I checked in and confirmed the captain's failure, it was time to retake control of my organization."

"You had outside contact?" Mason asked.

"Of course, but I used it sparingly. I was able to receive and send very basic encrypted messages. The updates I received gave a more positive report of our progress than was accurate. I have dealt with the ones responsible for that," Zebra Xavier said, a darkness coming over him.

Mason swallowed. The bold feelings he'd felt before slipped away. He was starting to understand why the Übel feared this man.

"I'm really a peaceful person. I'd rather work with people in partnership than force them," Zebra Xavier continued.

"Since we're working together, I'd like to explain more about who we are and what we have been trying to accomplish for more than one and a half millennia," Zebra Xavier said. "And why."

Mason knew that the Übel had been around a long time, but Zebra Xavier was talking about at least fifteen hundred years. Now nine years didn't seem all that long.

Zebra Xavier walked to a large screen on the wall and tapped it. A couple thousand colorful dots appeared in a series of columns, each with a name next to it. "This is a list of all the planets, moons, and orbital platforms under Federation control," Zebra Xavier said. He tapped the screen again. Half the planets listed were now highlighted. "This was the Empire." He tapped the screen once again, and all the planet names disappeared except for about fifty. "This is where it all began. These forty-eight planets and moons were the beginning of the Empire. But this fledging society, having just escaped from the dangers of our collapsing world, was threatened by a plague carried on one of the colonization ships from Ursprung. If not for the quick actions of a group of wise men, the same tragedy that had befallen Ursprung would have destroyed the new Empire." Zebra Xavier's hand moved to the silver skull pendant on his suit jacket, and he looked at Mason with an expression of sorrow. "This is the contamination list," he said with another tap on the screen. A red line slashed through nearly half of the remaining planets.

A plague? That didn't sound at all like what Austin had told them that Brother Sam had said, or what O'Farrell had told Oliver and Tiffany. Both had said that there had been a cover-up, a wiping of history. Brother Sam had specifically said that the men were purposely covering up the Truth and had replaced it with a story of prosperity and peace. This did not sound like prosperity or peace.

Zebra Xavier touched one of the planets in the list. It appeared as a slowly rotating holograph before him. "We believe the plague started here. It spread quickly." He tapped several more planets in rapid succession; each began circling Zebra Xavier as holographic globes. "These planets were primary resources for food; these supplied water to planets without it." He moved his hand from planet to planet, designating the resources they held. The planet names hovered below them. "These planets were important for natural resources used in manufacturing. These were oxygen supply planets. Suddenly all of them were unusable, along with all their resources, leading to shortages across the rest of the Empire. Many planets, moons, and orbital stations were without food, water, or oxygen and had to be abandoned. Famine grew, and unemployment rose. This caused uprising after uprising. The promising restart for mankind was turning into a nightmarish sequel."

Mason was starting to feel that this presentation had been used many times before. Zebra Xavier was well practiced in explaining this history. If what Austin had relayed about the cover-up was true, this was just one part of that propaganda.

Zebra Xavier closed his fist, and the circling planets disappeared. He tapped the screen, and nearly half the planets without red lines slashed through them began flashing orange. "Each of these planets had major uprisings. It was all we could do to quash each one and hold the Empire together without losing more habitable planets." He pressed his pale blue hands together. "The leadership of the Übel discussed abandoning the cause and leaving with supplies to found a new colony. Thankfully, they determined to *fight* for the Empire. They had the courage to take action and risk their own lives to save countless others."

Mason nearly choked at the ideas Zebra Xavier was spewing at him. Not for a second did he believe that the Übel were capable of putting others first. Could the situation really have been so bad that they had to choose to flee or fight?

Mason raised his hand. "Why did you have to abandon entire planets? Wasn't there a way to contain the plague?"

"We attempted to quarantine the infected planets, but people escaped. The fledgling Empire didn't have a system in place to control interplanetary space travel, nor did it have the vast military force the Federation has now. The greatest asset to the growth of the Empire had been its network of supply ships. Now that network was our greatest threat." Zebra Xavier shook his head. "This plague is airborne, unstoppable if those carrying it are truly overtaken by it. Once an infected citizen reaches a planet, there is little to do but quarantine the planet and destroy those residing there. Otherwise, we risk its spreading to another, and another."

Mason felt sick at the words. He knew what they meant. "*Destroy*? You mean *kill*?" he asked, his throat tightening.

Zebra Xavier ignored the accusation. "The plague can remain hidden. There's no way to know who has it until it begins to spread. One infected person can infect thousands before we know."

"Why have I never been told this?" Mason asked.

"The Empire buried any information related to the contaminated zone," Zebra Xavier said. "The plague was a terrible time in our history. Knowledge of what the Empire had been forced to do would lead only to questions, accusations, and distrust. We had to replace it with a vision of peace, prosperity, and equality for all." He looked darkly at Mason. "You see, we still have no cure for this plague. If our citizens knew of it, it would cause widespread fear: fear of death. We must contain the plague with all our might, working to find the antidote at the same time. This is why we have returned to uncovering our past. We must find the source of the plague in order to create the antidote. That is why we must find Ursprung. We can stop death."

Mason had heard about outbreaks of disease or plague before. Scientists and doctors always tried to find the source—called *patient zero*—since that offered the best chance of discovering a cure or antidote.

Zebra Xavier's last words were haunting. It was true then—the Übel were after the secret to eternal life, and they believed it was a cure held by someone or hidden somewhere on Ursprung. Their biggest goal was to get back to the place where it had all begun in hopes that they would find the answer.

4.15

Skull Box

Zebra Xavier tapped a keypad at his desk. The desktop slid open, and a large black box with the Übel skull insignia emblazoned on it rose to the surface. He touched the sides of the box so that all five fingers of both hands were against a silver plate. Electricity surged over his hands, and the box opened. Zebra Xavier pulled out two black metallic, rectangular plates and two black cubes. He held the first plate level with his face, staring at it until, with a soft beep, the plate became transparent. He set the plate down. Inside was a frail piece of yellowed paper, burned around the edges. Only one line was legible. Zebra Xavier turned the plate so Mason could see. "We didn't know Ursprung mattered until we found this clue, dated at more than twenty-five hundred years old."

Mason read the scrap of paper. "And I give unto them eternal life; and they shall never perish." He knew this phrase well. Vedrik had said it before. It was the reason the Übel had invested all their time and resources in discovering Ursprung.

"This one phrase revealed that there is an answer to the fears of the people. We just don't know where that answer is. Who is 'I'? We gathered scientists and historians, and again we were stuck. Our history had changed; no one knew any of the real past."

"What makes you think the 'I' is even still alive?" Mason immediately regretted his question. The conclusion the Übel had drawn was obvious.

"One does not know the secret to eternal life and not use it," Zebra Xavier said. "The citizens we serve need us to find the one who can give people eternal life. This will remove the fear of death, and once again the Empire will be free." Zebra Xavier stroked his pale blue hair. "We've spent centuries trying to find a scientific cure, and while our technologies and medicines can extend our lives, eventually death catches each of us." Zebra Xavier glanced toward the wall with a frown. Mason followed his gaze to a cabinet door with the letters *ZXDNA* etched in silver across it. The Übel leader twisted back, his eyebrows raised as if he'd forgotten that Mason was there for the briefest of seconds. "This remnant of a page long forgotten hinted at another way."

Mason was surprised by Zebra Xavier's explanation. He didn't doubt that the man believed it, but it sounded like a doctrine ingrained into his very being.

Zebra Xavier tapped the clear metal three times. It instantly went black. Mason crossed his arms and sat back in his chair.

"The cure we seek is on Ursprung," Zebra Xavier said. "If we can find our origin, we can unlock a cure to all that ails the fragile human body. We have turned our attention and efforts to finding Ursprung. To draw out people who might be infected by the plague but in hiding, we converted the Empire to a Federation that promised freedom, One of the first acts of our newly installed chancellor was to lift the ban on archeology. Archeos was established not long after that."

Mason considered what he knew about Archeos. It was indeed relatively new. His parents had chosen archeology because their excitement over its discoveries had brought them together. In fact, on one of their first expeditions together in university, they'd discovered nearly two thousand artifacts from an ancient civilization.

"My brother said that the Übel weren't involved with archeology until recently; you said you were involved since the Empire converted to the Federation," Mason pointed out.

"We were always involved, but we couldn't make our actions obvious. Some wished to stop us. We remained out of the light, compiling the data discovered and tracking the efforts," Zebra Xavier explained. "We raised the quarantines on several long-blockaded planets, and discoveries about the Gläubigen began to surface. Unfortunately, the work wasn't easy. So much destruction had been done to their settlements, and their history had been wiped clean. We were finding scraps among decimated ruins. After decades of piecing things back together, it seemed the settlements were linked in a continuous circle. We thought the Gläubigen's history would not lead us back to Ursprung. Then, just under ten years ago, this was discovered by your parents," Zebra Xavier said.

He raised the second black plate and stared at it until it became transparent. He set the plate down so Mason could see what was inside.

Mason looked closely at the artifact, which was in worse condition than the previous one. Sections had been torn from the blue paper or eaten away, and the text was not printed, but written in a sloppy scrawl.

> Tyler,
>   . . . safety on . . . travels. . . . bring peace to us all. We give . . . the hope we . . . your work as an emissary . . . our people. "For all flesh is as grass, and all the glory of man as the flower of grass. The grass withereth, and the flower thereof falleth away: But . . . Lord endureth forever. And this is . . . unto you" (1 Peter). For our task is beyond our physical body, it is to ensure . . . live eternally as our Lord has promised.

May you . . . as a reminder of our home. Always keep the . . .
in your . . . mind.
      . . . be with you.

"This artifact again confirmed the possibility of living forever. We believe that Peter is the creator of the cure for death, becoming a 'Lord' who will live forever. He may be an emperor or king. The writer of the note then reaffirms this in his or her own words and mentions something that is to be kept in Tyler's mind. We believe that the knowledge about eternal life is a secret passed only verbally from one person to the next." Zebra Xavier triple-tapped the plate, and it went black again. "This is why building trust with the king of the Blauwe Mensen was so essential."

"But how did this artifact lead you to Cobalt Gorge?" Mason asked.

"While running analysis on the paper's makeup, the database identified a mineral that we sourced to lumber produced on Jahr des Eises. It is a potent blue pigment called Blue Frost. Since it has no significant use or dangers, no search for the mineral's source had been conducted."

Mason recalled how everything within Cobalt Gorge was some shade of blue, including the people. The pigment had literally dyed everything and everyone in the valley blue, including Zebra Xavier during his time there.

"As my scientists researched Jahr des Eises further, they uncovered an artifact that the Übel had obtained in 1259. A man had discovered a book in the woods of Jahr des Eises that mentioned Ursprung at the time of the final exodus in AD 2559."

Zebra Xavier opened the cube to reveal a book in fair condition. "This was confiscated to maintain the revised history of the Empire. One of our leaders held it for his own private collection. We didn't realize how valuable it was. The book itself is a journal. Although it doesn't mention the cure, it pinpoints dates and locations on Ursprung that should be useful when we reach the planet. For example, it names the spaceport from which the author departed and is accompanied by a sketch of a large arch surrounded by domes." Zebra Xavier took out the final box. "Then came the discoveries at the Gläubigen's Dabnis Castle: the green globe with coordinates to a new location and a very important book. We now had coordinates to a previously unexplored settlement and the most significant artifact we'd ever discovered. The new location had the first unexplored ruins in three decades."

"You mean Evad?" Mason asked.

Zebra Xavier nodded and lifted out the crimson, leather-bound book Mason's parents had discovered at the castle. "When the captain recovered the artifact from your home on Tragiws, we were able to confirm its direct connection to Ursprung."

"Recover? You stole it!" Mason accused incredulously.

Zebra Xavier's expression darkened. "It was ours to begin with. We've been the ones allowing your parents to explore. We even found ways to fund them when they needed additional equipment or support, before we lifted the funding band. Do you think your parents could have afforded to send you and your siblings to Bewaldeter or your brother would have received early admittance to the Star Fleet Academy without our efforts? We have given far more to your family than you can ever imagine."

Mason's breathing picked up. Anger, fear, disbelief—the emotions were like a storm inside him. His family had been nothing but pawns in the chess game the Übel were playing against death. Had his parents even known that the Übel were helping them?

"Your parents found a way to surprise and defy us. They'd never trusted us, and then they turned down enough money to support your family and many future generations of Wikks," Zebra Xavier said. "We knew then that they were on to something significant. My teams are at this moment analyzing the book. It was in an unfamiliar language, and we do not have a full translation available to us."

Mason's mom hadn't mentioned having any troubles reading the text. Mason wondered if his parents knew what the book said or had begun to read it. But if so, how had they avoided letting Zebra Xavier know? They believed in pure honesty.

"We have discovered a story about a tree that might provide life," Zebra Xavier continued. "We believe that it grows a fruit that contains an ingredient in the elixir for eternal life."

"How much longer do you expect the search to continue?"

"Days, at the most, if the *Ark* is the final stop to Ursprung. Everything has accelerated beyond expectation." Zebra Xavier carefully set the book back in the box and sealed it. "We're headed to the valley, where we will acquire the remaining keys. Captain Vedrik retrieved only four of them previously. The others were stolen before we could secure them, I believe by the red cloaks."

Zebra Xavier noticed Mason straighten. A sly smile slipped across his face. His reaction had been exactly what Zebra Xavier had been hoping for.

"I want you to tell me all you know about the man in the red cloak. Captain Vedrik reports that you made contact with him on both Evad and Enaid."

Mason squirmed in his seat. He couldn't reveal anything about Brother Sam or the Veritas Nachfolger. Doing so would lead to discussion of the Truth.

"The man is part of a society attempting to cause confusion to those seeking Ursprung and the secret to eternal life," Zebra Xavier said. "His people are likely the ones responsible for the plague."

The Veritas Nachfolger were spreading the Truth. Zebra Xavier was the leader of the Übel, a group that sought a physical cure for death. Mason didn't doubt that they would lie to reach success.

"We want to be prepared in case these people are carrying the plague with them." Zebra Xavier leaned forward in his chair. "Don't think that you or your family would be immune. If my men are targeted, you will fall along with them."

Mason remained silent. He didn't like the idea of dying of a plague, but he couldn't imagine the Veritas Nachfolger or Brother Sam using one as a weapon. Of course, Brother Sam had said that this had been a long fight. There were always casualties in wars.

"Tell me what that man is after." Zebra Xavier's tone contained a warning.

"Sir," Mason began, trying to find words in a desperate attempt to deflect the question, "why do you believe these men would try to spread a deadly plague?"

"To disrupt the peace and prosperity of the Empire, to unseat those in control, and to take their power for their own," Zebra Xavier explained with conviction.

"If so, wouldn't they have spread the plague again by now?"

Zebra Xavier paused. "The Federation is careful to watch for any sightings of these red cloaks. More often than you would expect in the last few centuries, the Federation has arrested them and dismantled their organization. We are careful to remove any evidence of their actions. We don't want to create a panic." Zebra Xavier tapped the desk, and the black box sank back, its contents replaced and secure. "This had been the longest they'd been silent. Until the incident on Evad, we thought the last of them had died."

The Veritas Nachfolger were clearly tied to the Gläubigen. Brother Sam had spoken of protecting the path in order to preserve it, but the idea that they would fight back with a plague seemed in complete opposition to what Mason knew of them. Yet why did it seem that the Gläubigen's settlements were nearly always on a planet that had been quarantined or contaminated by the plague? Mason's parents had explored and made discoveries on many of the planets on Zebra Xavier's list. Was Mason wrong about the Veritas Nachfolger? Was it just one more ruse that he and his family faced?

Mason's thoughts turned to the e-papyrus the Übel had given him. He wanted to write this down so he could look for clues and piece together the puzzle. So much swirled in his mind that it was becoming too foggy to sort through. He needed to see it in front of him.

"Back to what you know, Mason," Zebra Xavier said. "Tell me about the man in the red cloak."

Mason rubbed his eye. "I have nothing to say about him."

"We know that he took you into the cathedral on Enaid and attempted to kidnap you on Evad. Captain Vedrik should have done more to protect you. He should have blasted that silver ship out of the sky." Zebra Xavier took a deep breath. "Now, I ask you one last time, who is this man?"

Mason bit his lip. He didn't want to lie, but he didn't want to talk of the Truth, and not just because of Branz's instructions. He could discern what was true and what was not; he knew in his heart and in his mind that Helper was guiding him. He knew that the Veritas would not spread a plague. He knew that the way of the Truth was the right way. He knew that this man was dangerous.

As if to confirm his fears, Zebra Xavier slammed his fist down on the desk. His expression changed so suddenly that Mason pushed back in his chair. The patience of nine years had worn on him, and Zebra Xavier had none left.

"You and your family will begin to cooperate. Are you ready to suffer for your silence?" he bellowed.

Letter

Austin was glowing with excitement. His reattachment of the cable to the generator appeared to have worked.

"Austin, did you do it?" Tiffany asked in case she was missing something.

"Yes!" he cheered. "Although we won't know if it's enough extra power to lift us until we try."

"Should we try to hover?" Tiffany asked.

"I don't want to test it and risk that it's a one-time shot. We might only get one powerful burst of thrust," Austin admitted. "We'll try as soon as Oliver and Ashley are on board."

"Do you think something might go wrong?"

"It's not 100 percent unlikely."

Oliver's eyes shot open. A man with a yellow orb in place of one eye stared down at him. Half of the man's face was constructed of metal and blinking lights.

"He's awake," the Corsair said, retracting a vial of waking agent from under Oliver's nose.

"Good," said the Corsair in charge. Her face appeared in his view. It was the Corsair Oliver had stunned. Her hair was raven black, and her tricorne hat was back in place. "To your feet."

Oliver didn't move.

"Get him up," she growled.

Firm hands yanked Oliver to his feet. Ashley's hands were bound, glowing swords held to her back. Like him, she was no longer wearing a protective spacesuit. They were in the immense bay of a huge ship—not anywhere as large as the *Black Ranger*, but far greater in size than the *Phoenix* or the *Eagle*. His mTalk was gone.

"Where are your siblings?" the Corsair demanded.

He said nothing.

"Where is Samuel Krank?" she yelled.

Oliver didn't speak.

The Corsair's gloved hand struck Oliver across the face. "Speak!"

"No!" yelled Ashley. "Don't hurt him. Let us—"

"Silence her." One of the Corsairs covered Ashley's mouth. "You will speak, or she will suffer."

Oliver opened his mouth.

"Commander DarkStone, report to the bridge. We've located a ship in the near vicinity," a voice called over the loudspeaker.

A victorious smile crossed the commander's face. "Throw them in the brig," she said.

The commander and two of her men disappeared through a set of doors. The remaining Corsairs escorted the two prisoners through a single door at the base of the large bulkhead separating the rest of the ship from the cargo bay. They shoved them inside a drab, gray room with three benches inside.

A moment later, they felt the vibration of the ship taking off.

Tiffany overlaid the hand-drawn star map from the cathedral's ceiling with a federally commissioned digital star map that displayed the position of Yl Revaw. The wooded planet displayed underground in the cathedral was in this same position. Cao was also in line between Enaid and YelNik Eisle and matched up with a digital star map. YelNik Eisle could not be matched.

"Of course!" Tiffany shouted.

"What is it?" Austin asked.

"The communication data recorder from the observatory!" she said. "When we were on Evad, Mason and I learned about the telescope in the observatory. It was also an optical communication transmitter and receiver. Oliver retrieved the data recording and storage cylinder. It must still be in his pack."

"Unless he took it out in his cabin," Austin said. "Then it'd still be on the *Phoenix*."

"Let's hope not," Tiffany said. "Have you seen it?"

Austin bent over and reached under the pilot's seat. "It's right here." He pulled out Oliver's pack and began to dig through it. "What's this?" He held up a pink and gray envelope. "It's addressed to Oliver from Ashley."

Oliver sat next to Ashley on a bench in the cell.

"Hey, nice fighting out there," he managed. "We almost had them."

"Almost." Ashley smiled, nodding to their cell around them. "I can hardly believe you came for me. I wasn't sure you'd get my distress signal."

"How did you send it to us?" Oliver asked.

"My parents had mentioned the *Phoenix* when we left to rendezvous," Ashley said. "I found it listed in the com directory."

"That makes sense. The *Phoenix*'s original owner is the Corsairs' beloved Supreme Admiral," Oliver said. "How did you escape?"

Ashley's eyes glistened. "The ship was trying to rescue Mr. O'Farrell. A shuttle got him and returned to the *Black Ranger*, but it was followed. The *Ranger* was attacked." Ashley paused.

"You don't have to tell me now. You can wait until you are ready," Oliver said.

Ashley shook her head. "No, I'm fine. Before the *Ranger* could escape by hyper flight, another ship docked to it. It was too late to disengage. When the *Black Ranger* performed the jump, the enemy ship came with it."

Oliver had heard of instances of that happening, but also of cataclysmic consequences for both ships if something went wrong. A hyper-flight docking was beyond risky.

"The soldiers blasted into the ship. They were after one thing: my parents." Ashley whimpered. "And they got them. My mom yelled for me, but several Corsairs got between us. They fought. The soldiers retreated into their ship with my parents and were gone."

Oliver was frowning. "I can't believe they were able to pull off a mid–hyper flight extraction and undocking," he said. "It's nearly impossible. How'd they know where to go?"

The question was meant rhetorically, but Ashley answered. "I don't know. They docked on the exterior of the ship in line with the prison level. When the enemy ship released itself from the *Ranger*, it left a gaping hole. It was chaos; the oxygen levels were plummeting. That's when I climbed into the escape pod. I hoped that if I got away, you and Tiffany would come for me." She looked at him thankfully. "And you did."

How had the Übel known that the McGregors were on the *Ranger*? Why did they want them? They had Oliver's parents. Perhaps his parents' resistance was frustrating the Übel. Hopefully not so much that they would dispose of them. The taste of bile seeped into Oliver's mouth at the thought of the Übel killing his parents. He shook it off.

"I'm glad to see you again," he said. "I'm just sorry we got recaptured."

Ashley smiled. "It's not your fault. There were a lot of them." She pulled two H2O bottles from her pack and handed one to Oliver. "What will they do now?"

"Take us back to the *Black Ranger*, probably," Oliver said. "After they capture Tiffany and Austin. I wish there was a way for me to warn them." He looked at his bare wrist.

"Wait, what happened to Mason?" Ashley asked.

Oliver felt a pang of sadness. "He's been taken by the Übel. They captured him and Obbin, the blue boy you met."

Ashley touched his shoulder. "Oliver, I'm sorry."

He looked at her and smiled. "We'll get him back, just like we'll get back your parents and mine," he promised.

Austin held the letter in his hand, his eyebrows raised. Tiffany looked at him, bemused. She wanted to ask him what it said, but then her better judgment kicked in. "Put it away, Austin. It's not for us to snoop."

Austin cocked his head. "Serious? It's got to be a love letter or something."

"Austin! Put it back," Tiffany said.

Austin scowled back at her and set the envelope back in the pack.

"Do you see the cylinder?"

Austin grunted and kept digging in the pack.

Tiffany looked at the map on the e-journal. Yl Revaw was highlighted. If the people on Evad had communicated with people at the XYZ coordinates for Yl Revaw, then the planet on the mural was indeed the same and Yl Revaw was likely the location of the Eochair.

Perhaps she could cross-reference all the coordinates of outbound communications with planets in the Federal registry. Then she could eliminate planets and locations already visited and determine places yet to be visited. She would be able to determine which of the planets that her parents had visited were likely connected to the Gläubigen and could eliminate ones that were not.

It wasn't perfect, because some settlements could have been abandoned before the establishment on Evad and some created after Yth Orod itself was abandoned. But the cross-referencing plan was the best she could come up with to narrow down the amount of information she needed to go through.

Tiffany was frustrated. Too many times in the last few days she had gotten a clue and failed to follow it up because events were happening so quickly. The Valley of Shadows, the cylinder from Evad, the maps from the Blauwe Mensen castle, the books from the ziggurat . . . each scrap of information could unravel the mystery of their destination and help them to keep one step ahead of the Übel. Yet she hadn't kept up.

She closed her eyes and sighed, remembering what her brothers had said. Getting down on herself wouldn't help. She'd done her best to read and search for information. She'd hardly slept, and she'd hardly remembered to drink and eat.

"It's not here," Austin said, pulling her from her thoughts.

"He must have taken it out." Tiffany frowned. She'd just have to work with what she had.

Who Is He?

Zebra Xavier's gaze seemed to pierce Mason's mind like daggers of cold blue ice. Mason didn't know what to say.

"Is this a game to you, boy?" The old man's eyebrows narrowed angrily. "Do you think I won't punish you or your family?"

Mason shook his head, trying to dispel the intensity of Zebra Xavier's anger.

"I won't hesitate to use any method to get the information from you that I need," Zebra Xavier threatened. "Understanding and unlocking the ability to control life will change everything. It will give us the power to create a perfect world without end. With no fear of death, peace will rule our society. We will provide those loyal to us with everlasting life so they can prosper forever."

The change had been so quick. When the man had explained the long history of the Federation and how the Übel had sought to make it a better place, he'd had the personality of Mr. Thule. Then the darkness of Zebra Xavier had come out roaring like a monster from the shadows. It was like he was two people trapped in the same body.

Had Mason's parents faced these threats, or was Zebra Xavier using them on him because he was a kid? If so, the old man was underestimating Mason's resolve. Mason was willing to do his part to protect the Veritas Nachfolger. He knew now why they had remained so quiet. They were few in number compared to the Federation. If word of their existence got out, the Übel would wipe out entire cities, even planets.

A knock at the door interrupted the standoff. Relief washed over him.

"Enter," growled Zebra Xavier.

The wooden doors opened, and Obbin was shoved in. The young prince's hands were bound, his mouth gagged. He wore only his black shorts.

"Sir, this one has information about the cloaked man. They call him Samuel," said the all-too-familiar voice of Captain Vedrik.

Mason gasped. Why would Obbin give in? He was the last one Mason would have expected to do so.

The captain stepped in, his black uniform and cape crisp, his boots shined to perfection. The silver skull pendant on his cap glimmered under the cabin's lights. Mason eyed the pistol at his side.

"I'd expected Branz to give in to logic before you got over your stubbornness, but then again you were always selfish and looking to save your own skin," Zebra Xavier said. "Ungag him."

Vedrik bowed his head. "Yes, sir."

"I knew you were a traitor from the day you came!" Obbin shouted. He jerked his wrists side to side in a futile attempt to free himself.

"You were two years old. You don't remember anything," Zebra Xavier countered harshly. "Get on with what you have to say, or we'll tie that gag tighter and send you back to the cooler."

Obbin's nostrils flared as he scowled. It took him a moment to compose himself. Vedrik slipped out his Zapp-It and let the

WHO IS HE? | 139

blue sparks sizzle between the two silver prongs on the end of the device. A metallic smell filled the air.

"Okay," Obbin said, rubbing his bare side. "I met Brother Samuel in the valley with the pyramids. He'd come there to oversee their discoveries." He nodded toward Mason. "He gave me tasks and, once I completed them, he would find me again and give me more. He said I would be rewarded."

"Sir, this one was responsible for the skelzax infestation," Captain Vedrik inserted.

Skelzax, Mason mouthed. He'd never heard of that. It sounded awful.

Zebra Xavier grunted, then waved his hand for Obbin to continue.

"We met him again under the great city, and he led us to the chamber with the painting," Obbin said.

Mason felt relieved. Obbin hadn't given them any information that they didn't already sort of know. He'd said nothing of the Truth or mentioned Sister Dorothy.

"You know more, boy. I've known you long enough to know when you are keeping something from me," Zebra Xavier accused.

There was a sickening crackle, and Obbin screamed. Vedrik pulled the Zapp-It away from the prince's exposed side. Two reddened circles smoldered just under Obbin's armpit. The boy didn't collapse, meaning that the charge was low, but hot.

"Yes, I released the skelzaxes into the troops' tents," Obbin admitted in a pained mumble. "I disrupted the defensive barrier around your base camp and led the black cats to you."

Zebra Xavier slammed his fist against the table. "That's not what I am talking about, and you know it!" he howled. "Leave him in the cooler until he's ready to speak. Bring me his brother."

Vedrik gripped Obbin's bare arm in black-gloved hands and yanked him from the room.

Zebra Xavier picked up the tablet device he'd touched earlier. "I know your sister took my other e-journal. Fortunately, I have all the information backed up on this device. While I doubt that you or your siblings could have gotten past the security protocol, I believe this Samuel might have. You will tell me what you discovered."

They hadn't been able to crack into Zebra Xavier's e-journal, and in the brief time they'd had with Brother Samuel, the device hadn't come up. Mason stopped a smile from crossing his lips; the e-journal was safe in the *Phoenix*. "Nothing, sir," he said honestly.

Zebra Xavier considered him. "I have a gift. I can read people. I can tell when they're lying. For the moment, you are not lying."

Mason took a shallow breath.

"Where is the e-journal?"

"Sir—" Mason started again. Using the term of authority might help to better position him with Zebra Xavier. Clearly the man demanded respect, and calling him *sir* could only help Mason's situation. "—it's on the *Phoenix*." Mason was happy to answer these questions. They meant that the conversation was moving away from the Veritas Nachfolger.

Zebra Xavier sighed. "We have yet to locate your brothers and sister after their escape from Enaid."

Again Mason fought back a smile. His siblings were still free.

"What do you know of this Phelan O'Farrell character?" Zebra Xavier asked next. "We caught up to his flagship, the *Black Ranger*, but the weasel escaped us again."

"Sir, I don't know that much about him. He funded some of our parents' expeditions." Mason didn't mind revealing what he knew of Mr. O'Farrell. Part of him hoped that the Übel would find and capture the man who'd betrayed the McGregors.

"And?"

"He's not working with us. He captured us when we left Jahr des Eises the second time."

"I'm aware." Zebra Xavier's cold blue eyes began to pry again.

Mason felt compelled to say more. "He's the one who gave us the *Phoenix* and the McGregors the *Griffin*."

"Yes, yes, we extracted the McGregors from the *Black Ranger*."

Mason took a breath. He already knew that the Übel had captured the McGregors. Rand and Jenn had been in the mural room under the Cathedral of the Star.

"Why didn't you capture the *Black Ranger* or at least Mr. O'Farrell?"

"It was just a tactical extraction team. A quick latch and grab," Zebra Xavier explained. "Nearly lost the ship during the undocking."

Latch and grab? Mason assumed this meant that the Übel had docked with the *Black Ranger*, broken in, and removed the McGregors quickly.

"Do you know where Ashley McGregor is?" Mason asked.

"My men were supposed to take the girl too, but she escaped them. Her parents were the primary targets," Zebra Xavier said. "I'm telling you, I prefer to have you kids with your parents. They are far more cooperative if they know you are safe. We can all work on this quest together. I can provide the materials and protection needed."

"What happened to the *Black Ranger*?" Mason asked.

"Evacuated, perhaps. My men left before they could see its fate."

Mason nodded.

Zebra Xavier had taken on a far different tone with Mason than the one he'd used with Obbin. Then again, Zebra Xavier had a lot more history with the Blauwe Mensen.

"Did you contact Archeos?" Zebra Xavier asked.

"No."

"The Federation?"

"No."

"So this O'Farrell was operating rogue from Archeos and the Federation?"

"I believe so." There was silence for a moment. "I don't know much else. I wasn't with him prior to being captured. By then he wasn't giving out much information," Mason concluded.

There was a knock on the door. "Come in."

"Sir, Prince Branz to see you," Vedrik said.

4.18

Swallowed

Austin was reworking the numbers when an alert flashed on the screen: *Unidentified craft approaching.*

The video feeds to the outside were useless, still shrouded by the thick green gases of the Cixot atmosphere. He tapped the screen, and the titanium heat shields slid up, clearing the view from the bridge windshields. It wasn't any better. The blip on the radar revealed that the craft coming toward him was large, bigger than the *Eagle*.

He held up his mTalk. "Oliver, Oliver, come in. Something is approaching us."

There was no response.

"Oliver, Oliver, this is the *Eagle*. Are you all right?"

Still nothing.

The green cloud swirled, and a wall of silvery gray filled his view. Lights blinked across it. Then the surface shifted; a massive hatch lowered like a gaping mouth.

A dozen troops swarmed out from the door and moved to either side of the *Eagle*, disappearing from his view. A large rover rolled out of the bay. A long mechanical arm with a clamp reached from the vehicle and latched on to the *Eagle*.

"Tiffany!" Austin cried. "We're under attack!"

"What? Who?" Tiffany hurried to join Austin at the console. "I thought we were cloaked."

Austin put his hand to his head. "The auxiliary generator. When I redirected the power, I may have shut off the cloaking."

A violent jolt knocked Austin to the ground. Tiffany gasped as she too hit the bridge floor.

"What in the world?"

"They're taking us," Austin said.

The gaping mouth ahead was about to swallow the ship whole.

"Do something," Tiffany said.

"Like what?" Austin's hands were on the console.

"Take off?"

"We'd nose-dive!"

Tiffany froze, her mouth hanging open. "Oliver?"

Austin shook his head.

"Lock down the ship. Make sure no one can get in," Tiffany ordered as she swung into the copilot seat. "If there was a cloak on this ship, there has to be some sort of security too."

Tiffany's fingers slid and tapped the screen.

"Ship secure," the computer voice said. "All hatches locked."

Oliver's toes ached. How much longer could he balance on the top of the thin doorframe, his sweaty palms pressed against the cold metal of the brig? Ashley looked completely at ease. She was poised and balanced and wasn't trembling like he was.

"How are you doing that?" he whispered through gritted teeth.

"Several years of ballet," she said. "It can't be much longer."

Oliver wasn't so sure. They'd already been on the doorframe for at least ten minutes, waiting for the guard to see that they were apparently missing. Their plan was then to rush the bridge and take control of the ship. It would be unexpected, and it would be their only chance to escape before they reached the *Black Ranger*.

The lock clicked, and the hatch opened. A Corsair stepped into the room directly below Oliver, sword glowing brightly.

Oliver jumped from his perch, bringing his foot down on the soldier's sword-wielding arm. The weapon clattered to the floor. Ashley dropped behind the soldier, and the Corsair twisted to see.

Oliver sent the soldier sideways with a firm kick. Ashley went for the sword, and Oliver jumped at the off-balance Corsair. The soldier fell to the ground, her tricorne hat falling off, loosing long locks of blond hair. Before the Corsair could recover, Ashley brought the sword against the soldier's arm, knocking her out. The attack had taken all of fifteen seconds.

Oliver and Ashley slipped from the brig and pressed a button to lock the Corsair into the cell.

Tiffany looked out the windshield. Lights blinked across the large bay. A black, diamond-shaped pod sat beside them. The rover had dragged the *Eagle* all the way into the bay on its skids. The screeching noise the skids had given off as they scraped against the charred earth and then the metallic floor of the bay had forced Tiffany and Austin to cover their ears.

She and Austin had discussed firing up the engines and attempting to fight capture, but it seemed futile. They were more likely to cause an explosion, stranding them on Cixot.

Tiffany was sure the pod beside them was Ashley's escape pod. Since they still had not heard from Oliver, she assumed that her brother and her friend were both aboard the larger ship.

The Corsair soldiers in their tricorne hats had stayed near the ship but not attempted to board. Tiffany was sure that would change the moment the bay's air was breathable and the doors were closed behind them, sealing the *Eagle* within the belly of the enemy ship.

She looked at a screen that showed the view behind the ship. Sure enough, the large cargo bay doors were slipping together. The last wisp of green cloud disappeared.

Any minute now, the Corsairs would begin their attempt to break into the *Eagle*.

Ashley handed Oliver the Corsair sword. "Are you sure this is the way to the bridge?"

"No, but the other way leads back to the cargo bay," Oliver said.

The corridor was fairly well lit by small points of white light. A door at the end was labeled *Stairwell*. Oliver opened the hatch and looked up.

"Looks clear," Oliver said. Ashley moved first, followed by Oliver, who closed the door softly behind him. They moved up the stairs cautiously but quickly.

At each flight, Oliver scanned the listing of what was on the level. The bridge was on the top level of the ship.

"Wait here," Oliver said. Ashley was about to protest, but he stopped her. "It'll be easier. I'll be right back."

Austin ran down the corridor and into the cargo bay. He knew where the extra weapons were. He wasn't sure if his sister was ready for a Zinger, but after her performance on Re Lyt, he knew she could hold her own. Maybe the bigger weapon would be suitable.

He took two Zingers and a Zapp-It, then raced up the stairs, down the corridor, and into the bridge. He sealed the hatch behind him. This was where they would make their final stand. He wasn't sure how long they could hold out in the *Eagle*. Now that they were inside the enemy ship, they had few options for escape.

"Austin, a skiff just hovered alongside us. I think it has some sort of laser cutting tool mounted on it," Tiffany said.

"We're going to be ready," Austin said.

"Do you really think standing against them is the wisest thing?" asked Tiffany. "We're outnumbered, and our ship is impounded. Once they cut into it, we won't be able to fly it."

"What do you suggest? Giving up?" Austin asked.

"Yes," Tiffany said. "It's not what I want to do, but resisting is pointless at the moment. They have Oliver. Maybe their ship is the only sure way we'll get off Cixot."

His sister had a point. Still, surrendering seemed to go against everything they'd done.

The long corridor was empty. Oliver recalled the steps and turns they had made from the cargo bay to the brig cell and then from there to the stairs. The ship's bridge should be to the left.

As Oliver continued down the corridor, he stopped at a half-dozen open hatches to cautiously check inside. This was taking him longer than he desired. The Corsair trapped in the cell below could be discovered at any moment.

When Oliver was about fifteen feet from the end of the corridor, he could read a sign next to the last door. *Engine Compartment.* He'd been wrong. It was odd that the door didn't lead to the ship's bridge. Usually cargo bays were at the rear of the ship.

He glanced at other hatches lining the hall; none appeared to be entrances to the ship's command area. The listing in the stairwell had said that the bridge was on this level.

Oliver turned and started back down the long corridor. He'd been unconscious when he'd been dragged to the ship. Perhaps the cargo bay doors were at the front of the enemy craft. It wasn't standard, but it wasn't uncommon either, especially on larger ships.

He heard a hiss, and the door at the far end of the corridor began to lift. Oliver dashed for one of the open hatches and dove into the cabin. He pulled himself up and slipped to the door. Several sets of footsteps were coming his way. He wanted to look but resisted.

The footfalls stopped. "Get the prisoners from the brig and meet me in the cargo bay." Oliver recognized the voice of Commander DarkStone. "Those two will let us board, or their brother will suffer. I want them to see it."

"Yes, ma'am." Oliver recognized Drex's voice. The young Corsair seemed to be showing up everywhere. A handle clicked, and a hatch closed with a hiss.

Oliver tightened his grip on the Corsair sword. Its silver glow brightened. *Interesting.* He loosened its grip, and the blade dimmed. It glowed stronger under a renewed squeeze.

One set of footsteps continued toward him. If it was Drex heading to the brig, his former Academy classmate would run right into Ashley. Oliver had to act.

He took a deep breath, then spun out of the room and sprinted toward his enemy, catching him off guard. Oliver closed another twenty feet before Drex came unfrozen and reached for his weapon.

Oliver was nearly to him, but not close enough. Drex fired his Zinger. The blue stun shot zipped past Oliver and took out a wall light.

Drex fired again; Oliver spun to his left and slammed against the corridor wall. He bounced off and continued his charge toward his enemy. He swung the glowing sword at Drex.

Drex blocked with the Zinger. An explosion of blue and silver sparks erupted between them, sending the two flying backward. Oliver hit the ground hard. The stench of singed hair and scorched metal filled the air.

Oliver rolled to his stomach. His ears were ringing. He pushed himself up and looked for the sword. The weapon wasn't glowing; its handle was charred. Drex was still on the ground, shaking his head.

The Zinger lay a few feet away. Oliver tried to run for it but only managed to stumble forward. He bent down to grab it.

Drex plowed into his side, knocking him to the ground. He was still shaking his head but had grasped the Zinger. He twisted it toward Oliver when a foot collided with the Corsair's hand. The Zinger smacked the wall and fell to the ground with a resounding clang.

Austin and Tiffany were praying together when they heard a voice come over their mTalks. "We have your brother and your friend. There is no escape," a woman said. "Open the hatch, and do not resist."

Tiffany looked at Austin and nodded. He shook his head, "We can't just give in. Oliver would want us to fight."

"So we can do what?" Tiffany scowled. "I'm not one to roll over and get captured. I might have had those feelings before, but I've changed."

Austin swallowed. "I know."

"Perhaps if we obey, they'll think we're not as much of a threat. We can use that to our advantage."

"Tiffany, they're Corsairs. They work for O'Farrell. I'm pretty sure they know we're a threat," Austin said.

"They have Oliver. And, like I said, this is a sure way off Cixot."

Austin took a deep breath. Half a dozen Corsairs stood before the ship. One of them held an mTalk in her hand. He was sure it was Oliver's. Their three mTalks were connected.

"You have sixty seconds to comply, or your brother suffers," the Corsair said.

Drex tumbled to his right and hit the wall, gasping for air. A hand pulled Oliver to his feet. It was Ashley. She grabbed the Zinger and fired two shots at Drex. The soldier went unconscious.

"Which way?" asked Ashley.

Oliver was shocked at Ashley's arrival, her performance, and her knocking out Drex without a moment's hesitation. His throat was constricted and felt swollen. He couldn't speak, so he pointed.

Ashley supported Oliver as they headed toward the far doors. He felt his strength creep back into his arms and legs. He rubbed his throat as he walked, trying to loosen the muscles.

"Hold on," he mumbled. He took a breath. "Do you . . . do you see a weapon locker or anything?" He pulled himself up, trying to stand on his own. Another deep breath. "There usually is one close . . . close to the bridge of a combat ship like this."

"Are you okay?" Ashley asked.

"I'm fine. Just look for a weapon for me," he said.

"You can use this one," Ashley offered.

"No, we each need something," Oliver said.

They scanned the walls of the corridor.

"Nothing on this side," Ashley said.

"I've got something." Oliver opened a cabinet and took out a Zinger.

They didn't know how many Corsairs they would encounter once they got into the bridge. Oliver couldn't imagine that too many soldiers were there, but there could be five or more. He hoped there would be fewer, since the ship wasn't flying at the moment.

Either way, they were about to find out.

"Time is up," the commander in charge said.

Tiffany wasn't sure if this was her call or her younger brother's. Being in charge wasn't about age anymore. Each of the four Wikks had proven themselves capable.

She nodded to Austin. He tapped his mTalk. "Hello," he said.

The Corsairs looked toward the ship. Their leader seemed bemused. "How old are you?" she asked.

"Eleven," Austin replied. "Why does that matter?"

The Corsairs outside chuckled. "You're surrounded, boy. We have your brother. We have your ship. Your parents are imprisoned with the Übel. And you're a child."

The words made Tiffany burn. If this woman had any clue what her brother had done in the last week, what courage he'd shown, what intellect. . . . She grunted.

Tiffany tapped her mTalk. "You have no idea who you're messing with. We've seen more action in the last several days than you have in your entire career. Just try to capture us!" she yelled.

That was it. Tiffany tapped an icon on the NavCom, and the heat shields slid back over the windshield. She took up the Zinger and flicked a switch, bringing it to life. "I'm ready."

Austin's bright green eyes were huge, his mouth open. She knew she'd surprised and impressed him with her turn from surrendering to fighting.

"Are you ready?" Oliver asked.

Ashley nodded and energized her Zinger.

Oliver reached over and tapped the control screen next to the bridge hatch. The outline of a hand appeared, along with the words *Palm identification required.*

Oliver glanced back down the hall. "Quick, we need Drex's hand."

He and Ashley charged back down the corridor. With their Zingers slung over their shoulders, they dragged Drex toward the bridge. Oliver lifted him up while Ashley pressed his palm against the screen. The screen glowed blue, then turned green: *Access granted.*

Oliver let Drex drop to the floor. The hatch lifted open with a hiss. Oliver was first in. He took aim and shot the pilot, who slumped forward before he knew what had hit him.

Ashley blasted a series of blue sparks across the console. One finally made its mark, and the Corsair copilot fell against the controls.

Oliver was already scanning the room for other threats. A third man—the navigator, most likely—leaped to his feet and pulled a Zapp-It from its holster. But the weapon was only good for close combat, and Oliver hit him square in the chest with his Zinger. The man fell to the ground.

There were no other Corsairs in the room. Oliver and Ashley quickly dragged the unconscious soldiers out to the corridor. Oliver removed their badges in case they had some sort of access scan or code on them. He closed the entrance hatch and looked for a way to lock it. The button he needed was labeled *Emergency Lockdown*. He tapped it. The lights in the bridge went from white to red, and an alert rang out overhead. He wasn't sure how "locked down" the place really was.

Austin heard a siren ringing outside the *Eagle*. This was it. The Corsairs were going to begin their attempt to breach the *Eagle*'s doors. He was proud of his sister's boldness to stand up to the leader and flattered that she felt the two of them were a match for the Corsairs, regardless of how many they faced. He'd been angered by the commander's belittlement as well.

He didn't want to doubt that they could be successful, but reality was playing in his mind. He and Tiffany would hold off the soldiers for at least a while, give them a run for their credits, and perhaps stun a few in the process. Of course, he'd likely be stunned as well.

The screen on the console flashed. *Incoming Message*. What was the Corsair commander going to threaten now? Austin tapped *Accept*.

"Austin, Tiffany, don't let them in!" It was Oliver. He was free.

Tiffany tapped the screen. "Oliver, where are you?"

"We've taken control of the ship's bridge," he said. "I can see the *Eagle* from the security cameras. The Corsairs have a laser cutter near the cargo bay. It doesn't look like they've started yet. At the moment they're confused by the lockdown of the ship."

"Oliver, do you have Ashley?" Tiffany asked.

"Yes. We're both armed. Just hold them off. I'm going to see what we can do from up here," Oliver said.

Austin tapped the screen, and the heat shields lowered again. The cargo bay was bathed in flashing red lights. A couple of Corsair soldiers were trying to force their way through a door at the base of the Corsair ship's cargo bay and into the rest of the ship. Three more were at the top of the staircase, trying to barge through another door.

"What'd you do?" Austin asked.

"I locked down the ship and sealed all the doors," Oliver said. "It's a common security measure for military ships."

The commander stepped back into view; she was glaring up at them.

"Who is this Corsair woman?" Austin asked.

"That's Commander DarkStone. Let me tell you, she's not real nice." Oliver chuckled. "Oh, and Drex is here. Unconscious at the moment, but here."

"Oh, good," Austin said.

"Hey, can I talk to Ashley?" Tiffany asked.

"Yeah, she can hear you," Oliver said.

"Ashley!" Tiffany called. "How are you holding up? I was so worried about you."

"I'm fine now," Ashley said. "How are you?"

"Alive." Tiffany sighed. "I can't wait to see you. We have so much to talk about."

"I know," Ashley said.

"First we have to figure out how to handle these Corsairs," Austin said.

"Any ideas?" asked Oliver.

"Security alert access point two," the *Eagle*'s computer said.

"That's the side hatch," Austin said and ran out of the bridge.

"We've got visitors banging at our door," Oliver said. "It's got to be Drex."

4.19

Damage Control

Branz wasn't saying anything. Zebra Xavier's frustration was growing, yet he hadn't lost it like he had moments ago.

"Why can't we talk like we used to?" Zebra Xavier asked. "You and I have so much in common. We desire to learn, to discover, to grow in knowledge."

Branz said nothing. Didn't Zebra Xavier realize that everyone could see through his good-guy act?

"Your dad has already started to assist me. Don't you think it's time his children did as well?" Zebra Xavier asked.

There was a knock on the door.

"Come in."

"Sir, we're about to come out of hyper flight," Captain Vedrik said.

"Fine, I'm almost finished here," Zebra Xavier said.

"Sir, we recommend that you stay in the secure chamber while we exit hyper flight," Captain Vedrik said. Mason heard concern in his voice, a tone he'd never before heard the dangerous Übel use.

"I assure you that won't be necessary," Zebra Xavier said sternly.

"The damage to the bay is significant. We're not sure how the exterior will hold—"

Zebra Xavier held up his hand. "I will go."

Mason felt a shiver of concern and pride at the same time. Obbin had dealt a blow to the Übel, even without a strategy. He could only imagine how much trouble the young prince was in if the damage was enough that they were ushering their leader into a protective chamber just in case.

"What of these two?" Captain Vedrik asked.

"Bring them with me," Zebra Xavier said.

"Sir, the chamber only seats three," Captain Vedrik said.

"One of them can have your spot," Zebra Xavier countered.

"Yes, sir."

A wooden panel slid up, revealing a solid-looking metal door. Captain Vedrik tapped in a code on the pad, and Mason watched closely. *102580.* He repeated the numbers in his mind: *10*—that was how old he'd been when Oliver had gone to the Academy; *25*—his favorite Kugel player's number; *80*—the year his parents had gotten married. The heavy door angled inward.

Zebra Xavier stepped in, followed by the two boys. The chamber was triangular in shape, a seat tucked into each of the points. Vedrik grabbed Mason by the shoulders and shoved him into a seat. He clasped Mason's wrists together in front of him. Before Mason had a chance to react, the captain had snapped shock-locks onto his wrists.

"You move, you get shocked," Vedrik warned. "You'll be out cold in a nanosecond."

Branz sat down, and Vedrik snapped shock-locks onto his wrists.

"Move, shocked, out cold," Branz repeated.

Vedrik sneered and backed out of the chamber. The large metal door slipped closed. The boys were alone with Zebra Xavier.

"We'll be out of here in just a few minutes." Zebra Xavier looked toward Mason. "I'm looking forward to overseeing your parents' work methods and increasing their productivity. Apparently they're thorough."

Though his words seemed diplomatic, Mason got their underlying meaning. His parents were too slow for Zebra Xavier's liking.

Zebra Xavier turned to Branz. "And your father has been most helpful. He's put forth a lot of knowledge that he didn't share with me during my stay in the Cobalt Gorge. Intriguing how new surroundings and loss of power can influence one."

"My father isn't intimidated by you. He only wants his family to be free of this ordeal as soon as possible," Branz argued. "If getting you to your goal does that, so be it."

"Is that so?" Zebra Xavier said.

Branz nodded, glaring at the old man.

The chamber jerked violently.

"What was that?" Mason blurted out.

Zebra Xavier's expression wasn't as confident as it had been seconds ago. Mason's eyes grew large as he looked around the small chamber.

"Nothing, I'm sure," Zebra Xavier said. He glanced down at the e-journal in his hands. His scowl deepened. A half-second later, the chamber's light turned dim red. A siren warbled.

The seat seemed to drop out from beneath Mason, then catch him and lift him up again. The dramatic movement reminded him of Oliver's first flights in the *Phoenix*. They'd nearly died. Was the *Skull* ripping apart mid–hyper flight? He thought of being stranded in space in this minuscule capsule. The walls closed in around him. He shut his eyes, trying to fight back his phobia. Who would come for them? Were there other Übel?

Then he thought of his parents. They weren't in a safe chamber like his, and they didn't know Creator yet.

Mason's stomach turned. He was going to be sick. The chamber shook.

"What's happening?" Branz asked. "Did the ship explode?"

Branz's words hit Mason harder than he would have expected. Mason had been through a lot, but everything had always worked out.

Zebra Xavier looked up from the e-journal. "We've dropped out of hyper flight and come under fire from a federal destroyer." He stood and punched in a code on the keypad next to the hatch. It opened. Two Übel soldiers were outside. Mason recognized them as Sekelton and Frantivic.

"Sir, you really should sta—"

"Get me the captain of that destroyer! *Now!*" Zebra Xavier ordered.

"But, sir, with the damage to the bay exterior—"

"I gave an order! Obey it, or face my wrath!"

Frantivic nodded and dashed out of the cabin. Sekelton remained. "Ready to serve."

"Get me Captain Vedrik," Zebra Xavier ordered. "Have him release these two."

The soldier ran from the cabin.

"Wait in the chamber until Vedrik comes. Don't try anything." Zebra Xavier nodded at the shock-locks.

Mason looked at his wrists. The restraints glowed red. Too much movement would indeed result in a nasty shock across his wrist that would temporarily paralyze his arms—possibly his entire upper body if they were set high enough. He doubted he'd be rendered unconscious, as Vedrik had implied, but it was likely they would deliver a serious jolt of electricity.

Zebra Xavier tucked his e-journal under his arm and left.

"Mason, are you okay?" Branz asked. "You looked like you were going to throw up."

Mason nodded. He still felt queasy. "I need to get out of here."

"Rescuer, free us from this danger; Helper, bring peace to my friend," Branz called out.

Why hadn't Mason thought of that? He closed his eyes and whispered, "Rescuer, please keep us safe. Helper, take away my fear of this closed space." Mason looked up, and Branz smiled at him.

"We're not alone. Someone greater is watching over us," Branz explained. "This is all part of Creator's plan."

The confidence with which Branz said this struck Mason. Did he believe as fully as Branz?

Vedrik appeared at that moment. "Enjoy that, boys?" He laughed. "Haven't quite gotten your space legs."

Neither of them responded.

"I'm taking you to your families. They're being held together in an escape pod," Vedrik said.

"Are we abandoning ship?" Branz asked.

"No, it's only a precaution. Zebra Xavier will handle the mindless federal captain," Vedrik spat. "You'll wait with your families until we're ready to depart for Cao."

Vedrik removed the shock-locks from each of the boys. The cuffs lost their red glow the instant they were unlocked. Vedrik led Mason and Branz from the cabin, followed by Sekelton.

The ship shook again. Red lights flashed everywhere; the siren continued to warble; alerts were announced one after the other. It seemed like chaos, yet Vedrik didn't appear overtly concerned.

"Sounds like the *Skull* is in trouble," Branz said. "I don't think it can take much more of an attack."

"The *Skull* is one of the heaviest armored ships in all the Empire," Vedrik countered without turning to look at the boys directly behind him. "A destroyer would normally not be a match for us, but your brother's reckless firing weakened the bay wall from the interior."

"So we're in trouble," Branz argued.

"Did you say *Empire*?" Mason asked.

"Empire . . . Federation, the same," Vedrik said. "And, no, we've turned. Our undamaged side now faces the destroyer."

"Alert. Prisoner escape. Priority level 1 recapture. Alert. Prisoner escape," another warning added to the announcements.

Mason looked at Branz, wondering if the chaos was their chance as well. What if their families had escaped in the pod? Branz shook his head, signaling Mason not to attempt anything. That was a big difference between Obbin and Branz: the younger was always looking for opportunities, but Branz seemed to always play it safe.

Was the escapee Obbin? A brief smile crossed Mason's face at the thought, but it disappeared as he wondered if Obbin would do more damage to the ship, truly stranding them all in the cold, dark depths of space.

Vedrik entered a code to the lift. The doors opened. They headed down to the level where their families' cabins were. There were no guards when the doors opened. Down two corridors they came to a round hatch guarded by four soldiers. Mason recognized Cruz, Rutledge, and Currie.

Vedrik nodded, and Cruz turned and tapped in the code. The round door swirled open. Mason caught a glimpse of his mom and dad. Branz followed him in, and the hatch closed.

Mrs. Wikk pulled Mason close. "I was so worried when the attack started and you were still gone."

Mason's dad came over and ruffled his hair. "You okay?"

Mason nodded.

"What'd Zebra Xavier ask?" Mrs. Wikk asked.

"He wanted to know about the people in the red cloaks," Mason said. "But mostly he told me all about the real history of the Federation, the Empire, the plague, and the renewed search for Ursprung."

Mrs. Wikk nodded. "I expected the history lesson. And the people in the red cloaks . . . what did you say?"

"Nothing," Mason said. "He didn't like it; he got angry. But we were interrupted by the drop out of hyper flight."

Mrs. Wikk looked at her husband. "We've got to protect him."

"We will. The king and queen will look after him while we're in the Valley of the Shadows," Mr. Wikk said.

Mrs. Wikk looked at her son regretfully, then hugged him again. "Don't try anything while we're gone."

Mason nodded.

The ship shook again, and Mrs. Wikk wrapped her arm around Mason, pulling him close. Mason looked toward the Blauwe Mensen. The king was hugging Princess Mae, and the queen hugged Princess Grace. Branz was welcomed into the circle. There was no sign of Obbin. The McGregors were sitting together. Where was Ashley? Mrs. McGregor had tears on her cheeks, and Mr. McGregor looked sad.

Each family was divided. The Blauwe Mensen were missing Rylin and Voltran; the McGregors were missing Ashley; and the Wikks were missing Oliver, Tiffany, and Austin.

Would they all be reunited again? He knew that his siblings were on the hunt for the clues, but was Ashley all alone? How could Rylin or Voltran ever find the Übel?

Incoming

An alert flashed across the screen: *Surface launch. Incoming projectile. Projected trajectory in course with Cixot. Forty minutes until impact.*

Tiffany tapped the screen. A green dot arced from Ledram. Its dotted trajectory line crossed through Cixot. Austin had set the *Eagle*'s tracking system to use a federal communications beacon orbiting Ledram to monitor anything launching from the flaming planet.

And now it had happened. She wasn't surprised, but she was frightened.

Tiffany tapped the communications link to the bridge of the Corsairs' ship. "Oliver, did you see that? An explosion on Ledram sent a projectile toward Cixot."

"How long?" Oliver asked.

"Forty minutes."

"Where's Austin?"

"He's still checking the hatches and entry points to the *Eagle*."

"Does he know?"

"Not yet."

"The Corsairs are trying to get through the hatch," Oliver said. "They're not having much success."

"Are you armed?"

"Yes. You?"

"Yes."

"Do your best."

"We will! Oliver?"

"Yes?"

"That object from Ledram just has to pass through the atmosphere of the moon. It doesn't have to hit the surface," Tiffany said.

A second passed. "I know."

"Oliver, you've got to take off."

"Right," he said.

"Oliver, you can do it. This ship might be bigger, but you can do it."

"First I have to figure out how to access the controls."

"Austin, come in," Tiffany's voice crackled over his mTalk. Austin lifted the device near his mouth. "I'm here."

"We've got a problem," Tiffany said. "Incoming from Ledram."

"You mean—?"

"Yep!"

"What should we do?"

"Oliver's going to try to take off," Tiffany said.

"Is there anything he wants us to do?"

"Not yet. Just keep the Corsairs from taking control of the *Eagle*."

Austin looked toward the side hatch. The Corsairs hadn't broken through with the laser. But once they did, he'd take out as many as he could. After that, he'd have to retreat up to the bridge with Tiffany.

The ship shook.

"Tiffany, what's going on? Can you see anything on the cameras?"

"Most of the Corsairs are still trying to regain access to the rest of the ship. They haven't engaged the laser yet, as far as I can see. The rover just unhooked from the *Eagle*."

"What about that commander?"

"She looks livid. She's ordering her troops around, but none are having much success," Tiffany said. "Wait. Two Corsairs are running down the flights of stairs."

Kaboom! The floor of the ship vibrated beneath Austin.

"What was that?" Austin called.

"They just took out the hatch at the top of the stairs with an explosive. The commander and the Corsairs are swarming up."

An explosive inside the ship? This was nuts.

The door thumped with renewed efforts from the Corsairs. So far they'd not been able to access the bridge. The lockdown had isolated the bridge, cutting off easy entry through the hatch. The only way in was to take out the door.

Oliver sat in a chair in the center of the bridge. A half-arc console covered in screens sat before him. The flight system was loaded, but a flashing red line waited for the passcode to start the ignition. He stared at it.

Ashley hovered at his shoulder. She held the Zinger at the ready, glancing over her shoulder at the banging on the door.

"We need the passcode," he said. "I can't engage the thrusters or ramp up the generators without the passcode. All I've got is access to security and navigation information."

"How about the badges?" Ashley asked.

"I tried," Oliver said. "We need the passcode."

"Might it be written somewhere?" Ashley asked.

Oliver shook his head. "I doubt it."

"I'll look."

As Ashley scanned the nearby consoles, Oliver browsed the screens before him. Was there another way to bypass the code? A loud thump rang from the bridge hatch. He wasn't sure they'd be able to take off before the Corsairs made it through. He only hoped they wouldn't risk a detonation for fear that it could damage the flight systems.

"Nothing," Ashley said. "What can I do?"

"Let Tiffany know we need the passcode. Ask her if she has any ideas." Oliver knew it was a really long shot.

Ashley nodded. "Tiffany, come in."

Oliver switched to another display, looking for another way in: a manual override, a different program, anything.

He'd connected to the federal communications beacon orbiting Ledram. The projectile was now thirty minutes out from the atmosphere and thirty-five minutes from surface impact. He had to act quickly. How long would it take to clear Cixot? Had the Corsairs done the calculations on how much thrust it would require to take off in the dense atmosphere, or how much energy the engines would need? Could they even take off? The thought was chilling.

"Ashley, it's Tiffany."

"There's a passcode stopping us from getting into the liftoff sequence," Ashley explained. "Any ideas?"

There was a brief silence. "I'll get Austin."

The speaker buzzed. A second communication icon flashed on the screen. "You will stand down," Commander DarkStone ordered. "If you open the bridge hatch immediately, you will be placed under restraint in the brig. If you do not, you will suffer physical consequences." Her words were sharper than an energized saber.

Oliver thought. Letting the Corsairs in might be the only way they could escape before it was too late. But it was unlikely the commander had any idea about the danger hurtling toward them. Commander DarkStone might not believe him. Instead of doing an emergency takeoff, she might wait until she got Austin and Tiffany out of the *Eagle*, undoubtedly by threatening to harm Oliver.

Yet Oliver needed the Corsairs. Why had he not kept the pilot or copilot in the bridge? He could have found out the code from them.

"Ashley, it's me," Austin said over the speaker.

Ashley tapped the icon representing communication with the *Eagle*.

"Austin, can you override a ship's passcode?" Oliver asked.

"It depends," Austin said. "There should be a transponder code, a BDE number, and a sequence ID somewhere beneath the console."

Oliver ducked down and nearly bumped heads with Ashley. They both scanned underneath the console.

"Got it." Ashley quickly read off the three items for Austin.

"Great. These will help. It's not automatic access, but now I have something to work with," Austin explained.

"Austin, we don't have much time," Oliver warned.

"I know. But I don't know how long it will take."

Oliver pictured his brother at the console, swiping his fingers across the screen in an attempt to access the systems of the Corsair ship.

"You have five minutes," Oliver said. "If you can't do it, I'll have to give in to the Corsairs."

He expected Austin to protest, but he didn't. "I understand."

"Ashley, I didn't tell you before, because I didn't want to alarm you," Oliver said. "There is something soaring toward this moon right now, and if it crosses into the atmosphere, it's going to ignite all the gases into a ball of flame."

She stared at him. "What?"

"But we're getting off here, one way or another," Oliver promised.

She nodded. "Okay. I trust you. What can I do to help?"

It was time for Oliver to prep his contingency plan. From Commander DarkStone's communications thus far, he didn't believe it would go well.

"Ashley, open up the communication with the Corsairs," he said. She tapped the screen.

"Commander," Oliver said.

"Open the hatch!" she shouted.

Clearly she was not one who understood negotiations.

"You should know that at this moment there is—"

"There will be no parleys. Open the hatch!"

"Commander DarkStone!" Oliver shouted. "At this moment a projectile is flying toward the planet. If it crosses into the atmosphere of Cixot, the gases will erupt into a fireball, incinerating us and the ships." He was speaking rapidly. "If you want to live, you'll give me the passcode so that I can take off and get us out of here."

A brief silence. "Open the hatch! I will enter the passcode, and a real pilot will get us off this planet."

"I can't do that," Oliver said.

"You will, or we all die," she warned.

Oliver looked at Ashley. "She's bluffing."

Ashley cleared her throat. "What if she isn't?"

Oliver wasn't sure. "Get Tiffany."

Ashley tapped the icon for the *Eagle.*

"Tiffany, how is Austin doing?" Oliver asked.

"He's trying. He located the server, but the security is really high."

"He hacked into the Corsairs' escape pod," Oliver said.

"Yes, but you want a rescue team to be able to access an escape pod," Tiffany countered. "There is no security."

She had a point.

"Your fellow cadet here, Drex, says you're not capable of flying the *Vulture*," Commander DarkStone cackled.

The *Vulture*?

"Get me Austin," Oliver said.

Ashley opened the link.

"Austin, the name of the ship is the *Vulture*," Oliver said. "Is that helpful?"

"Uh, no, not real—"

"Did you say *Vulture*?" Tiffany asked, interrupting him.

"Yes."

"It wasn't the Übel!" Tiffany exclaimed.

"What wasn't the Übel?" Oliver asked.

"The Corsairs have the keys!" she exclaimed.

"Tiffany, you're not making sense."

"Mom and Dad . . . Ashley, your parents too," Tiffany said. "They were at a place called the Valley of Shadows. They discovered some keys, but some of the artifacts had been stolen from the valley by a ship called the *Vulture*."

"There could be other ships called—" Oliver tried.

"No, it's been O'Farrell all along. Shortly after that, he offered the *Phoenix* and the *Griffin* to our parents," Tiffany said. "He's got some of the keys, and my guess is they're on the *Black Ranger*."

"You have thirty seconds to open the hatch," interrupted an unwelcome voice. "We have set explosive charges, and we will detonate them. You'd best take cover if you don't wish to be skewered by shrapnel!" Again the commander laughed eerily.

Oliver reached over and tapped the icon. "We'll let you in. But you have to get us off this moon immediately. You'll see what I mean."

He hit the icon for Tiffany and Austin. "We're letting them in. We have to get out of here, and we're running out of time. Hide whatever you can, and then don't resist. Let them on board."

"Oliver, are you sure?" Tiffany asked.

"Has Austin broken in?"

"No," she said.

"We have to get off this moon, or we'll not see another day," Oliver said. He swallowed the hard lump forming in his throat. "There's no use fighting them. They'll bring you to us."

"Okay."

"We'll talk about the keys once we're together," he added.

Valley Plan

Branz called Mason to where he and his sisters were sitting. "Sit down," he said. He looked toward the hatch. Next, his gaze flitted toward the security cameras mounted at opposite corners of the room.

Princess Grace was busy writing something on her e-papyrus. "I wish I had mine," Mason said. "I wanted to write down a couple of things that Zebra Xavier mentioned."

Branz shrugged. "Use Obbin's. It's in my pack, and you can have it. Obbin didn't want it." He pulled out the extra e-papyrus and stylus and gave them to Mason.

"Do you know how long they'll keep Obbin in the cooler?" Mason asked.

"You didn't hear?" Princess Mae asked, then guarded her mouth with her hand and whispered, "He's missing."

"Missing?" Mason asked softly.

"Apparently he escaped during the drop out of hyper flight and the commotion with the Federation ship," Princess Grace said with a smile.

Mason had been right. Obbin was definitely skilled at escaping.

"I hope he frees Feng," Princess Mae said.

"I wish he'd just quit with all the heroics," Branz said bluntly. "Grace said they are still working on getting the fires under control."

"But that happened a while ago," Mason said.

Grace nodded. "I saw it with my own eyes."

"Amazing how the two of you can go anywhere you want," Branz said with a smile.

"We're easily overlooked," Grace said.

"Especially since we're not perceived as a threat." Mae flashed a smile that seemed to cut through the thin air between her and Mason.

"Princesses aren't expected to have anything but good etiquette." Grace laughed.

Mason looked at the girls. Wasn't being blue pretty noticeable?

"The three of us have accomplished a lot more, and collected far more information for Dad and Mom, than Obbin has accomplished with all his reckless antics," Branz said.

"We did not get to speak much while you were in our palace," Grace said before Mason could ask what sort of information they'd collected.

"You departed a bit sooner than we expected," Mae said.

"Yes, with our brother," added Grace.

The two girls seemed to be challenging Mason. Did they blame him for their current circumstances? Should he apologize? The queen hadn't blamed him, and the Übel's attack would have happened sooner or later. Still, he knew his and Austin's actions had sparked it.

"We didn't mean to cause any harm," Mason began. "We only wanted to get back to our brother and sister and find our parents. We didn't know the magnitude of the quest we were on."

Grace looked to her sister, frowning.

"If we'd known that our escape would bring such danger to you, we would . . ." Mason's voice trailed off. His next words would have been a lie, the opposite of the truth. "I'm sorry for what has happened to your family."

Grace cleared her throat. "Mason, don't be sorry. We're not mad. The evil was already among us. We would have ended up here with or without you eventually."

"Better with you than without," Mae added with a smile.

Mason smiled back. Then he looked at Grace. "You mean Mr. Thule."

"Yeah, the traitor," Branz interjected.

"Don't you mean the great Zebra Xavier?" Grace said in a deep voice, stiffening her shoulders and moving her head side to side. She and her sister laughed.

Mason smiled. Their joking put him at ease.

"We needed something to bring our family out of our prison within the gorge," Mae said.

Branz frowned at her.

Mae raised a hand. "Okay, it wasn't a prison, but it's far more exciting to see the larger world around us for once. Obbin and Rylin were always leaving the gorge."

"Yes, but we left too," Grace corrected her.

"A few times a year with Feng and the guards does not count," Mae said.

"We had everything we needed in the valley," Branz said. "Why did we need to leave?"

"Fresh air, for one," Mae said.

Grace and Branz both laughed.

"You mentioned Feng. Is he in the cooler? You said you hoped Obbin would free him." Mason had forgotten about the captain of the Blauwe Mensen. The soldier had been his and Austin's escort during their stay in Cobalt Gorge.

"Apparently, he was too great a threat," Grace said. "He made a handful of attempts to help our family escape, but none panned out, and the Übel don't feel that they need him for their expeditionary work and research, so they locked him up."

"Oh. That's too bad."

"It really is. He's always been so loyal and kind to our family. Our father tried to plead for his release, but the Übel never once considered it," Mae said. "Now Dad has enough trouble just keeping his kids out of the cooler."

"It's better than being dropped off on the nearest planet or moon," Branz countered.

"They wouldn't do that," Mason said.

Branz cocked his head. "Oh, they did. We heard one of the guards talking about how Zebra Xavier had three of the commanders who he left in charge while he was in our valley marooned on a moon."

"That's horrible," Mason said. "You're joking."

Neither of the princesses was smiling.

"Afraid not," Branz said.

That didn't sit well with Mason.

The conversation slowly trailed off. Mason turned on the e-papyrus to begin recording what Zebra Xavier had said about the Federation's history and to make note of a few important things from the past several days, things he didn't want to forget in case he was never able to access his mom's e-journal again.

Surrender

"Austin, you can stop trying," Tiffany said. "We're letting them in. We have to hide whatever we can: the e-journal, our packs, any artifacts . . ."

"We don't know everything that Brother Samuel put in the cargo bay," Austin countered. "There could be valuable things there that can't fall into the Corsairs' hands."

"I know," Tiffany said. "But Oliver's right. He has to let them into the bridge for us to get off Cixot. Once he does, they might hurt Oliver and Ashley unless we give in. We can't let that happen."

"I understand."

"Let's go," Tiffany said. "I'll take care of our stuff on the main deck. You double check the cargo bay, and do a quick search on the inventory console. See if anything catches your attention and hide it!"

"Don't resist when we let them in," Oliver said. Ashley nodded. "The less we fight back, the less likely they are to harm us. After all, it's still in O'Farrell's best interest to keep us cooperating."

"Are you sure?" Ashley asked. "Commander DarkStone doesn't seem restrained."

"We don't have a choice," Oliver said. He tapped the icon to cancel the emergency lockdown.

Immediately, white light replaced the red emergency glow. The siren ended, and the hatch lifted open. Drex and another Corsair rushed Oliver, grabbing his arms and slamming him against the nearest wall, nearly knocking all the air from his lungs. Two other Corsairs grabbed Ashley and restrained her arms behind her back. She had taken down both DarkStone and Drex, and the Corsairs weren't discounting her a third time. The pilot, copilot, and navigator dashed for their places.

Commander DarkStone had taken his information about the incoming threat seriously. The pilot entered the passcode immediately, and Oliver caught the slightest smile in Ashley's eyes. She'd seen what he'd entered.

"Commander, engaging thrusters," the pilot said.

"Fourteen minutes until inbound projectile crosses into Cixot atmosphere," the navigator added.

"Projecting seventeen minutes to exit Cixot atmosphere," the copilot said.

"That's not good enough," Commander DarkStone shouted.

"Commander, requesting permission to use vortex progression," the pilot said.

Commander DarkStone hesitated for the slightest moment. "Granted."

"Vortex progression?" Oliver asked. "That's—"

The bridge began to shake. A low rumble emitted from the engines.

"Get them out of here!" Commander DarkStone ordered. "To the brig!"

Drex twisted Oliver around and pulled his arms together at the center of his back. "She'd have given you the code," he told Oliver as he restrained his wrists. "You just don't have the nerves for this."

"Silence, lieutenant," Commander DarkStone ordered.

Like a dog obeying a command, Drex released his hold on Oliver and came to immediate attention. "Yes, commander."

Oliver's restraints weren't fastened. He threw up his elbow and caught Drex under the chin so that he stumbled backward. Oliver had no intention of trying to escape. That would cost them too much time. He'd just wanted to put Drex in his place.

Austin scanned the cargo inventory listing. Nothing stood out. He didn't like the idea of surrendering, but his older siblings had made a good case for it.

A knock resounded against the smaller of the cargo bay doors.

"Go ahead and let them in," Tiffany called from the landing. She started down the stairs. "I've hidden everything as best I can. Most of our stuff is on the *Phoenix* anyway."

Austin smiled at his sister and extended his hand. She took it and held on. He tapped the screen, and the hatch slid open. Five Corsairs rushed in. Two took Austin, and two took Tiffany. The fifth nodded her head.

"Good of you to obey," she said. "I'm Lieutenant Peterson. Don't try anything. Your brother and friends are already locked in the brig."

Austin nodded.

"Yes, ma'am," Tiffany said.

"We are to secure you in place during launch." The lieutenant led them to the bench by the cargo bay wall, just beneath the stairs.

Once Tiffany and Austin were secured, the lieutenant and two guards sat. The remaining two dashed from the *Eagle*. The floor shook.

An announcement echoed from the *Vulture's* bay, "Prepare for vortex progression."

"Vortex what?" asked Austin. But his words were lost as his voice was suddenly sucked from his lips. Whatever the vortex progression was, it had caused him to go mute. He only hoped it was temporary.

The time could not have passed quickly enough as the *Vulture* flew straight up in its desperate attempt to escape the impending explosion. It was probably only ten minutes, but it felt like an hour.

There was a powerful jolt and a thunderous boom. The straps of Austin's seat dug into his shoulders. He looked at his sister but still couldn't speak. She looked worried. The ship shook violently twice, then jolted again.

"*Vulture* is clear," came an announcement that echoed through the side hatch and into the *Eagle's* cargo bay.

The Corsairs escorted Tiffany and Austin to the brig. As the hatch shut behind them, Tiffany was pulled into a warm hug. Long brown hair swept around her as Ashley held her close. "I'm so glad to see you," she said.

"And I'm glad to see you," Tiffany said. "Are you okay?"

"I just miss my parents," Ashley said.

"We saw them," Tiffany said. "They're with our parents. They looked fine."

The girls held each other at arms' length.

"My mom is probably so worried about me," Ashley said.

"I know," Tiffany said. "It'll be okay. We're going to get out of this."

Oliver was ruffling Austin's hair. "You okay?"

"I'm fine. I just wish we hadn't lost our ship," Austin admitted.

"I know," Oliver said. "We'll work on getting it back. My guess is they'll return us to the *Black Ranger* and O'Farrell."

"But you and Tiffany pulled a fast one on him before," Austin said.

"Yeah, but he needs us," Tiffany said. "I have a lot to tell you. While you were gone, I read up on the Valley of Shadows."

Ashley looked toward the hatch. "I'd love to hear what you've done."

"And I want to know how you and your parents were captured," Tiffany said. "We saw the *Griffin* in a warehouse in Mudo."

Austin looked toward the door. "The guards said we have under an hour."

"Then let's get started," Oliver said.

4.23

Unified Opposition

Holographic images floated across a large, circular screen that lay flat like a table in the impressive Übel expedition command chamber. The team gathered around was made up of the McGregors, the Blauwe Mensen, Mason's parents, a handful of Übel scientists Mason didn't recognize, Captain Vedrik, and Zebra Xavier. Übel guards ringed the chamber, all armed and ready. The gathering of so many potential opponents seemed to be putting them all on edge. More than one soldier had his finger on his trigger.

"A squadron of fighters and shuttles has been dispatched to secure the air space and neutralize any ground threats," Captain Vedrik said. "The federal destroyer is now in orbit on the opposite side of Cao. They will inform us if the Corsairs arrive."

Zebra Xavier had indeed taken care of the destroyer; it was working for him now. It made sense. Apparently the Federation, Empire, and Übel were all interconnected.

"Their orders?" Zebra Xavier asked.

"To capture," Vedrik answered.

"Good," Zebra Xavier said. "I want O'Farrell alive, and I want those crosses."

"We will need them," King Dlanod said.

"Yes, so you have said," Zebra Xavier sneered. Mason wondered how he had kept up an act of servitude for nine long years.

A hologram appeared before them of a wide valley with long spikes towering from its walls.

A scientist pointed at the center of the valley. He wore a white lab coat and black wire-rimmed glasses. His tousled white hair stood out against his dark brown skin. "First to the crosses," he said. "The captain secured three during his mission to the valley. If our suspicion is correct and the Corsairs have captured four of the crosses—"

"We will get those back," Captain Vedrik snarled.

"Hold your tongue," Zebra Xavier commanded. "They shouldn't have been lost in the first place."

Mason caught his dad's quick glance at Rand McGregor.

"Continue, Professor Norton," Zebra Xavier ordered impatiently.

"According to King Dlanod, that leaves five crosses in the valley," Professor Norton explained quickly. "Using the map created by the Archeos archeological exploration team, we have identified tunnels that we expect will lead to the other chambers."

A second scientist tagged in; like Professor Norton, she wore a long white lab coat, although hers was over a blue dress; her blond hair was tied into a tight bun. "Based on the Wikks and McGregors' initial expedition, we know that the crosses are housed within chambers inside the spires. We have identified spires with hollow cores that match the shape of the chambers in which the crosses were stored." She tapped five points across the map, and the three-dimensional columns of rock began to glow green.

"Unlike the Corsairs, who simply destroyed the tops of the spires, we will take a more methodical approach," Professor Norton continued. "We will remove the top sections of the chambers with a laser cutter and then extract the crosses that way."

"How long until the five keys are secure?" Zebra Xavier said.

"Estimated time for extraction is seven hours," Professor Norton said.

"Unacceptable," Zebra Xavier barked. "Do it in five!"

"Yes, sir," the two scientists said in unison.

Mason's dad pointed to the holographic spires. "Be sure that someone checks the chambers for additional artifacts. Remember, we discovered a map in each chamber that corresponds specifically with each cross. We will want to have as many matches as possible. We should also check the previous chambers; the Corsairs may have left artifacts behind during their hasty extraction."

The scientists nodded.

"The McGregors will be assigned to the tactical extraction teams," Captain Vedrik said. "The Wikks will come with me to explore the chamber that we believe contains the Eochair."

"This is the one." Professor Norton pointed to a chamber on the map. It was larger than the others and had twelve sides. "You see it's the same shape as the spire chambers, a dodecagon. Unfortunately, our scout drones were unable to reach the chamber due to an extensive collapse."

"I will have my demolition expert with me on the mission," Captain Vedrik said. "Nothing will stand in our way, I assure you."

"Have you determined the origin or meaning of Eochair?" Zebra Xavier asked.

"No, sir, not at this point," said the scientist in the blue dress. "But we are very thankful, sir, for the information you recovered from Jahr des Eises about the Eochair."

Zebra Xavier didn't smile at her praise. He looked at Mason's mom. "You?"

Mrs. Wikk straightened. "The word isn't associated with any of the languages I've studied."

"You've studied many ancient languages," Zebra Xavier said. "Are you sure this word isn't from any of them?"

186 | UNIFIED OPPOSITION

Mr. Wikk stepped closer to his wife as she spoke. "Sir, I know many languages, but most of our knowledge of ancient languages is incomplete. If I come across the word in my notes, I will let you know. But most of my notes are still on my e-journal on the *Phoenix* and inaccessible to me."

Zebra Xavier glared at Vedrik. Mason knew what he was thinking. Vedrik had let the Wikk kids escape on the *Phoenix* with all the Wikks' tools and artifacts, including the e-journal.

Zebra Xavier looked at Mason. "Was the e-journal still on the ship?"

Mason nodded. "Yes, sir."

Zebra Xavier touched his temple. He glanced back at a scientist by the wall, then shook his head. "Captain, continue."

"*Raven*," Vedrik said. A holograph of a ship appeared. "The *Raven* will take us here." He pointed to a place on the map, and the section of map expanded. The holographic *Raven* flew to the spot the captain had touched. "We will land at this entrance and follow this route to the chamber. We're prepared to deal with any blockages in the tunnel. We estimate three to five hours to reach our destination."

"Make it three, captain," Zebra Xavier said, his voice heavy with frustration.

"Yes, sir," Captain Vedrik said. "Once we determine the size of the Eochair, we will prepare for extraction. We will extract it the same way we entered."

"That might not be possible," Mrs. McGregor said. "When we explored before, we had to follow canals that flowed in one direction only."

"I'm aware of the canals. That is why we will have hover carts available," Captain Vedrik said.

"Are you prepared to deal with the Saharvics?" Mason's dad asked.

"We will have two dozen escorts," the captain said. "I don't want this artifact to fall into the Corsairs' hands."

"Wikks, McGregors, do you have any theories about the Eochair or its use?" Zebra Xavier asked.

Mrs. McGregor spoke first. "We have yet to identify what the crosses unlock, but we expect that somehow the Eochair will be used with them."

"The *Ark* then?" Zebra Xavier said.

"We believe it's a very real possibility that the keys will unlock the *Ark* or be used to launch it," Mrs. McGregor said.

Zebra Xavier grunted. "Fine. King Dlanod, Queen Dotty, any input?"

"No," King Dlanod answered plainly.

The royal family knew a lot more than they were letting on, Mason was sure. After all, they hadn't mentioned their ship, the *Ontdekking*. Perhaps the king was not assisting the Übel as he suspected. But why had he given up the total number of keys? Was he trying to stop the Corsairs?

"What do we have on YelNik Eisle?" Zebra Xavier asked next.

A heavyset Übel soldier wearing a captain's hat stepped forward. "We are just starting to get data back from the Sky-I-411s. There have been no sightings of a ship as of yet."

Zebra Xavier looked hard at the king. "You are sure of your legends?"

"Yes. Was not the *Ark* painted on the walls of the cathedral?" the king asked, a tone of defiance in his voice.

Zebra Xavier scowled back at the king, then turned his icy gaze on the captain. "Captain Ryker, I expect results."

"Sir, we dispatched three dozen 411 scout drones. We will find it," Ryker said reassuringly.

"Take a scout team now!" Zebra Xavier said. "I want that ship found before I arrive. You have one day. Dismissed."

Captain Ryker bowed his head. "Yes, sir." His black cape swept behind him as he hurried out of the chamber.

"What else are you doing to locate the *Ark*, Captain Vedrik?" Zebra Xavier asked darkly.

188 | UNIFIED OPPOSITION

"Sir, I have sent agents to the settlements to interrogate leaders there," Captain Vedrik said.

"And?" Zebra Xavier asked, his patience thin as a razor's edge.

"Nothing yet, sir," the captain said.

"Fine. If Ryker fails, I am holding you accountable."

"Yes, sir," Vedrik answered.

Zebra Xavier looked at Mason's parents. "Your son will be coming along to make sure you cooperate," he warned. "I'll have no more delays. I am authorizing the captain to *keep you on track*."

Mason felt something hard in his throat as he swallowed. Zebra Xavier's earlier words of punishment came to mind. Would he make good on the threat?

"Dr. Blue, you will escort Mr. and Mrs. Wikk," Zebra Xavier said. The scientist in the blue dress nodded. "You will ensure that they are looking in the *right* places and uncovering *actual* artifacts with real clues." Mason wondered what false things his parents had presented to the Übel to slow their progress.

"King Dlanod, you and the queen will work with Professor Norton to uncover the location of the *Ark* on YelNik Eisle," Zebra Xavier said. "My notes from Cobalt Gorge have been fully uploaded. You will use those and the scans of the books we recovered from your palace." He motioned toward the three royal children sitting in the corner. "If you don't want your other three children in the cooler, you'll be helpful."

Queen Dotty seemed shaken. The king tightened his arm around her.

"You two will work with Drs. Chase and Coal to extract the remaining crosses and artifacts from the spires," Zebra Xavier said to the McGregors. "Captain, is the *Black Widow* ready?"

As in the spider? Zebra Xavier seemed to be referring to a ship, but Mason hadn't seen this one yet. The name made him wonder.

"Yes, sir. The ship is loaded with gear. Drs. Chase and Coal await the McGregors," the captain responded. "Repairs on the extraction arms were successful. They are operating at 100 percent."

"I want two dozen escorts assigned to the McGregors as well," Zebra Xavier said.

"Sir, I have assigned Lieutenant Jaxon to lead the mission," Captain Vedrik said. A soldier stepped forward and saluted.

"Fine. We are finished here," Zebra Xavier said. "Captain Vedrik and Lieutenant Jaxon, I want updates every fifteen minutes."

"Yes, sir," Vedrik and Jaxon said.

"Dr. Green, if you'll come with me," Zebra Xavier said. A woman in a white lab coat stepped out from the corner of the room. She carried an e-journal and a silver briefcase with several lights blinking atop it. On its side was the same series of letters that Mason had seen in Zebra Xavier's chamber: ZXDNA.

What did that stand for? Why was Dr. Green carrying the case with her? The question would have to wait, because the two left the room together.

Vedrik waved a gloved hand. Three Übel soldiers stepped forward: Currie, Rutledge, and Sekelton. "Take them to the *Raven*. We leave in five minutes."

"Yes, sir," said Rutledge.

At that, Branz and his sisters rushed toward Mason. Vedrik grabbed the prince, arresting him in an armlock, and Rutledge stopped Grace, but Mae reached Mason. She wrapped him in a brief hug until one of the Übel soldiers pulled her away.

"Do you three want to go to the cooler?" shouted Vedrik.

"They only wanted to say good-bye to our son," Mrs. Wikk said, stepping forward.

Captain Vedrik grunted. "Return to your parents," he told the royal children.

The Übel guards assigned to the Wikks moved forward and ushered them toward the exit. Mrs. Wikk waved to her friend Jenn McGregor, and Mason followed his parents to the *Raven*.

The black ship stood out against the other fighters and shuttles. It had a long, sharply pointed nose and four wings at ninety-degree angles from each other. Its name was scrawled across it in luminescent silver letters next to the Übel's skull emblem. Two Übel soldiers with muzzled celtyx were walking toward the ship. Mason didn't like the idea of the lizard-like creatures coming along on their mission, but that was what was happening.

The guards and celtyx moved toward the rear of the ship, where the beasts were loaded into cages. The Übel soldiers assigned to escort them were coming through the back of the ship as well.

Closer to the bay doors, Mason saw what must be the *Black Widow*. With its eight extraction arms, the ship indeed reminded him of a spider: a black pod at the front was probably the ship's bridge, and a massive black cargo bay sat behind it. He imagined the arms reaching down and grappling with their target before lifting it into the ship's bay.

Mason and his parents boarded the *Raven* on a set of hovering stairs, under the escort of Currie, Rutledge, and Sekelton. They entered a wide cabin with several purple couches lining the walls. Two doors stood side by side at the aft of the cabin and a single door at the bow.

When Dr. Blue boarded the *Raven*, she'd changed into a gray shirt and black pants and wore a gray pith helmet. She held an e-journal with the silver Übel skull etched into its cover. The scientist did not look up as she took a seat in the cabin.

The captain entered a moment later. The demolition expert, Pyrock, boarded last. The sight of the man put Mason on edge; he could still hear his maniacal cackle from the underground chamber on Evad.

"Take your seats." Captain Vedrik lifted the device on his wrist. "Take us down."

Mason was off on an expedition with his parents again, though under very different circumstances from before.

Ransom

Ashley was explaining what she'd experienced aboard the *Black Ranger* when the brig hatch opened and Drex entered with seven other Corsairs. His lower lip was bruised from his earlier scuffle, and he glared at Oliver.

"Welcome back to the *Ranger*," he said sarcastically. "The Supreme Admiral would like a conference with you."

Drex cuffed a set of restraints around Oliver's wrists, and additional guards restrained Tiffany, Austin, and Ashley the same way. Two guards were assigned to each prisoner. Clearly the Corsairs were not underestimating their opponents again. Oliver wanted to comment on the fact that Drex needed backup, but he didn't want to antagonize Drex into taking advantage of the current situation and making it more painful for Oliver.

Drex leaned close. "Don't worry. I'll be taking care of you." He grabbed Oliver under the shoulder, pulling him up from the bench, and shoved him forward.

When the prisoners were moved out of the *Vulture* onto the flight deck of the *Black Ranger*, Commander DarkStone started toward them like a charging rhinoceros. She didn't look happy.

"What's taken so long? The Supreme Admiral is waiting," she bellowed.

Drex shoved Oliver forward, and Tiffany's guard pressed his hand against her back as Commander DarkStone turned and led them through an open hatch. The Corsair guards stayed with their assigned prisoners at every step. Had the kids really become such a threat? Tiffany smiled at the thought. She had been more than they expected of a fifteen-year-old girl.

Commander DarkStone berated Drex a few more times as they walked the familiar corridor, then took a lift to an upper level of the ship. Soon they stopped before a room labeled *Supreme Admiral's Quarters*. Two guards stood on either side of the door. Commander DarkStone placed her hand on a translucent grey plate outside the door. It glowed blue, then turned green. With a hiss, the door before them opened. They stepped into a foyer bathed in purple light. Commander DarkStone closed the door behind them, sealing the prisoners and escorts inside. A second door blocked their path. The commander stared into a white light bar. A blinding light flashed several times. Tiffany blinked a half-dozen times before her vision returned. The light bar flashed green, and the door opened. This time they stepped into a large office.

Mr. O'Farrell sat behind a wide desk. His back was to them, and he was watching a large display on the wall. Tiffany caught glimpses of ruins and soldiers moving about a forest. As Mr. O'Farrell swiveled around to greet them, the video froze, then went black.

The dig site on the screen had seemed familiar.

The old man clucked his tongue. "No need for the restraints. Release them; this is not a way to treat children."

Frowning, Commander DarkStone nodded to the guards, who obeyed.

"Take a seat," Mr. O'Farrell said. "Welcome to my command office."

The four kids each found a seat in front of the wide desk. Tiffany sat next to Ashley. O'Farrell scratched just beneath the front of his emerald flat cap, releasing a tuft of white hair.

"First, I want to start by apologizing for our hasty actions on Enaid," he said. "I was only trying to stop you from running back into the Übel's trap."

"You nearly had us eaten," Austin blurted.

Mr. O'Farrell's bushy white eyebrows furrowed. "No, not at all. Wartocks are taught to stop and restrain their targets, not eat them."

"Didn't seem like that," Austin countered.

"The four of you haven't been making things easy." Mr. O'Farrell tapped his fingers on the desk. "It's bad enough that the Übel have all your parents, but now Mason has been taken from you." He shook his head with a sympathetic sigh. "I've dealt with these soldiers before. You wouldn't want to be their prisoner."

The thought sent worry through Tiffany as she thought about Mason and her parents. Austin mumbled something that she couldn't make out.

"The Übel are after one thing and one thing only: the secret to life everlasting. They will stop at nothing to get it. They will not hesitate to threaten, torture, or . . . *discard* those who stand against them."

Ashley took Tiffany's hand, sensing her concern.

"But if we work together, I can protect you and rescue Mason and your parents. I have the resources and the manpower to do so." O'Farrell nodded to the soldiers behind them.

"Is that how you got off Re Lyt?" asked Oliver.

Mr. O'Farrell frowned. "After you and your sister abandoned us"—Tiffany thought his choice of word was interesting—"we ran into GenTexic security and a contingent of Übel soldiers.

We had no choice but to call in the *Black Ranger* for extraction. We hardly escaped."

Austin spoke up. "Did you retrieve the soldiers we kicked out of the *Phoenix*?"

"No, we were unable to rescue them or Megus."

"You just left them?" asked Austin.

"You left us no choice. Surely you saw the battle waging in the sky over the Hatchery," Mr. O'Farrell said. "They weren't the only Corsairs captured that day. I understand you may not trust me at the moment—"

"Ha! We *definitely* do not trust you." Austin jumped to his feet and pointed his finger at the old man. "You're a liar."

Mr. O'Farrell glowered at Austin. "That is your perspective," he said in a raised voice. "Your activities put our mission at risk. I did what I needed to do. Drastic actions are required when fighting against a group like the Übel."

Oliver put his hand on Austin's shoulder and moved him back to his seat.

"To be honest, we're not sure who to trust or who wants what," Oliver said. "None of us had any idea of the depth of our parents' work. We just want to be reunited with them."

"I'm your best shot at reuniting you with your families, and I'm also your best shot at reaching Ursprung," claimed Mr. O'Farrell.

"What if we don't care about Ursprung?" asked Ashley.

Mr. O'Farrell looked at her unbelievingly, "My girl, that has been the goal of all your parents' years of hard work. To take Ursprung from them now would leave their mission incomplete. Their quest would end without any reward for their labors."

O'Farrell's explanation was a bit overdramatic, Tiffany thought. Then again, the man was known to put on a show.

"How will you get us there?" Ashley asked.

A bright, genuine smile crossed the old man's face. It was the exact question he'd wanted to be asked. He turned, tapping the mTalk on his wrist. An image of a large ship, larger than any they'd encountered before, appeared on the screen before him and began to rotate.

"This is *Sylvia's Hope*," he declared.

The name *Sylvia* struck Tiffany oddly. It had been the name of Mr. O'Farrell's automated home assistant in Brighton.

"Ursprung will be at a greater distance than any planet in the known Federation," O'Farrell said. "The *Hope* will travel faster than any other ship in the Federation and will carry the required supplies for long-term and possibly permanent settlement. I've been working on it for more than three decades; it has the most advanced propulsion technology and navigation possible."

Tiffany realized that O'Farrell was not aware of the *Ark*. She wasn't sure that it mattered one way or the other, but she figured she would discuss it with Oliver, Austin, and Ashley before telling him about it.

O'Farrell turned back to face the kids. "When we arrive, I will need you and your parents to help me uncover the artifacts in the ruins on Ursprung to learn the truth. We will all work together."

Tiffany had heard this before. She was sure it was true that everyone would work together happily and peacefully—as long as they were doing exactly what Mr. O'Farrell wanted.

"Further, my teams have been securing many artifacts that we will need for our exploration," Mr. O'Farrell continued. "We have secured four large crosses from the Valley of Shadows. I have on good authority that the Übel are about to launch another mission to the valley. Either the Übel are unaware that we have already extracted the four crosses, or they are after something else. Regardless, we will be there, and I will rescue your parents myself." O'Farrell folded his hands and took a deep breath. "Children, I know you do not trust me. I surprised you, and I realize that the drastic measures I took to protect the McGregors were confusing. But I will prove to you that I am your ally and that I do indeed want to work with you. When I return with your parents, you will see that my intentions are true and always have been."

The speech stung Tiffany like a scorpion's stinger. Surely everything he said was a lie, but she had trusted him before and for some odd reason wanted to trust him again. He had the resources to pull off the whole expedition, and his offer was more tempting than she had expected. But it had to be too good to be true. Actions always speak louder than words, and O'Farrell had already clearly revealed his true self.

"I will personally see to your parents' rescue while you go with Commander DarkStone on an expedition to a previous dig site on Yl Revaw. We are attempting to uncover what might lie in a chamber there."

Tiffany smiled. She'd been right: Yl Revaw was an important location.

O'Farrell continued, "If the Übel aren't aware of the artifact yet, they will be soon. We can't let them steal it. I have a team of former Archeos experts on Yl Revaw right now, preparing to excavate."

Oliver spoke up. "Why do you need us there?"

"The *Ranger* was severely damaged when the Übel kidnapped Rand and Jenn," O'Farrell said. "Should the Übel or Federation discover the ship's location again, we may not be able to stand against them. I can't have you all captured or stuck on escape pods, so I'm sending you to the securest place I have, besides the *Hope*. No one is going on the *Hope* until we're ready to depart for Ursprung. I cannot risk its being destroyed or captured."

For the first time, Tiffany heard genuine concern in Mr. O'Farrell's voice. She now knew for certain that any previous concern had been a façade.

"Sir, the *Vulture* and *Eagle* are ready," Commander Dark-Stone said.

Mr. O'Farrell nodded and stood. "Kids, think about what I've said. I'm confident you will make the right decision. I will return with your families shortly, so keep that in mind as you cooperate with my team at the dig site."

Oliver jolted up from his seat, and Tiffany noticed Drex's hand underneath his arm. Oliver shook it off. Tiffany was sure a fight was about to break out, but instead Oliver said, "Mr. O'Farrell, how can you expect us to cooperate with you when we're being treated harshly?"

Drex straightened. Tiffany heard more shuffling among the other guards behind her.

"How do you mean?" O'Farrell seemed oblivious to the previous treatment of the prisoners. Tiffany was nearly sure it was an act. He didn't seem the type to not know every action of his subordinates.

"Your commander has been pushing us around since she captured us. Drex has been violent since our first meeting on Evad."

"Commander, is this true?" O'Farrell asked in fake surprise.

DarkStone cleared her throat. "Sir, recapturing them was not easy. We had to use force."

O'Farrell raised his hands. "Enough. Do better from now on. These kids are part of our team. They're not our enemies. Don't treat them as such."

"Yes, sir," DarkStone said grudgingly.

"Oliver, is that satisfactory?" Mr. O'Farrell asked.

"Only time will tell" was his simple reply.

4.25

Obbin's Shadow

ason was on a dig with his parents again. They were
deep inside dusty catacombs, marching toward an unexplored chamber. It would have felt normal, if not for the
soldiers of darkness prodding them forward and for the fact
that Oliver, Tiffany, and Austin were still missing.

As the *Raven* had cruised into the Valley of Shadows,
Mason had seen the blackened remnants of several stone spires
destroyed during the Übel's and Corsairs' previous visits to Cao.
Mason imagined the valley was quite unique and picturesque
before the destruction. The destroyed spires made the valley
look like a fractured remnant of what it once must have been.
Still, he could see how the valley had gotten its name. The
spires' shadows darkened the valley floor, and shadows lurked
across the ridges in the valley walls. The valley held many
areas that the sun's light could not touch. It gave him the chills.

Vedrik and eight escorts were at the head of the exploration party. Dr. Blue came just behind him, and Mason and his
parents followed a dozen feet after, with eight escorts of their
own. Eight more escorts brought up the tail of the group. The
celtyx had been left on the *Raven* after Mason's parents had
raised concerns about their being difficult to control on rafts.

Vedrik had seemed annoyed but had agreed. Mason was thankful that the monstrous creatures would not be in the confined space of the tunnels with him.

Unlike the rooms that had contained the crosses, the chamber they sought was deep underground, preventing easy extraction. Already they had descended stairs and floated down two canals, one of which was partially blocked. After the blockage, a portion of the canal was covered in thick mold that gave off a noxious poisonous gas, requiring the entire party to don Oxyverters.

Vedrik raised his hand. "Halt, everyone."

Stones blocked the tunnel ahead from top to bottom.

"Sekelton, take the Wikks and Dr. Blue one hundred feet back with eleven of the soldiers," Vedrik ordered. "Rutledge, take the rest of the soldiers and post two men every ten yards from the Wikks back to us. This might be a trap. Be vigilant, and stand your ground."

The team walked back and waited in the cold, dry tunnel. Pyrock and Cruz disappeared around the bend to set the charges to remove the cave-in. Other soldiers set LuminOrbs along the tunnel.

Cruz seemed hesitant to go with Pyrock. Mason understood. Pyrock was always laughing at odd times. He seemed crazed. Likely the concussions of years of detonations had taken their toll on him.

As Mason waited, his parents and Dr. Blue discussed the map they had on the new e-journal they'd been given. Apparently they'd found a map at a previous dig and were comparing notes on the information.

Austin and Tiffany had been matching the same map with the paintings from the Blauwe Mensen castle. Now his parents used a map created with information that the Übel had collected and compiled. While Mason didn't like seeing his parents cooperate with Dr. Blue, he didn't like the alternative either. At least the doctor was a scientist, not a soldier. She might be interested in the discoveries for the right reasons.

Mason kicked a loose rock at his feet, and it ricocheted off the opposite wall. No one seemed to be paying attention to him. After all, where could he go with even more soldiers blocking his only escape? He had been given back his mTalk, but the communication function appeared to be blocked—not that it would have done a lot of good this deep in the catacombs. There was no chance of reaching out to his siblings, wherever they might be. A dismal sense of loss slipped across his mind like a chilly, wandering breeze. Mason missed them more than he ever had before. He trusted that they were with the Veritas Nachfolger, safe with Brother Sam.

Lowering himself to the ground, Mason felt the e-papyrus in his pocket. He'd already noted everything Zebra Xavier had told him about the Übel's version of the Federation's history, as well as what he and his siblings had experienced, learned, and concluded over the last several days. He'd enjoyed reliving their triumphant moments. They'd already accomplished something spectacular, and it wasn't over yet.

As he slipped out the e-papyrus to write some more, a little black ball with a red button fell to the ground. A label said *Recovery Beacon*.

Recovery Beacon? These devices were used to locate someone or mark a location in an emergency. Whoever had the tracking receiver would receive an alert if the beacon was activated and could then locate it. But how had this gotten into his pocket?

Of course! Mae had slipped it into his pocket during their good-bye. Branz, Grace, and Mae had been trying to get it to him—that was why they'd rushed him.

He rolled the beacon in his hands but avoided pressing the button. This could come in handy.

Two Übel soldiers drifted past, their weapons at the ready.

"I don't like it," the first soldier said. "It's been too quiet."

"The Saharvics probably want nothing to do with us since Captain Vedrik didn't fulfill his end of their bargain," the second soldier said.

"Or they want revenge," the first replied. "He should've just paid them what they asked. He may not have gotten all seven crosses, but at least he got four."

"Yes, but you know the captain. If he doesn't get his way . . ."

Mason looked back down the dark tunnel. Several smaller chambers had riddled the paths along the way, but the party had been given no time to stop and explore. Even now they were just yards from a small alcove hewed from the stone. It was empty of artifacts as far as he could see, but there were markings on the walls. Suddenly he jumped. In the dim light of the LuminOrbs, he'd seen something move in the alcove.

Mason shone his mTalk light at the alcove. As the beam danced along the wall of the tunnel, he saw the movement again. He swung the light back quickly, but it was already gone. Was it the Saharvics, or something else? He shivered to think what sort of creatures might inhabit these dark tunnels. On a previous dig, they'd encountered large eyeless rodents with long yellowing teeth. One had been nearly as large as six-year-old Mason.

Someone called Mason's name. He looked toward his parents, but they were still in discussion with Dr. Blue. He looked toward the tunnel and saw a blue face crowned with green hair.

"Obbin?"

As he started forward, an announcement came from behind him.

"One minute until detonation," called Cruz as he hobbled around the bend in the tunnel.

Mason glanced back to the alcove. The blue face was gone. He wanted to investigate, but conversations had ended and the tunnel was relatively quiet.

A high-pitched squeal echoed down the tunnel. Light bounced off the walls ahead. A moment later, Pyrock came into view, cackling, a light strapped to his forehead. "Sir, charges are set. Twenty-three seconds."

Mason's dad partially shielded his mom. She pulled Mason under her arm. The ground shook, and the sound of the explosion rumbled through the air. A cloud of dust floated ominously toward them.

"Pyrock," Vedrik said.

The soldier dashed off into the dust. A moment later he called over Vedrik's mTalk, "Clear."

"Let's go," Vedrik ordered. He lifted his mTalk. "Rutledge, bring your soldiers back. We're ready."

Mason glanced down the tunnel again, hoping to spot Obbin once more. Had he really found his way onto the *Raven* during the confusion? Was he going to try to rescue Mason and his parents? The thought gave Mason mixed feelings. Obbin's last plan had almost gotten a lot of people hurt and Mason thrown in the cooler. Then again, he'd previously worked with Brother Sam to help them escape and evade the Übel on Evad.

The question was simple: *when would Obbin make his move?*

4.26

Zapp-Tap

"We're leaving!" Commander DarkStone bellowed to a waiting squad of Corsairs as she led her prisoners and crew across the *Black Ranger*'s large flight deck. "Lieutenant Tallion, your squadron is to escort us to Yl Revaw."

A Corsair wearing a bright green tricorne saluted and turned toward three lines of Corsair pilots. "You heard our orders. Prepare for takeoff." The pilots dashed for their awaiting starfighters. Tiffany noticed that the ships were not uniform in type like the Übel's.

Another soldier stepped forward. She wore a heavy-looking helmet and mask that obscured her face. "Commander, all three crosses are loaded into the *Eagle*."

If the Corsairs had only three crosses, who had the rest? Or were they still in the valley? O'Farrell was headed back there on a "rescue mission," but perhaps he was also going to collect the remaining crosses.

"Have both ships been resupplied?" Commander DarkStone asked.

"Yes, commander," the soldier said. "We have loaded the requested supplies, including payment for the Saharvics, and have resupplied the *Vulture*'s assault weapons."

"And the generators and engines are fixed?" DarkStone asked, referring to the work Austin had done to redistribute the power for takeoff from Cixot.

"Yes, commander," the soldier said.

"Very good. Dismissed," Commander DarkStone said. "Drex, tag each of those four with a Zapp-Tap."

Tiffany didn't like the sound of that.

"Then take them to their cabins so they can change and rest if needed. I'll call for them when I am ready."

Drex ushered Tiffany, Oliver, Austin, and Ashley toward the *Eagle*. He opened a metal locker, removing a dark green case with a yellow lightning bolt etched on the front. Drex smiled as he removed a silver syringe and dropped a miniscule, flashing orange pellet into the cylinder. His smile grew as he approached Oliver.

"This will only hurt a little, unfortunately." With the last word, Drex pulled back the collar of Oliver's shirt and stabbed the needle into the top of his right shoulder.

Tiffany cringed as her brother winced. Drex suppressed the plunger, and a glowing orange dot traveled down the transparent needle. The orange light changed to purple and began to pulse the instant it was under Oliver's skin. Oliver gritted his teeth and briefly slumped.

"Guess I was able to make it hurt worse," Drex said. "But I'll keep it painless for your sister and girlfriend, per the Supreme Admiral's orders."

Tiffany couldn't tell if Oliver was blushing because he was angry or just embarrassed by his reaction.

Drex removed a new syringe and slipped an orange pellet in. Tiffany pulled back the collar of her shirt herself, and Drex pressed the needle into the flesh directly behind Tiffany's right shoulder. She felt a twinge and some warmth, but nothing overly painful. Normally she wouldn't have wanted to look, but she wanted to see the glowing purple pellet. Indeed, her shoulder was illuminated from within.

As Drex moved to Austin and then Ashley, neither suffered the same pain that Drex had bestowed on Oliver. It made Tiffany angry that Drex had purposely hurt her brother even after Mr. O'Farrell had forbidden it. As soon as Drex was finished, the guards relaxed.

Tiffany looked at her brother; he was as surprised as she was. She had a pretty good idea what the Zapp-Tap would do, and she suspected Oliver knew for sure. But neither of them had expected to be left unguarded.

"What now?" asked Austin.

Drex grunted. "You're free to go to your cabin."

"Free?" asked Ashley curiously.

"We're not free," Oliver said. "They've inserted a shocking pellet into us. If we do something they don't like, they'll tap an icon and the surge of electricity will either bring us to our knees or knock us unconscious."

"Like this," Drex said. He touched the screen of the device on his wrist, and Oliver's body jerked as he dropped to one knee.

"Stop!" cried Ashley. She put her hand on Oliver's shoulder. "Are you okay?"

"I was just giving you a visual," Drex said. "I could have increased the power."

Tiffany shifted between Drex and Oliver and stood straight. "I think we get the picture."

Oliver groaned and let out a heavy sigh.

"I'll be tracking all of you," Drex said.

"Why not just lock us up?" Austin asked.

"Freedom," Drex said with a mocking air.

Tiffany watched as Drex walked back to Commander Dark-Stone. His demeanor changed the moment she began barking orders at him. In the seconds it took Drex to walk from them to her, he went from a cruel, power-crazed soldier to a cowering, rundown servant.

"Does that mean we can grab something to eat from the galley?" asked Austin.

"Yes, I believe," Oliver said. "But we must remember that he's always watching. He'll be looking for an opportunity to activate these. Don't give him one."

"So much for Mr. O'Farrell's orders," Ashley said.

Oliver nodded with a forced smile.

Before heading to the galley, Ashley and Tiffany went to the cabin to change into their newly provided expedition clothing. Tiffany smiled. The outfits were Ultra-Wear invented by her grandpa, Theodore William Wikk, a serial entrepreneur.

"I'm glad to be out of my prisoner jumpsuit, but these weren't designed for teenage girls," Ashley said. The khaki cargo pants, pocket-strewn button-up shirts, and bulky brown boots weren't the most flattering.

"I couldn't agree more," Tiffany said.

The girls rejoined Oliver and Austin in the galley, where they'd already begun eating. An announcement over the speakers notified them that the ship was taking off.

"Should we get our stuff out of hiding?" Austin whispered once hyper flight was stabilized.

Oliver looked toward the door. "I don't see why not. O'Farrell already knows most of what we do."

Tiffany shook her head. "He doesn't know about the *Ark*, and I'm not sure how much he knows about the Veritas Nachfolger."

The metal clanking of a Corsair soldier stopped her. The guard looked in with one eye and one blinking blue light, then turned and moved on. Austin waved his hand as he forked beef stroganoff into his mouth.

Tiffany smirked at her little brother's show of opposition. "I'd like to get the e-journal at least," she told him.

He nodded. "I'll go get it."

"Be discreet," Tiffany warned.

Austin smiled. "Of course, sis."

Austin headed to the cabin where he had stashed the e-journal. As he approached, he overheard Commander Dark-Stone's voice.

"Lieutenant, you will have to restrain yourself," Commander DarkStone said. "The Supreme Admiral's orders are to be obeyed. If the Wikks continue to complain, I will have no choice but to reassign you. I don't like placating them any more than you do. But the Supreme Admiral believes they have information that we do not, and we're not going to get it from them without their cooperation."

"Why not electro-flogging?" asked Drex. "It works on insubordinates."

"Nephew—"

Austin jerked back. *Nephew?*

"—the Supreme Admiral will not resort to that on non-Corsairs. The results we desire have never warranted torture. It only creates more resistance."

"Yes, commander."

"Have we made any progress in unsealing the locked cabin?" Commander DarkStone asked.

Austin covered his mouth. They had to be talking about the cabin that he'd not been able to breach either. He was as curious as the Corsairs about what was inside, but he didn't want them to be the ones to get in. Who knew what the Veritas Nachfolger had stored there?

"No, commander. We have not been able to bypass the security," Drex said.

"You'll never move up the ranks if you don't get your head together," Commander DarkStone said. "Now, bring those kids to me."

"Yes, commander."

Drex stepped into the corridor just as Austin slipped back into the galley.

"What is it?" Oliver asked.

Austin took a seat. "Nothing. Drex is coming to get us."

"You didn't get the e-journal?" Tiffany asked.

"No. It's in the cabin that DarkStone is using as her office," Austin explained. "And get this: Drex is DarkStone's nephew."

"What?" the three older kids practically shouted.

"You four, with me!" Drex appeared in the doorway. "What are you staring at?"

Oliver, Ashley, and Tiffany did have strange expressions on their faces as they processed Drex and DarkStone's relationship.

The bunks in the cabin had been removed. Other than chairs in a semicircle before DarkStone's desk, the room contained a cryostore unit and an examination table set under two large machines. The last item gave Austin the chills. Did it have anything to do with cybornotics or biotronics?

"Welcome, comrades," Commander DarkStone said. "Take a seat."

Austin grunted. He wasn't her comrade.

Drex took an end seat, and Austin quickly sat next to him. He'd show Drex that he wasn't afraid of him. He'd just like to see the bully mess with him. He wasn't as restrained as Oliver. Plus, while Oliver had tolerated cruelty to himself, he wouldn't tolerate cruelty to his little brother.

"It's time to discuss our expedition to Yl Revaw," Commander DarkStone said. "We will begin our expedition on Everwood Ridge, then move to the grotto where the artifact is located."

Tiffany bumped Austin. This was exactly where she had believed the Eochair would be.

"May I ask what is so important to recover?" asked Oliver.

The commander paused. "We've scoured the research documents provided by your parents and other teams. Due to the high security of this underground vault, it must contain something valuable. Of course, you already know this. I believe you're calling it *Eochair*."

Tiffany gasped, and DarkStone smiled as she revealed their parents' e-journal. She handed it to Tiffany. "You can have this back now. We've copied its data into our system."

Austin stared at the device, a sense of guilt overcoming him. They'd not hidden it well enough. Of course, nearly everything in the room had been dismantled to make room for the commander's temporary office. If he'd expected that, he never would have picked the room for a hiding place.

"Now that we're working together, perhaps you can figure out how to access the chamber," DarkStone said.

While Austin was mad that the Corsairs had pirated their information, he knew that it didn't really matter. They were stuck with the Corsairs for the foreseeable future. Finding their parents and Mason was most important, and part of him hoped that Mr. O'Farrell would succeed in his mission and recapture his parents from the Übel. Austin would rather the Corsairs had the Eochair than the Übel. If they lost the path to Ursprung, they'd lose Mason and their parents.

"Your parents have failed at each attempt to gain access to the vault. We will not," DarkStone continued.

"How do you know?" Austin blurted.

Drex shifted defensively at Austin's reaction, and Commander DarkStone raised her chin. "I have orders to acquire the Eochair at all costs. We will use all the tools at our fingertips to gain entrance. Explosives, drilling, cyber, whatever it takes. We have good reason to believe the Übel will come here soon."

"You risk destroying whatever is hidden inside the chamber," Tiffany warned.

"It's better to destroy the artifact than to let it fall into the hands of the Übel."

"I disagree," Ashley said. "We seem to be getting close to the end of the trail. This artifact may be invaluable. Why not work with the Übel to discover it? Aren't you all looking for the same thing?"

DarkStone gave a hearty laugh. "The same thing? No, not at all. The Übel wish to use the cure to control others and gain more power and wealth. We want to provide the cure to all, so that all can be healed."

Healed? Was that the simple difference between the two? What about the Veritas Nachfolger?

"Destroying the artifact could end the quest," Ashley continued. "At least if the Übel discover Ursprung, you'll have a chance of discovering it too."

"Your point is made, but we do not have unlimited time. We are open to your suggestions before we resort to more drastic measures."

Austin nodded. He was up to the challenge.

"We'll do our best," chimed Tiffany, and Ashley agreed.

"Excellent," DarkStone said.

"Do you expect the Übel soon?" Oliver asked.

"It could be hours—or days. If they come to the planet, there will be little we can do but destroy and evacuate."

The word *evacuate* made Austin think of Cixot. "Commander DarkStone, how close were we to being incinerated on Cixot?"

Her reply was quick. "Twenty-three point four seconds."

Austin felt sick to his stomach. They'd come very close to being obliterated.

"Mr. O'Farrell mentioned that the *Black Ranger* was unusable. How bad was the damage?" Ashley asked.

The commander snorted. "I think you know the answer."

"I didn't take the escape pod for safety. I took it to get away from you," Ashley said.

"That didn't work as planned, did it now?" A scowl quickly replaced Commander DarkStone's victorious smile. "The *Black Ranger* suffered significant damage to its fuselage and structural integrity. Repairs could take the engineers several days."

"How did the Übel know where to attack the ship to get the McGregors?" asked Oliver.

"You're responsible for that." DarkStone's eyes flared with frustration. "During the shootout at the Hatchery, one of our men was captured and divulged the information."

"That's how they knew you had us too?" asked Ashley.

"Yes," the commander snarled. "Your parents were their primary targets, although they probably desired the artifacts from Cao as well. The *Black Ranger* can't jump into hyper flight due to the gaping hole they left in it, which is why the Supreme Commander has taken the *Vulture* and we must take the *Eagle*. Is that all your questions?"

Oliver looked at the others. "Yes, for now."

"Fine. I expect full cooperation from you. Don't think for a moment that I will hesitate to bring you to the ground should you try any sabotage or escape," warned DarkStone. "Do you understand?"

"We do," said Oliver.

"Commander, I do have one request," Ashley said.

"What is it?"

"That you restrain Drex. He has continued to be unnecessarily cruel to Oliver."

Drex shifted in his seat to stare at Oliver. Austin thought the commander looked unsettled. Were her threats even valid? Perhaps she had been bluffing, though Austin didn't want to test her limits.

"His continued violence does little to give us reason to cooperate with you," Tiffany said.

The conversation was beginning to sound like a negotiation, with Tiffany and Ashley holding the bargaining chips.

"Done! Lieutenant Drex, you will behave or you will be electro-flogged," Commander DarkStone said.

Austin gave Drex a glowing, victorious smile.

"Commander?" cried Drex.

"Silence!" she shouted. "In just over two hours, we will land and get to work, so if you plan to sleep, sleep now. Get dressed in your new clothing before we arrive. Eat before debarking. When we land, Tiffany and Oliver will come with me to the grotto. Austin and Ashley will remain at camp."

Austin gave a grunt of disapproval but didn't protest any further.

"We're returning your mTalks. We're monitoring them, and I can shut them down at any moment, so don't try anything," Commander DarkStone said. "Dismissed."

They took their devices and left for their cabin.

"Well, that went all right," Austin said. "You think Drex will cool it?"

Oliver shrugged. "I doubt it. But thanks, Ashley, for mentioning it."

"Electro-flogging sounds horrible," Tiffany said.

"Well, he deserves it," Austin said. "He's caused plenty of pain to us."

Tiffany didn't seem so sure. Austin pulled at the collar of his shirt and showed the pulsing purple light under his skin.

4.27

Collapse

The ceiling of the tunnel rose. A moment later, the expedition party came to a halt as their lights landed on a double door made of copper. Each door was at least twenty feet high and ten wide.

Vedrik ordered Currie and Rutledge forward. The two soldiers moved hesitantly, and Mason could tell they were nervous, perhaps even scared. They jumped as their commander ordered them to hurry.

"Sir, shouldn't we check for booby tr—" Dr. Blue began.

"They're still alive," Vedrik said, pointing at Currie and Rutledge.

"The doors could—"

"Zebra Xavier's time limit isn't only for me. It's for you and the Wikks as well," Vedrik growled. "Don't think I'll be the only one taking the fall if we fail." The doctor was silent. "Now push the doors open!"

Currie and Rutledge leaned against the doors. They didn't move.

"Put some muscle into it!" Captain Vedrik shouted.

The men threw their weight at the doors. Still they didn't open.

"You two, help them!" the captain ordered.

Cruz and another soldier moved forward, and Pyrock started to unload explosives from his satchel. Dr. Blue moved away from the doors, and Mason's parents motioned him to do the same.

"Captain, may I, may I, may I?" Pyrock asked.

The captain rubbed his chin and looked at the doors. The soldiers grunted as their bodies slammed against them.

"You may," Vedrik said. "Everyone, back around the bend."

Once they'd gotten out of sight of the large doors, Mason slid to the ground. He looked back to see if the blue prince was waiting for them. He wasn't.

"One minute," Vedrik said as he walked into view.

Pyrock followed. "All set."

There was a resounding bang. The walls shook. Pyrock disappeared around the bend. A moment later, they heard a long howl. Vedrik dashed forward. "What is it?"

Silence for a moment.

"What is it?" Vedrik shouted.

"Sir, the doors are still standing," said Pyrock sullenly.

Everyone returned back around the corner. Sure enough, the copper sentinels still stood guard over their chamber.

Although Mason's parents weren't working for the Übel, they were admiring and scouring every inch of the large doors. There was an intricate pattern etched into the metal.

"Dr. Blue, how do we get in?" Vedrik asked.

"I have not ascertained the answer yet," Dr. Blue said. She pressed her hand against one of the large copper doors, then her ear.

Vedrik rolled his eyes as he sighed. The captain stood impatiently behind the scientist.

Mason moved to the side of the tunnel and began to sit again but stopped suddenly. In the lantern light he saw a cross shape embedded into the stones rimming the door. He gasped, drawing the attention of Vedrik and his parents.

"What is it, Mason?" Mrs. Wikk asked.

Mason shook his head. "Nothing."

But he had said it too quickly. Vedrik came to him in three quick strides, tearing the collar of Mason's shirt as he yanked him to his feet. "What do you know, boy?"

Mason looked past Vedrik. Currie was holding back his dad.

"Tell me, boy!" Vedrik shouted. He looked desperate. The three-hour limit was running out.

"I . . . I just noticed something," Mason said. He didn't have the cross necklace they'd used to unlock the doors on Evad, so it wasn't like they'd be able to get in anyway. "That indent," he said. "They were on Evad too."

"Ah, yes." Vedrik dropped Mason on the ground. "Rutledge, the pack."

The soldier ran over and pulled a pack from his own gear. Mason recognized it immediately. It was his. His heart sank as Vedrik emptied its contents onto the dusty ground and used his foot to scatter Mason's things: the transponder cylinder from Evad; the book, *The Path to Creator*, with its cover bent backward; the blue jewel from Cobalt Gorge. The cross-shaped necklace lay exposed on the floor.

Vedrik lifted the pendant out of the dirt and held it to the indent.

Everyone stepped back from the doors as loose rocks and dust fell from the ceiling of the tunnel. With a teeth-chattering rumble, the large copper doors began to slide sideways into the walls. Light shone down from overhead. Mason's mouth dropped open.

A large spaceship was bathed in light, held up by several braces. It wasn't like anything Mason had seen before. There were no windows or wings as far as he could see, and instead of engines it had large propellers on one end. Two curved tail fins arched from the center of the oval ship and nearly touched the underside. The skin of the ship was a swirling blue and gray.

This was no spaceship. Was the *Ark* actually a submersible?

4.28

No Sleep

Tiffany was unable to fall asleep, her mind swirling with the information she'd gathered over the past week. The e-journal's screens glowed next to her. She'd found nothing new about the Eochair, so she'd started to read more about Yl Revaw. Now she'd turned her thoughts to YelNik Eisle.

Just moments before Mason had been captured, he'd told her that the map from the observatory on Evad, the star map from the ceiling in the library at Dabnis Castle, and the mural and star map in the Cathedral all showed YelNik Eisle. Brother Sam had confirmed it as their destination. What was there that would unlock the final clues to Ursprung? The Corsairs were analyzing this information as well now, but that didn't stop her from creating her own theories.

She stared at the underside of the bunk above her. Could they really be coming to the end of their quest? How long had her parents been searching? Now it seemed that all the pieces were in place, and her parents' years of work were finally about to pay off. Everything was coming together like a well-orchestrated plan.

Orchestrated plan. . . . She thought of Creator. Obbin had explained that He was the one who had created them. Was this all part of His plan? The notion went against everything she'd been taught in school. At Bewaldeter she'd studied the science of the natural world.

Now she was being challenged to consider what—or Who— had made everything work so perfectly together. Her teachers might call it fantastical, but it was beautiful and hopeful to think that Creator loved her and that life could go on eternally.

Tiffany knew she didn't have it all figured out. The books that the Blauwe Mensen had given Oliver were on the *Phoenix*, as were all the other artifacts they'd collected so far and the LibrixCaptex, which contained even more information. Did those things even matter at this point? Did they contain clues that would help them to find Ursprung?

There was a knock on the hatch. Tiffany climbed down from her bunk and pulled the hatch open. A Corsair with a metallic faceplate greeted her.

"Commander DarkStone requests the four of you in the cargo bay immediately," the Corsair said. She tapped the controls, switching the lights on in the cabin. "Everyone, up! Now!"

Groans echoed from the bunks. Austin nearly fell from his spot on a top bunk, barely catching himself. Ashley sat up and yawned. Oliver pulled back his covers and swiveled to get up.

"Up!" the Corsair shouted again.

Austin hopped down and pulled a shirt on over his head. "Relax!"

The Corsair's sword flashed.

Tiffany shifted between Austin and the Corsair. "We're coming," she said firmly.

The guard seemed cautious about challenging Tiffany. Her sword dimmed as she stepped back through the hatch and waited in the corridor.

Oliver gripped Austin's shoulder. "Careful, brother."

Austin nodded. Oliver took Ashley's hand and pulled her up from the bunk.

"You boys were to change into the expedition clothing provided," the Corsair said.

"We'll change and catch up," Oliver said.

"Shall we?" Tiffany asked her friend.

Ashley locked arms with her. "Let's go."

Extended Dig

Before stepping out to call Zebra Xavier, Vedrik ordered the archeologists to look around the chamber but not to enter the ship. Mason gathered his items back into his pack again. They'd let him keep it, perhaps because whatever he had on him was theirs for the taking if they needed it.

"Dad, what's a submarine doing down here?" asked Mason. "This is a mountain in the middle of a desert. The canals aren't deep enough for it."

"The ship may have a control mechanism for a hidden exit," Mr. Wikk said.

Captain Vedrik strode into the chamber. "We have two hours. An extraction team is being sent in to help."

"They won't be able to get this out in two hours," Dr. Blue said.

Vedrik grunted. "That's their responsibility. You may enter the ship now, but remember I'm watching."

Mason followed his parents toward a hatch in the submersible's side. He read the name aloud. "The *Black Lagoon*."

There was no handle or entry keypad to open the door.

"Perhaps there's a control room," Mr. Wikk said.

Mason stepped closer to the ship. "Wait. Look." A vertical line of five small squares crossed with a line of three horizontal squares was embedded in the side of the submersible: a cross like on Evad. He touched the squares one by one, and they lit up green.

The hatch shifted and lowered outward on hinges at its base.

"Good work," Mrs. Wikk said.

"Let's find the bridge," said his dad.

They walked up stairs on the inside of the hatch. At one end of a corridor, toward the bow of the ship, was a spiral staircase. Going up it, they arrived at what appeared to be the bridge. A series of screens were laid into a console at the front, with several control sticks. There was no windshield.

"Let's see if we can get this thing to turn on," Mr. Wikk said. He pressed a green button labeled *Ignition*.

WHUUUUUZZZZ.

A humming sound echoed from underneath the ship. They'd activated the propellers. Lights flickered on around the room, and the screens on the console came to life.

"You did it, Dad!" Mason said. He tapped a screen that said *Exterior View*, hoping to see the archeologists and soldiers outside. Every inch of unoccupied wall space became transparent. The entire chamber was visible, but none of the people outside seemed to notice a change.

"What just happened?" Mrs. Wikk asked.

"I tapped *Exterior View*," Mason said.

"Interesting," Mr. Wikk said. "I've never seen this technology used in a ship's interior."

"Can they not see us?"

Mr. Wikk waved at Dr. Blue. The scientist made no acknowledgment. "Guess not. This might be useful."

"Quick, turn it off. Vedrik is coming onboard," Mrs. Wikk said.

Mason tapped a button that said *Abort Exterior View*. A moment later, the captain came up the spiral stairs. "Have you found anything yet?" he asked.

"Nothing of expedition value," Mr. Wikk said.

"Dr. Blue has located some sort of control room," Vedrik said.

"We'll continue to search the data here," Mr. Wikk said.

The captain grunted. "You'd like me to leave, wouldn't you?"

"Of course," said Mrs. Wikk. "But we know better than to ask, so at least be useful and help."

Mason was not surprised by his mom's directness. Neither was the captain.

"Your attitude toward me has soured considerably," he joked.

"Really," she said. "I don't recall a time when I didn't despise you."

"What do I care about your opinion?" Vedrik asked, but something in the way he said it seemed wounded.

Dr. Blue's high voice came over the mTalk. "Captain, I need you to see this."

Vedrik took a frustrated breath. He tapped the screen of his mTalk. "I'll be right there." He tapped the screen again. "Cruz, come up to the bridge and keep an eye on the Wikks."

"And where might we take a submersible in the middle of a waterless cave?" asked Mr. Wikk.

"With you people, anything is possible," Vedrik said.

Mason took that as a compliment.

"Don't try anything," Vedrik said as he left.

4.30

Everwood Ridge

"What were you looking at?" asked Ashley.

Tiffany looked up from the e-journal. "Just the information from our parents' earlier visits to this place. There isn't much to help us. Not even the most powerful scanners have penetrated the vault's walls to get a glimpse of what's inside."

"My parents feared a collapse of the room if they forced entry," Ashley said. "They were patient, believing they'd discover the key at another archeological site."

Tiffany smiled. "That's the thing. Our parents weren't on an urgent timetable. This was their career."

Oliver and Austin came into the cargo bay. Their outfits were similar to the girls', just a slightly different fit.

"You guys look nice," Ashley said.

"Just like twins . . ." Austin's words trailed off in sorrow. His true twin was still missing.

"We're going to see him again." Oliver patted Austin's back.

Funny how connected the three of them were now. Never before had they been so in tune.

"We will, Aus," Tiffany said. "Though these people aren't our friends and their mission isn't ours, they're trying to reach the same place as the Übel. We will find Mason and our parents."

Austin's green eyes locked on hers, and she saw a renewed strength. "You're right."

"Three minutes until reentry," a voice said over the intercom. "Find secure seating immediately."

The drop out of hyper flight was hardly noticeable. The ship landed perfectly. A dozen armed Corsairs moved toward the large cargo bay door as it opened. Their actions made it seem like there was imminent danger outside, but no shots were fired when the doors opened.

Soldiers began unloading supplies. Another half dozen stood armed and ready next to the containers holding the crosses. Where had they all come from?

"Looks like there could be trouble," Austin said.

"I suspect they're weary of how often their path is crossing with the Übel's," Ashley said.

"Do you think they're intimidated by them?" Austin asked.

"No, they've taken them head-on more than once," Oliver said.

"You four," called Commander DarkStone. "With me!"

Ashley and the Wikks joined the commander near the open bay door. Outside, a camp was quickly being assembled around the ship.

"We've landed at our base camp. The three of us will proceed to the grotto now." DarkStone looked at Austin and Ashley. "You two will remain here. Don't try anything, or you'll wake up three hours later with a severe headache." She snapped her fingers. A large Corsair walked up with four Zingers in his hands.

"You're arming us?" asked Austin.

"Cooperation is expected," the commander said. "Should you—"

"Yes, I know. Three hours," Austin sneered.

"You are quite bold, young man," Commander DarkStone said. "But I will only tolerate your attitude for so long."

Tiffany eyed her brother. He didn't back down.

"Let's go." Commander DarkStone escorted Oliver and Tiffany out of the *Vulture* to a skiff. It wasn't quite like the one the Übel had used on Evad, but it was similar. Commander DarkStone let them into the back row, where she sat across from them, facing backward.

The Corsair skiff zipped forward. The pilot maneuvered among the trees with ease. The forest was warm and damp, although not as humid as Evad's. A piney, earthy scent filled the air, and birds chirped all around. A white bird soared above them as if racing them. The trees were not nearly as high as the ones on Jahr des Eises, maybe a hundred feet at most. Low walls of moss-covered stones lined the path. Tiffany recalled them from her previous visit.

They flew into the clearing, where a settlement had once stood proudly before the underground chamber. The village was now in shambles, but the sun shone brightly.

At least twenty Corsairs were manning guard posts around the perimeter of the ruins. Four skiffs hovered in the middle of the site, each armed with large blaster cannons.

"Preparing for something?" asked Oliver.

"It's no secret that we must remain vigilant against the Übel," Commander DarkStone said. "Also, federal activity has recently increased at a nearby outpost, Pocket Falls. They have a new brigade commander."

The Corsairs' enemies were mounting.

They stopped by a rocky slope at the edge of the forest. Fifty or more trees had been cleared, only their stumps remaining. Branches had been piled high to the far right of the slope. Remnants of the stone buildings had been dragged around it to create a wall. The Corsairs clearly didn't mind disturbing the historical site or destroying the environment.

An arch of rock was set into the hill. The last time Tiffany had seen the entrance to the grotto, she, her brothers, and Ashley had been more interested in exploring the nearby woods.

Oliver was first down from the craft, his Zinger and satchel slung opposite each other across his back. Commander Dark-Stone climbed down, followed by Tiffany.

Two men approached. The first wore a khaki outfit and a helmet with a tinted visor that covered his eyes but left his round nose and purple lips exposed. The man next to him was taller. Dark brown sideburns and a mustache accented his angular face and bright green eyes. He looked like he might venture into the forest and come out holding a wild animal in his bare hands, having wrestled it into submission.

"You have news?" the commander asked.

"The artifact recovered by Lieutenant Drex was not a key," the first man said.

Commander DarkStone grunted. "Good-for-nothing nephew."

Tiffany was sure they weren't supposed to have heard her. The furious look on DarkStone's face made her wish she hadn't. What a cruel family.

"We're preparing to access the grotto via plasma drill," the taller man said. "We're just waiting for the crew to arrive from Pocket Falls."

"You're bringing our enemies here?" Commander DarkStone said. "You're to run anything affecting security past me."

"Cool it, commander," the man said. "We work for Mr. O'Farrell, not you."

Commander DarkStone looked like she was about to explode. "I'm in command of the Corsair activity on Yl Revaw."

The man shrugged. "We're not Corsairs."

Commander DarkStone turned, marched to the nearest defense skiff, and began bellowing orders. "Fly that cannon skiff here. If the site is attacked while we're inside and defeat looks imminent, destroy the entrance and seal us inside," she said.

"Seal us inside?" asked Tiffany.

"We cannot risk losing whatever is in there," DarkStone said. "Collapsing the entrance will provide enough time for the rest of my troops to sweep in and repel the attackers."

"What's the likelihood of an attack?" Tiffany asked.

The first man raised his tinted visor, revealing graying bangs. "Based on recent federal troop movements, we project a 29 percent chance."

Oliver looked at him closely. "You look familiar."

"Richard Hixby," he said, extending his hand. "I worked with your parents."

"Traitor!" Oliver lunged for the man. The taller archeologist intercepted him, grabbing his wrists.

"STOP!" shouted Commander DarkStone, mTalk raised and finger ready. Oliver relaxed.

"Before I release you," the taller man said, "I should tell you that I also worked with your parents. The name is Phillip Skalker."

Oliver didn't react. Skalker let go of him, and he shook out his shoulders and glared.

"Now that we're past the introductions, let's get on with it," Skalker said gruffly.

Commander DarkStone moved toward a group of her soldiers. The others ducked under the low-hanging outcropping of rock and earth. A solid metal door stood before them.

"We've attempted several forms of cyber assault, a technique that has worked in the past, but this system is either incompatible or so ancient that we can't access its cyber language code," Hixby said. "That's why we're preparing to excavate."

The earth seemed ready to consume the door; roots and rocks protruded from the sides of the grotto. Oliver swept his hand along the dirt, knocking several chunks loose. He shifted as if embarrassed, covering up what he'd disturbed.

"We've used terrain mapping to analyze the chamber as best as we can. The walls form a perfect dodecagonal shape, similar to the chambers in the valley," Hixby said.

"You were there with our parents," Tiffany said. "But you went missing."

"We're not here to discuss that," Skalker said.

Hixby cleared his throat. "We believe your parents discovered that they could access the grotto with a key, and therefore opted out of excavation."

"They didn't want to damage whatever was inside," Tiffany said.

"Do you know of a key?" asked Hixby.

Tiffany opened her mouth, but Oliver nudged her shoulder before she could reply. "It's a shame the Übel destroyed Yth Orod," he said. "We left the rubies and planks from Dabnis Castle in the chamber. They were the only keys we had from our parents."

Tiffany eyed her brother. It was a truthful statement. Their parents had not given them the cross pendant keys. Clearly her brother wasn't planning on cooperating with the Corsairs.

"Might we see the terrain map you created?" Oliver asked.

"Yes, of course," Hixby said. "It's on my e-papyrus. I'll go and get it."

"Mr. Skalker, I think Commander DarkStone needs something," Oliver said.

The Corsair commander was indeed waving her arms and yelling.

"She's getting on my nerves," Skalker said. "If she or her soldiers damage any of our equipment again . . ." He stalked off.

"Good, we're alone. Look at this." Oliver shifted, revealing a hardly noticeable cross-shaped indent beside the door. "Don't mention the cross necklaces."

Tiffany nodded, understanding why he'd acted so funny when he'd disturbed the wall. "Okay. But we need whatever is in there."

"I know."

"The sooner we get it, the sooner we'll be off to YelNik Eisle."

"I know." Oliver glanced to see if either of the archeologists was coming back. "We're taking whatever is in here ourselves."

"How?"

"Brother Sam is here," Oliver said. "In the forest. I saw a red cloak. If it's not him, it's someone from the Veritas Nachfolger. How many other people run around in red cloaks?"

Tiffany laughed. "True." She stared out at the Corsairs. "We're heavily guarded, Austin and Ashley are back at camp, and we're Zapp-Tapped—remember?"

"I know; I'm still working on some of the plan," Oliver said. "But we shouldn't let them into the chamber."

"They're bringing a plasma drill. They'll destroy whatever is inside."

"We won't let them. We're coming back here tonight and entering the grotto."

"And then?"

"We escape," Oliver said.

4.31

Chaos

They had turned on the exterior view inside the *Black Lagoon* again, but now Cruz was coming, and this time there wasn't enough time to turn it off.

"As far as he knows, it's not a function we can turn on and off," Mrs. Wikk said. "Vedrik was just here, so he'll assume the captain already knows."

Through the transparent walls they could see a large crane mechanism sitting in front of the *Black Lagoon*. It was too large for loading crates, and it was stationary, so it couldn't reach the cargo door near the rear. Currie and Rutledge were opening several dozen crates stacked along one wall. They were making slow progress, and so far it seemed they were uncovering only spare parts. Sekelton and the remaining guards had spread out in the chamber, searching for other doors that might be hidden within the walls. As far as Mason could tell, the only other door was the one Dr. Blue had called Vedrik to see.

Cruz climbed into the bridge. "What are you three doing?"

"Searching the ship for artifacts, clues, the usual," Mrs. Wikk said.

"You should help us," Mr. Wikk offered.

"Maybe if you discover something significant, you won't be suspended anymore," Mrs. Wikk said kindly.

Cruz nodded. "That's a good idea."

Mason wondered how this man had survived in the Übel for so long. He wasn't the brightest, but he also wasn't cruel like the rest. Maybe he was related to a higher-ranking Übel or something. Why else would his failures be continually tolerated?

The four went back down the spiral staircase. The corridor was still dark.

"Looks like we need to find the lights for the rest of the ship," Mr. Wikk said. The corridor went two ways: left and straight. "Let's split up. Cruz and I will go this way."

Mason and his mom continued down the corridor. It was interesting to see through the exterior wall of the ship. Since the corridor was several feet off the chamber's stone floor, it appeared that Mason was walking on air.

A corridor branched off, and Mrs. Wikk took it. Mason continued until he came to a cargo hold. A few crates were strapped down along the walls. In the center was a metal dome seven feet in diameter that appeared to be another hatch. It had not gone transparent. A short cylinder stretched down from the dome. Was it meant for docking? Why else would there be a hatch in the center of the bay?

Mason gasped as the stone floor below the ship suddenly began to shift and separate. In a matter of seconds, a wide black gap appeared. If not for the fact that they were far underground, Mason would have thought he was seeing into deep space. Small lights twinkled all around.

Dr. Blue and Vedrik stepped out from the doorway to stare at the opening in the ground. The soldiers gathered around the edges as the movement halted.

Not one but two blue streaks dashed through the copper doors leading into the chamber. They ducked behind the crane. No one but Mason noticed. All the others were preoccupied with the newly created gap in the chamber floor. Obbin and a nearly identical boy dashed from the crates to the hatch to the ship. Obbin wore the clothes he'd been given on the *Skull*, but the other boy wore fur shorts and a fur jacket like the people wore in Cobalt Gorge.

Mason ran from the bay toward the entrance and flashed his mTalk light at the prince. "Obbin! And Rylin?"

Rylin nodded. He was only slightly taller than Obbin and had nearly identical green hair and turquoise eyes.

"Where did you come from? How did you get on the *Raven*?"

"I've been stowed away on the *Raven* since they captured my family," Rylin said.

"And I overheard that the captain was leaving on another expedition, so I snuck onto the *Raven*," Obbin explained. "I found Rylin as I was looking for a place to hide."

"Thank Creator we think alike," Rylin said.

"Praise Creator, amen," Obbin added.

"Why were you hiding?" Mason asked Rylin. "I thought you were going to make a trade with *The Chronicles of Terra Originem*?"

"It didn't take long for me to realize that would be foolish," Rylin said. "These men do not know Creator. It's clear that they can't be trusted to keep their side of a deal."

A light overhead flickered on. Someone had discovered how to turn on the interior lights.

"Where are the books?" Mason asked.

"Hidden. The *Raven* has many compartments," Rylin said.

"Obbin, how did you evade the Übel?" Mason asked.

"I waited in an air duct. There was an alert to look for me, but everyone became preoccupied when the ship was attacked."

Somehow the prince was as adept as a chameleon at blending in, despite his bright blue skin and green hair.

"How did you follow us here?" Mason asked.

"Easy," Rylin said. "We just kept to the shadows."

"We were nearly caught when you all came back around the corner," Obbin added. "Good thing there was a room in the wall."

"I saw you," Mason said.

"We know," Obbin admitted. "We wanted to talk to you, but the soldiers were too close."

"Well, I'm glad you're here," Mason said.

"As always, Creator came through by placing you on the ship to wait for us," Rylin said.

Out of the corner of his eye, Mason saw Sekelton and his squad of soldiers moving back toward the large copper doors, his weapon at the ready. "Quick, we need to get the two of you hidden."

Rutledge, Currie, and Pyrock were jogging toward the doors to join Sekelton. Shouts came from the tunnel. Footsteps echoed in the corridor.

"Quick, hide," Mason said. "I'll find you as soon as I can."

The soldiers outside had drawn their weapons. Vedrik was ushering Dr. Blue toward the ship. Cruz started down the stairs on the hatch when an explosion caused him to stumble forward. He fell flat on his face, nearly toppling into the gaping hole beneath them.

Most of the other Übel soldiers had been thrown to the ground. Vedrik pulled out his pistol and fired toward the doors. Dr. Blue lay on the ground, covering her head and screaming.

A streak of orange hit the chamber floor in a fiery explosion. The ground shook beneath Mason. Something splattered against the underside of the ship. *Water?*

Pyrock was moving toward the *Black Lagoon* with his satchel over his shoulder. The other Übel soldiers were still firing through the doors. Sekelton was bellowing at his men.

Cruz was trying to help Dr. Blue up. She looked panicked. Vedrik was shouting; Currie and Rutledge turned to him as he fired again and again.

Another streak of orange, and the crane exploded. Rutledge was on the ground; Currie pulled him up. Captain Vedrik was waving his men back. He turned and fired toward the *Black Lagoon*. The ship rocked forward. He fired again. The nose of the ship dropped sharply, knocking Mason off his feet. He was taking out the braces that held the ship in place.

Dr. Blue climbed through the hatch, fighting to get her balance. Mrs. Wikk assisted her with an agility and calm that surprised Mason—he wasn't used to seeing his mom in action.

"This way," called Mr. Wikk from the stairs leading to the bridge. Mason, his mom, and the frazzled doctor hurried toward him.

The ship shook again, partially balancing out. A deafening creak echoed throughout the chamber. Vedrik leaped into the ship. Moments later, Cruz toppled backward through the hatch as the remaining support for the ship crumpled.

The ship fell on its side through the gaping hole in the floor.

Mason watched through the exterior as water surged up around the ship, sloshing wildly. Water poured in through the open hatch, but the ship bobbed to the surface. A few more waves splashed in. Then the ship began to turn, throwing everyone against the corridor wall. The *Black Lagoon* righted itself. Water flowed across the threshold of the hatch.

Currie and Rutledge still struggled toward their only escape. Sekelton was backing toward the ship, recalling his remaining troops while continuing to fire rapidly into the gap. Then his gun stopped. He ran headlong toward the ship.

A swarm of people in long brown tunics and capes rushed through the opening: the Saharvics. They overtook the retreating Übel soldiers with fists and wooden staffs. Sekelton turned to fight but was quickly subdued.

Orange streaks blasted the walls of the chamber in ear-splitting explosions. Several hit the side of the *Black Lagoon*, blackening the view through the damaged portion of the wall.

In that brief moment Mason saw him—the Supreme Admiral, Mr. O'Farrell himself. He wore gray body armor and held a weapon in his hand. Dozens of Corsairs stood around him. The biotronically adjusted soldiers stood out against their less technologically enhanced allies, the Saharvics.

Pyrock leaped for the opening of the *Black Lagoon* and tumbled through, laughing hysterically as explosions erupted all around him. Rutledge poised himself to jump, then hesitated and reached out, grabbing Currie for balance. The two fell flat into the water with a painful smack.

"Close the hatch!" shouted Vedrik.

Cruz hesitated. "Sir, Rut—"

"CLOSE IT!" Vedrik bellowed.

Pyrock yanked the hatch closed.

"DIVE the ship!" Vedrik called toward Mr. Wikk.

Mason's dad beckoned to Mason and his mom from atop the stairs.

4.32

Alerts

Though Austin and Ashley had to remain at the camp while Oliver and Tiffany went to the dig site, the two were allowed outside the ship. They had climbed atop the *Eagle*. The scene reminded Austin of his and Mason's first moments on Jahr des Eises: a silver surface beneath, shadowy trees ahead, and the threat of the unknown surrounding them. He gazed through his Zinger's scope. Every shadow could cloak an enemy. As the bright orange sun set, shadows from the forest crept closer like predators wanting to take them.

"Austin, look at this," Ashley said.

He lowered the weapon. "What'd you find?"

"The Corsairs only control three of the keys from the valley," Ashley said. "Four others were identified by our parents, but they went missing before Archeos could extract them."

"Is Archeos working for the Corsairs? Why do they have the keys that Archeos recovered?"

"They're Corsairs. They probably stole them," Ashley said.

Austin nodded. "Where are the rest?"

"I'm not sure. Mr. O'Farrell is trying to retrieve the ones left in the Valley of Shadows. Tiff said there were five. The mission isn't going well."

"How do you know?" asked Austin.

Ashley raised her mTalk. "I'm getting updates. It's the Corsairs' information feed on what is happening." She showed Austin her screen: *Übel extraction team onsite. Keys' locations unknown. Engaging Übel.* "The Übel must be attempting to secure the five remaining keys from the valley."

"How far back does the information go?" Austin asked.

"Not very. A couple of hours." Ashley reached over and touched a flashing red *E* on Austin's device. A feed of information displayed on the screen.

"Why do you think they're letting us in on this?" Austin asked.

Ashley smiled. "O'Farrell wants our cooperation. He wants us to believe that his is the right side. Besides, what good could it do us? We're not in a position to escape."

Austin laughed. "If I've learned one thing in the last few days, it's that we're always in a position to escape. These guys are so focused on their mission. They keep taking us for granted because we're kids. But we've shown them before, and we will again."

Ashley leaned back on her elbows. "Looks like I'm in for a ride with you guys. I always knew you and your brothers were trouble, but Tiffany surprises me."

"She surprised all of us," Austin said. "But she's got it in her. She didn't say much about it, but she saved herself and Oliver from a bunch of Übel soldiers and dinosaurs at the GenTexic-RepFuse facility. It was our greatest escape yet."

The screens on their mTalks flashed. A new update had appeared: *SA attempting rescue of Wikks/McGregors. Saharvics assisting.*

"Rescue?" Austin's stomach lurched. "Do you think our parents are in trouble? Mason?"

Ashley shook her head. "It sounds like they're trying to free them from the Übel like O'Farrell promised."

"I'm not sure if that makes me feel any better. Isn't O'Farrell as bad?"

"It could have said 'attempting capture,'" Ashley said. "At least the Corsairs think they're helping them."

"Still, they'll be in the middle of a battle."

"Aren't we all? Look around. These troops are ready to fight. None of us is safe."

"At least we can trust Helper."

Ashley looked at him curiously. "Helper?"

"You don't know yet, do you?" Austin asked. "Our greatest discovery has been to learn of Creator, Rescuer, and Helper."

"Who?"

They were interrupted by a series of commands. "You five, that way quickly! You five, over there now!" shouted Drex. "We want to flank whatever it is."

It seemed there had been a disturbance in the woods to the east. Austin hadn't heard or seen anything. He and Ashley watched with interest as Drex marched to a large skiff, climbed aboard, and took a seat behind the weapon. He aimed carefully.

Was there a threat in the woods?

Hixby returned, his e-journal out to show Tiffany the screen. "You see, the walls are thick and solid. We don't know *how* thick. Our sensors can't penetrate them to give us a glimpse of what's inside."

Oliver shifted to block the cross indent, moving roots over the doorframe.

"Tiffany has figured out that it's called the Eochair," Oliver said, "but we still don't know its shape, size, or location in the chamber."

"Good point." Hixby scratched his chin. "It's DarkStone— she's pushing us. Says the Übel will be on their way soon. I

tried to explain that this sort of thing can't be rushed. Even
Skalker tried to reason with her. He asked why the two groups
couldn't get past their selfish ambitions and work together.
The Corsairs and Übel would be far more efficient if they combined their resources. But I gather they don't want that." Hixby
cleared his throat. "I did enjoy working with your parents, you
know. But that's neither here nor there."

Oliver clenched his fists. How dare this man mention
his parents? Either Hixby had been in cahoots with Mr.
O'Farrell all along or he'd sold out later. He was no friend of
the Wikks. Oliver was confident he could take him, but why?
To cause the man pain? It seemed below him. His earlier
knock to Drex's chin hadn't made Oliver feel like a hero either.
Hixby seemed so unaware that Oliver could be angered by
the betrayal of his parents. It was just business as usual to
the archeologist.

"Did your parents mention anything about this place?"
Hixby asked.

Tiffany shook her head.

"Well, I'm not sure what use the two of you will be," Hixby
said. His tone didn't imply disrespect. He sounded matter-of-
fact. He sighed. "There is little use for children in the field."

Oliver was getting tired of being called a kid, but he held
his tongue. "When will the drill arrive?" Oliver asked.

"In a few hours," Hixby replied, "but we won't start until
tomorrow."

"Will the commander really wait until then?" asked Tiffany.

"Phillip and I have put in a long day. These Corsairs are
part machine, but I'm a mere man. I can't go hour after hour,"
Hixby said. "I'm sick of the sprint we're on. Übel, Corsairs,
Archeos, Federation—why do I care? One way or the other,
we will unlock the secret to life everlasting."

That was it. This guy didn't see one group as worse than
the others. He was willing to use whatever means necessary
to fuel his exploration for eternal life.

The stream bordering the south side of the camp added a peaceful babbling to the chorus of birds. The natural world didn't have the same concerns as the Corsairs. The soldiers were still on alert, and Drex had ordered another six men into the forest, but Austin wasn't worried. If the Übel attacked, he expected they'd conduct an all-out aerial assault on the site, not sneak through the trees.

"I first heard about Creator, Rescuer, and Helper from Brother Samuel. He called Rescuer the Truth," Austin explained. "But the rest I learned from Obbin." He looked at the forest around him. An example of Creator's work was right before him. "You see these woods?"

"They're right in front of me."

Austin smiled. "How'd they get here?"

"They grew."

"How?"

"Sun, water, nutrients, and time."

"They came from seeds that contained the plan for how they would grow."

"I didn't think you paid much attention at school."

"I like to know how things work."

"So a seed has a plan. Its genetic code."

"But someone had to create that plan, right? I mean, the odds are astronomical that the code could randomly sort itself so that a seed could grow. How many randomized mutations would have to occur for the cells in the seedling to come into a perfect order? One wrong piece of code and the whole system would fall apart."

"That's a fair assessment. But we have an infinite amount of time."

"So a happenstance explosion of rocks and space matter created life? Rocks aren't alive. Space is a vacuum. How did the first cell come to be? From sunlight shining on rocks? Where did the rocks come from? Or the sun, for that matter?"

"Okay, you have me there," Ashley said.

"So what if someone created that design?" asked Austin. "Suppose someone planned our entire universe."

Ashley laughed. "You're talking about a mystical being."

"I guess so, but Creator isn't a fairy tale. He created everything around you." This was harder than Austin had expected. "I think Obbin explained it better."

"I'm listening, Austin. You're doing a good job."

"Obbin told us that Creator made the whole universe. And Rescuer was sent to die for us, because we all do bad things. Obbin called it *sin*. We have sin when we are first born."

"You mean we have the tendency to behave badly," Ashley said. "No one's perfect."

"Exactly. The first humans ever created didn't have sin. But then they messed up and disobeyed Creator. That caused everyone born after them to be sinful in nature and face death someday. But Creator, through Rescuer, made a way to be free from sin and to live eternally with Him. Rescuer died for us as a sacrifice, no matter how bad our sin is," Austin said. "Rescuer is the path to eternal life."

"You're telling me you have the answer that the Übel and Corsairs are searching for? The secret to living forever?" Ashley's eyes were wide with excitement. "We can end this quest now. Get back our parents, your brother!" she said excitedly. "We have to tell the commander and get hold of Mr. O'Farrell." She stopped. "Why haven't you done this already?"

"It's not that easy. I mean, receiving the gift of eternal life is easy, but not explaining it to the Corsairs or the Übel," Austin said, his voice solemn. "These soldiers want something they can hold in their hands or a recipe for concocting an elixir. They want to live forever right here, right now."

"Have you tried to explain?" Ashley challenged.

"We haven't had the chance. They don't seem open to it."

"What do you mean?"

"We have to believe that Rescuer died for us and invite Helper to guide us. Helper stays with us each day, speaking to our hearts," Austin said. "We don't see Him."

Ashley sighed and looked out at the darkening clearing. "And you believe this?"

"Yes."

"And Tiffany? . . . Oliver?"

Austin nodded. "All you have to do is ask Rescuer to forgive you of your sins. When He forgives you, you're free."

"This is such a new concept for me," she said. "What proof is there?"

"I told you about the seedling's design."

"Yes, but what proof is there that He forgives us?"

Austin thought for a moment. Ashley asked good questions. "After Rescuer died, He was raised from the dead. He defeated death. When He did that, He overcame sin."

Ashley seemed to be considering this.

"A feeling of relief came over me when I began following Rescuer," Austin said. "I feel as though someone is guiding me."

Ashley smiled, but it was clear that Austin had lost her.

"Perhaps Tiffany can explain better when she comes back."

"Maybe," Ashley said. "But you have done quite a good job. It's just a really big idea. I need some time to take it all in."

"Yeah, I suppose it would be a lot. It was to me too, but I knew it was right. I believe it."

A white bird flitted just over their heads and landed a few feet away atop the bridge of the *Eagle*. Austin stared at it. The bird looked at him, squawked, and took off, flying back into the woods.

"Well, we're not going to accomplish much right here," Hixby said. "I need to survey the slope again and make sure our markers are set for when the drill arrives."

"It looks like Commander DarkStone is shoring up defenses," Oliver added. "She must be worried."

Hixby chortled. "Yes, she is. Worried that one more mistake will get her demoted . . . or worse: exiled."

"Exiled?" asked Tiffany.

"Long story," Hixby said. "But yes, she's worried. The Federation recently issued an alert authorizing lethal, unrestrained force against all Corsairs."

"Isn't that a standing order?" Tiffany asked.

"Usually the Federation prefers to capture and try criminals," Oliver explained.

"Alas, the altercations between the Übel and the Corsairs have brought their battle to light," Hixby said. "A newly arrived brigade commander in Pocket Falls is cause for concern, though it could just be a standard rotation."

"Then why did you risk drawing attention to the dig?" asked Oliver.

"Until the *Eagle* arrived with additional troops, Corsair presence was minimal. Skalker and I are in an Archeos ship under an Archeos expedition permit. The Corsair contingent assigned to us all wore Archeos security uniforms and badges. Unfortunately there are armed skiffs everywhere now. The commander isn't concerned about remaining hidden now; she wants to be ready for the pending assault." Hixby adjusted his visor. "I'll be just above here should you come up with something."

Once the archeologist was gone, Tiffany spoke up. "We have to get the Eochair before they start drilling tomorrow and ruin it."

Oliver smiled. "Don't worry. We will."

Black Water

M r. Wikk took the steering handles in his hands. The screen glowed before him. The submersible floated just at the surface of the thrashing water. Rutledge and Currie were dog-paddling their way to the edge of the hole.

"Propellers activated," Mrs. Wikk said.

"Diving," said Mr. Wikk as he tapped the screen before him, then pressed the handle in his right hand forward. Water surged around the *Black Lagoon* as its nose dropped. Mason's mom went to work, and soon five beams of white light blasted out in front of them.

How did they know how to pilot the submersible? It was clearly different from the *Phoenix* and even *Deep Blue*.

"Son, try to locate a map or nautical chart," Mrs. Wikk said. "Elliot, I've activated the sonar."

Mason slid his fingers across the glowing screen. He looked up. A large column of stone stretched down before them, with openings on either side.

"I'm holding steady," Mr. Wikk said. "I don't think they can get us down here."

Through the ceiling, Mason could see a rectangle of dim light above. The gap was smaller now. The twinkling lights

Mason had seen before were gone. The surface was far above him. No weapon the attackers were using reached the ship.

"Elliot," Mrs. Wikk said, "I've located a map. Go left."

Mason had lost concentration, and his mom had done the work. His parents didn't say anything to him, but Mason chastised himself for not focusing. He wanted his parents to see him as a capable partner on the quest, like his brothers and sister had.

Loud footsteps signaled the arrival of the captain. His long black coat was torn, his hat missing. "Where are we headed?"

"We're not sure yet, just away from the attackers above," Mr. Wikk said.

"I've found a cabin for the doctor to rest in," Vedrik said, slipping his pistol from its holster. "Pyrock and Cruz are scouting the ship to ensure that none of the Saharvics or Corsairs got aboard."

Mason thought of Obbin and Rylin. Would the soldiers find them?

"Why don't you help to determine the course we should take," Mr. Wikk said.

Mason expected the captain to protest, but instead he walked to Mason's chair. "Give me your seat."

The submersible was moving down a long, straight tunnel.

"We'll be approaching a fork. Go left," Captain Vedrik said, studying the map.

The fork came and passed, as did another five. Each time Vedrik gave the direction to go. Mason desperately wanted to find the princes. If the two boys had been discovered, though, Cruz and Pyrock would have brought them to the bridge.

Suddenly a cloud of greenish light swept through the inky blackness toward them.

"What's that?" Mason asked. His parents looked up from the navigation screens.

"Reverse props!" shouted Vedrik. "Bring her to a stop!"

Mr. Wikk obeyed. Mason steadied himself against the nearest armrest. "What is it?" he whispered.

"Could be a number of things," Mrs. Wikk said honestly.

"Dangerous?"

"Probably not," she said, but Mason could tell she wasn't confident.

The luminescence shifted back and forth in the water, growing larger as it neared.

Vedrik was working the screen before him. "There doesn't seem to be any weapons system. Who were these people?" He answered his own question: "Unprepared."

The green glow swirled and shifted. Occasionally gaps appeared in its midst; it wasn't a solid object.

"I know what that is," Mason said at last. "I think it's bioluminescent phytoplankton. We worked with some in the science lab at school."

The green cloud seemed to expand in size, growing fainter. Then it pulled back together, growing brighter.

A moment passed before his dad spoke. "Yes, I do think you're right."

"What should we do?" asked Vedrik.

"Nothing. It's not dangerous," answered Mason. "At least the ones we studied weren't."

"Why are they moving like that?" the captain asked. "They seem to be preparing to attack."

The glowing green cloud did look like a phantom coming for its prey. "The current, perhaps."

A moment later, the green haze swallowed the ship. The plankton's bioluminescence overtook the ship's interior lighting, giving everyone a swampy green skin tone. Mason gazed at the swirling green glow, contemplating the intricate design of the small creatures. His breath caught. This was creation; this was the work of Creator.

No one spoke until the swarm of plankton passed.

"Full speed!" shouted Vedrik. "I've mapped a complete course that will take us to a possible exit."

Had the captain even paid attention to the creatures? Had he recognized their beauty?

"This exit is at least twenty miles from the valley," Mrs. Wikk said. "Estimated remaining time is forty-seven minutes."

Had his mom?

"We'll need an extraction for the entire ship," said Mr. Wikk.

His dad?

"We can't let the ship fall into the Corsairs' hands," continued Mr. Wikk.

"I know that!" Vedrik lifted his communication device. There was no signal. "Do either of you think this is the Eochair?" he asked.

Mrs. Wikk shrugged. "It could be. We won't know until we've determined the craft's purpose or the Eochair's use."

The captain began searching through the rest of the computer system.

"I can see how people survived in the Valley of Shadows. The subterranean water system was more than enough to provide all they needed," Mr. Wikk said. "I wonder what eventually drove them out."

"Isn't Cao one of the formerly quarantined planets?" Mason asked.

Vedrik turned to him. "How do you know that?"

"Zebra Xavier told me about the Federation and the Empire."

Mr. Wikk spoke up. "Mason, is your theory that the Empire drove out the Gläubigen?"

Mason nodded.

His dad smiled. "That's my conclusion as well. By accessing the quarantined planets of the Gläubigen, we've made so much progress. Once these places were opened to us, we began finding treasure troves of new ruins and artifacts."

Mason felt emboldened with his parents beside him. He eyed the lone Übel. They could take him. If Oliver and Austin were here, he was sure they would have made the attempt by now.

As if to quell the rebellious flicker in his heart, Pyrock's maniacal laugh echoed up the stairs. "Captain, look what we found!"

Mason's heart sank as the two soldiers stepped into the bridge. But his fear was misplaced. The men didn't have Rylin or Obbin in hand. Instead Cruz was lugging a black, oval case.

Cruz stumbled, and the case dropped open, dispersing its contents. At least ten vials rolled across the floor of the bridge. One bumped against the bottom of Vedrik's chair. He reached over and took it with a gloved hand. "Fool!" Pyrock gave a low gurgle of laughter.

Another bounced against Mason's shoe. He picked it up. It was full of what looked like dirt.

"Don't stand there. Pick them up!" Vedrik ordered.

Cruz and Pyrock dropped down to all fours and began gathering vials.

Mason's eyes remained locked on the small vial.

"Return it now!" Vedrik shouted.

"Mason, do as the captain says," Mr. Wikk said.

Mason looked to his father, who winked at him. On the other side of his dad's shoe was one of the released vials.

Mason handed the vial to the captain and stepped away. "What are they?"

Vedrik looked at the label on the glass tube. "We'll need to analyze them before we know, but they carry the name of the lost planet, Ursprung."

4.34

Love Letter

The troops Drex had ordered into the woods had returned a half hour ago. Several now patrolled the perimeter. Austin and Ashley remained perched atop the *Eagle*, watching the Corsairs set up camp.

A black and gray camouflaged hexagonal pod sat several feet off the ground in the center of fifteen newly erected, similarly bedecked tents. A perimeter of silver stakes, each with a glowing purple orb atop, had been placed around the entire encampment.

Drex paced below. He occasionally ordered a Corsair around, but mostly he cleaned his weapon and unpacked and repacked a satchel of equipment. The physical similarities between Drex and Oliver were uncanny. Both boys were about the same height and muscular, with short brown hair, squared jaw, and straight posture. When it came to personality, they were completely different.

Austin could see how rigorous training might change a person. Oliver understood compassion and love; Drex did not. Of course, love might not be an easy feeling for the Corsair to display. He was surrounded by cruelty and darkness, even from his supposed aunt.

A new alert appeared on Austin's mTalk. *Wikks/Übel captain escaped. Unit 4 en route to McGregors'/keys' crash site.*

255

Austin's breath hitched. Ashley sat quietly, looking out toward the woods. She'd not seen the update yet. Should he tell her, or should he wait until they got more positive news? He'd want to know, but he tried to think like a girl. What would his sister want?

"Ashley," he said, reaching his hand out to her shoulder. "There's another update."

Ashley tapped her mTalk's screen. He saw the worry come over her. He shifted closer, putting his arm around her. She didn't speak. She tapped the screen again, but nothing changed. She bowed her head and began to cry.

"Ashley, I . . ."

She sniffled. "Austin, I know what you want to say. But you can't, because you don't know. I don't know. None of us know anything. We're just stuck on a journey that we have no control over." She looked up, tears streaming down from her eyes. "I just want it to be over."

"We all do. We're going to get there."

A beep on the mTalks pulled each of their eyes toward their screens: *McGregor/key ship recovered by* Skull. *McGregors alive/recaptured by Übel. SA and Saharvics exiting VOS tunnels.*

"It's hard to be happy that my parents have been recaptured," Ashley said, "but at least I know they're okay." She wiped her eyes. "I'm just tired. I want to go back to Bewaldeter. Life was simpler there."

"It was," Austin said. "But I wouldn't want to go back. I . . . I feel like I've grown so much. And I know my brothers and sister so much better than I ever did before. Now you're one of us."

"You're right. I'm glad you guys found me."

They looked out at the woods in silence.

"I'm sorry," Ashley said after a few minutes. "I didn't mean to get so upset."

"Don't worry about it. We've all had those moments. Believe it or not, even hero soldier Oliver has shed some tears during this quest."

Ashley's smile brightened. "I'm not happy he was sad, but if someone as strong as Oliver has had moments, I guess it's okay that I have too."

Ashley certainly had a high view of Oliver. "I have a question," Austin said. "Oliver . . . what do you really think of him?"

Ashley's lips curled into a soft smile. "What do you mean?"

"Well . . ." Austin wasn't one to beat around the bush. "I found a pink envelope in his pack addressed to him from you. Tiffany wouldn't let me read it."

"Because she's a good friend," Ashley said, ruffling Austin's hair.

Austin raised his eyebrows.

"It wasn't anything mushy, like what you're thinking. I wanted to encourage him when he left for the Academy," Ashley said. "We're friends."

Austin smiled wryly. "Sure."

A playful giggle told Austin that there might be more between the two.

Oliver had put on the cross pendant necklace when he had changed. He wanted to test his theory that it would unlock the door, but there were too many eyes watching.

"We're going to need to create an electromagnetic pulse to escape," Tiffany said.

Oliver shook his head. "The Corsairs shield against EMPs."

"But the Zapp-Tap isn't designed that way," Tiffany said. "It's a hunch, but a low, targeted EMP would be the best way to disable an implanted device. Otherwise, removal would require a medic."

"You assume the Corsairs are willing to free their prisoners."

"Yes, I do. Plus, the devices are too small to shield easily. We need to ask Austin if he can make an EMP."

"Zapp-Taps, covered. Accessing the grotto, covered. Now we just have to find a way to come back here with Austin and Ashley, remove the Eochair, commandeer a ship, and hightail it out of this place with the crosses," Oliver laughed.

"We have to take the *Eagle* then," Tiffany said. "The crosses are on the ship."

"You're right. We'll have to get any Corsairs off the ship," Oliver said. "If the Zapp-Taps are disabled, but the Corsairs don't know it, we can use that to our advantage. Fake a shock. Then take DarkStone and Drex when they think we're down."

"You two, come on!" called Commander DarkStone. The Corsair had climbed aboard the skiff. "Were heading back."

Oliver and Tiffany started for the craft.

"Wait, wait." Hixby nearly tumbled down the hill above the grotto. "Commander, stop."

DarkStone sighed irritably. "What is it?"

"Those two need to remain nearby," Hixby said. "Skalker and I want to go over what we know with the girl and see if it reminds her of anything she knows."

"We're returning to the base camp to wait for the drilling to complete. If you'd like to speak with them, you can join us there," Commander DarkStone said.

"Why not leave them here?"

"You can't handle these two," DarkStone said. She waved the pilot forward as soon as Oliver and Tiffany were aboard.

The trees were flying past when Oliver saw a red blur. Brother Sam was near. *When would he come for them? What sort of plan was already in motion?*

Austin and Ashley climbed down from the *Eagle*.

Drex stood before the contingent of Corsairs. "New orders from the commander," he said. "You are to remain hidden within your tents. Only Sanders and Peterson will stand guard. If we're attacked, take your predetermined positions. The artifacts and children are more valuable than your lives. We must have them if we wish to live forever and become whole once more. They are the keys!"

Austin looked at Ashley. "For people Drex apparently hates, we're awfully valuable to him."

"Yeah, it's a bit confusing," Ashley said.

"Clear out!" shouted Drex. He turned. "You two, follow me."

Austin and Ashley followed Drex to a domed tent. Four cots were set against the walls. A silver orb sat on three glowing green columns in the middle of the space. On the far end were two silver crates, a column of canvas, and a rack with several more sets of clothes.

"Food and beverages are in those crates. Your toilet is within the canvas," Drex said. "I assume you know what this is."

Austin nodded. "An Enviro-Stabilizer."

"The temperatures fluctuate significantly here. It will get cold tonight," Drex said. "Your tent is close to the ship. We don't expect to be attacked, but if we are, board the *Eagle* immediately."

Austin eyed Ashley.

"I wouldn't suggest trying anything. I'll be the first one here if we're attacked." Drex pressed a finger into Austin's shoulder. "You'll be out before you know it."

"And for a second I started to think you weren't as cruel as you seemed," Austin said.

"You don't know the half of it," Drex crowed. "Yet you'll need us if you want to see the rest of your family ever again."

Austin glared. "We don't need you."

Drex stood to his full height. "I'll put you in your pla—"

The device on Drex's wrist beeped. He tapped the screen.

"I want you in my pod now!" said Commander DarkStone's voice.

"Sounds like your boss is about to put you in a place you won't want to be." Austin smiled.

Drex rushed out of the tent. A slight commotion followed. Oliver and Tiffany had returned, and Drex was being his usual rude self.

Tiffany was first in. "We met some of our parents' coworkers."

Oliver backed into the tent. "Yeah, we'll see if you're so tough after your aunt gets through with you."

Austin laughed. "Maybe he'll get his electro-flogging."

Tiffany clucked. "Now, Austin, we don't need to fall to his level." She embraced Ashley. "What did you do while we were gone?"

"Talked," Ashley said. "And thanks."

"For what?"

Ashley smirked. "Later." She held up her mTalk. "We discovered a feed that tells us what the Corsairs are doing."

"O'Farrell didn't rescue our parents. They're still with the Übel," Austin said. "And they didn't capture any additional keys from the Valley. The Übel must have gotten all of them."

They showed Oliver and Tiffany how to set up the feed. Then Austin remembered. "While you were gone, Drex had a bunch of Corsairs searching the woods, but they returned empty-handed."

"That confirms it!" Oliver motioned everyone to the opposite side of the tent, presumably away from wherever Drex had been summoned. "Tiff and I have a plan to escape. We know how to get into the chamber and get the Eochair."

Oliver reached inside the collar of his shirt and slipped out the cross necklace. "There was an indent in the frame of the doorway, but it'd been covered by dirt and roots."

"Plus, the indent is so shallow that you'd have to look for it to find it," Tiffany added.

"So we can get in," Austin said. "But escape? Drex was just reminding me about our Zapp-Taps."

"You're going to make an EMP," Oliver said.

Austin looked at his older brother. "I think . . . I might be able to do that, actually."

"Okay, but even if that works, how are we going to get out of here? We're surrounded by Corsairs," Ashley said.

"I saw Brother Sam in the woods," Oliver said. "At the very least, someone from the Veritas Nachfolger is here."

"We think," Tiffany said.

"I know what I saw," Oliver insisted. "Austin, you said Drex sent his men to search the woods."

Austin nodded. "The Übel would have swarmed in, but Brother Sam is good at waiting in the shadows for the right moment."

"Exactly," said Oliver.

"How would he know where we are?" Ashley asked.

"The *Eagle* is his ship. He must be able to track it," Tiffany said. "He was O'Farrell's friend, and I think he worked on the ships."

"Friend?" Ashley asked. "Should we trust him?"

"Brother Sam doesn't want to help Mr. O'Farrell in the way you're thinking," Austin said. "He's a follower of the Truth. He believes in Creator, Rescuer, and Helper too."

Before Ashley could respond, Tiffany grabbed her friend and hugged her. "You believe?"

Ashley pulled away. "No. I mean, I don't know. Austin's been telling me about it, but I'm not sure I get it."

"I'd love to answer the questions you have as best I can," Tiffany said.

"That'd be great," Ashley said. "You and I think a lot alike."

"While you two talk, Austin and I will figure out how to get what we need for the EMP," Oliver said.

Austin pointed to the Enviro-Stabilizer. "Actually, I think I already have what I need."

4.35

Two Princes

Sunlight glinted in the water ahead. As Mr. Wikk drove the *Black Lagoon* forward, a nearly perfect circle of light came into view.

Mr. Wikk brought the ship to the surface, and the view through the ceiling cleared even more. The walls of the vertical cavern were covered in long tendrils of green vines. The place looked more like the jungles of Yth Orod on Evad than like the arid desert climate of Cao.

"This is as far as I can take us," Mr. Wikk said.

"This is Vedrik, requesting immediate extraction. Coordinates sent. I repeat: Captain Vedrik, requiring immediate extraction. Our coordinates are sent," Vedrik said into his mTalk as he approached the console. He'd been looking over the contents of the black case.

The speaker buzzed. "Transmission received. Requesting approval from the Supreme Commander. Stand by for confirmation."

Vedrik grunted and looked toward Mr. Wikk. "Move us toward the middle of the pool. I don't want the ship getting wrecked against the side of this cavern."

263

"Extraction request granted," the voice said over the speaker. "ETA: thirty minutes. Confirm coordinates X11, Y12, Z13?"

Vedrik held up his mTalk. "Confirmed."

"May I be excused?" Mason asked.

Vedrik glared down at him. "Why?"

"Restroom."

"Fine," Vedrik said. "I'm going to take these to the doctor for analysis. Cruz and Pyrock, watch over Mr. and Mrs. Wikk."

"Yes, sir!" the men replied.

Vedrik followed Mason down the stairs but turned off the main corridor toward the cabins. "I warn you, kid. Don't try anything."

Mason nodded. "Yes, sir."

The captain's tattered cape swirled as he marched down the corridor.

Mason stopped at the restroom. He hadn't wanted to lie; he did have to go. However, his real goal was to find Obbin and Rylin. They needed a better plan for hiding the princes until they could meet again. Their secret presence was of huge strategic value, and Mason planned to use it.

The cargo bay was dim; someone had turned off the main lights. As Mason rounded the docking hatch in the center of the room, the green-haired boys stepped out from a recessed compartment.

"What happened?" Obbin asked.

"You didn't see?" Mason asked. "The Corsairs and Saharvics came for us. We have a lot of enemies."

"What now?" Rylin asked. "Should we turn ourselves in?"

Obbin straightened. "No!"

"No, no," Mason agreed. "You're like a . . . secret weapon. They don't know you're here, and that might be really useful."

"I'm getting low on water and food," Rylin said. "I'd brought enough for me, and I got some extra supplies from the stores on the *Raven*, but now I'm sharing with Obbin."

"I'll see what I have left in my pack," Mason said. "I'm really glad you guys are here. It's good to have more people on my side."

"It'll be just like in the valley with Brother Samuel," Obbin said.

Rylin touched Mason's shoulder. Their eyes locked. "Look how Creator has brought us together. This is all part of His plan."

"This is true," Mason said.

"My father always said, 'He is all we need. With Him we are victorious already,'" Obbin added.

"I never thought you were paying attention," Rylin said.

"Far more than you know," Obbin said.

"Speaking of paying attention, did you see the glowing plankton earlier?" asked Mason.

"What's plankton?" asked Obbin.

"Small water organisms," Mason said. "The green cloud that surrounded the ship earlier was made of bioluminescent plankton."

Rylin nodded. "I thought that was something the ship released."

"Me too," Obbin said. "I'd like some of those for pets."

"When we get out of this, remind me. I think I can get you some from our lab at school," Mason said.

"That would be great," Obbin said.

"I'd better get back," Mason said. "The *Skull* is coming for us."

"What about the *Raven*? The books are on the *Raven*," Rylin reminded him.

"I'm sure it's already returned to the *Skull*," Mason said.

"We must get those back," Rylin said.

"We will. The two of you had better hide again," Mason said. "I'll sneak back some food and water as soon as I can."

4.36

Building the Bomb

Tiffany cried with her friend. When Ashley had said, "I do," a feeling of complete joy had overtaken her.

She and Ashley had had many discussions at Bewaldeter about the cosmos, the theory of evolution, and Notrub's particle prime theory, but never had they considered a Creator. Yet in a few short days, they had come to know with overwhelming clarity that He was the way and the only real truth.

The two had many more questions. However, Creator was the simplest concept to believe in. He didn't involve complex algorithms or scientific theories based on billions of chance happenings. The truth was all around. It was impossible for the complex makeup of everything to come from random chance.

As they spoke, even scientific ideas fell into place. A Creator could and would make a perfect system, whereas a chance collision of particles could never create the intricate processes necessary for life. How could two inanimate particles come together to spontaneously create life? Though they'd been taught all their lives that this was logical, it didn't make sense.

Having her best friend believe in the Truth and confirm the infallibility of the Creator made Tiffany's own belief even more exciting to her.

Oliver watched Austin disassemble the Enviro-Stabilizer, discarding nonessential pieces and collecting important ones. His diligence was impressive when it came to building devices. He never flinched, even when sparks exploded out as he removed a capacitor from its location.

Oliver was currently stripping wires and creating a coil with them. He was pretty sure Austin had assigned him the job so that he'd stop hovering over him.

"Is this enough?" Oliver asked, holding up what Austin had called the *load coil*.

"That'll work," Austin said. "Bring it over."

"What else do you need?"

Austin looked at his supplies. "Switch, capacitor, power source, connection wires, load coil . . . I think we've got what we need. This won't be a big pulse, so we'll all have to stand really close and lean in."

"How long until it's assembled?" Oliver asked.

"I can have it done in five to ten minutes," Austin said.

"Really?

"Yeah!"

"I'm going to try to put this back together . . ." Oliver looked at the parts that had once been an Enviro-Stabilizer. "Um, maybe I'll just hide the scraps under the cots."

"Good idea." Austin smirked.

Shadows stretched across the clearing. Tiffany shivered as the temperature dropped. The two archeologists had returned with a few Corsair escorts, which meant that others remained on guard at the grotto. Tiffany was glad they hadn't come to speak to her. She had no desire to give Hixby and Skalker, Archeos traitors, any more assistance on their quest for fame and money.

She turned her attention to the commander's pod. Drex still hadn't left Commander DarkStone, and Tiffany was growing oddly worried for him. She didn't like him, but the more she interacted with him and those he served, the worse she felt for him. Their lives had been so different, and she felt sorry for him.

The door to the commander's pod opened.

Tiffany let the tent flap drop so that she had just a sliver to look through. Drex's head was down and his shoulders drooped. He started for their tent, then stopped and took a deep breath. What was he thinking? A second later, he turned and walked toward a different tent, disappearing inside.

ZIP! SIZZLE! ZAP!

Tiffany spun around as Austin bounced back against a cot, smoke rolling from the EMP device he'd been working on. "Austin!"

Austin's eyes were closed; there were small black marks on his fingers. Oliver knelt next to him, listening at his lips. Then he smacked Austin's cheek.

Austin gasped, and his eyes shot open. "Whoa! That'll wake you up."

"Or put you to sleep permanently," Oliver said seriously. He ran to the tent flap to check whether anyone had heard the explosion. "Coast is clear."

"Are you okay?" Ashley asked.

"My arms and legs tingle, and my fingers sting." Austin held up his hands. A couple of his fingernails were partially melted.

"Austin, your eyebrows," Ashley said as she stroked back his bangs. Most of Austin's eyebrow hairs were missing or curled, as were his blond eyelashes.

Austin tilted his head left and right. "My ears are ringing."

"It's a wonder you're not dead," Ashley said.

"I guess we're going to need a new plan," Oliver said.

"No, no, no, it's done," Austin said.

"But it exploded," Ashley said.

"I got my wires crossed," Austin explained. "The device didn't explode. I just released the energy incorrectly. It will still work."

"Will it do that to all of us?" asked Ashley.

Austin shook his head. "I know what to do now."

"Austin, you can't touch that thing again," Tiffany said. "I doubt your body can take another hit like that so soon."

"I'll do it," Oliver volunteered.

"You were just fried too," Austin said. "I'll be fine. I know what I did. I won't do it again."

Tiffany was impressed by how strong and resilient her brothers were. The Wikk kids would have quite the story to tell their parents when this was all over.

"Okay, we're almost ready," Austin said as he fingered the last unconnected wire.

Ashley laughed nervously. "You might be, but I'm not so sure I am."

Oliver took her hand. Then, realizing what he'd done, he patted it awkwardly. "I trust him. You can too."

4.37

Extraction

"The *Skull* is on approach." A satisfied grin crossed Vedrik's face. "Cruz, Pyrock, we must secure the *Skull*'s extraction cables to the *Black Lagoon*. Let's go. Wikks, remain here. Don't try anything."

As the men disappeared down the stairs, Mr. Wikk motioned Mason to come and look at the fallen vial in his hand.

"*Ursprung Verification Key*. What does it mean?" Mason asked.

"It could mean all sorts of things," his mom said. "This could be used to unlock the *Ark* in some way, much like the cross necklace that let us in here."

"Is this the Eochair?" Mason asked.

"Possibly," Mr. Wikk said. "It's not the kind of artifact we expected, though."

"We don't know what *Eochair* means?" asked Mason.

"I have a suspicion," his mom said. "It's not in any language I've discovered yet, but I believe it means 'key.'"

"Still, we won't tell that to Captain Vedrik," Mr. Wikk explained. "They don't take well to theories that don't prove correct. We'll reveal the information at the right time."

Mason nodded. "I haven't had a chance to tell you every-thing that happened over the past week," he said. "Only bits and pieces."

"Once things are calm again, we'll have plenty of time," Mrs. Wikk said.

"But some of it is important, Mom."

The clanking of boots on metal echoed up the stairs.

"Mr. Wikk, the captain needs you," Cruz said.

Mason's dad sighed as he stood up. "Let's all go."

Mason's heart raced as they gathered in the cargo bay. There was no sign of the princes. Where had they hidden now?

"Bring it down!" Captain Vedrik said into his communicator.

A large black silhouette was above them—the *Skull*. A gap opened in its belly, and several long tendrils began to reach toward them.

"Open the hatch," Vedrik commanded his men. He removed his cape and jacket. "I assume you can hold your breath," he said to Mr. Wikk.

"I can." Mason's dad sounded annoyed but expectant.

"Then you'll be assisting me in securing the lift cables around the *Black Lagoon*."

"Why can't your men?" Mrs. Wikk protested.

The two soldiers were laboring to open the hatch, which was screwed closed. Each had taken hold of a long bar and were pushing it to open the seal.

Vedrik grunted. "These two aren't capable without proper gear."

"Fine." Mr. Wikk pulled off his vest and shirt, then started to roll up the bottom of his pants.

Captain Vedrik folded his tattered cape and set his hat and shirt on it. He was muscular like Mason's dad, and there were several scars across his back to match the one on his face. The Übel's symbol, the skull, had been tattooed in silver on his left shoulder. On his right shoulder, the words *And I give unto them eternal life* had been tattooed in thick black ink.

The seal broke with a pop, and the lid opened on a hinge. "I'll take the left side, you take right," Mr. Wikk said.

Vedrik grunted but didn't argue. The two men climbed up and dropped into the water. Was it hot or cold? The Aqua Cathedral had been hot, and the Valley of Shadows was a desert.

His dad didn't react but dove underneath the ship. The two men swam to opposite sides and retrieved the first set of cables floating in the water. They swam back together and connected the large clasps at the end of the cables. Mr. Wikk swam back up the hatch and took a breath, but Vedrik had already retrieved the cable closer to the bow of the ship.

Mr. Wikk wasted no time getting his own second cable and swimming to Vedrik. Then Vedrik and Mason's dad both swam up for air.

The two men continued until two dozen connections were locked from bow to aft under the belly of the *Black Lagoon*. Both men were exhausted as they climbed back through the hatch. Vedrik looked particularly weak. Could the Wikks take control of the situation?

"They're prepared to lift us, captain," Cruz said, handing Vedrik his clothes and curtailing Mason's hope of escape. The captain scowled. "Sorry, sir, we don't have any towels."

"I'll air dry," Vedrik hissed. He held up his device. "We'll be ready in one minute. Cruz, inform the scientist that we are being extracted and remain with her. Pyrock, stay here and keep an eye on the harnesses at this end. Wikks, you're coming with me to the bridge."

4.38

EMP'd

Oliver looked out the flap. He'd been watching for the last twenty minutes. The clearing was dark. There was no moon and only a few dwindling stars. No Corsair soldiers had been stationed inside the *Eagle*, and the small hatch at the cargo bay had even been left open in case they needed to evacuate during an attack. Helper was on their side: these were the absolute best conditions for an escape.

Oliver checked the Corsair feed on his mTalk one more time. He was sure that O'Farrell would be coming soon.

The EMP device was ready, tucked safely under Austin's cot. The girls had been concerned that the shock would replicate Austin's incident or that the Zapp-Taps would malfunction and knock them all unconscious or worse, but Oliver and Austin had convinced them that the risk was worth taking.

Commander DarkStone had checked in on them, as had Drex. He'd looked oddly discouraged and hadn't even tried to compensate for this with cruelty.

Oliver waved everyone over. "One more time through the plan," he said. "Austin?"

Austin used his hands as he explained his movements. "I slip into the *Eagle* and up the bridge. Next, I activate all systems except for the engines, then wait for your signal."

"Tiffany?"

"I follow Austin into the *Eagle*. First, I secure the side hatch, then the large cargo bay door. Next, I locate the rope ladder and cables, then wait until you give the signal."

Oliver nodded. "Ashley?"

"I plant my mTalk at the opposite side of the clearing," she said. "I turn off the power supply to the perimeter scanners. Then I return to you and the sky scooter."

"What does the power supply look like?" Austin asked, checking to make sure she'd paid attention.

"It should be a white oval, like an egg," Ashley said.

"You're sure the Übel and Corsairs use the same systems?" asked Tiffany.

Austin nodded. "I saw them unloading one from the *Eagle* and setting it up. It looked exactly like the one of Evad," he said. "We call the mTalk only if the patrols start to investigate the *Eagle*. If they do, we go to plan B. Oliver?"

"I secure a sky scooter and hover it near the perimeter to wait for Ashley," Oliver said. "Once she's with me, we push the hovering scooter until we're far enough from the clearing to start the engine."

"How far is that?" asked Tiffany.

"That's a good question," Oliver said. "I was thinking a quarter mile."

Ashley looked at him. "That far?"

"Aren't you up for a little hike?" he teased.

She smiled and punched his shoulder. "You'd better believe it."

"We fly outside the grotto and land, then we sneak to the door," Oliver continued.

"Once inside, I locate the Eochair while you keep watch," Ashley said.

"If it's small, we sneak back to the scooter, then signal Austin and Tiffany from another clearing deep in the woods," Oliver said. "If it's too big to carry, we signal you and wait for you to arrive at the ruins."

"When we get the signal, I seal the side hatch of the cargo bay and join Austin," said Tiffany.

"I activate the engines and thrusters and fly to the rendezvous point you'll give me," Austin says.

"I open the underbelly hatch and drop the rope ladder and a harness for the Eochair," Tiffany says.

"Ashley starts up, and I hook the Eochair, then hightail it up the ladder," Oliver said.

All eyes turned to the tent flap as a silhouette moved past. They held their breaths until it continued on.

Oliver checked his mTalk. "It's half past ten. That was one of the guards. It'll be at least fifteen minutes until the other gets to us."

Oliver had carefully studied the guards' patrol pattern; they followed the same path. One walked along the entire exterior perimeter while the other zigzagged across the interior of the camp, then continued around the exterior as the other began zigzagging across the interior. They alternated this way all night as far as Oliver could tell and were perfectly synchronized in their timing and steps—part of their robotic programming, perhaps.

"No sign of Drex and DarkStone since they last checked in. DarkStone's lights are off, Drex's are still on," Oliver said. He looked toward Austin's cot. "I think we're ready."

He could feel the nervous tension in the room. Tiffany and Ashley still weren't keen on the EMP, but it was the only way to disable the Corsairs' hold on them.

Tiffany collected the mTalks and set them as far away as possible. Austin pulled out the homemade device and brought it over. "Get as close as you can, and lean your tapped shoulder in, okay?"

They nodded, bending lower toward the device. Oliver took a deep breath. Ashley grabbed one of his hands, and Tiffany his other.

"Closer," Austin said. Everyone shifted in.

Austin held up the switch. Long wires waiting to surge with sparks slithered down to the coil and capacitor. "Here it goes."

A flash of sparks erupted in the middle of the huddle, making everyone jump. The lights in the room hadn't even dimmed.

"Did it work?" Tiffany asked.

Austin pulled up his shirt so everyone could see his bare shoulder. There was no pulsing purple glow. Oliver and the girls pulled down their collars to look, each nodding a confirmation. Their Zapp-Taps had been disabled.

"Great job, Austin!" Oliver said.

"Great idea, Tiffany!" congratulated Austin.

"Now comes the hard part," Oliver said.

Ashley fetched the four mTalks and handed them out. "I'm ready."

"Can we pray first?" Tiffany asked.

"I think that's a great idea," Oliver said.

Nose Job

The frame of the *Black Lagoon* creaked as the harnesses tightened and the *Skull* began to raise the ship. Water drained off the sides, and the pool of water lapped against the chasm walls.

Mason stood next to his mom, watching the procedure. Lights blinked across the bottom of the large Übel cruiser. A wide bay was open to receive the *Black Lagoon*. Through the swirling sand kicked up by the engines, Mason could make out the large gun turrets across the bottom of the ship, though it hovered high overhead.

He wanted to tell the king and queen that Rylin and Obbin were both okay. At the same time, Mason still hadn't figured out how to get fresh supplies to the princes. The boys would likely remain hidden on the *Black Lagoon* just as Rylin had on the *Raven*.

The *Raven* was another issue. *The Chronicles of Terra Originem* were hidden somewhere on board. Mason needed to retrieve them before the Übel did. For that he would employ Branz's or perhaps Grace and Mae's help.

Suddenly one of the cannons on the underside of the *Skull* discharged. With a resounding boom, a streak of green flew from its muzzle. Immediately the rest of the weapons began firing.

Vedrik lifted his device. "What's going on up there?"

Static. The cannons continued to fire.

"Sir, we're under at—" The voice cut off.

A shower of orange sparks exploded against one of the long cables.

SNAP! TZOOO! The cable harness ripped in half. The floor beneath Mason shook.

Another explosion, another sliced cable.

The bow of the ship dropped forward. The nose of the *Black Lagoon* slammed against the side of the wall, throwing Mason to the ground. His mom slipped backward, slamming against the front console with a bone-jarring thunk. She screamed out in pain.

"Laura!" cried Mr. Wikk as he held tight to the seat in front of him. A violent jerk sent him tumbling over the pilot chair and toward the consoles.

An unnerving sound of metal grinding against rock rattled throughout the bridge as the front of the *Black Lagoon* dragged against the stone wall of the shaft.

A wide tear slithered across the ceiling of the bridge.

Mason scrambled toward his mom and reached out to grab her hand. Their fingers had only just locked when the nose of the *Black Lagoon* angled sharply, breaking away from the rest of the submersible. The consoles remained intact, but everything beyond was gone.

"I've got you," Mason said, one arm wrapped tightly around the navigator's seat, the other extended to his mom as a lifeline.

Mr. Wikk was bear-hugging one of the consoles, feet dangling through the gaping hole at the front of the submersible. Even more shocking, the captain was holding tightly to Mr. Wikk's legs, his long black cape waving in the updraft of the cavern.

"Save me!" shouted Vedrik.

The ship began to swing away from the wall. Almost as quickly, it twisted and started back toward the rock face. The submersible still twisting, the side of the ship slammed against the wall.

SNAP!

Mason's side of the bridge dipped violently. His mom dropped lower as the top of the remaining bulkhead slammed against the cavern wall with a shower of sparks and a metallic crunch. Had the ceiling's upper support beams not lodged against the rock wall, she and Vedrik would have been crushed.

"Mom! Reach with your other arm!" Mason yelled.

"I can't move it," she called. "It's broken."

"Everyone, hold on!" yelled Mr. Wikk. "Including you, Fritz!"

Mason had never heard Captain Vedrik's first name used. Elliot let go of the console with one hand.

"What are you doing?" Vedrik panicked.

"Trust me!" Mr. Wikk called.

Mason watched as his dad fought to get something from the front pocket of his vest. His muscles pulsed in the arm that still held on to the console.

The *Skull* had stopped lifting the *Black Lagoon*. The submersible dangled perilously over the water below.

"Dad, hurry . . . I . . ." Mason gritted his teeth. His breathing was labored, and his muscles were sore. He couldn't let go of his mom. She didn't know Rescuer.

The metal creaked against the stone, but the ship didn't swing away from the wall again. The bridge floor held at a forty-five-degree slope.

Mason looked around the cabin for anything he could grab. His only idea was to somehow use the chair safety harnesses, but he didn't have a free hand or a knife to cut one loose. Sweat dripped down his face and dampened his palms.

"Mom!" he cried. She was slipping from his grasp. The gaping hole looked ready to swallow her.

SCHOOP! A taut line extended from Mr. Wikk's grappling gun to the railing of the spiral staircase. "Captain, you must trust me," Mr. Wikk said again.

Mason barely saw Vedrik's nod.

"I'm going to slide the gun to you," Mr. Wikk said. "Take it, and let go of my legs."

"Okay," Vedrik said.

Mason's dad dropped the gun to the captain. Vedrik grabbed it with both hands. Kicking the captain's shoulder or cutting the line would have rid them of Vedrik at that moment. But Mason knew that his dad was a man of his word. Instead of attacking the Übel leader, Mr. Wikk pulled himself up around the console so that he was on the front side of it.

"I've got you!" Mason shouted to his mom with renewed strength, yet his arms ached and his palms grew ever sweatier.

Mr. Wikk leaped to the chair that Mason was holding. Gripping the chair with one hand, he extended his free arm toward his wife, pulling her toward him. Her other arm dangled helplessly.

Mason didn't let go of his mom's hand until she was safely beside him. The chair groaned under the Wikks' combined weight.

Vedrik was making quick work, climbing up the grappling line hand over hand.

"Mason, I want you to jump for the center chair, then the third. Use the line to climb to the railing."

Mason swallowed. "Dad . . ."

"You can do it, son. I believe in you!" Mr. Wikk said. Mason looked at his mom; she nodded back.

Vedrik had nearly pulled himself all the way to the pilot's seat using the line from the grappling hook.

Mason looked at the middle seat and took a deep breath. He jumped, bear-hugging it as he landed. "I've got it!"

"One more," his mom said encouragingly.

Mason leaped again. His hands felt the solid frame of the chair. A feeling of accomplishment poured over him like cool water as his footing steadied.

"Now use the line to climb to the rail," Mr. Wikk ordered. "After you and the captain are there, release the hook and fire the grapple to us."

As the words left his mouth, the pole that the chair sat on began to buckle. The seat twisted. Mr. Wikk pulled his wife against his chest, fighting to keep hold of the chair. "Hurry!"

Vedrik was pulling himself up just behind Mason. "Go!" he ordered, but his tone held something Mason had never heard in his voice before: encouragement.

Mason quickly pulled himself up to the rail. Vedrik followed. The two wound up the wire and unhooked the grapple.

"To the side!" the captain shouted. Mason shifted along the railing, using it for support.

Mr. Wikk turned to shield his wife with his body as Captain Vedrik aimed and fired. The grapple clanked on the far side of the chair, then began to slide toward Mason's parents.

"Grab it!" Vedrik shouted.

Mr. Wikk took the grapple in his free hand. The captain anchored their end to the railing.

"It's secure," he called.

Mason watched with nervous admiration as his dad pulled himself and his wife up the sloping floor of the bridge. As soon as the two were in arm's length, Captain Vedrik pulled Mrs. Wikk to the safe side of the rail, and Mason extended a hand to his dad.

4.40

The Escape

The lights in their tent were turned out. Oliver peered through the flap one last time.

"We're clear. Austin, go," Oliver whispered, tightening the strap on his left glove.

Austin darted past Oliver and dashed for the *Eagle*. As he ran, he saw no sign of the two patrols. The commander's pod was dark, as was Drex's tent. A cold breeze blew across the clearing. Austin's mTalk light bounced before him. They had dimmed their lights as much as possible so as to not attract the attention of the Corsairs walking the perimeter. He'd have gone without, but the few stars and the scattered lights remaining on in the camp were not bright enough. The mTalks' light would attract less attention than one of them stumbling over something.

Austin dove into the grass on his stomach as a snap echoed to his right. He glanced in the direction of the noise, covering his mTalk with his hand. Barely visible in the darkness, Oliver stood as still as a statue, looking in the direction of the sound.

One second, then two, then three passed. Austin's heart pounded in his chest. Then, to his relief, Oliver moved his mTalk up and down, signaling Austin to go.

Austin pushed himself up and moved quickly to the hatch. He slipped into the *Eagle*. The interior was dark, but he knew this ship like he knew the *Phoenix*. There had been no sign of a Corsair guard or pilot remaining onboard, but he went slowly just in case.

"Tiffany, you're up," Oliver called. She got up from the cot like a player leaving the bench before a kugel game. Taking a deep breath, she tapped on her light. She was ready.

"You can do it," Ashley said. "I'll see you soon."

"Be safe," Tiffany replied.

She moved to the tent flap. The first thing she noticed was the chilly air. Her target was straight ahead, a silver reflection of the dimly lit camp.

She took off at a sprint, never stopping until she'd crossed into the cargo bay. She turned and waved her light—Ashley's signal to start her mission. Tiffany locked the larger cargo bay door and ran down the corridor to the side hatch. It was already closed. She secured it by tapping on the control pad.

She spun on one foot and ran back to the cargo bay. Her next mission was to find a rope ladder and some long cables, in case they were needed to extract the Eochair, Ashley, and Oliver.

Ashley ducked into the shadow of a nearby tent, then slipped behind it. Oliver's mission had begun. He exited the tent, looking for the patrols. No sign of them.

Oliver dashed toward the commander's pod, to the dozen sky scooters and skiffs that sat behind it. He dove into the trampled grass as he heard the pod's door click.

The door opened. Boots thumped across the grass. Oliver held his breath. If the commander found the empty tent, the entire plan would be over. She'd never let them out of her sight again, regardless of what Mr. O'Farrell said. He exhaled slowly, trying to make as little sound as possible. What did she want? What was she thinking?

A soft series of beeps sounded. "Commander DarkStone here."

A pause.

"Yes, sir. No, sir. I'm sorry to hear that, sir. And the McGregors escaped?"

Another pause.

"I see. And the Wikks?"

Pause.

"Yes, the other keys are secure here. The Eochair is still sealed in the grotto."

Pause.

"No, sir. I will, sir."

Pause.

"Five hours? Yes, sir. We'll be ready."

Oliver's arms tingled. The Supreme Admiral was on his way? He glanced at his mTalk. There was no new update. If O'Farrell was on his way, Commander DarkStone would likely want to rouse her soldiers, get the Wikks, and head back to open the grotto.

The hatch clicked as the door closed again behind her. How long did he have?

Oliver ran around the back of the pod. He grabbed one of the wings of the nearest scooter and started to push it. The perimeter fence still glowed purple. Ashley hadn't completed her mission yet.

Suddenly it struck Oliver: the patrols would notice when the purple orbs dimmed. They'd raise the alarm; the entire plan would fall apart. Why hadn't he considered it before? Everything had been rushed. All they'd been thinking was "Escape, escape, escape."

Oliver let go of the scooter and ran. He had to stop Ashley before she took out the security system. He darted around a tent, then another. He saw Ashley's silhouette reach the large white oval. He couldn't shout—that would raise the alarm as well.

Ashley tapped a screen, then prepared to yank something from the system. Oliver grabbed her and slipped one hand over her mouth. Her muffled scream echoed under his hand, and a sharp elbow struck him in the chest.

"Ashley!" he half groaned, half whispered in her ear. "It's me." He turned her so she could see him. When he saw the relief on her face, he slipped his hand away.

"What happened?" she whispered.

"If you shut down the perimeter system, the purple lights will go out. The patrols will know something's happened," Oliver explained in a hushed voice.

"What should we do?"

"I don't know."

"We have to tell Tiffany and Austin to get back."

"Yeah, and quickly. O'Farrell is on his way here."

Ashley grabbed Oliver's shoulders. "Austin's EMP," she said. "We can use it on the perimeter scanners we need to get past."

"That won't work."

"Sure it will. It's the same concept. The localized pulse will wipe out the electrodes in the scanners we want, just like it took out just our Zapp-Taps and not the overhead lights."

Oliver rubbed his face, eyes to chin.

"I'll sneak back to the EMP. You get the scooter," Ashley said. "Go!" She took off for their tent.

Oliver made his way back to the scooter and began pushing it toward the fence. A minute later Ashley joined him, the small homemade EMP in hand. He was impressed with her speed.

Ashley held the EMP near one of the stakes and pressed the trigger. A flash of sparks erupted with a soft *zhoooop*, and the purple orb dimmed instantly. Ashley moved to the next scanner and repeated. The orb went black.

"Through here," Ashley said.

Oliver pushed the scooter between the two shut-down scanners. There were no alarms, no sirens, nothing.

"You did it!" Oliver said.

"We're not clear yet," she reminded him.

He nodded, and they pushed the scooter into the trees.

Blasted

"WHAT HAPPENED?" Vedrik screamed into his communicator.

Static crackled on the radio. No answer.

"Looks like we're stuck for the moment. Might we check on Dr. Blue?" Mr. Wikk asked.

Vedrik eyed Mason's dad. "Why didn't you let me fall?"

Mr. Wikk half smiled. "I might not agree with your tactics or the Übel's ideals, but you're a human just like me. Everyone deserves life."

Vedrik seemed to consider that. Mason was sure he was about to say something like, "I owe you one," but instead he scowled. "Shows what you know. You'd make a terrible soldier."

Was Vedrik talking about himself as if he didn't deserve to live? The Übel had done many bad things, but what Mason had been learning about Rescuer told him that it didn't matter what you'd done. It only mattered that you began to follow Truth.

A beep sounded on Vedrik's communicator. "Sir, we took heavy fire from the Saharvics. They have been repelled. Engineers are trying to visually assess the damage to the lifting straps to determine if we can continue the operation."

"I order you to continue," Vedrik shouted. "We have injuries, and there is heavy damage to the *Black Lagoon*."

A moment passed.

"Yes, sir. The Supreme Commander will be notified."

Vedrik scratched his chin. "Let's get out of this section. I'm not sure we can make it to the scientist, but we should get near a bulkhead."

Mr. Wikk helped Mrs. Wikk down the oddly angled spiral stairs, followed by Mason, with Vedrik bringing up the rear.

The ship jerked, and Mason's breath caught. But the *Black Lagoon* began to rise through the air again. Through the clear bottom of the submersible, Mason watched the water grow farther and farther away.

His eyes shot closed as bright light filled the submersible from every angle. He forced himself to squint. Large white sand dunes stretched for miles, reflecting the sun. As his pupils adjusted, Mason made out darkened sand where the *Skull*'s cannons had blasted. Several smoking pieces of wreckage smoldered from the brief but fierce battle.

A shadow overtook the *Black Lagoon* as the ship entered the flight deck of the Übel Cruiser. The large bay doors shifted closed, and the submersible was set on the floor. Soldiers and personnel rushed toward the ship.

"Let's go," Vedrik said as he walked down the now-level corridor. The hatch was crooked and damaged. Two solid kicks knocked it off its hinges.

"We've got an injury," Vedrik said, pointing to Mrs. Wikk.

Three medics loaded Mason's mom onto a hover stretcher. Mr. Wikk gripped Mason's shoulders and moved him through the crowd so they could be near her.

"Sir, we'll be taking her to the medical ward," the medic said. "You'll need to remain here."

"I'll see you in a bit," Mrs. Wikk said.

Mason nodded. "Okay, Mom. I love you."

"I love you too," she replied. The medics pressed a button on the side of the stretcher. Red light flashed beneath it, and the medics jogged alongside it as it flew toward a door.

Mason watched until she was gone, then looked back at the damaged ship. The nose of the submersible was missing, but what was more frightening was the huge split at the top of the ship. The entire front section of the *Black Lagoon* had nearly ripped off and fallen into the water. Would he have survived?

Dr. Blue emerged from the ship with several medics surrounding her, followed by Cruz. Neither looked injured. Mason waited with his dad while Vedrik spoke with Dr. Blue.

A medic backed out of the ship, his arms locked under Pyrock's arms. Another medic carried the soldier's legs. They lifted Pyrock onto a hover stretcher and started for the doors. There was blood on the man's face. Mason hoped he wasn't injured too badly. He could imagine how easily passengers would have been thrown around the open cargo bay if they weren't harnessed in.

"Rylin! Obbin!" Mason gasped. He started for the hatch.

"Son, what is it? You can't go back on the ship," his dad said.

Mason's father was one of the few people he could tell. "Dad, the missing Blauwe Mensen princes are on board—Prince Rylin and Obbin. They're on the ship."

"Are you sure?"

"Yes, I saw them. I spoke with them," Mason said.

"Why didn't you say something?" his dad said.

"There wasn't time," Mason said.

"Cap—"

"No, we can't tell him! They're hiding," Mason said.

"They could be injured," Mr. Wikk said.

That had been Mason's first concern too. "I know, but if they can keep hidden, we can use their presence to our advantage at the right time."

Mason's dad rubbed the stubble on his chin and took a slow, contemplative breath.

"Dad, please," Mason said. "You have to trust me. We know what we're doing. Obbin hid in the *Phoenix* while we were on Evad, and Rylin's been hidden on the *Raven* since the Übel extracted Zebra Xavier. These two are great at sneaking around."

His dad clicked his tongue. "We have to make sure that neither of them are hurt. I want to reassure their parents that I saw them and that they're safe. But I believe the king would agree with you. He's growing tired of placating the Übel."

Mason nodded.

"Let's go," Mr. Wikk said.

"How will we get back in?" Mason asked as they walked.

"Vedrik will let us," Mr. Wikk said. "He owes me one. More than one. I'll tell you about the incident on Re Lyt with the triceratops later. It was wild."

Mason laughed. "Oliver and Tiffany ran into a tyranno-saurus and some velociraptors."

Mr. Wikk turned on him and grabbed his shoulders. "What?" he asked with utter surprise. "They were there?"

"Yes, Dad. We were all there with the Corsairs. Oliver and Tiffany went to the Hatchery; Austin, Obbin, and I took over the *Phoenix*. Then we escaped. That's how we got to the Cathedral of the Star without Mr. O'Farrell."

His dad smiled. "I want to hear everything." They neared Vedrik. "Captain, I'd like to take a look around the bay of the *Black Lagoon* and see if we missed anything before the engineers and soldiers damage something."

"Fine, but be quick," Vedrik said. "Cruz!" The bulky soldier turned and faced his captain. "Escort these two to their cabin once they're done."

The words had barely left Vedrik's lips when his communicator beeped. "Captain Vedrik, the Supreme Commander orders your immediate presence," a raspy voice declared.

Vedrik raised his head and cleared his throat. "Mr. Wikk, be prepared to give a *full* report on the incident in the chamber."

Mason's dad nodded. Most of the soldiers had already cleared out. Several engineering teams swarmed over the front section of the ship, lining up contraptions on all sides of the submersible. A web of green lines of light crisscrossed the ship, analyzing the *Black Lagoon*'s structural integrity. A large crane secured straps across the ship, locking it down so that it wouldn't shift during flight. Unlike the other Übel ships in the bay, the submersible didn't have magnetic locking systems.

"You can wait here if you'd like," Mr. Wikk told Cruz.

"The captain said—"

"He said to escort us to our cabin, not to babysit us. Take a rest. Where are we going to go? We're in your fortress," Mr. Wikk said. This seemed to satisfy Cruz, who leaned against the ship's side.

Once inside, they passed a scientist carrying out the case that contained the Ursprung verification keys. The bay of the *Black Lagoon* was deserted.

Mason saw blood near the hatch. "Rylin! Obbin!" he called out in panic.

"That's probably Pyrock's," his dad reassured him.

"Rylin?" Mason called again. "Obbin?"

There was a click, and a compartment door opened.

4.42

The Spot

Austin sat in the pilot's seat. He'd left the heat shield over the windows so that the patrols wouldn't see him in the bridge. Everything was on. He'd mapped his flight path to the grotto, even though it was hardly more than a minute away on the *Eagle*. It would take more time to lift off and land than to fly to the dig site.

A small blue blip on the radar represented the sky scooter leaving the camp. Oliver and Ashley were already about halfway between the *Eagle* and the grotto. Maybe ten or so minutes left.

"Austin," Tiffany said as she stepped into the bridge. "Could you help me? I've found a rope ladder, but I need help getting it out of the case."

Austin didn't want to leave his post, but what good would it be to not be ready to extract Oliver and Tiffany if he couldn't land?

Together they got out the heavy rope ladder and anchored the top next to the hatch in the bay floor. Tiffany would just have to roll it, and it would open as it dropped to the ground. Next, they prepared several large tethers that could be used to reel in the Eochair if needed. They still weren't sure how large it was, but the size of the hill over the grotto suggested that it might be sizeable.

When they were finished, Austin dashed up the bay stairs two at a time. He sat at the console and immediately noticed that something had changed. A second blue dot had appeared on the screen. The system hadn't picked up any identification; all Austin could tell was that it was larger than a sky scooter. A second later it was gone.

Austin tapped the screen once, twice. The blip didn't return.

Lights off, Oliver flew the sky scooter along the trail to the ruined settlement. The path was straight, and he went slowly so as not to crash. He watched the tree line, hoping he might catch a glimpse of Brother Sam in the darkness, but they neared the edge of the settlement without the Veritas Nachfolger's stopping them to assist in the next part of the mission.

Oliver let off the throttle. At least a few Corsairs had remained to guard the dig site. The area was bathed in a dim blue light— enough for the guards to spot movement, but not so much as to give the appearance that a major excavation was underway.

Dismounting the scooter, Oliver and Ashley coasted it just inside the tree line, facing the front outward in case they needed to make a quick getaway.

"We've got to be stealthy," Oliver said. "Some of the Corsairs might have night vision in their enhanced eyes."

Ashley nodded and followed Oliver as he started forward in a low crouch. They let their eyes adjust to the dim light instead of using their mTalks.

"We're almost there," Oliver said. "The grotto is in that direction." He pointed ahead and to their right. Ruins blocked the view of the entrance. He scanned the clearing for the guards. The only Corsair he saw stood near a turret mounted on a skiff, an orange light blinking on his head.

A large stone wall was their first waypoint. Oliver ran, followed by Ashley. He pointed to another set of ruins. The building's foundation was all that remained, save the stone frame of the front door, which stood like a sentinel. They moved to the foundation and crouched. Oliver looked for patrols, pointed, and the two moved again. They followed this rhythm for nearly twenty more stops, covering more than two hundred feet.

Once inside the threshold of the grotto, Oliver looked around the dig site. Other than the guard he'd spotted earlier, he saw no one.

"That went well," Ashley said.

Oliver nodded, shifting aside dirt and a few encroaching roots with his hand. He reached under the collar of his shirt and lifted out the cross-shaped necklace, then leaned toward the cross-shaped indent, hoping it would work.

SHHHHHEW!

A gasp echoed from the chamber as the door slid into the ground. Oliver looked back toward the ruins. The noise had been loud. Had anyone heard? They weren't about to wait around to find out.

Slipping into the dark, damp-smelling chamber, Oliver pressed the pendant to the doorframe. Nothing happened. He leaned to the other side. The door started to rise but stopped with a clunk.

"Why won't it shut?" Oliver gripped the top edge of the door and pulled. It wouldn't budge.

"It's old," Ashley said. Together they pulled up on the door. Still, it wouldn't move.

"We have to leave it," Oliver said. "Let's just be quick about this."

Ashley tapped on her mTalk light and started into the room. The chamber wasn't much larger than the Wikks' living room at home. Oliver and Ashley stood across from each other in the hollow.

"Oliver, there's noth—" Ashley stopped mid-step. "Wait."
She kneeled down and knocked against one of the flat, angular
stones.

Oliver heard it too. It was hollow underneath. He tapped
a nearby stone: solid.

Ashley tapped all around the angular stone before her,
then tucked her gloved fingers in the crevices surrounding
it. "Not deep enough," she said. She slipped her pack off and
pulled out a hand pick. She tried wedging it in the crevice
without success.

A smirk crossed Oliver's lips. Ashley had gone into action
mode without any guidance. This mission was hers as much
as his. She wanted the Eochair, and she wanted to escape.

"Let me try."

Ashley offered him the pick, but he shook his head. "Stand
back." He lifted his foot and slammed it against the center of
the stone.

"Again," Ashley said. "There's a crack."

Oliver stomped again and tumbled forward onto Ashley
as the stone crumbled beneath him. She fell backward, and he
rolled to the side. "I'm sorry. Are you okay?"

She rubbed her elbows. "I'll be fine. I'm just glad you didn't
fall completely through."

Only a few shards of the stone remained, leaving a hole
large enough to swallow him. "Whoa."

Ashley pulled Oliver to his feet. She gagged at the musty
smell seeping into the room. Holding her nose with one hand,
she stooped over the hole and shone her light in. "Stairs."

They used their feet to break away the final shards of stone.

Oliver looked down at their new path and took a last deep
breath of what was certainly fresher air before stepping into
the darkness.

The staircase was solid stone, so Oliver didn't fear that it
might collapse. Instead he had concerns about what might lurk
below. The air was chilly and heavy with a rotting stench that

reminded him of a half-eaten animal he'd once found in the woods behind their home on Tragiws. Yet his confidence that the Eochair was there overcame his hesitation, and he moved lower into the chamber with Ashley just behind.

Austin wanted Tiffany to speculate about the blip with him, but using the mTalks to communicate was too risky. He'd have to do it the old-fashioned way and find her.

Then the blue blip appeared again. He glued his attention to the screen. It moved close to the campsite and stopped. Austin watched it, listening for a siren to alert the Corsairs. Oliver and Ashley had taken out the perimeter security, but he expected the patrols to spot the intruder soon. But a minute passed and no alarms rang out, nor did the blip move.

Austin wished he could see it with his own eyes. He considered leaving the ship. The camp was dark, the patrols had not seen him before, and he could maneuver among the tents to spot the intruder.

But before he could go, the blue blip moved backward and disappeared from the screen again. Austin rolled his shoulders as he stood and started for the cargo bay.

Just steps down the corridor, Austin stopped dead in his tracks and stared.

The air grew colder and more putrid smelling, and the stairs became slick. Oliver and Ashley proceeded at a snail's pace; thick, slippery green grime on the walls left nothing for them to use for balance.

The staircase opened, spiraling along the outside of a large chamber. There was no railing, making their descent even more treacherous.

Oliver shone his flashlight into the space below. The beam caught on a tall, flat stone structure in the center, about twenty feet tall, with two sides wider than the other two, like a table-top set on end.

An odd gurgling noise stole Oliver's attention. He cast his light around the chamber again, then back at the structure. The beam glinted on something green and moving.

Oliver halted and held his hand back to stop Ashley. He slipped his pack from his back and pulled out the Zinger.

"What is it?" asked Ashley.

"A snake maybe, or something worse," Oliver warned.

His weapon began to charge; blue sparks at the end showed that it was ready. If Oliver hadn't believed that the Eochair was down there, he'd have turned them around and headed back up. He had no desire to face swarms of slithering serpents or the ensnaring vines from the ziggurats. He and Mason had barely escaped the first time.

"Be ready," Oliver whispered.

"Always," Ashley answered. A sizzle told him that she'd charged her weapon. He was glad that he wasn't alone.

Oliver stepped onto the slimy chamber floor. Then he heard the sound again.

GURGLE GULP. GURGLE GULP GULP.

Oliver and Ashley aimed their lights and weapons at the sound, which had come from the stone structure. A stream of thick, slimy, green goop shot out from a spout halfway up the structure—it was a fountain—and pooled in a basin below. The awful smell increased with the new discharge.

"Is that your snake?" asked Ashley.

Oliver exhaled with relief. "It looked bigger from up there."

"Right—well, if you're not scared, let's find whatever it is we're looking for," Ashley teased.

Oliver cleared his throat. "You take the fountain, I'll check the walls."

"Thanks." Ashley groaned playfully.

Ashley headed toward the center, and Oliver marched back to the wall. He wasn't sure what he was looking for as he walked along the perimeter of the room, or if he'd be able to see anything on the wall. The covering of slime might cloak it completely.

Of all the locations he'd visited so far, this one was in the greatest disrepair. Perhaps because it was one of the last stops on their path to Ursprung, it was one of the oldest locations to hold a clue. Age had not treated it well.

"Oliver, check this out," Ashley called. He joined her at the fountain. Words had been carved into a wide stone placard over the fountain's basin. The sign was either made of or coated in a material that had not let the grime grow.

"'Enter ye in at the strait gate, for wide *is* the gate, and broad *is* the way, that leadeth to destruction, and many there be which go in thereat,'" Ashley read. She stepped up onto the edge of the basin to reach the placard and used her glove to wipe the surrounding grime away from the area around it. "Nothing else," she said and stuck her tongue out with a sickened expression. Long, green strands of goop dripped off her glove. She wiped her hand on Oliver's shirtsleeve as she stepped down. "Yuck!"

Oliver grunted. "Thanks."

He moved to the opposite side of the fountain, shining his light over every inch. "Here," he called. "'Because strait *is* the gate, and narrow *is* the way, which leadeth unto life, and few there be that find it.'"

"It has the same terms we've been encountering so far," Ashley said. "'Leadeth unto life.' We're in the right place."

"But where is the Eochair?" Oliver asked.

4.43

My Brother

Tiffany startled at Austin's shouts and took off for the second level of the *Eagle*. Her brother wasn't in sight when she reached the top of the stairs. Her Zinger before her, she started down the corridor. Had a soldier been on board the *Eagle* or somehow gotten past her? She didn't want to shoot anyone, but . . . She sighed. She would if she had to.

"Tiffany!"

Tiffany jumped. Her heart raced. "Austin, quit shouting. I almost stunned you!"

"Tiff, it's open. The sealed cabin is open."

Tiffany realized that Austin was hanging out from the cabin that had been locked. She'd all but forgotten about it in the constant stream of events that had occurred.

Turning into the room, she was amazed at what she saw. On the far wall, three large screens blinked with live images from all sorts of places. A suite of control screens lay embedded at three consoles beneath the displays, much like the NavCom on the bridge for the ship. Three chairs sat empty at the stations. A large locker lined the left wall, filled with red robes and a myriad of weapons, gadgets, and other uniforms. The last wall was covered in drawers and cabinets, all closed. Most had locks.

"It's some sort of control room," Austin said. "There was a video of Yth Orod a moment ago." His voice was glum; the city had been destroyed. "But I also saw Dabnis Castle."

Tiffany watched as different feeds rotated on the trio of screens. "This is how Brother Sam knew everything that was happening. This is amazing. You know what sort of information we'll have now?"

If the videos were showing areas where the Veritas Nachfolger had hidden artifacts or clues, then . . . Tiffany shook the thought away. She didn't want to get her hopes up. "Austin, this is really great. How did you open it?"

"I didn't. I was coming to get you, and the hatch was already open."

"That's strange," Tiffany said.

"Not really. Oliver thought he saw Brother Sam nearby. He built these ships, or at least retrofitted them, and he gave us the cloaking device. Don't you think he has a way to control the *Eagle*?"

Tiffany was hesitant to buy into that so quickly.

"I was coming to get you because I noticed a blip on the radar earlier," Austin said. "It wasn't Oliver and Ashley, it was someone else. They could have remotely opened this door."

"But why?" asked Tiffany. "Why now?"

"Maybe there's something in here that we need, or need to see," Austin said. "Or maybe they are coming for us and the ship like Oliver suggested. They might be helping him and Ashley right now at the grotto."

Her brother made a fair point, but he was possibly too optimistic. "If we don't find anything right away, you should get to the bridge and wait. Oliver could signal us anytime," Tiffany said. "We can come back and look further when we've got him and Ashley." She started toward the cabinets.

"Wait, Tiffany! It's Dad!"

Oliver had taken pictures of the two placards. Now he and Ashley were scouring the fountain.

"Do you think this whole thing is the Eochair?" Ashley asked.

"I don't think so. If it's a key, how would they get it out?"

"A plasma drill is on its way. We'll have to commandeer it."

"That's harder than you think."

Oliver stepped back as the fountain sputtered and the gunk poured into the basin. He looked at Ashley. She was considering the words etched on the placards. She was so similar to his sister.

"Perhaps the words are an entry code?" she asked.

"Or the key is hidden behind the placard, like the entrance was hidden beneath the stone," Oliver suggested. He straddled the basin to reach the placard, tapped it with his fist, then stepped down with a grunt. "Not there. It's solid."

"Wait, Oliver, look at that." Ashley flashed her light at Oliver's foot. Just above the basin was a faint cross-shaped indentation.

Oliver grabbed the necklace and held it against the indent. The tall fountain began to spin, sinking slowly into the ground.

"Another secret passage," Ashley said.

Oliver saw the top of a ladder in the newly opened hole. "I'm going down. You stay up here."

Ashley nodded. As Oliver stepped in, she squatted and provided extra light for him.

The ladder was made of stone. Grime squished underneath Oliver's gloves as he descended.

The air began to change; it was warmer and smelled of smoke. Oliver didn't see any flames. He continued to descend; the smell and warmth grew stronger.

Where was the fire? How had it burned all this time? Had something they'd done ignited it?

When his feet finally touched down, he was standing next to the basin of the fountain. Before him was a wide, arched door with another indent. He raised his cross and then stopped. Something wasn't quite right.

Oliver glanced up at the fountain. The placard facing him read, "'Enter ye in at the strait gate, for wide *is* the gate, and broad *is* the way, that leadeth to destruction, and many there be which go in thereat.'" He looked at his mTalk and read the other phrase. "'Because strait *is* the gate, and narrow *is* the way, which leadeth unto life, and few there be that find it.'"

There was a narrow gap between the fountain and the side of the pit. Oliver attempted to climb through but couldn't fit. Perhaps his theory was wrong. He took the pendant in his hand and started to press it toward the door, then stopped. Something wouldn't let him go on. He needed to check the other side.

His light glinted on the stone ladder as he climbed up. He stopped at the top of the fountain; another ladder led down the other side. Previously he'd been at the wrong angle to see it.

"What did you find?" Ashley's question startled him, and he almost lost his balance.

"A door," he said.

"What was in it?"

"I didn't open it. I think there's another door on this side."

She didn't respond for a moment. Then she said, "While you were down there, I felt certain that something bad was happening."

"Why didn't you shout to me?"

"I thought I was just feeling jittery."

Oliver looked up at her. "Don't be scared. Helper is watching us." It felt good to verbalize the feeling he had. "We're being guided, protected. Something stopped me from opening that door." Oliver hoped she understood. "I think Helper was warning me, giving me hesitation."

Ashley nodded. "I'll tell you if I get a feeling like that again."

"Me too." Oliver smiled, then slipped to the other ladder. The smell of smoke still filled the chamber, and the air continued to grow warmer. Near the bottom he turned and confirmed that the other placard was visible on this side. There was no door on the wall. A dead end?

A symbol was etched into one of the stones: XII. On Evad the wall before the chamber had been covered in strange numbers. This time there wasn't an opening for a ruby but instead a cross-shaped indent.

Oliver reached out to touch the stone with his pendant, then paused. "Helper, please guide me, give me peace."

He placed the cross pendant against the indent next to the one-foot-by-one-foot stone. It began to slide backward, then dropped out of view. An icy blast of air surged out, causing Oliver to jump back, nearly tripping over the edge of the basin.

When he'd recovered, he looked at the dark hole. The light of his mTalk seemed to dissipate the second it hit the cupboard's threshold. What sort of technology was that?

Oliver swallowed and reached his hand forward, hesitating as he noticed jagged icicles ringing the interior of the space. He paused, but this time he didn't sense danger.

Oliver fought to keep his arm from shaking in the cold air. When he thought his hand wouldn't go any farther, his knuckles hit something. He extended his fingers and gripped the back of it and pulled it toward himself. Icicles cracked off as a box slid out. It was so cold that Oliver was glad for his gloves.

The cube was silver. He turned it over in his hands but couldn't see a way to open it.

Their dad stood next to Mason in what looked like the inside of a ship's bay.

"Do you see mom?" asked Tiffany.

Austin shook his head.

The video feed switched, and Austin jumped into one of the control seats.

"Can you bring it back?"

"I . . . I don't know." Austin tapped an icon labeled *Security Feeds*, and a new screen popped up before him with a couple hundred new icons. Most of the images were of planets, moons, and even asteroids, but about fifty or so were ships, and four ships looked just like the *Phoenix*. They were labeled *Phoenix*, *Eagle*, *Griffin*, and *Falcon*. Austin recognized the names of some of the planets—Evad, YelNik Eisle, Enaid, Yl Revaw, Jahr des Eises—but there were many others he didn't recognize.

"Click on *Eagle*," Tiffany said. "I want to see how Brother Sam did it."

Austin obeyed. Several options came up: Bridge, Galley, Cargo Bay, Control Suite, and so on.

"That one," Tiffany said, pointing. Their backs appeared on the screen. Tiffany turned, and Austin was suddenly looking right into her brown eyes. "This is how they know," she said. "This is how we find our parents and complete this quest."

"Let's see if we can find Dad and Mason again," Austin said. He tapped back to the screen with the ships.

"*Ark!*" Tiffany shouted.

Austin went to tap on the icon, but a warning appeared: *No Access*. He tried again, but the same warning appeared.

"Security passcode?" Tiffany asked.

Austin shrugged. "Maybe, but it didn't ask for one when we started using the system. It was already on."

"Let's look for Mason and Dad again," Tiffany said. "Try Cao."

Oliver held up the box for Ashley to take. By the time he had pulled himself up, Ashley was already turning it over, trying to discover a way to open it.

"Try my cross," Oliver said.

Ashley pressed it against each of the box's six sides, but nothing happened. "Weird."

"This was hidden behind a stone marked XII. I can't recall what number that—"

"Twelve."

"You and Tiffany are two of a kind." Oliver laughed. "Anyway, the stone had to be unlocked with my cross. That's a good sign that it's something of value."

"But the Eochair?"

Oliver shrugged.

"What about the other door?"

"I don't think so. The placards made it clear that the wide door involved destruction of some kind. This was the correct choice."

"We should get going. Tiffany and Austin are probably worried," Ashley said. She slipped the box into her pack.

There wasn't a place to wave the cross necklace, so Oliver couldn't return the fountain to its previous location. There was no way to cover their tracks, but it didn't matter. As soon as he called Austin, the game would be up.

The two climbed the stairs to the upper chamber of the grotto.

"Stop right where you are!" exclaimed a raspy voice that Oliver didn't recognize.

Ashley paused halfway through the opening.

Oliver slipped the Zinger off his shoulder and hit the charge. Ashley held steady.

"Now come up slowly with your hands in the air," the voice called.

Ashley's foot tapped Oliver's arm. Was she urging him to do something, or did she want him to not do anything? Though

Oliver did have the element of surprise, he didn't know how many enemies there were or what weapons he faced.

Ashley climbed out of the hole with the pack containing the Eochair, her not-to-be-used Zinger slung over her shoulder.

"Who are you?" the voice asked. "What are you doing in here?"

"My name is Ashley McGregor," she said. "I am looking for the Eochair just like everyone else."

"Where are your comrades?" the voice asked.

"Where are yours?" Ashley responded.

That was the signal. The soldier was alone. Oliver popped up, took aim, and fired before the owner of the voice even knew he was there.

The Corsair slumped to the ground.

"Good work," Ashley said.

"Thanks for the tip." Oliver grabbed the Corsair's weapon and tossed it back into the chamber. "We'd better go. Surely he alerted others."

The door was still in a half-raised position. They squeezed over it.

Three lights approached from separate directions. A Corsair shouted, "Halt!"

Before he went entirely still, Oliver tapped the screen of his mTalk.

Austin's and Tiffany's mTalks beeped simultaneously, and the voice of a Corsair soldier hissed over the speakers. They were hearing a conversation.

"You two, arms in the air!"

"Sir, we were doing what Commander DarkStone asked. We opened the grotto," Oliver said. "There was another chamber below. We took your comrade down."

"They've got it!" shouted Austin. "They need us."

Tiffany ran for the cargo bay and Austin for the bridge. It was the quickest sprint of his life. He took his seat and activated the thrusters. In moments the Corsairs would be all over them and Commander DarkStone would activate the Zapp-Taps. His eyes flicked to his shoulder. Hopefully they really were disabled.

A message on the screen told him that the cargo bay door had closed, and he activated the security lockdown, sealing the ship. Moments later Tiffany hopped into the copilot's seat and strapped in. "Ready."

Austin took the controls. The *Eagle* began to rise. He lifted the heat shields, and purple flashes erupted across the front of the silver spaceship. The Corsairs were already firing on them. Austin turned the ship toward the grotto.

Commander DarkStone was tapping the device on her wrist. Austin looked at his sister. She raised her eyebrows. Another second passed, and both were still conscious.

"Excellent work, little bro!" Tiffany celebrated.

DarkStone turned on her nephew and screamed, then shoved him to the ground.

Austin adjusted the thrusters, and the *Eagle* cruised right toward the commander and a squadron of Corsairs, who immediately dove in all directions. A resounding scraping sound across the bottom of the ship indicated that they'd taken the roof off DarkStone's command pod.

The trees zipped past them. Austin kept the ship low until the *Eagle* had disappeared from the Corsairs' line of sight and was no longer a target for their weapons.

The grotto was just ahead. Every security light had been turned on. Oliver and Ashley had awoken a hornets' nest.

"Get ready to deploy the ladder!" Austin shouted, "We're going in hot!"

Tiffany unstrapped and took off for the bay.

Tiffany slipped a harness over her shoulders, then locked the safety strap to one of the anchors she'd used for the rope ladder. She tapped the controls to open the floor hatch.

The ship suddenly bucked forward. Tiffany fell to the ground, sliding toward the gap until Austin pulled the nose of the ship back up.

Was he using the ship to create space between the Corsairs and his brother and Ashley?

"Rope ladder!" Oliver called over her mTalk.

Still on the ground, Tiffany kicked her foot. The rope ladder spilled out through the underbelly hatch. She raised her mTalk. "Eochair?'

"In my pack," Ashley said.

The *Eagle* bucked again. Tiffany scrambled to the edge and looked down. Her friend was climbing quickly up the wildly swinging ladder, with Oliver right below. Austin was shifting the ship back and forth, trying to keep Oliver and Ashley from being easy targets.

"Come on!" Tiffany cried.

A purple flash struck the underside of the ship, forcing Tiffany back. But she was ready. She swung her Zinger forward and aimed at the soldiers below.

Whoop! Whoop!

Several Corsairs ducked, but one took a direct hit and crumpled to the ground. She fired again and again.

The remaining Corsairs directed a barrage of fire at her while scattering for cover. She quickly twisted to the side as dozens of stun shots exploded across the top of the cargo bay, showering her in purple sparks.

"Tiffany, keep firing!" Oliver's yell sounded distant against the onslaught of stuns.

She moved to the edge and fired several more stuns. Oliver threw down a small black ball.

Tiffany let the Zinger hang by its shoulder strap as she reached out and took her friend's hand, pulling Ashley through the opening. Together the girls turned their weapons on the Corsairs, laying down a flurry of purple stuns as Oliver fought his way up the last few feet of rope. An orange light had begun flickering across the ground below. A fire?

Oliver's hand gripped the edge of the opening. Tiffany reached for him.

Without warning, the *Eagle* rolled to the side. Oliver's hand disappeared. Tiffany clawed toward the opening to look for him. Had he fallen all the way down?

No. Oliver held tightly to the ladder. His Zinger lay smashed and sparking below him, but he was unharmed. Tiffany and Ashley pulled him into the *Eagle*'s bay as a series of purple zips of light shot through the open door.

Tiffany got to her feet. With a touch of the controls, the hatch began to close.

"To the bridge. We've got to get out of here!" Oliver commanded. The three took the stairs, holding tight to the rails as the ship bucked and shifted.

Austin was either trying to avoid being shot at or working to keep the Corsairs on the defensive. Tiffany couldn't imagine the exterior of the *Eagle* holding up against the firepower of the Corsairs' gun turrets for long.

"What did you throw?" she asked as they ran.

"That large pile of chopped wood. I threw a fireball into it," Oliver said.

4.44

Takedown

Oliver sat in the copilot's seat, leaving his youngest brother at the controls. The *Eagle* was reporting damage all across its sides and belly. The Corsairs had locked their gun systems on the *Eagle* and must have gotten permission to attack, because they were laying down a barrage of rapid fire unlike anything Oliver had experienced before.

"Take us up!" ordered Oliver.

Austin yanked back on the controls. Oliver remembered the first night of the quest and his initial flight to escape the Übel. This time, though, the ship didn't approach a stall or even slow. It increased speed, gaining altitude and powering through.

"Watch out!" yelled Oliver. A missile-lock notification appeared on the console before him.

Austin twisted the controls, and a hazy white contrail zipped past them.

"Again!" Oliver shouted, and Austin twisted the other way. The *Eagle* bucked.

A deafening roar exploded all around. The entire ship shook, and a siren rang out overhead. The screen in front of Oliver filled with warnings and indicators of damage.

The nose dropped forward as the shaking increased.

"We're going down!" yelled Austin. "It's the left wing."

The sky was aglow with purple flashes and sparks.

Oliver had to act. He released himself from his harness. The ship jerked, and Oliver stumbled, bracing himself on the console. He forced himself forward. Wrapping his left arm around an armrest on the pilot's chair, he grabbed the controls with his right.

"I've got this," he said to Austin. The *Eagle* began to roll. "Quick, switch with me!"

Austin unharnessed and dove for the copilot's seat as the ship veered hard right. Oliver lodged himself into the pilot's seat, taking full control of the *Eagle*. He worked the screens and adjusted the thrusters. The ship began to level back out.

"We're near the base camp," Austin said.

Falling back into the hands of Commander DarkStone would be unpleasant. Oliver doubted she'd restrain Drex this time.

More zips of purple blasted the *Eagle* and filled the sky around them. Blue and white sparks erupted from the lights overhead as they shorted out and went black. Red emergency lights flashed on.

Oliver worked the flaps and engines and adjusted the thrusters individually. The *Eagle* began to rotate into a flat spin.

Austin was secure in his chair, watching with interest. "What are you doing?"

"Crashing," Oliver said.

In the Academy, Oliver had learned that certain types of ships could be put in flat spins to slow their descent during a crash landing. Though the *Eagle* didn't match the exact fuselage design he'd trained on, it was close enough. The real trick was using the multidirectional thrusters correctly.

An explosion of white smoke burst from a vent behind the seats. One of the consoles flickered, then went black. Sparks exploded from the right wall of the bridge.

The spin wasn't fast but slow and level. Oliver didn't feel out of control, though the entire cabin around him seemed to be melting down. He knew what he was doing, and he knew Helper was with him.

"Brace yourselves! Seven, six, five . . ."

4.45

Stowaway

"This is my dad," Mason told Rylin.

"Your parents are worried about you, Rylin," Mr. Wikk said, "but they're also proud of you for escaping."

Rylin looked up at him. "I only wanted to help."

"We know, and we think you and Obbin should remain hidden," Mr. Wikk said. "If you're discovered, you'll be taken to your parents, but for now your secret presence might be a powerful tool. I'll tell your parents that you're safe, and if they want to find you, they will."

"Take positions for hyper flight in five minutes," a voice echoed over the loudspeakers.

"We're headed for YelNik Eisle now," Mr. Wikk said. "It sounds like it will be our final destination. All clues suggest that the so-called *Ark* is there."

"Should we try to get back onto the *Raven*?" Rylin asked.

Mr. Wikk thought. "I believe, as do the Übel, that this submersible will be needed to access, pilot, or interact with the *Ark* in some way," he said. "That's why they extracted it and are working feverishly to fix it. When it docks with the *Ark*, you should get off. I won't let you remain hidden if it seems that you won't be reunited with your family."

The princes nodded.

"Boys, it's going to be okay," Mr. Wikk said, and though he was speaking to Obbin and Rylin, Mason took comfort in the words as well.

"Here, take my mTalk," Mr. Wikk said, unstrapping it. "Only use it if Mason sends you a message. Otherwise don't access its functions. The Übel are monitoring it."

"Thank you," Rylin said.

"We'll see you soon," promised Mason.

Cruz was waiting for Mason and his dad as they exited the *Black Lagoon*. "I was about to come and get you," he huffed. "We need to find some seats. Hyper flight."

"We have a few minutes," Mr. Wikk said. "Let's take the lifts to the medic ward."

"I'm to escort you to your cabin," Cruz said.

"My wife was injured. I think I have the right to see if she's okay," Mr. Wikk said sternly.

Cruz grunted. "The captain—"

"The captain's getting chewed out by Zebra Xavier at the moment," Mr. Wikk said.

Cruz seemed to consider that, and Mason's dad pounced on the chance to sway the soldier further. "Who do you think is more valuable to the Supreme Commander: a group of archeologists specializing in locating Ursprung, or a replaceable captain?"

Cruz scratched just above his right eyebrow.

"In fact, the new captain could be you," Mr. Wikk added.

Mason bit his lip, suppressing a laugh. Though he wanted to see his mom, his dad's argument was really overdone. There was no way the soldier would buy it.

"Fine, but after we're in hyper flight," Cruz said.

Mason looked at his dad, impressed.

As they started for the lifts, Mr. Wikk stopped dead in his tracks.

The *Black Widow* sat in the cargo bay. Its bridge pod was crumpled, and several of its extraction arms were missing.

The large bay seemed relatively intact, however, and engineers and soldiers were working around it, focusing on the huge bay doors.

"Cruz, do you know if the McGregors are okay?" Mr. Wikk asked.

Cruz scowled. "The crew and archeologists got a bit knocked around, but I heard no injuries were serious."

"What are they doing now?" Mason asked.

"Removing the artifacts they recovered. They got all the crosses," Cruz said. "Now, let's go. We're running out of time."

As the three hurried across the bay to the lifts, Mason glanced back at each of the damaged ships once more.

Red Cloaks

Branches splintered against the side of the silver ship as it spun through the tops of the trees like a circular saw.

" . . . four, three, two," Oliver counted.

Tiffany and Ashley held hands as the view through the windshield filled with dense, green foliage.

"One . . ."

Tiffany's body jerked, her safety harnesses dug into her shoulders, and her hand lost hold of her friend's. With an ear-splitting metallic rip, the back end of the bridge dropped and slammed against the ground, forcing the front into the air. Her head slammed against the back of the seat.

"Ahhh!" shouted Austin.

The entire bridge of the *Eagle* had just been torn from the rest of the ship.

"Is everyone okay?" Oliver called out. He'd already unharnessed himself and was poised to drop toward Tiffany and Ashley.

"I'm good," Austin said, climbing from his seat. "Oliver, grab my Zinger and pack."

Oliver took the items from underneath the pilot's seat and tossed them one by one to Austin. Austin grabbed Oliver's pack and threw it back to him.

Ashley's pack had stayed on her lap the entire time. Tiffany knew why. It contained the thing they'd worked so hard to retrieve.

"We've got to get out of here," Oliver said. "The ship could explode, and Corsairs will probably be here any second."

A loud creak echoed somewhere outside the ship. Another shower of orange and blue sparks exploded from the ceiling.

"Girls, are you okay?" Oliver asked.

"I'm all right," Ashley said.

"Me too, but my pack is in the surveillance cabin," Tiffany said.

"The what?"

"The locked cabin opened. It was a surveillance room," Tiffany explained.

"The Veritas Nachfolger had eyes on everything," Austin said. "Still do."

A shower of sparks erupted from a shattered console screen.

"We'll talk later," Oliver said. "It looks like there's a gap between the ship and the ground over there."

The two girls moved around their seats, then slid down the sloped floor to the ground. Dirt and branches were tangled with the ripped metal and structural elements of the *Eagle*.

"Careful not to cut yourself," Ashley said.

Ashley was first through the gap, then Tiffany. Austin was next. He dashed away from the ship, his Zinger out and ready to fire as he surveyed the nose and tail of the ship. Tiffany appreciated her youngest brother's readiness. Oliver crawled out last.

The newly created clearing glowed with the flickering light from several small fires in the underbrush. A white glow emanated from underneath the *Eagle*, where several spotlights had turned on; likely they had been set to turn on automatically in the event of a crash. A light at the back of the ship cast eerie shadows into the woods.

"Oliver, my pack has the e-journal in it," Tiffany said.

A hole had been ripped a short way down the side of the ship, leading into the engine room.

"I'll get it. Austin, keep watch. Tiffany and Ashley, have your Zingers ready." Oliver ran for the hole and disappeared inside.

"Tiff, you watch the right flank; Ash, the left. I'll move around to the other side of the wreck," Austin said.

The word *wreck* struck Tiffany oddly. She'd just experienced a crash landing—controlled, yes, but a ship-obliterating crash. She glanced back at the destruction and felt queasy. Her adrenaline was wearing off, the stress of the moment catching up with her. She couldn't look again.

As she turned back toward the woods, her eyes brightened. They were here.

Oliver crawled through the gap, doing his best to avoid being sliced by long slivers of metal. Sparks showered down in spurts, and gases poured out from pipes.

He was on the lower level of the ship. A large section of the corridor wall had buckled in, creating another barrier. If the e-journal weren't in the pack, he'd have already abandoned the mission.

He tapped his mTalk light on and noticed that the screen was cracked. He'd thought the things were indestructible.

He kicked at the wall until he'd bent a gap large enough to squeeze through. The rest of the corridor was fairly clear, with the exception of several unattached power cables that sent out sizzles of blue energy.

He started for the bow stairs. The entrance to the corridor was completely blocked. He rounded back toward the cargo bay and the stairs there.

When he entered the large bay, he saw the cross-shaped containers.

The keys. They couldn't abandon them, but how could they take them with them? The Corsairs would be here any moment. He and the others couldn't hold them off indefinitely. After all that, would the crosses really fall back into their enemies' hands?

Tiffany sighed with relief as three people in red cloaks stepped out from the trees. The first held his hands in the air, a small white bird perched on his shoulder. "We are here to help."

Tiffany didn't hesitate. She recognized the voice, and though she hardly knew him, she felt as connected to the man as if he were her grandparent. She let her Zinger drop and ran toward him, tears beginning to stream down her cheeks. "Brother Samuel!"

The old man hugged her. It was like being held by her father; she felt such security and trust. "My child, everything is going to be just fine."

Sister Dorothy stood beside a man with silvery short-cropped hair and wire-rim glasses.

"Call the others," Brother Sam told her. "Let them know we have the children. We need ten minutes at least."

"Yes, Brother Samuel," Sister Dorothy replied.

"Brother Thomas, secure the perimeter, then meet back here."

"Yes, Brother Samuel." Brother Thomas dashed toward the tail of the fallen *Eagle*.

"Tiffany, you may want to let Miss McGregor know that it's okay to lower her weapon," Brother Sam said.

Tiffany turned. Her friend held the Zinger up but didn't look ready to fire. "Ashley, this is Brother Sam, the man we told you about. He's part of the Veritas Nachfolger."

Ashley slowly lowered the Zinger. Was her reaction one of shock? Distrust?

There was a shout from the other side of the ship.

"Austin!" yelled Tiffany. "Austin, he's with Brother Sam."

"We'd best go to him," Brother Sam said. The small bird hopped into the air and flew up over the broken *Eagle*.

When a man in a red cloak had suddenly dashed into view, Austin's hair-trigger response was to fire first and ask questions later. He knew what Oliver, Tiffany, and Ashley were wearing, and it wasn't red.

By the time Austin realized that he was one of the Veritas Nachfolger, the cloaked man lay crumpled in a heap. A second later, Tiffany, Ashley, and Brother Sam came around the ship.

"Oh, dear," gasped Brother Sam. The man ran toward his friend and kneeled down. A small white bird landed on the unconscious man's chest. "Brother Thomas will be okay, but we're going to have to carry him."

"I can help," Austin offered.

"Yes, I'll need you," Brother Sam said. "Where is Oliver?"

A series of loud pops echoed from the woods as orange flames climbed up the trunk of an old, dead tree.

Oliver had found the surveillance cabin. Most of the equipment was still intact: the screens were lit and video feeds were cycling. The power to the rest of the ship had gone out, so the room clearly had a separate power supply.

Tiffany and Austin hadn't explained what the room contained, but he'd had a pretty good idea. This was how Brother Sam had known where the kids were at all times.

A rumble in the lower level reminded him to get out of the potentially explosive ship. He saw his sister's pack and grabbed it, then opened a weapons cabinet and took out another Zinger.

He headed back to the cargo bay. Instead of going for the hole in the fuselage, he hit an emergency release on the cargo bay door, grabbed the handle, and yanked. A moment later, the large door was open enough for him to get through.

As he squeezed out, he found Tiffany, Austin, Ashley, and two cloaked figures. One was standing; the other was on the ground.

"What's going on?"

"Brother Sam has arrived," Tiffany said.

"And Brother Thomas," Austin added, motioning to the unconscious Veritas Nachfolger.

"Brother Sam, the keys are still in the ship," Oliver said. "They're too large to carry."

Brother Sam nodded and raised his wrist. "Sister Rose, send in the *Phoenix* and the *Falcon*. Prepare for extraction of the crosses. Brother Douglas, we're going to need you to hold off the Corsairs for another fifteen minutes." He looked at Oliver. "Are you okay to go back in?"

"Yes," Oliver said.

"We need to set charges to destroy the command cabin," Brother Sam said. "We can't let the Corsairs or Übel get hold of the information displayed in that room."

"Yes, sir."

"Tiffany and Ashley, would you wait for the others to arrive? When they do, direct them into the bay to get the crosses."

"Of course," Tiffany said.

"Austin, will you go to Sister Dorothy and tell her about Brother Thomas?" Brother Sam asked. "Then watch the perimeter with her. The others should be able to hold off the Corsairs, but one might get through."

"Yes, sir," Austin said.

"Now we'd best go," Brother Sam said. "Come with me, Oliver."

4.47

It's Happening

The shift of the hyper jump was hardly noticeable. Mason, his dad, and Cruz unharnessed from the bench where they'd sat during the countdown.

Cruz's communicator beeped. "Cruz! Do you have the Wikks?"

It was Vedrik. He didn't sound happy.

"Mr. Wikk and his son, yes, sir."

"Bring them up here immediately," Vedrik roared.

"I have my orders," Cruz said. "Let's go."

"Lead the way." Mr. Wikk's quick agreement seemed tactical. He probably wanted to maintain the trust he'd been building with Cruz.

They took a lift, then walked down a familiar corridor with wood-paneled walls and potted plants. A shout came from behind two large wooden doors just before Cruz knocked on them.

"Come in!" ordered Zebra Xavier. "Cruz, wait outside the door."

The Übel leader sat behind a wide desk, Captain Vedrik standing before him, his head lowered. Mason spotted the

333

cabinet labeled ZXDNA. It was partly open, and a red globe with blinking lights was tucked inside.

"Mr. Wikk, the captain was just telling me how he lost nearly two dozen of his comrades," Zebra Xavier said. "Take a seat and tell me the true turn of events."

Captain Vedrik remained standing, his face dark and angry, as Mr. Wikk told of the underground caverns and Saharvic attacks.

"Do you believe that the captain did all he could?" Zebra Xavier asked. "Tell me of his incompetence, and he'll be demoted and sent to the cooler to stay!"

"The captain did what he could, given the situation," Mr. Wikk said. "He sacrificed his men to protect me, my family, and the ship."

Watching Vedrik out of the corner of his eye, Mason saw the slightest twitch in his lip as if a smile had fought to surface. Why *was* his dad helping this guy out so much? Sure, what he'd said was true, but Vedrik had taken Mason's parents captive and set these events into motion. Wasn't his cruelty a good reason for him to be punished?

"Are you telling the truth?" Zebra Xavier asked. "Perhaps you hope that his incompetence will be your key to freedom."

"Sir?" Mason said. "My dad saved the captain from falling out of the ship. We could have escaped, but we didn't."

Zebra Xavier grunted. "Captain Vedrik, if you fail me again, you will not receive such a fair trial. You are dismissed; get out of my sight."

The captain bowed his head. "Yes, sir."

Zebra Xavier leaned back in his chair as the door clicked shut. "Captain Vedrik acquired several crosses from the indigenous people on Cao, but he betrayed them too soon and lost the remaining ones," he said. "Had he been smart, he would have waited until all were secure. Fortunately, the recent extraction the McGregors led—"

"Fortunately?" Mr. Wikk interrupted. "The McGregors were hurt. Next time, someone might be killed."

"Don't lecture me," Zebra Xavier spat. "Risk comes with reward. You of all people know that."

Mason wondered what Zebra Xavier meant. He made it sound like Mr. Wikk had once taken an extraordinary risk.

"As I was saying, we have nine crosses," Zebra Xavier said, calming himself again. "Your benefactor Mr. O'Farrell will have acquired any of the crosses that Archeos may have had, putting all three remaining crosses in the possession of the Corsairs. The submersible from the catacombs appears to have some sort of value, though we are unable to determine if it or the soil inside is the Eochair."

Zebra Xavier slid a device across the desk to Mr. Wikk. It displayed a live image of a massive lake surrounded by a thick forest or jungle. "Captain Ryker's team discovered a large vessel about two hundred feet beneath the surface of an inland sea on YelNik Eisle. We believe it is the *Ark*," he said.

"May I ask what you hope to accomplish through this *Ark*?" Mr. Wikk asked.

Zebra Xavier scowled. "You know the answer."

Mason's dad sighed. "I'm not sure I do, and I don't think you do either."

"You think my goals lead to nothing more than a myth."

Mr. Wikk held up his hand. "These bodies of ours, they weren't designed to last forever. Organs shut down, bones break, muscles weaken, our brains slow."

Though Mason hadn't shared the Truth with his dad, Mr. Wikk seemed to be coming awfully close.

Zebra Xavier shook his head. "The scientist who discovered the cure gave it to his people. We found his exact words: 'And I give unto them eternal life; and they shall never perish.'"

"You've shown me those words. Yes, you have evidence," Mr. Wikk countered. "But what you believe the evidence leads to is fiction."

Fiction? The word struck Mason like a slap to the face. Clearly his dad didn't know the Truth. There was indeed eternal life, just not like the Übel sought.

"It is not fiction," Zebra Xavier said. "My predecessors believed it was possible. Hundreds of years have been spent searching, preparing. I spent nearly a decade with descendants of the Gläubigen."

"Did they have the cure? Did anyone die while you were there?"

Zebra Xavier grunted. "You have me there."

Mason was surprised that Zebra Xavier was allowing Mr. Wikk to challenge him. Was there some respect between them? Though his dad hadn't liked being taken against his will, perhaps he was doing the work he had always done: exploring, discovering, analyzing.

But hadn't he and Mason's mom purposely slowed the Übel's expedition? *Hadn't they?*

"Then they didn't have the answer," Mr. Wikk said. "At least, not the answer you want." *What was he driving at?*

The two men stared at each other.

"It took years to get access to the palace, and several more to become a trusted advisor to the king," Zebra Xavier said. "Only then did I gain access to the library. It was immense. I spent years combing through their books. I discovered maps, clues, history."

"But not how to gain eternal life," Mr. Wikk said. He paused; Zebra Xavier's face was turning purple. "Can I be completely honest with you?"

Zebra Xavier glared. "Aren't you already?"

"You were hiding for those nine years," Mr. Wikk said.

"Hiding?" Zebra Xavier asked, his tone dangerous. "From what?"

"You found the Blauwe Mensen's book," Mr. Wikk said. "You read the words from the artifact in it, and you began to wonder. The book presented you with a choice. You couldn't make up your mind. You were beginning to believe what the Gläubigen believed. If you told your allies what you'd discovered, they'd call you a fool. If you tried to leave Cobalt Gorge without telling them, they'd hunt you down. You acted as though you were still searching, but you were actually hiding. The gorge was the safest place for you."

Mason felt short of breath.

"I've read the book you took from us," Mr. Wikk continued. "I know what it says."

"And yet you refused to help us translate it," Zebra Xavier said.

"We didn't refuse," Mason's dad said. "Vedrik didn't believe we were translating it correctly. He thought it was complete fantasy: a man calming storms, walking on water, feeding thousands with a small amount of food. He feared your wrath if he used the archeologists' valuable time to translate such outlandish stories, so he gave the book to the scientists."

Zebra Xavier scratched his neck.

"But you already knew that," Mason's dad said. "You've let your scientists waste their time so that you wouldn't have to face the truth—the real Truth, the Truth that will set each of us free. Life *can* go on for eternity, but not in the physical realm in which we currently exist."

A sense of utter joy overtook Mason. His dad knew. He believed.

But Zebra Xavier leaped to his feet and pointed at the door. "Get out! Get out now! Cruz!"

Zebra Xavier's reaction didn't surprise Mason. It was clear he had been fighting the urge to silence Elliot Wikk while allowing him to speak. If Zebra Xavier knew what Mason did, why was he fighting it so much? To Mason and his siblings, the Truth had come as a hopeful, joyous relief. To Zebra Xavier, it seemed dangerous.

The door swung open.

"Take these two to Vedrik. Vedrik is not to let them out of his sight!" Zebra Xavier commanded.

4.48

The Key

Two silver ships cruised over the crash site and hovered, their bright white spotlights illuminating the wreckage. Wind whipped around the newly created clearing, and Ashley shouted, "Watch out!" as the burning tree crashed against one of the *Eagle*'s tail fins, tearing it from the ship.

A rope ladder dropped from the *Phoenix*. Four Veritas Nachfolger climbed down it: two women and two men. Two were younger than any of the Veritas Nachfolger Tiffany had encountered before.

"Brother Jostin, get Brother Thomas to the harness," said the first woman. She was probably Tiffany's parents' age.

Brother Jostin was even younger, with olive skin and bangs of dark hair that peeked from under the hood of his cloak. He crossed the clearing and took Brother Thomas under the arms, then dragged him toward a harness that had been lowered from the *Phoenix*.

The other man had a long metal pole across his back that came to a sharp point with a small red crystal at the tip. He lowered goggles over his eyes, swinging the pole around. "Stand back and close your eyes," he warned.

Tiffany and Ashley obeyed. Metal sizzled; Tiffany could feel heat in front of her.

"You can open your eyes," called the man a second later. "Sister Rose, we can proceed."

"Stay there," the first woman, Sister Rose, warned.

The Veritas Nachfolger slipped through the gap between the cargo bay door and frame. The door fell away from the ship, landing with a loud crash. The brother's device had cut through the exterior of the ship like a knife through butter.

Cables lowered from the second ship—the *Falcon*—and were pulled into the *Eagle* one by one. Ashley and Tiffany moved inside as the Veritas Nachfolger attached cables to the cases containing the crosses.

Brother Jostin came beside them. "Is there anything else of value to you on this ship?"

Tiffany shook her head. "I don't think so."

"No," Ashley said, and whispered to Tiffany, "I was never fond of that green jumpsuit."

Brother Jostin smiled and left for the stack of crates at the side of the cargo bay. He opened them and began removing weapons.

"Let's see if we can help," Ashley suggested, and the girls ran to assist.

Back in the control cabin with Oliver, Brother Sam took a couple of totes and a box out of a locker. He quickly piled items from the shelves and drawers into the containers, then set them next to the door.

Brother Samuel handed Oliver several small silver balls. "Place two of these on those lockers. Press the red circle on top; it'll light up once it's activated."

Oliver attached the silver explosives to the lockers containing the remaining robes and other gear. "Don't you want the rest of this stuff?"

Brother Sam shook his head as he placed his own devices. "No time. I've got the important items. We need to get out of here."

Austin stood next to Sister Dorothy as the *Phoenix* and the *Falcon* flew into view.

"It won't be long now," Sister Dorothy said.

"How many of you are there?" asked Austin.

"Just fifty Veritas Nachfolger," she said. "We're the official protectors."

"Why so few?"

"Our task is not an easy one; our lives are dedicated to protecting the Truth. There are many more whom we would call *Gläubigen*, believers."

"Where have you been? Why not rescue us and our parents sooner?"

"We are scattered across the Federation and beyond it. We each have our areas to protect and serve, and Gläubigen to shepherd," Sister Dorothy said. "Only when the Übel destroyed Yth Orod did we pull everyone together. The Übel had gotten close before but eventually lost the trail. Now they have nearly everything they need to find and activate the *Ark*. They will find Ursprung. Too many lives are in danger now."

Something snapped in the woods. Austin and Sister Dorothy raised their weapons. Nothing moved in the tree line ahead.

Whoop! Whoop!

Two streaks of purple zipped from the woods and struck Sister Dorothy. She fell backward with a gasp.

Austin stood in shock.

Whoop!

Austin dove to the ground as purple light zipped past him. He swung his weapon and fired haphazardly into the woods. A splintered branch provided a quick barrier for him to crawl behind.

"Ha! You've never been a good shot, Austin," called Drex's familiar voice. "Give up."

Austin fired several more stuns. He glanced toward Sister Dorothy. She was breathing. He looked at the silver ships that still hovered above, their lights providing the light he needed to see Drex.

Two purple zips blasted the ground, sending a shower of sparks.

Austin fired three more shots of his own and lifted his mTalk. He tapped Oliver's picture, then fired toward Drex. "Oliver, come in."

"Austin, what's going on?"

"I'm pinned down. It's Drex!"

"I'll be right there," Oliver said.

Austin fired again and again. He hoped he could keep Drex stuck behind a tree long enough for Oliver to get there.

"Austin's under fire from Drex," Oliver said, then took off down the corridor. The screen on his mTalk still didn't work, but at least Austin had been able to call him.

Only one cross remained in the cargo bay. Oliver dashed down the stairs, Brother Sam behind him. "Brother Jostin, left flank; Brother Andrew, right."

Oliver didn't stop but rushed into the lower corridor. He moved past the wires and debris. His goal was to fire at Drex from the gap between the bridge and the body of the *Eagle*.

He crawled, twisted, and climbed his way through the tangled wreckage of the corridor. As he reached the jagged opening, he saw his brother. Austin was in the dirt just ahead, tucked behind a large branch.

Oliver held up his weapon, searching the woods for any sign of Drex. A purple glow shot from the right. He didn't have a good angle. Shifting slightly, he could see his target's upper right arm.

He took aim, holding his weapon steady. It was a small target, but it was all he had.

Drex spun to the opposite side and fired again.

Austin ducked.

Drex was completely out of sight now.

Oliver waited, his patience thin but necessary.

A moment later, Drex's arm was in view again.

Oliver fired. The blue streak zipped toward its mark, and Drex crumpled to the ground.

Victory!

4.49

Chow and Shut-Eye

ruz escorted Mason and his dad to a well-lit common room. At least a dozen Übel soldiers milled around; some sat on comfortable-looking benches, some ate, and others cleaned weapons. All of them wore insignia showing that their ranks were higher than frontline soldiers like Cruz.

Cruz marched the Wikks to a rounded silver door at the far end of the room. He knocked, and Vedrik's voice answered. "Who is it?

"Zebra Xavier has sent the Wikks to remain under your supervision."

"Come in."

The cabin was smaller than Zebra Xavier's, but larger than the one Mason's entire family had been sharing. There was a rack of weapons on one wall and a bed to one corner.

Mason followed his dad into the private chamber.

"Take a seat over there," the captain ordered, motioning to some chairs. "We have seven hours until we arrive on YelNik Eisle."

"Captain, may we get some rest?" Mr. Wikk asked. "We haven't stopped since we were in the catacombs."

Vedrik glanced at the device on this wrist. "Cruz, take them back to their cabin."

"Sir, Zebra Xavier ordered them to remain under your supervision," Cruz said respectfully.

Vedrik paused, and Mason wondered if he would disobey the command. Then he stood. "Well, let's go then."

Mason was surprised. Letting the Wikks go forced Vedrik to leave his own quarters, but perhaps making them stay in his own cabin would have felt like an invasion of his personal space.

They marched back toward the lifts.

"Sir, may I be excused?" Cruz said. "I too have not rested or eaten."

"We'll head to the galley first," Vedrik said.

"Captain, might we stop in the medical ward to check on my wife?" Mr. Wikk asked.

"She's in surgery," Vedrik said. "They're repairing damage done to her tendons."

"Why wasn't I made aware?" Mr. Wikk asked.

"I only just learned myself." The captain's voice betrayed him with an apologetic tone, but he quickly recovered. "You are fortunate I told you at all." He glanced at Cruz as if to make sure that the soldier's respect for him had not changed.

The galley was on the deck below. It was filled with perhaps a hundred tables with bench seating. About a third were occupied by soldiers and crew.

They sat at the nearest table. Vedrik touched the center of the table, and menus appeared before each of them. Mason selected a roast beef sandwich, baked potato, and steamed broccoli. He looked through the drinks, but there was no Energen. His favorite fizzy, all-natural drink made him think of his twin. In the end he chose a Limon-H20.

Their food arrived, and they ate in silence. When they had finished, Vedrik dismissed Cruz and led the Wikks back to their cabin.

"Mason, try to get some rest if you can," his dad said, dimming the light in the room.

The captain took a seat on the couch, and Mason took the bed he'd first woken up in. It had been remade with clean linens. Mr. Wikk slipped onto another bunk not far away.

Mason's eyelids were heavy, and his mind was at ease. Sleep came quickly.

4.50

Welcome Sight

The *Phoenix* was a welcome sight to Oliver. He pulled himself up its rope ladder, Ashley and Tiffany climbing just above him. Cables lifted the unconscious Sister Dorothy, equipment salvaged from the *Eagle*, and items from the control cabin. Austin climbed another rope ladder several feet away, while Brother Sam and the remaining Veritas Nachfolger set more explosives across the *Eagle*. The ship was destined to become nothing more than an ashen crater.

Several sky scooters had zipped out of the woods, piloted by the Veritas Nachfolger who had been fending off the Corsairs while the explosives were set. Drex had gotten through somehow, probably by sweeping far outside the perimeters set up between the grotto and the Corsair base camp. The pilots and riders had quickly hoisted the scooters into the hovering ships and climbed to the *Falcon*. Oliver doubted that they had much longer.

Just before Oliver climbed aboard the ship, he saw three more Veritas Nachfolger backing into view from the direction of the grotto. They were firing rapidly into the woods. Four more came from the direction of the Corsair camp. Oliver threw his leg into the ship, and Ashley grabbed his arm and helped him the rest of the way in. Austin was in a second later.

The *Falcon*'s side hatch and small hatch to its cargo bay opened, and two Veritas Nachfolger leaned out, shouldering Zazzer blasters, multibarrel cannons that could lay down a rapid-fire barrage of stuns. They fired into the woods while the retreating men, led by Brother Douglas, climbed the rope ladders into the *Falcon*. Dozens of soldiers dressed in gray body armor charged through the trees. They'd been held off, but not indefinitely.

Hundreds of purple zips shot back from the trees. The *Phoenix*'s belly hatch closed.

Tiffany had a huge smile on her face and a ball of black fur in her arms. She'd been reunited with her cat, Midnight, without a moment's delay. "They want us on the bridge," she said.

In the bridge, the pilot and copilot were preparing for takeoff.

"Course set. We can hyper jump as soon as we're out of the atmosphere," the copilot said.

"Excellent. I want full power dedicated to the takeoff," the pilot said. She tapped the screen on the console. "How long until all brothers and sisters are on board?"

Brother Sam's voice came over the speaker. "Ten seconds."

"Count down," the pilot said to her copilot.

"Ten, nine, eight . . ."

"Take your seats," the pilot said without looking. The kids strapped in.

"Six, five, four, three, two . . ."

"Hatch secure," Brother Sam said over the speaker.

"Set vector to one-hundred eighty degrees," the pilot said.

"Ninety, one twenty, one fifty, one eighty," the copilot said as Oliver watched him work the screen. Oliver was impressed with their thorough communication and the perfection of their teamwork. The ship was now pointing straight into the sky.

A purple flash hit the windshield, but the pilot never flinched. She tapped the screen. "Secure for liftoff." She tapped the screen again, changing the communication. "*Falcon*, this is *Phoenix*. We are ready for planetary exit."

"Roger that," came another voice. "*Falcon* is a go."

"Synchronize launch in three, two, one," the *Phoenix*'s pilot said. She pulled back on the controls as the copilot engaged the thrusters' full power.

An alert blared. "Missile lock. Impact in five, four, three, two . . ."

"Evasive action," called the pilot. She twisted the controls as the engines blasted their full power into the thrusters. The ship jolted forward as the pilot spiraled the ship like a corkscrew.

The spinning stopped. No missile impact. The pilot brought the *Phoenix* out of the twist, and the ship sailed into the night sky, toward the edge of the atmosphere.

Brother Sam stepped onto the bridge, a white bird on his shoulder. "Ready for hyper jump?"

"Coordinates for YelNik Eisle set. Hyper jump in seventy seconds," the pilot said.

"That bird landed on the *Eagle* earlier today," Austin said.

"I sent it to check on you," Brother Sam said, taking a seat next to him.

"It talks?"

"It communicates through tapping its beak on this screen." Brother Sam revealed a one-screened e-journal in a holster under his cloak.

A bird that could investigate situations inconspicuously and report back would be an amazing tactical asset—a literal bird's-eye view. The possibilities buzzed through Austin's mind.

He could probably mount a camera to the bird and send the live video feed to his mTalk. "How do I get one of those birds?"

The old man smiled. "You can take care of this one while we're together."

Austin's eyes widened. "Really?"

"Yes." Brother Sam put his finger in front of the bird, whistled a short tune, and tapped Austin's shoulder. The bird hopped from his shoulder to Austin's.

"Does it have a name?"

"You may give it a name if you like."

"I will," Austin said. "How do I talk to it?"

"Through this device. You can speak your command or type it." Brother Sam removed the single-screened e-journal. "A chip on the bird's skull will create brain waves to communicate with it."

"I can't wait to test that out," Austin said.

"Yes, but wait until after we've entered hyper flight."

Austin felt the all-too-familiar push and pull of the jump.

A moment later, Brother Sam unclipped himself. "We'll be in hyper flight for about six and a half hours. Oliver, Tiffany, Ashley, and Austin, will you join me in the library for a bit? Then you can all get some rest."

The four kids followed him down the corridor and into the *Phoenix*'s once-familiar library. The room had been retrofitted with several large displays and control consoles—a makeshift version of the control cabin on the *Eagle*.

"First, may I have your mTalks?" Brother Sam asked. "We need to ensure that the Corsairs cannot track us. We'll fix them up and remove any applications or components that might send our location to them."

The kids handed their devices to him.

Brother Sam motioned to some chairs by a table. "Take a seat, please. I'll be right back."

He left with the mTalks. Only a few minutes after they'd sat down, Brother Sam returned and took a chair. He lifted up a GlobeX Glowmap, and it activated, floating about three feet above the table.

"YelNik Eisle," he said. The purple disc dissolved. In its place appeared a glowing orb covered in swirls of blue, green, and tan. "This is our destination," he said. "YelNik Eisle has a breathable atmosphere and a tropical climate. It was an ideal new world for the Gläubigen to settle."

Brother Sam pointed to a large body of water on the planet's side. A ridge of mountains created one shoreline. A smaller mountain with a deep basin at its top sat at one side, and a multitude of small rocky islands jutted up from the water.

"The *Ark* is deep within this inland sea," Brother Sam said. "A dozen keyholes surround it, and the twelve crosses must be inserted to release the ship. For this to work, however, we must first turn on the power, which means we must find the thermal generator plant and activate it. The plant's location is known only to the Guardian, so we must first find him."

"The Guardian?" asked Austin.

"Brother Noah, the Veritas Nachfolger who guards the *Ark*," Brother Sam explained. "The Übel may have most of the items they need to release the *Ark*, but they don't have Brother Noah, nor are they aware of their need for him."

"We have three of the keys," Tiffany said, stroking back Midnight's thick black fur. The cat purred loudly.

"We also have the Eochair," Ashley said, taking the small silver box from her pack. She set it on the table beneath the holographic planet.

"We couldn't figure out how to open it, though," Oliver said.

"Based on the records we've been able to preserve, it's our understanding that we won't be able to open it until we've entered the bridge of the *Ark*," Brother Sam said.

"Understanding?" asked Austin.

"The *Ark* landed many centuries ago, and while the Veritas Nachfolger have tried to keep detailed records, information has been lost over time, and some of our tracking systems have failed or degenerated," Brother Sam explained. "Some information was intentionally not passed on."

"What's in it?" asked Ashley.

"We do not know," Brother Sam said. He looked back at the map. "We'll also need to get a submersible to access the *Ark*. The original submersible, the *Black Lagoon*, was stolen from its bunker by the Übel. We sent a team to retrieve it, but they were intercepted and barely escaped. The Corsairs and Saharvics had infiltrated more of the Valley of Shadows than we knew, because several of our surveillance systems had failed."

"But all the pieces will end up on YelNik Eisle," Tiffany said.

"Retrieving what we need shouldn't be hard now that we have the Veritas Nachfolger," Austin said.

Brother Sam smirked. "We don't even need to retrieve it. We simply need the Übel to put the artifacts in place."

"What if they don't know what to do with them?" asked Ashley.

"We're confident that your parents will figure out the clues," Bother Sam said. "Creator gave your parents their skills and diligence; unfortunately, they've been controlled by people who want to misuse their gifts. Only through your parents' persistence have the Übel reached the *Ark*'s resting place." Bother Sam looked as though he were carrying a great weight. "Now, after two thousand years, the soldiers of darkness will find the planet of our origin. We, the Veritas Nachfolger, have failed in our mission."

4.51

Mission

"I understand that our parents are persistent and talented," Ashley said after a moment's silence. "But there's so much to explore. How did they figure it out?"

"Archeos provided many resources, and Phelan O'Farrell and his Corsairs funded your parents generously," Brother Sam said. "Meanwhile, the Übel monitored their progress and discoveries and made sure that your parents had the permissions they needed. Combined, these resources and the recent lifting of the archeological ban allowed them to investigate more abandoned settlements and ruins over the last decade than others had in the century before.

"Hundreds of sites had been off-limits to exploration, so we had been able to monitor all exploration that occurred. Then came the discovery at Dabnis Castle. By the time your parents found the wooden planks, the rubies, and the Book, they had the keys to unlock the first door on the path to Ursprung. We could do little to reverse the course."

"Why not destroy the artifacts?" Austin asked. "Wouldn't that have been the best way to hide the path?"

Brother Sam shook his head. "Our mission is clear. We are to protect the path from darkness, but it is to remain open for the day of great revival."

Brother Sam's tone gave Austin chills. The Übel and Corsairs had repeated their missions in the same way: as if the words were so engrained in their minds that they could think nothing else.

"An awakening is coming, when the Truth will go to the masses," Brother Sam said. "But the Übel have worked so hard to keep us at bay. Whenever they discover our activity, they attack, sometimes wiping out whole settlements and declaring a quarantine to cover their tracks. That's why we have been quiet." Brother Sam looked at Oliver. "Do you recall the vines on Evad?"

"How could I forget?"

"The Übel genetically engineered those vines for accelerated growth rates and carnivorous, aggressive behavior. They planted them on Yth Orod to force the settlers to abandon the settlement. They were forced to flee so quickly that almost everything had to be left behind. Fortunately, the Gläubigen always incorporated clues at the beginning of a new settlement."

"So that's why we found so many items in the ziggurats and observatory," Tiffany said. Midnight meowed, and Tiffany scratched behind her ears. "Did the Übel send the black cats too?"

"Actually, the panthers were brought by us," Brother Sam said. "When the Gläubigen first left Ursprung, many animals were saved, then placed on the planets they settled and set free to become part of the new ecosystem. Along with terraforming a planet to create a breathable atmosphere and plant life, we needed to create a working ecosystem. That required animals."

"The path to the underground chamber, the clues—they'd been placed there before you left?" asked Oliver.

"Yes. When the Gläubigen established new settlements, we always pointed back to the location we'd come from," Brother

Sam explained. "The planet Atin's moon, Aerilyn, also held clues that would have led you to Evad. But sadly Aerilyn was pushed from its orbit and passed into an asteroid belt, becoming uninhabitable for our people. We lost contact with our monitoring systems. The ziggurat on the moon containing the clues has likely been obliterated."

"You said 'our mission,'" Ashley began. "Who gave you the mission to protect this path?"

Brother Sam folded his hands and took a deep breath. "The Veritas Nachfolger were established long ago to protect Ursprung for the Gläubigen's descendants. When the Ark left Ursprung, the planet was in shambles, its atmosphere poisoned, the lands and oceans destroyed. A dark evil was over the world. Our ancestors' lives were in danger. They were unable to live out their beliefs. They were persecuted to the point of death for following the Truth." Brother Sam's voice was soft.

"The Gläubigen pooled their resources. They sent terraforming pods to YelNik Eisle to accelerate the creation of a breathable atmosphere. It took three decades. While they waited, they built a ship large enough to carry all those who followed the Truth."

Brother Sam looked up at the still-glowing holograph of the planet. "YelNik Eisle promised a new start. They took plants, animals, supplies, technology, building materials. In order to protect their new world, the elders of the Gläubigen placed the Ark deep in Assilem Sea. The coordinates to Ursprung were stored only in the ship's navigation system. By hiding the Ark, they hoped to remove the temptation to ever return.

But life in the new world was not easy. Certain materials broke and could not be replaced. Some technologies could not be replicated, nor were certain medicines rediscovered to cure previously treatable illnesses." A grave expression crossed Brother Sam's face. "The people wanted to return to the comforts they'd known, even though they existed in a terribly broken world. Some were prepared to renounce their beliefs just to get their old lives back. When they called for the *Ark* to be restored, the council of elders took drastic measures, fearing a return to the path that had destroyed Ursprung."

"This doesn't sound like freedom," Ashley said.

Brother Sam sighed. "The elders were chosen to protect the people and provide guidance. They knew the truth about Ursprung—a planet so abused that it was dying—and the dangers of the evil that opposed the Truth, those who believed more in themselves than in the Creator. The elders were the ones who found ways to secure the ship, barring anyone who didn't have certain access keys. They built the *Black Lagoon* to access the *Ark*. They had large holding arms placed on the ship, only to be unlocked by the Schlüssel buried in the Valley of Shadows. Then they installed a system that needed keys to activate the ship's propulsion—the Eochair—and a verification key to unlock the ship's navigation separately. They wanted to ensure that future generations would not be able to return to Ursprung easily. They spread keys throughout the twelve settlements so that the Gläubigen could return only if they were united, if they made the decision to return and unlocked the clues as one body. It had to be a challenge so that no one would easily give up new freedom to return to old comforts."

"Why not destroy the *Ark*?" asked Austin.

Brother Sam shook his head. "The elders did not feel it was their right to hide the origin of mankind forever. They left the decision to future councils and assigned the Veritas Nachfolger to maintain the clues and guard them from darkness. We take an oath forbidding us from personally seeking the *Ark*."

Austin thought about the oath that the Blauwe Mensen had had him take. The oaths of protection seemed to be a tradition—perhaps an outdated one, given the circumstances.

"You said there were twelve settlements?" asked Tiffany. "That number shows up everywhere."

"It's an important number to us," Brother Sam said. "The Book says there were twelve tribes of Creator's chosen people.

Rescuer chose twelve followers called disciples. The number seemed important to Creator, so the council used it."

"Are there other Eochair, Schlüssel, verification keys, and submersibles in the other settlements?" Tiffany asked.

"Yes. Some were destroyed, but thankfully some stayed intact," Brother Sam said. "Only once was it necessary for us to remove an endangered clue and hide it elsewhere. We had to place the final remaining verification keys on the *Black Lagoon* in Cao."

"Were Yth Orod and the Cathedral of the Star two of the twelve settlements?" asked Ashley.

"The Cathedral of the Star was, but Yth Orod was established when the Gläubigen started forming new settlements beyond the original twelve."

Brother Sam coughed; when he spoke again his voice carried a remorseful undertone. "That's not the whole story. Others had fled Ursprung as well and established colonies on planets beyond Ursprung's solar system. Over the next two millennia, these colonies and the Gläubigen's were consolidated by the Übel through war, annexation, alliances, and need. The Übel painted a history of peace and prosperity by destroying all mentions of Ursprung, including its coordinates."

"O'Farrell mentioned the conspiracy when we first met him," Oliver said.

"The Übel were threatened by the Truth that we taught and believed. The Gläubigen would not remain quiet, so they banned our beliefs. When we practiced in secret, they put our people in prison. Still, the Gläubigen could not be contained. The Übel began destroying our cities, forcing us to flee or disperse. Entire planets were 'quarantined' so they could attack us. We were imprisoned, killed, or forced into hiding."

"Hold on," Austin started. "Why were they so opposed to your beliefs? Don't they desire eternal life? "

"At the time they were trying to remove what they saw as a threat to peace, prosperity, and stability," Brother Sam said. "Belief in a mystical being was irrational to them. We were considered fanatics who might cause the Empire to meet the same fate as Ursprung. But centuries later, when Übel leadership had all the wealth and power they desired, they realized there was one thing they did not have: the ability to defeat death. Advancements in biology and genetics allowed many to live long, healthy lives without ailment or sickness, but their bodies would still suddenly fail not long after a century of life. That was when they discovered an artifact from the Gläubigen that mentioned 'eternal life' and their quest began."

Other artifacts had been uncovered before, but always they had been destroyed. Still, knowledge of the artifacts remained among the top Übel leadership. Why they saw the artifact in a new light, we don't know. Having driven the Gläubigen into hiding, rewritten mankind's history, and destroyed nearly all the Gläubigen artifacts, the Übel had no way to discover the rest of the artifact or research who had written its words. They took the artifact as confirmation that eternal life was possible. Because the artifact was written on paper from Ursprung, they began searching for Ursprung in hopes they could discover the scientist who they believed had created the death cure." Brother Sam smiled. "You and I know that there is indeed a *cure* to death, made possible by Creator, but the Übel didn't know that. They have been looking for a cure that can be made in a laboratory and dispersed as an anecdote."

"We weren't taught much about the Empire," Tiffany said. "In fact, we were told to refer only to the Federation."

"But the Übel controlled both from the beginning," Oliver said.

"We believe so," Brother Sam said.

Austin sat up straight. "Once the Übel found the artifact, you could have told them about the Truth, right? You could have come forward and showed them?"

Brother Sam's chin rose. "It's not that easy."

"You had the Book," Austin said. Frustration was bubbling inside him. Why had no one told the Übel the Truth or shown them the way? "You could have made copies for the Übel. They could have read about the Truth for themselves."

"My son, it isn't so simple. They thought our beliefs were weak, unscientific. They were entrenched in their search."

"A search for eternal life," Austin said. "You had the answer all along. You had the rest of the text."

Tiffany looked uncomfortable. "Austin, hold on. Let Brother Sam explain." But the old man remained silent.

"Why did you keep it from them?" Austin asked.

Brother Sam seemed to be looking for the right words. "The Veritas Nachfolger are to protect the path from darkness. The Übel are the embodiment of evil."

"Obbin said it didn't matter how bad we've been—Rescuer died for everything we have done and will do," Austin said.

The white bird jumped from his shoulder and flew over to a bookshelf, squawking as it landed. No one spoke. Austin looked at Tiffany, then Ashley, then Oliver.

"We didn't know the Truth; it was entirely new to us," Austin said. "Brother Sam, you told me I had to have faith."

Oliver bristled. "All right, Austin. I think that's good, buddy. We get the point."

"No, I don't think so. How many Übel died without knowing the Truth? How many were searching for eternal life, yet you held on to the secret because of your mission?" Austin realized he was standing, his fists clenched. His words rose up inside him and fired from his tongue. "Perhaps you've been keeping the revival from happening by hiding the Truth. Look how quickly the four of us believed! So many others like us want to know the Truth. Yet you have kept it to yourselves. So have the Blauwe Mensen, hiding in their valley. It's time to stop hiding!"

"Enough!" Oliver leaped to his feet. "This is no way to talk to—"

Brother Sam raised his hand. "Oliver, your brother is right. He has opened my eyes. I am open to his suggestions and deserving of his admonishment."

4.52

Sylvia

"Austin, how do you believe we are hiding?" Brother Sam asked.

Unexpected relief came over Austin, and he and Oliver sat down again. "I don't mean physically," he said, "though maybe the Blauwe Mensen are doing that. It seems that you're hiding behind rules and traditions established by men thousands of years ago."

Brother Sam was listening.

"The elders wanted you to protect the path so that your people would have time for their beliefs to become firmly rooted," Austin said. "They weren't telling you to stop talking about the Truth."

"But the Gläubigen were chased off, imprisoned, or killed for what they believed," Ashley said.

"That was before the Übel began looking for the secret to eternal life," Tiffany said, and Austin knew she had come around to his viewpoint.

"The Übel are dangerous," Oliver said. "They aren't ones to listen. They take what they want and destroy what they don't need."

Austin looked at Brother Sam. "You said I needed to have faith. You should have had faith that Rescuer would protect you and that Helper would give you the words to tell the Übel. Whatever seed you planted before them would grow."

Tears formed in Brother Sam's eyes. "Austin, I've needed to hear your words for so long. Your new, innocent faith has opened my eyes to our failure to share the Truth with others. Thank you."

"There is no need," Austin said. "You were the one who first shared it with me." He hugged Brother Sam, and Brother Sam patted his back.

"Do you think the Veritas Nachfolger should have let the Übel find the *Ark*?" asked Oliver.

"I'm not suggesting they needed to give them the keys to the *Ark*," Austin said, "just the keys to knowing Creator, Rescuer, and Helper. Once they had those, why would they even want to return to Ursprung?"

"Good point," Tiffany said. "We could stop this quest now."

Brother Sam smiled. "I do think the Übel and Corsairs will desire to find Ursprung either way. Even if they weren't seeking eternal life there, the planet's discovery would be significant. Your parents have spent their entire careers searching for the origin of mankind. I doubt they'd want to stop now."

Oliver nodded. "That's true."

"You know, Austin, I'd like to tell you one thing," Brother Sam said. "I don't share it to excuse myself, nor do I share it to boast.

"As you know, Phelan O'Farrell and I are friends—well, we were friends once, for many years. I doubt he regards me as such any longer."

Austin nodded.

"You already know that Phelan is not who he seems to be, but he is much more than you could know. Though we look it, we are not the same age. He is much older than I. In fact, I met him when I was in my late twenties. Even then he looked the age he does now."

"Didn't you say you were sixty when we met you?" asked Tiffany.

Brother Sam nodded.

"So if you met him when you were nearly thirty and he looked the same, he must be like ninety-three," Tiffany said.

"Yes, but just because he looked a certain age when I met him doesn't mean he was. We became friends through his wife, who sought me out and asked me to speak to him. She was in her late eighties when we met."

"So how old is he?" asked Austin.

"I don't know exactly, but over 120."

"Whoa!" Austin said.

"He certainly doesn't appear that old," Tiffany said.

"As the leader of the Corsairs, he probably has extensive biotronic and cybornotic enhancements," Ashley said. "I was on the *Skull* long enough to see a wide variety of work."

"But most of the Corsairs' enhancements and repairs are visible, not covered up," Oliver said.

Brother Sam shook his head. "The Corsairs have a system. The longer you serve, the greater the enhancements that are available to you. Loyalty guarantees improved transformations over time, and Phelan has had extensive work done. But what I wanted to explain is that Phelan and Sylvia were very wealth—"

"Did you say *Sylvia*?" asked Tiffany. "Like his home assistant? And his colonization ship?"

"Yes, those were named for his wife," Brother Sam said. "Sylvia used her wealth to help those who had nothing. Our paths crossed, and we became friends. I shared the Truth with her, and she believed. She was ill and ready to depart from this world, but before she took her last breath, Phelan had her cryogenically frozen."

"That's terrible," said Tiffany.

"It's banned," Oliver said. "Though so are Corsairs."

The most basic form of cryostorage was used to preserve food, as on the *Phoenix*. Back when spaceships had been slower and less advanced, the technology had also been used to put human bodies into hibernation during long intergalactic voyages. But that was cryostasis, not cryogenically freezing. Freezing a human for long-term or permanent storage had been deemed morally unacceptable and made illegal.

"Phelan told me that as a young man he had discovered an artifact that had mentioned eternal life," Brother Sam continued. "He had sold the artifact for wealth, losing the only clue he had to find victory over death. In his mind, the artifact represented a way to save his wife." Brother Sam took a deep breath. "I tried to explain what the words meant, but he would have none of it. He wanted his wife to be well, physically with him, so they could live together forever. He didn't like my interference and told me to leave."

"I'm sorry, Brother Sam," Austin said after a moment's silence.

"No, Austin, I am sorry. You were right. I should have done more to reveal the Truth to others," Brother Sam said. "But not all accept the Truth so easily. Some harden themselves against Him."

"But you two were friendly at your shop," Oliver said.

"Our relationship healed over time, but I never spoke to him about the Truth again," Brother Sam said. "I was waiting for the moment when he would have no other options."

"When he's at death's door?" asked Ashley.

Brother Sam nodded. "I also needed to keep track of what he was doing, since he sought the clues I guarded."

"Thank you for sharing that," Ashley said.

"My pleasure. I realize that this is what we were supposed to be doing," Brother Sam said.

"What happened to the elders?" asked Tiffany.

"Their council disbanded several centuries ago," Brother Sam said. "After the Empire sought to destroy every last Gläubigen, there was no longer a connection among the settlements or followers. They had been scattered like leaves in the wind, most never again to be reunited in their lifetimes. Many, including the Blauwe Mensen, went into hiding. The Veritas Nachfolger focused on protecting the path instead of facilitating unification amongst the Gläubigen. In our view, gathering all the Gläubigen would only lead to danger for our people."

Austin yawned. He was tired from the late-night escape, and it was now the early hours of the morning.

"I agree," said Brother Sam. "Everyone, try to get some rest. If you have more questions, we can continue the conversation later. Oliver, I hope it's okay, but I'm using your cabin. Do you mind sharing with Austin?"

"No, sir," Oliver said.

"Tiffany, your cabin is the same. We assume Ashley will share it with you."

"Just like Bewaldeter," Tiffany said with a smile. Midnight hopped from her lap, staring up at the white bird that had returned to Austin's shoulder. Austin leaned away, putting a bit more distance between the two animals.

"Come on, Midnight, leave Austin's new friend alone," Tiffany said.

The girls left, Midnight padding along behind them. Oliver, Austin, and Brother Sam remained seated.

Oliver pointed to the holograph of YelNik Eisle. "So this is where everything converges, where this whole mess is untangled?"

"Only if we find a way to reveal the Truth to these two groups," Brother Sam said. "Their leaders will fight for their goal with force; they will oppose each other and even us. We must seek to explain and bring peace. I do believe a final showdown is near."

Code

Midnight perched on the edge of the dresser as Tiffany opened the top drawer. In it were two items she'd left before trekking to the Cathedral on Enaid: Zebra Xavier's e-journal device and the laboratory bag holding the glowing red sphere they'd taken from the Hatchery.

She took out Zebra Xavier's device. "Ashley, look at this."

Her friend came over to her. "What is it?"

"Oliver and I found this in Zebra Xavier's study on Re Lyt." Tiffany handed the device to her friend. "We'll probably learn a lot about the Übel with the information in here."

Ashley opened the device and tapped the screen. Nothing happened. She felt along the edges—still nothing. "How do you turn it on?"

Tiffany shrugged. "We hadn't tried yet."

"Yeah, maybe we can use this to figure out the Übel's next moves. We just have to get access to it."

"Austin's good at cracking codes. He might figure it out."

"We can ask Brother Sam too," Ashley said. She peered over Tiffany's shoulder. "What's in the bag?"

Tiffany emptied the contents onto the top of her dresser. The glowing red sphere rolled out.

"Do you know what this is?" Ashley asked, astounded.

"No. You do?"

"We learned about these in Advanced Nano-Helix Genetics," Ashley said.

"I didn't take that course," Tiffany said.

"I know," Ashley said. "It wasn't nearly as fun without you." She leaned toward the sphere. "This is a DNA-Helix NanoVault for storing an editable, pre-mapped version of a living organism's DNA. They're common in genetics labs. It probably contains the DNA of a test creature at the lab. Didn't you mention dinosaurs?"

Tiffany bit her lower lip. "Z X DNA," she said softly, and took a long breath. "Ashley, this is Zebra Xavier's DNA."

"What?"

"The Übel leader, this is his DNA. It was in a chamber labeled ZXDNA." She gasped. "There were bodies inside huge glass cylinders, a dozen at least."

"Clones?" asked Ashley.

"I think so," Tiffany said.

"Human cloning has never worked," Ashley said. "The technology is impossible *and* illegal. We can form genetically identical humans, but replicated babies have lives and traits that are entirely unique. No scientist has transferred memories from a parent clone to a replicated baby."

"Nor should they," Tiffany said. "It would be unfair to force someone to take on another life with no opportunity to have his or her own."

"I remember learning that they even attempted to wipe babies' minds to implant memories, so the babies would have no sense of self." Ashley stopped and looked at her feet. "It's terrible. That's why it was banned."

"The bodies we saw were adult," Tiffany said.

"Adult cloned bodies grow, and their organs work, but there's never brain activity," Ashley said. "Why would they waste their time with them?"

The ideas passing through Tiffany's mind were dark and frightening. "To harvest from them," she said slowly.

Ashley shook her head, backing away from the sphere. "That's illegal. Individual organs can be created, but not entire bodies."

"All I know is what I saw," Tiffany said.

"Tiffany, we need to ask Brother Sam about this. He needs to know what the Übel have been doing."

The girls found Brother Sam in the library.

"Brother Sam," Tiffany said, "may we show you something?" She set the laboratory bag on the counter next to him. "We took this from the Hatchery on Re Lyt. I think it's Zebra Xavier's DNA." She paused. "We also found large cylinders with bodies in them."

Brother Sam nodded slowly, frowning. "I hoped they had abandoned this practice."

"Were they people? Living people?" asked Ashley.

"They were clones created at the adult stage, never to come to life," Brother Sam explained.

"Then why do they have them?" asked Tiffany.

"This sphere is indeed Zebra Xavier's DNA," Brother Sam said. "The Übel have been manipulating his DNA repeatedly in an attempt to unlock the secret to life."

"The secret to life—Creator, Rescuer, and Helper?" Tiffany asked.

"You refer to eternal life. Creator has given our bodies *souls*. Our souls shape our minds, wills, and emotions," Brother Sam said.

"Souls?" Ashley repeated. She shook her head, and Tiffany was worried that this was the tipping point that would send her back to disbelief. "It makes sense why no scientist or technology could ever solve this problem. There was always something missing . . ." Ashley trailed off, and Tiffany reprimanded herself for doubting her always-loyal friend.

Brother Sam smiled. "I'm glad you understand. If only others would realize that there's more." He stood, lifting the laboratory bag. "We should put this in the cryostore. You can see that the red is darkening. That means its coolant is growing low."

"Sir, there's something else." Tiffany held out the device.

Brother Sam's eyes brightened as he took it. "Where did you get this?"

"Re Lyt," she said. "From Zebra Xavier's study."

He held his palm over the screen, and the Übel's skull insignia appeared. Its mouth began to move.

"To whom do I speak?" A deep, gravelly voice from the screen sent chills through Tiffany.

Brother Sam shut the lid immediately. "It is as I feared."

"What—who was that?" asked Tiffany and Ashley in unison.

"I'll explain soon, but for now we'll leave this alone," Brother Sam said. "Get some rest. Thank you for bringing these items to me."

Tiffany wanted to press; she wasn't tired. But she trusted Brother Sam. He'd already explained so much earlier. If he was putting this off until later, he had a reason. "We will," she said. "I just want to get the LibrixCaptex."

Brother Sam pointed to the device, which sat just down the counter from him. "I've been scanning the data in the books you imported. Much of the information was already in our files, but there were a few scattered titles that provide some insight into the Namreg colonies."

"Oh," Tiffany said. Taking the device seemed pointless now. "I was just going to begin searching to see if there was something to help us on the quest."

Brother Sam must have picked up on her disappointment. "I'm sorry," he said. "I don't mean to discourage you. You've been of great help to us on this mission." He looked at her, head tilted, then clicked his tongue. "I have something for you to read," he said. "Follow me."

The girls followed him to Oliver's cabin. He took a black case, set it on his dresser, and opened it. He revealed a book bound in dark blue leather. The pages looked worn. "This is a Bible."

"A what?" asked Tiffany.

"This book—we call it a *Bible*—is the same as the one your parents discovered at Dabnis Castle."

She shook her head. "That one had a crimson cover."

"That was a different copy of the same text," Brother Sam said. "Take it and read it, but get some rest first."

Tiffany nodded. "I will."

As they left, Tiffany looked at the thick book in her hands.

"So this is the book that set all this off," Ashley said.

"I guess it is," Tiffany said.

"I look forward to reading it with you," Ashley said.

The friends smiled and continued on to their cabin.

4.54

YelNik Eisle

Vedrik sat across from Mason and his dad in a storm unit, a large chamber designed to quickly deploy soldiers into action. All the Übel teams were being called to rendezvous on YelNik Eisle, and at least fifty Übel soldiers surrounded them, wearing body armor and helmets. Mason wasn't sure whether their weapons were still set to stun.

How large was the Übel's military?

How long would they be on YelNik Eisle before the *Ark* was ready to launch?

Mason glanced at his dad. What did he know? Was he a follower of the Truth?

"When we land, the three of us will head to the site immediately," Vedrik said. "Your wife will remain at base camp under guard."

"Mason is coming as well?" asked Mr. Wikk.

"Yes," Vedrik said. "His presence will ensure that you cooperate. And Mason, if you attempt to escape, you can rest assured that your parents will suffer."

"After what we did for you on the sub?" Mr. Wikk asked.

Vedrik seemed pale. "After the incident on the sub, I have all the more need to succeed in this mission."

"So we come with you, but what's our objective?" Mr. Wikk asked. "I'm an archeologist, not an engineer. I doubt I'll be much use making the *Ark* work."

"You'd like me to let you go," Vedrik said, "but you're going to remain beside me until we're on Ursprung."

Those had been Zebra Xavier's orders.

Mason looked at the captain, trying to determine whether he was in the mood to talk. He couldn't tell. "What about the three missing crosses? Won't you need those?"

"We've ensured that your friend O'Farrell is aware of the *Ark* and its location on YelNik Eisle," Vedrik said. "He and his Corsair armada will bring the crosses right to us."

"Is that why you need all these troops?" Mason glanced at the heavily armed men around him.

"We must be able to finish off the Corsairs in battle." Vedrik paused. "But we also must fulfill a guarantee. Those who swear allegiance to the Übel are given the guarantee that they will share in the secret to eternal life. All are being recalled from their posts around the Federation so that they may board the *Ark* and travel to Ursprung."

"Does that mean the other leaders of the Übel will be on YelNik Eisle?"

"They will come once the Corsairs are dealt with," Vedrik declared.

"And the Veritas Nachfolger?"

"Who?" asked Vedrik.

"The people in the red cloaks?" Mason asked. If the Übel had a plan for dealing with Brother Sam and the others, he wanted to know.

"Should those people appear, we'll get them," Vedrik growled. "They'll surrender, or we'll drive them off."

"Captain, one more question," Mason said.

"Your son is inquisitive, isn't he?" Vedrik snarled.

Mr. Wikk smiled. "He gets it from his mom."

"Why don't you ever kill anyone?" Mason asked. "You're soldiers. You wear skull patches on your uniforms."

Vedrik's eyes narrowed. Then he smiled slyly. "Death is the disease we're trying to cure. Why would we help it to spread?"

"Don't the Corsairs want eternal life too?" asked Mason.

"They do, but they want it for themselves," Vedrik said.

"And you want to share it?"

Vedrik's eyes darkened. "This secret has been discovered at a great cost. We alone have the right to it. We alone will distribute the cure after we've received our recompense."

Mason looked at his dad, trying to gauge his thoughts, but Elliott Wikk's expression was stony. He understood. The Übel could pretend that their intentions were good. But the bitter truth was that they selfishly wanted the secret so that they could use it as a reward for those who were loyal to them and withhold it from those who didn't submit to their reign. They might not *take* people's lives, but they weren't going to extend the lives of any who opposed them.

"Any more questions, boy?" Vedrik snapped.

Mason knew that meant he'd better not have any.

Escape

Water sprayed through a growing hairline crack in the wall. Soon the fracture would burst open, flooding the interior of *Deep Blue* and drowning her.

Tiffany's seat restraint remained locked, the buckle jammed. Her Oxyverter had fallen from the console and slid across the floor of the submersible, far out of reach.

Purple light blasted across the bubbled windshield. A web of cracks branched out across the glass. Another blast, another explosion of cracks. Beyond circled a school of hungry hammerhead sharks. Tiffany tried to fight her panic, but it was growing too strong. Death was moments away.

"Rescuer, please send help. Please free me from this watery grave."

A bolt burst from its place, ricocheting off the ceiling and just missing her head. Water poured through the hole. The back of the ship was underwater. Water covered her feet.

"Rescuer!" she screamed. "Rescuer!"

Where was He? Why had He not come for her?

The ship suddenly went dark as its power system shorted out.

Where was she going? What had Obbin and Brother Sam said about what came after this world?

Water covered her legs, then her chest.

It rose to her chin. Her breaths were shallow and quick now. This was the end. She took one last breath.

Suddenly, white light made her squint. She was in a room now, shivering but dry. There was frost on the walls. She wore a yellow jumpsuit; her hands were locked in glowing red rings. There were no windows, no bench—nothing but walls, floor, and ceiling.

Darkness fell again, broken with an orange glow. She stood at the end of a precipice. Beneath her raged a torrent of lava. Alone on a small island amid the molten rock, a young man was frantically searching for a way to escape.

"Drex!" Tiffany called out, but no sound came from her mouth. "Drex!"

"Tiffany! Tiffany, wake up!"

Tiffany's eyes shot open.

"Tiffany, are you okay?" Ashley asked.

Tiffany's breathing was labored. She sat up and looked around.

"You were yelling the name of that Corsair," Ashley said.

Tiffany took a deep breath, trying to calm her turbulent emotions. A black shape hopped up on her bed and pressed itself across her. Midnight was trying to comfort her.

"Are you okay?" Ashley asked.

"I think so. I was just having the most awful dream."

"About . . . Drex?"

"Yes."

For a moment they said nothing.

"Well, we should get you some water, and maybe something to eat," Ashley said. "Maybe something with chocolate."

Sitting shirtless on the lower bunk in the twins' cabin, Oliver traced the word *courage* between Austin's shoulder blades in large black letters. He had already used a Scrawler to write *truth* on Austin's right bicep and *untouchable* on his right forearm; on his left bicep, *honor*; on his left forearm, *peace*. This was a tradition, the way of the warrior. Austin was an equal in the fight, and this symbolized his rite of passage. He was no longer a little boy—Oliver's actions said as much.

Stacked across Austin's chest were the words *strength*, *speed*, *perception*, *agility*, *compassion*. *Fearless* was written down his left side; on his right side, *focused*. The words were meant to be reminders in the heat of battle. And Oliver was certainly preparing for a battle.

Oliver had already been nearly eaten by dinosaurs and vines; he'd been electrocuted, almost blown up, shot down in a spaceship; he'd fought in more hand-to-hand scuffles than he cared to recount. Yet anxiety had crept over him as they'd talked to Brother Sam. Through the Empire, the Übel had dominated the fight against the Veritas Nachfolger for the last several centuries. Now that the Corsairs were joining the mix, they'd be facing two heavily armed enemies who were unwilling to listen to the Truth. He'd wakened feeling on edge about the coming battle.

But scrawling these words on Austin relaxed him. He had used the ritual to focus himself before kugel matches back in Bewaldeter. Its familiarity gave him a small dose of peace, and Austin's excitement gave him a boost of camaraderie with his brother.

Austin began to write the words across Oliver.

"Austin, are you ready?" Oliver asked.

"Yeah," Austin said. "I am. This is awesome."

Oliver had been hoping for more after Austin's long speech to Brother Sam, but he didn't press. If Austin was ready, Oliver would leave it at that.

But why was Oliver so unsettled?

There was a knock at the door.

"Come in," Oliver said.

The hatch opened, and Ashley popped her head in. She raised her eyebrows at the sight before her. "Um . . . painting at a time like this?"

"It's a guy thing," Austin said.

Oliver laughed. "No, it's a warrior thing."

Ashley pulled back. "Well, I was just stopping in to let you know that Tiffany and I are headed to the galley. It won't be long until we land."

"Food always sounds good," Austin said.

"We're done here anyway," Oliver said, grabbing his shirt. "Wait a few more minutes to make sure nothing smears."

"I'm not planning on wearing a shirt at all," Austin said. "I want to show those Übel and Corsairs that I'm a warrior. I want them to run when they see me!"

"We're going to need to restrain him," Ashley joked.

Oliver shrugged as Austin took off through the hatch. "You go ahead. I want to go by the bridge and get an update."

"All right." Ashley turned and left.

Oliver closed his eyes and said a brief prayer. "Rescuer, be with us on this mission. Protect us from harm. Help us to find this man, Noah. Most of all, help us to rescue our families."

When he got up, he grabbed his pack and went to the cabin that had been his. His stuff was still in there, but so were a myriad of other things belonging to Brother Sam and the Veritas Nachfolger. He walked to his dresser to find a second change of clothes.

On top of the dresser were books that Speaker Ovon El had given Oliver. Then he remembered: the Speaker had given him a way to contact the Blauwe Mensen via the *Ontdekking*. Oliver had forgotten all about it until now. He wondered if the Speaker was worried, if he'd been waiting for a message.

Oliver lifted his mTalk. The screen had been fixed. He searched for the entry he had made with the ship's serial code, which would also act as the transmission location code. He found the code, 5002-01-TCO-7002-60-NUJ, and transferred it to the communications application.

Oliver knew the Speaker wouldn't be there to pick up the incoming transmission, so he tapped out a message for him to read later. He briefly explained what had happened in the past days. Then he said where they were headed and gave the Speaker the coordinates for the sea on YelNik Eisle. He also told Speaker Ovon El that the Übel would be there too, probably with the Blauwe Mensen royal family. He promised to rescue the royal family if it was at all possible.

He felt bad that he couldn't give a more positive report or provide more detail. But time was short, and he hoped this would be enough to suffice. It was better than no information at all.

Austin found his sister sitting at the table, an H20 and untouched brownie before her. She looked deep in thought. "Hey, sis," he said as he went to the cryostore and plucked out an Energen. "Are you ready?"

"Yeah, as much as can be," Tiffany said.

"Well, Oliver and I are prepared." Austin flexed his muscles, but Tiffany still hadn't looked up. He grunted, gaining his sister's attention.

"What did you do?" she asked with surprise.

"Prepared for battle!"

"Wow, looks like it."

Ashley walked in. "You've seen your brother's work? Oliver looks the same."

Austin smiled, but Tiffany still looked distracted.

"You've got to get it out of your mind," Ashley said. "Let it go."

Austin looked at his sister. "What are you talking about?"

"Oh, nothing," Tiffany said quickly.

"Sis, we can't start hiding things now."

Tiffany bit her lip, her brown eyes glossy.

"It's okay. We're almost there. We're almost to Mom, Dad, and Mason," Austin said. He wasn't sure what had happened, but it must have been pretty bad to make her like this.

Tiffany nodded. Austin didn't push it anymore. He popped back the top of his Energen and guzzled it down. "YEOW! That's what I've needed."

The girls chuckled. At least he could still make his sister laugh.

When Oliver stepped onto the bridge, Brother Sam was pointing to a map displayed on the console. "We'll land there."

"Sir, that's approximately three miles from the Übel cruiser," the copilot said.

"That's fine. Activate cloaking prior to coming out of hyper flight."

"Sir," the pilot said, "one of the generators is still not operating at full capacity."

"We'll be okay," replied Brother Sam. "Notify the *Falcon* of our landing coordinates. Tell them to cloak."

Neither the pilot nor the copilot countered him. Oliver sensed the trust between the three Veritas Nachfolger.

"Is there anything I can do, sir?" He pulled his shirt over his head. The words across his body were finally dry.

Brother Sam turned. "No, son, not until we land. Be sure to eat something. We'll have a bit of a hike ahead of us."

Oliver nodded. "Yes, sir."

As Oliver walked down the corridor, he wondered what would happen when they came against the Übel again. He was ready to fight, but he'd made up his mind to obey Brother Sam, and thus far the Veritas Nachfolger had not been ones for assault—defense, yes, but not assault.

Tiffany still struggled with the feeling that she was supposed to help Drex, yet she had no idea how. Was this a leading from Helper? Was Drex trapped on an island in the middle of a river of fire at that very moment?

Tiffany wanted to ask her brothers, but she knew where they stood when it came to Drex.

Brother Sam entered the galley. "We're just a few minutes from disengaging hyper flight. Gather any gear you need and meet me in the cargo bay." He smiled and left, his red cloak sweeping behind him.

Tiffany grabbed her backpack as she sprang to her feet and hurried after him. "Sir?"

Brother Sam turned. "Yes, Tiffany?"

Tiffany stopped a few feet away. Second thoughts rushed through her mind, but she forced herself forward. Brother Sam was wise. She trusted him to make decisions based on the way of the Truth, not feelings. "I have a question. May I walk with you?"

"Of course. Please do."

They started down the stairs into the cargo bay.

"I had a dream about Drex," she said.

"The Corsair who attended the Academy with your brother?"

"Yes," Tiffany said. Now that she'd seen the control cabin, she finally understood how the Veritas Nachfolger knew so much.

"What was in the dream?"

"At first it was about me. I was in *Deep Blue*, and it was sink . . ." Her voice trailed off as she stepped to the cabin floor.

Sitting before her was *Deep Blue* itself. Fear surged through her at the sight of her family's trusty submersible.

Brother Sam braced her with his arm. "Are you okay?"

She took a breath and nodded, forcing herself to recall the many times *Deep Blue* had been used. It had never failed her parents in all their explorations.

"You were in this ship?"

"Yes, and it was sinking. I was about to drown when suddenly I was in a cold cell, and then . . ."

"Yes, Tiffany?"

"Then there was a river of lava, and alone, stranded on a small island, was Drex."

Brother Sam looked at her, his face unreadable.

"He looked frightened."

Brother Sam nodded slowly. "I have sensed that this young man is hurting. He lashes out because of fear. You've picked up on this as well."

Tiffany understood. "And the submersible? The room?"

"Fears, my daughter. Your fears are manifesting themselves in your dreams," he said. "Drowning, being alone, being without the Truth. Drex's life hangs in the balance. Without the Truth, he will never see heaven."

"Heaven?"

"There is much for you still to learn," Brother Sam said. "We will discuss this further after we have located Brother Noah."

"Yes, of course."

"Tiffany, you may find that Helper is nudging you to make a bold move to rescue this boy by sharing the Truth with him," Brother Sam said, surprising her. "Austin has reminded me that Rescuer's sacrifice is to be shared with all. Don't be foolish with your actions, but trust Him."

"How will I know what to do?"

"Creator is not the author of confusion. You will know."

This wasn't the definitive answer she had sought, yet Tiffany took comfort in the old man's words.

"One minute until hyper flight disengaged," a voice said over the intercom.

"Let's find a secure seat," Brother Sam said.

4.56

The Beach

"Prepare to disembark."

The Übel soldiers grabbed their weapons from overhead racks and lowered their helmet visors.

"Team leaders, go!"

The large door lowered, creating a ramp. Before it was all the way down, the platoon swarmed out, leaping off the end.

Mason stood with his dad and Captain Vedrik until the troops had exited the ship. Then the captain started forward. "Follow me."

Mason squinted as he took in his surroundings.

The *Skull* took up a large swath of wide, sandy beach. Blue water lapped against the shore thirty yards away, and a thick, misty jungle sat just behind the large Übel cruiser.

Several other storm units opened, and more soldiers poured out onto the beach along with rovers, skiffs, and scooters. A few dozen celtyx and wartocks were held in separate phaser-beam enclosures, hissing and roaring at each other. The grisly sounds sent chills up Mason's spine.

Work crews were assembling pods and tents across the beach. Several men deployed turrets and wire mesh fencing, which would probably be electrified. How long they would be at this location? This didn't seem like one of the quick in-and-out missions of the last several days.

The body of water before them was large, though Mason could see a mountain ridge on the opposite shore. The beach and jungle stretched out on either side of the base camp in a gradual curve. Several rocky islands rose up from the water. One looked like an elephant, complete with a trunk made of rock slipping into the water as though it were sucking it up to spray. A single tree sprouted out from the top, with one long, leafy branch angled out over the water. Mason imagined swinging off it.

"Come with me," the captain called, bringing Mason back to reality. The captain headed toward the first black dome that was erected. Two soldiers pounded a pipe into the ground nearby. As the captain pulled back the tent flap, a black flag with the Übel insignia rose over the camp.

"Captain, your diving gear is here," a soldier said as he exited the dome. "The skiff will be ready momentarily."

"The skiff should be ready now!" Vedrik barked.

"Sir, we have a lock on the *Ark*'s location, but the *Black Lagoon* is still delayed in repair," the soldier said.

"That will be all, Lieutenant Sykes," Vedrik growled. "Change, and we'll meet outside," he ordered Mason and his dad.

On a shelf, Mason found a stack of items labeled *M. Wikk*. He stepped into a changing area. He'd been given orange swim shorts, orange flippers, a black dive suit, an Oxyverter, a set of aqua-oculus, an Audiox, and a knife inside a holster.

Mason changed quickly, strapping the knife to his left ankle. Walking in the flippers would be awkward and difficult, so he carried them. When he stepped out of the changing booth, his dad and Vedrik were already changed and waiting for him.

Cruz dashed toward them as they left the pod. "Sir, I need to speak with you."

Vedrik scowled. "What is it?"

"In private, sir," Cruz said, and he and Vedrik pulled farther away.

The sand was burning Mason's bare feet, so he retreated to some shade by the tent. Cruz kept glancing at him as he spoke; it made him nervous. Had they found Rylin and Obbin? Was his mom okay?

Vedrik walked back to Mason and his dad. "Remain here with Cruz," he said and stalked back to the *Skull*.

"Dad, do you think they've found Rylin and Obbin?" Mason asked.

"Possibly. If they have, they'll be reunited with their family."

"Can I ask you a question?" Mason glanced around. "Maybe in the changing pod?"

Mr. Wikk nodded. "Hey, Cruz, it's getting warm in these dive suits. Might we wait inside the pod until the captain returns?"

Cruz looked up at the hot sun. "Yeah, just be ready to come out when the captain returns."

No one else was in the chamber. Mason hoped the canvas exterior was thick enough to muffle their voices. Still, he spoke in a whisper, getting straight to the point. "Dad, when you were talking to Zebra Xavier, you said the secret to eternal life is contained in a book. You said you'd read it. Do you believe it?"

Mr. Wikk smiled. "Son, what we read in that book opened your mom's and my eyes. The book tells of Jesus, a selfless hero who died to save those who had scorned Him."

"Jesus?"

"That's his name," Mr. Wikk said. "What's wrong? A moment ago you looked delighted."

"I thought you believed in Rescuer, the Truth," Mason said.

"I do," Mr. Wikk said. "I've had many conversations with the king of the Blauwe Mensen. We compared our two translations of the book. The stories are the same."

"So you do believe?"

"Yes, and so do the McGregors."

"What you said to Zebra Xavier . . . does he know the Truth as well?"

"He's aware of what the book says, though he tries to hide what he knows from everyone else," Mr. Wikk said. "He's become afraid that his life's mission is for nothing. To give up the mission to follow Jesus, to become a humble servant of those around him . . . I guess it's just too much for him. He's afraid, I think."

"Wow," Mason said. He wasn't exactly sure what he thought of all this.

"I continue to remind Zebra Xavier of a passage from the book: 'O death, where is thy sting? O grave, where is thy victory? The sting of death is sin; and the strength of sin is the law. But thanks be to God, which giveth us the victory through our Lord Jesus Christ.' This gives the solution to the Übel's mission, yet he still won't accept it."

"Who is God?" asked Mason.

"That's another word for Creator."

Cruz opened the flap. "Mr. Wikk, the captain has returned. Please hurry."

Mason looked at his dad, who smiled and promised, "He has us."

Finding Noah

A wall of greenery surrounded the *Phoenix*. Dangling vines crisscrossed branches, stretching and winding until they found the ground; tall green poles stuck up from the jungle floor like prison bars. The hot air was thick with moisture. Droplets formed on Austin's bare chest, yet the words remained solidly marked across his body.

Both the *Phoenix* and the *Falcon* sat cloaked in the clearing. Austin had been the first to disembark, and his new pet—which he'd called Frost—had flown to a perch a short distance away.

Austin whistled to the bird, but it cocked its head and clicked its beak at him.

Oliver stepped out next, a Zinger across his chest, a machete at his waist, and a pack on his back. Austin smiled. His older brother had ditched his shirt, proudly displaying the words Austin had scrawled.

Tiffany and Ashley were next out. They'd changed from Corsair clothing into Tiffany's better-fitting Ultra-Wear shirts and pants in green, gray, and brown. Each had her pack and a Zinger. The girls were really stepping it up. This was the second time they'd taken more powerful weapons. After the battle with the Corsairs on Yl Revaw, Austin knew they wouldn't hesitate to use them.

Brother Sam approached Austin with a machete and Zinger. "Take these. I see you have your pack already." He whistled a short up-down melody and tapped Austin's shoulder. Frost glided to Austin and settled its small talons on his bare shoulder.

"Whistle that tune and tap where you want her to land. She'll be to that spot as quick as she can," Brother Sam said.

"How far of a trek is it to this Noah?" Austin asked.

"Several miles, and the terrain isn't exactly easy," said Brother Sam.

Austin squared his shoulders. "I'm up for it."

"Of that I have no doubt."

Brother Sam left to help several Veritas Nachfolger who were setting up perimeter-monitoring stations. Some would be staying behind, while others would be carrying out other missions. Austin walked over to join Oliver and the two girls' conversation. Tiffany had the e-journal out.

"What are you looking at?" Austin asked.

"The map we found in the observatory," Tiffany said. "It shows several islands called the Washed Stones. According to Mom's journal entries, there were similar maps with the two crosses they found. Each island corresponded to a cross."

"They have the exact same layout as the holograph that Brother Sam showed us," Ashley said. She pointed. "You see these twelve? They make a long oval across the sea. They're all nearly the same size and shape."

Austin peered at the screen. The oval was there, but many other islands dotted the map. If they hadn't been looking for a pattern, they probably wouldn't have found it.

"Clues have been everywhere," Ashley said. "All the pieces to the puzzle are out there, and we're the first to come this far in more than a thousand years."

"We're part of a plan—a plan Creator put into motion," Tiffany said.

"This map is missing the numerals that match the crosses with their islands," Austin pointed out.

"Still, we have a copy of the locations, which might be helpful. We'll know where the Übel have to go to place the crosses," Tiffany said.

Brother Sam and Sister Dorothy came over, cutting the conversation short. Brother Sam turned to Tiffany. "It's my understanding that you have experience piloting *Deep Blue*."

Tiffany straightened, and Brother Sam put his hand on her shoulder. "I'm not asking you to pilot it, just to stay behind and provide assistance to Sister Dorothy if needed. She'll use it to scout out the *Ark* while you monitor her progress from a video feed on the *Phoenix*."

Tiffany seemed relieved. "I won't be going to find Noah?"

"No, but your task is important," Brother Sam said.

"I'm not concerned about that," Tiffany said. "It's just that I'll be separated from Ashley and my brothers again."

"I understand," Brother Sam said. "I assure you, we are taking all precautions to avoid the Übel and Corsairs."

Tiffany nodded, and Ashley put her arm around her. "Do you want me to stay?"

"No, I'll be fine," she said.

Austin felt like he should stay behind, but he wanted to find Noah. The quest sounded a lot more exciting. The conversation moved on, saving him from volunteering.

"You all have your weapons and mTalks?"

The kids all nodded.

"It's essential that we maintain communication silence," Brother Sam said. "Though we have encryption, the Übel and Corsairs are always finding ways to overcome it. We can't risk their locating us. You might still get the Corsairs' feed, but they won't be able to find you."

"Boys, are you sure you don't want to wear shirts?" Brother Sam asked.

"No, sir, not unless I have to," Austin answered. Frost chirped softly.

Oliver shook his head. "If Austin wants to do it, then I will too."

"In that case, you'll need extra of this," Sister Dorothy said. She squirted several small dollops of white cream into everyone's hand. "Put this InsectX on any exposed skin. The climate here lends itself to large and aggressive insect species."

Austin didn't like the sound of that.

"Is everyone ready?" asked Brother Sam.

"Yes, sir," Oliver said. He crossed his Zinger back over his chest.

Austin instantly mimicked him. "Yes, sir." He and his brother were soldiers ready for battle.

"Ashley, would you mind navigating for us?" Brother Sam asked.

"Not at all," Ashley said.

Brother Sam handed her a single-screened tablet with a blue triangle attached to its top. "This will constantly ping the area around us and create a real-time map for us. Our destination is marked with the flashing yellow target. This green arrow will always point toward it."

Ashley nodded.

"Oliver, you take the lead at fifteen paces," Brother Sam said. "I'll guard the rear fifteen paces back. Austin, you're responsible for guarding Ashley while she navigates. Stay with her at all times. If we are overtaken, destroy the device. We mustn't let the Übel or Corsairs get hold of Brother Noah's location."

"That way," Ashley said, and she pointed into the maze of light-green poles.

Tiffany followed Sister Dorothy into the *Phoenix*'s bay. *Deep Blue* was suspended by four metal arms in the center of the bay, just over the ship's belly doors.

"The ship will remain cloaked," Sister Dorothy said. "We'll fly over the sea, I'll board *Deep Blue*, and we'll launch it directly from the bay."

That meant the submersible would be dropped through the door into the water. Tiffany was relieved that she wouldn't be piloting the craft; a fall like that was not something she wanted to experience.

"We've set up a communications suite," Sister Dorothy explained. "You can monitor my progress from it. We'll be in constant communication so I can get assistance from you as needed."

"Don't the Veritas Nachfolger have a submersible?" Tiffany didn't want to sound disrespectful, but she was curious. How come an organization as resourceful as the Veritas Nachfolger required the use of a modest sub like *Deep Blue*?

"Ours hasn't arrived yet, and we need to have eyes on what's happening down there right away," Sister Dorothy responded. "The Übel are already there, and the Corsairs will arrive any moment."

"Noah doesn't have a sub?"

"No. Only the *Black Lagoon* can dock with the *Ark* without setting off a myriad of disabling security measures. Leaving a submersible in the vicinity of the sea might have suggested that something was hidden beneath its surface."

That made sense to Tiffany.

"You've had experience with *Deep Blue*, and although I don't foresee any issues, it'll be better to have you overhead, just in case."

"The *Phoenix* will hover over the sea?"

"Yes, the ship will stay close in case I need to be extracted in an emergency. It's important that the Übel not capture one of us." Sister Dorothy stared at Tiffany. "The stakes have never been higher. I know where I will go if I perish, but many of the soldiers we fight against do not."

That hit Tiffany harder than she expected. She'd discovered the Truth just days ago, and still her parents didn't know. What if something happened to them? Again she thought about Drex. Why he kept passing into her thoughts, she wasn't sure. Still, the dream had been so vivid. It was humbling that Sister Dorothy was prepared to lose her life in an effort to protect others without the Truth. Had Brother Sam told Sister Dorothy what Austin had said? Or had she just not had the opportunity to share the Truth with the Übel herself yet? The kids had met her in the depths of Enaid, where she had been actively serving others.

"Sister Dorothy, are we ready?" a voice asked over the mTalk on her wrist.

"We're ready."

Oliver gripped the Zinger, ready to fire at a moment's notice. Ashley hadn't reported any threats; still, he was ready. He felt like he was walking on a sponge: the jungle floor was thick with dense mulch that had accumulated for years and was slowly decaying. It silenced every footfall.

Brother Sam had called the stalks *bamboo*. They formed a nearly impenetrable forest. The poles were close together and too strong to be cut down with a swipe of a machete. The group was forced to weave through them. Thankfully, Sister Dorothy's cream was working. Oliver had stopped keeping track of how many giant bugs he'd seen. Swarms of the insects, three to four inches in length, buzzed by. He could only assume that the cream was warding them off.

A few times Brother Sam had brought the party to a stop, waiting and listening. Once he instructed Austin to order Frost to fly ahead. Austin spoke instructions into his device, and the bird flew off in obedience. She didn't report any danger upon her return, so they continued.

About a mile later, Brother Sam suddenly motioned for everyone to crouch. He pressed his finger to his lips. Oliver heard the eerie, familiar growl of a black cat creature. They waited.

A moment later, a large panther charged toward them.

Oliver fired, as did Austin and Brother Sam, but the cat was quick and dashed back into the tight stalks of bamboo. A half-dozen growls erupted in an unbroken perimeter.

"It's an entire pack of them," Austin said.

"They've surrounded us," Ashley said.

"Quick! Into that cluster of bamboo," Oliver ordered. He swung his Zinger side to side, searching for a target.

Ashley slid sideways into the cluster. Austin stood with his weapon ready. Brother Sam was now scouting the area behind them.

"Austin, you next," Oliver said once Ashley was fully inside the protective ring of bamboo. His younger brother obeyed.

"Oliver, watch the branches above," Brother Sam warned.

A branch nearby shook. Oliver looked up and fired just as a panther dashed along a branch overhead and leaped at him. The shot hit the creature on the underside, and it fell to the ground in an unconscious heap. The attack was too close for comfort.

"Come on!" shouted Austin.

As Oliver turned to squeeze through, he saw a panther above Brother Sam and another dashing toward him on the ground. The old man was aiming low, so Oliver aimed at the one up high.

Both men fired at the same time, and both panthers crumpled to the ground unconscious.

400 | FINDING NOAH

"Brother Sam, hurry!" called Oliver. The man's red cloak swirled as he darted to the bamboo enclosure. Oliver pushed through as more panthers appeared. How many were there now?

Another charged Brother Sam, but Austin and Oliver fired at it, stopping it in its tracks.

A moment later, Brother Sam was safe inside the wall of bamboo. Though there were gaps, none was large enough for a panther to fit through, and no branches crossed directly overheard.

They were trapped.

4.58

Into the Water

Waves rolled in, splashing across the sandy beach. The bright white sun glared in the sky overhead. Mason couldn't imagine that the waters of the vast sea ahead of him were as warm as the water of Aqua Cathedral, despite the tropical surroundings.

Mason and his dad had stepped out of the pod just as Mason's mom came out of a large medical pod. Her injured arm was rewrapped in a fresh sling. Mason dashed toward her and carefully embraced her. "Mom, are you okay?"

She gave a half smile as she hugged him back. "I'll be fine. A broken bone, but the Nano-injectors have already started working. I'll be as good as new in a few hours."

"You aren't coming with us?" Mason asked.

"No, she's not," Vedrik said, surprising Mason with his presence. He stood a dozen feet away, glaring.

Mr. Wikk kissed his wife's forehead. "I love you, honey."

"I love you," she returned. "Be safe, and take care of Mason."

"This guy? He's proved that he's pretty good at looking out for himself."

Mason swelled with pride, his cheeks flushed.

"Enough. We have a mission," Vedrik said. "We need to get moving. The Corsairs are on the move and will likely be here soon."

"Should you be out on the water when they arrive?" Mrs. Wikk asked.

"I am not intimidated by these pirates, nor should you be. You're under the protection of the fiercest combat force in the universe," Vedrik boasted.

The word *protection* seemed at odds with the threats the captain had been making.

"Sir, we're ready," called the deluxe scooter pilot from his craft at the shoreline.

"Let's go," Vedrik barked.

Mason hugged his mom one last time. He followed his dad and the captain to the skiff.

Five Übel soldiers were already on the ship—two at turrets, the others in a seat reverse from the pilot and copilot. Mason took a seat beside his dad just as the craft shot forward. He looked up at Vedrik. The scar across his face stood out against his pale skin.

Mason craned his neck to look at his mom as the scooter turned and shot out across the water. He watched until she disappeared in the distance. The *Skull* was still visible, but it too had grown smaller. A warm, salty breeze whipped through his hair. The sun was high in the azure sky.

"The communication functions on your mTalks have been restored," Vedrik said. "But any attempt to escape will be punished."

Mason nodded.

"Thanks," his dad said. "What urgent situation called you away?"

"Apparently the Blauwe Mensen are more advanced than we believed," Vedrik said. "Believe it or not, a spaceship left the valley about fifteen minutes ago and was captured by the federal frigate we had blockading Jahr des Eises."

"The Blauwe Mensen had a spacecraft?" Mr. Wikk glanced at Mason. Mason hoped he wouldn't have to answer.

"The king believes it may be his son, the crown prince. We're still trying to confirm with the captain of the frigate."

"So what will the Federation do?" Mason asked.

"Bring it here, of course," Vedrik answered. "Zebra Xavier has called the Federation's chancellor already. The federal frigate will deliver the *Ontdekking* to us."

"Why bring the ship here?" asked Mason.

Vedrik frowned. "As bad as you may believe us to be, we will reunite the crown prince with his family before we travel light-years out of reach of any other ship in the Federation."

"Maybe you just want to have potential clues in your possession," Mr. Wikk countered, "and not allow them to fall into someone else's hands."

Vedrik gave a half chuckle.

If the Federation brought the Blauwe Mensen to the Übel, it put more people on Mason's side. But the Federation was more corrupt than he had imagined.

"We're closing in on the colonization ship," the pilot interrupted. Two idle skiffs hovered over the water. Soldiers sat motionless as turrets aimed at the sky.

"Captain Ryker's team and Lieutenant Jaxon's team have begun searching for the docking site," the copilot added.

Vedrik frowned at the device on his wrist, reading an update. He slammed his fist against the seat. "Incompetence! Your friends Skalker and Hixby have failed to get an important artifact from Yl Revaw."

"Skalker? Hixby?" Mason's dad sounded shocked.

"I know you thought they were working with you, but they were the first to take our payout. Only they don't have the resourcefulness or the instincts you have." Vedrik cracked his knuckles. "It should have been a quick job—O'Farrell thought they were working for him the whole time, especially after they called for his assistance on Cao. But that was where they first failed me. They allowed three of the crosses to be captured by the Corsairs instead of hiding them so I could get them later."

"And they failed to get the artifact on Yl Revaw too?" Mason asked.

"Yes. You can be proud of your siblings for that. They stole the artifact from underneath Hixby and Skalker's noses, then delivered it to the red cloaks and escaped."

Mason smiled brightly, and Mr. Wikk had a huge grin across his face. He nodded at Mason.

Vedrik rubbed his chin. "Oh, I don't mind you celebrating your family's success. If it's in their hands, I can use you as leverage to get it back. It's the crosses under the Corsairs' control that we will have to take by force."

"So my brothers and sister are okay?" Mason asked.

"Yes, and the McGregor girl, Ashley," Vedrik said.

"Do the McGregors and my wife know?" asked Mr. Wikk.

Vedrik nodded. "They will be informed."

"Do you know where the red cloaks are headed?" asked Mr. Wikk.

"We expect here, but we have no way of knowing for certain. We don't have anyone inside their organization."

Mason was happy to hear that his siblings were okay, but even happier that they were with the Veritas Nachfolger. They were safe if they were with Brother Sam's people. His dad's mood had also brightened considerably.

"Captain, how long until the *Black Lagoon* is ready?" Mason's dad asked.

Vedrik glared out over the sea. "The engineering team can't give me a time."

"What was the delay?" Mason asked. The captain's patience was thin. Perhaps he could distract Vedrik from his real mission, force him off-balance so he would make mistakes. If the right opportunity came, they could turn the tables on Vedrik.

"The ship's exterior material resisted our engineers' patches. They're sending a shuttle to retrieve the front section from the hole they pulled the *Black Lagoon* from," Vedrik said.

The deluxe scooter slowed to a stop. Six black egg-shaped devices splashed into the water as an Übel soldier unlocked them from the side of the craft. They had handles arcing out from them like oxen horns.

"Captain, Aqua-Zips deployed," the soldier said with a salute.

"You're both with me; you three follow at fifty," Captain Vedrik said. He glared at Mr. Wikk, then at Mason. "Either of you try anything, and you'll find I have no further use for you."

Mason's dad tapped his shoulder. "Son, stay close to me."

"What are those?" Mason asked as the soldiers took spiraled blue devices from a weapon locker.

"SwirlZaps," the soldier replied.

The soldier next to him grunted as he activated the weapon. "We're going to need them, too."

A fierce fight with the Corsairs was sure to come.

Mason pressed an aqua-oculus lens into each eye. His parents had used them on expeditions before. The small lenses made it easy to see underwater. They also contained sensors that monitored the wearer's vitals and provided a plethora of information about their surroundings. If the Corsairs arrived, they'd be highlighted on the lenses as unknown targets until they were identified. Next, Mason stuck the Audiox in his left ear so he'd be able to hear communication from the others. The Oxyverter contained a small communications mic. Mason's knife was already holstered on his leg.

Mason looked at his dad and nodded. Vedrik motioned to Mr. Wikk, and Mason's dad jumped into the water. Mason was next, followed by Vedrik.

Each took an Aqua-Zip in hand.

"Follow me." Vedrik dipped below the surface of the water.

Mason dunked his head and pressed the trigger on the Aqua-Zip's handle; something within whirled, vibrating softly. The Aqua-Zip moved forward, pulling Mason smoothly through the water. A green arrow appeared on his aqua-oculus: *Ark 1200 feet.*

A reef covered in bright coral lay directly ahead. Vedrik turned, and they slid deeper into the sea. An opening in the reef appeared, and they followed through it. The reef dropped away, and a dark depth lay below.

Mason paused as long green tendrils twisted up from below. No warnings appeared on his aqua-oculus. Still, the green arrow pointed directly into the swarm of tendrils, and he wanted to know. "Sir, what are those?"

Vedrik's words came over the Audiox. "Sea grass. Not a threat unless you get tangled in it."

An underwater ridge ahead took on more shape; the green arrow was pointing directly at it. Soon the long-sought *Ark* lay before him. The ship was larger than he had imagined. How would something this immense ever rise out of the watery bed it lay in?

"Captain, incoming!" The warning came over the Audiox.

Mason twisted to look back at the soldiers. His aqua-oculus lit up with a dozen red Xs, each labeled *Unidentified Creature.* Most were fairly close—a thousand feet away or less. Mason couldn't make them out, but they were some sort of under-water beast.

"Take care of them," said the captain. "Wikks, we will continue to the *Ark.*"

The three Übel escorts stopped their Aqua-Zips and turned, each slipping their SwirlZaps from their straps and holding them out before them.

"In range in thirty seconds. Fire on my count," Lieutenant Sykes said.

"Come on, Mason," his dad said. Anxiety flooded Mason as he noticed the sizeable gap between him and his dad. He had stopped, but the two men had continued cruising forward on their Aqua-Zips.

Mason accelerated.

"Five, four, three, two, one."

Mason craned his neck to look, not wanting to fall farther behind. The water flashed in pulses of light behind him, but he couldn't see the soldiers or their targets.

Mason focused on reaching his dad and the captain. His dad slowed as he neared the forest of sea grass and waited.

"We're going through," Vedrik said.

"Mason, stay right behind me," his dad said. "At the first sign that you're becoming tangled, stop and don't move. Take your knife and cut yourself free. The more you move, the more you'll become ensnared."

"Okay."

"Captain, one got past!" Lieutenant Sykes shouted over the Audiox.

The captain and his dad were staring behind Mason. He accidentally released the Aqua-Zip as he twisted to see.

A massive silver shark with a hammer-shaped head surged toward him, closing faster than Mason could have imagined. Streaks of green light shot through the water, but none hit their mark, though one nearly hit Mason. He turned to reach for the Aqua-Zip, but it had coasted out of reach.

Mason swam. His already labored breaths increased; his heart beat out of his chest. Every inch of his body tingled; he knew the beast was close.

Mason's dad cruised toward him; Vedrik hadn't moved. This was it.

Mason turned. The shark's gaping mouth of jagged, razor teeth opened wide enough to swallow him whole.

Mason's heart stopped. After all they'd been through, all the moments he could have been killed, he'd never have expected it to end this way. Hadn't Helper been with him so far? "Rescuer?" he murmured.

Everything seemed to slow as the gaping jaws of the hammerhead neared.

Bwoof! Bwoof! Bwoof!

Several blasts of green light exploded with circular pulses as green streaks zipped over his shoulder and hit the shark's head. Mason rolled backward, head over feet, as the concussive bursts of water hit him. The shark dived sharply, and its lengthy hulk of a body swept past just beneath him. The shots had not only stopped the creature, but also deflected its speeding maglev momentum. The massive shark sank into the deep bed of sea grass.

Mason turned back; Vedrik held a weapon in his hand. He'd been the one to stop the shark's attack. For the first time, Mason was thankful to the captain.

"Sir, the swarm has turned." The soldier's voice hinted nervousness.

"How did you let one past? You had one job."

"Sir, there were fifteen."

"Baker! You're in charge. Sykes, you'll get your punishment when we return," Vedrik said. "Now catch up to us. We are nearly there."

4.59

Search for Noah

Austin stared at the panthers circling the cluster of bamboo. "Should we just start firing?"

"No, I've got something else," Brother Sam said. "The more of these creatures roaming the jungle, the better. They'll distract the Übel and Corsairs." Brother Sam pulled out a blue glass pyramid. "Close your eyes."

Austin did. First there was no sound, then a chorus of frightened howling and branches breaking.

"It's safe to look," Brother Sam said.

"Flash bang?" asked Oliver.

"A frequency bang. I set it to the right noise frequency so it would affect the cats and not us," Brother Sam said. "It also flashes a blinding light."

"Won't they just come back?" asked Ashley.

Brother Sam shook his head. "They should stay away from us for a while." Brother Sam squeezed out through the protective bamboo, followed by Oliver, Austin, and Ashley.

Ashley pointed to the left, and they proceeded again.

The bamboo forest thinned. They were soon walking among thick trees with wide networks of branches. The trunks were at least ten feet across. Their canopy blotted out the sun so much that the party turned on their mTalk lights. For the most part, the forest floor was wide open. The larger trees were between thirty and forty feet apart, their thick branches interlocking and weaving among each other high above. The ground was covered with dry leaves and a few ferns; otherwise, it was barren.

Their progress increased significantly now that their path was more open, but they were more exposed. If the panthers came again, Austin wasn't sure how they'd climb the large trees. Their trunks were too wide to bear-hug and shimmy up; their branches were too far from the ground.

"There's a wall ahead, or a cliff face," Oliver said.

"The arrow is still pointing straight," Ashley said.

"Keep going. We're going to have to climb," Brother Sam said.

The cliff face stretched side to side as far as Austin could see. It reminded him of the ridge on Evad, except it wasn't as thickly covered in plants.

"Is there a tunnel?" asked Austin.

"No," Brother Sam said as he removed a grappling gun from his pack.

"We used one of those on Evad," Austin said.

"Then I won't have to explain much," Brother Sam said.

"I haven't used one," Ashley admitted.

"Have you ever repelled or climbed a rope?" asked Oliver.

"Yes," Ashley said.

"Then you'll do fine," Oliver said. Austin caught Oliver smile at her. "I'll be right behind you."

"I will take the lead," Brother Sam said. "Austin, bring up the end."

He would be last to climb. Austin looked around at the forest. Were the panthers near?

Brother Sam aimed the gun though the canopy. He fired, and the grapple shot into the air and did not return. The old man gave it a tug, then a harder one. "Secure. Oliver, you give it a try."

Oliver stepped over and jumped up, planting his feet against the stone and putting all his weight on the line. He yanked on it while remaining suspended a few feet above the ground. "Locked."

"Then let's go." Brother Sam and Oliver switched places. Brother Sam began his ascent and disappeared into the leaves about twenty feet up the side of the cliff. "Go ahead and start, Ashley," Brother Sam called down.

Ashley took the line with gloved hands and started up the cliff.

Austin kept his Zinger at the ready. No sign of any creatures yet. A soft mist was moving across the forest floor.

When Ashley was about ten feet up, Oliver started after her. "Austin, once I am through the underside of the canopy, start up."

Austin nodded. He wasn't going to wait any longer than he had to.

When it was his turn to climb, there had still been no sign of any panthers, so he slung the weapon across his chest and took the line. He pulled himself up into the branches and leaves. They tickled his bare chest and back so much that he had to fight to keep hold of the line. He'd not anticipated being tickled by leaves when he'd made his decision to go shirtless. He supposed it wasn't possible to anticipate everything.

He was relieved when he passed out of the leaves and into the open sky. He looked out over the vast treetops. In the far distance he could see the top portion of the *Skull*. He could also see the sea and several small craft whizzing across its surface about half a mile away.

There wasn't much farther to go. His brother had just reached the top, but where were Ashley and Brother Sam? Suddenly Oliver disappeared from sight. Panic struck Austin as he sped up his ascent.

"Oliver!" he called, but there was no reply.

Austin heard buzzing and looked over his shoulder. An Übel fighter was hovering over the sea. As Austin reached the top, Oliver and Brother Sam pulled him down into a small crevice.

"Stay still," Oliver warned.

"The fighter?" Austin asked.

Brother Sam nodded.

A moment later, the buzzing dissipated.

"It's gone," Ashley said. "I was sure it saw us when it turned and hovered facing our direction."

"Better cautious than not," Brother Sam said. "Let's hurry and get down into the basin."

"I didn't see anything down there," Oliver said.

"We are in the right place. See this?" Brother Sam pointed to a cross etched into the stone.

"The sign of Truth," Ashley said.

Austin looked at the perfectly symmetrical carving. "This is where the Guardian is?" he asked.

4.60

Sea Grass

Mason moved slowly, hardly pressing the Aqua-Zip's accelerator. He was afraid of being entangled in the sea grass, an event that would surely set off his claustrophobia and make him panic.

The long tendrils of green swayed in the underwater current, waving back and forth. Vedrik was still in the lead, with Mr. Wikk just feet ahead of Mason. He constantly looked back at his son, making sure he was all right.

"I'm okay, Dad," Mason said into his Oxyverter.

"Okay, bud," Mr. Wikk said. "Just keep on my tail."

There hadn't been any more alerts for any other creatures or enemies that might be lurking in the depths of the sea. Yet his dad was keeping a closer eye on him now.

The sea grass thinned and cleared. The *Ark* came into full view. Two teams of Übel divers were already onsite. Most of the sea grass closest to the *Ark* had been cut away, and huge lights had been set up, shining into the *Ark* through portholes, windows, and a massive glass dome atop the ship. Though the lights were external, the *Ark* seemed to glow with light from the inside.

Vedrik's voice hissed across the Audiox. "Lieutenant Jaxon, report."

A second passed.

"Sir, we have located the docking port. There is no clear mechanism to cyber hack," Jaxon said. "Based on the engineers' assessment, the docking collar on the *Black Lagoon* is of the same circumference as the port."

"Other entry points?" Vedrik asked.

"Negative, sir," Jaxon admitted. "We have placed Orbstrobes across the ship at locations for possible entry, but so far it's primarily windows and a few bay doors. Any attempt at forcing entrance could flood the ship. It does not appear to have been initially built for underwater access."

Mr. Wikk, Mason, and the captain continued to cruise toward the *Ark*. A black submersible was busily mowing the sea grass surrounding the *Ark*, revealing an arched cradle that the large ship sat in. Twelve arms arched up from the base, six on either side of the ship. Two other black submersibles searched the *Ark* with spotlights. Divers scoured the ship and appeared to be setting up weapon stations across the *Ark*'s surface. The ship was immense.

"I'm bringing Wikk and his son to look over the port and see if we're missing anything," Captain Vedrik said.

"Yes, sir," Jaxon replied. "Port location sent to you."

The ship grew in size, soon filling Mason's vision. It struck him that this ship had been built at least two millennia ago, if not more. Had people in the past really been able to build a ship capable of crossing galaxies? Of course, he knew the answer: the proof sat right before him. It made it all the more clear how hard the Übel had worked to destroy the Gläubigen and cover up their history.

The docking port was indeed the size and shape of the port Mason had seen inside the *Black Lagoon*. The submersible surely had been built for this purpose. The fact that it had been hidden so far from the *Ark* fit the tradition of the

Veritas Nachfolger's requiring seekers to follow a hidden path to the *Ark*. Yet it was curious that none of the clues they had uncovered had mentioned the *Black Lagoon*. Only the Übel scientists' observations and assumptions had caused them to investigate the chamber. There had been mention of an artifact called the Eochair, but no clues to its location, and Mason wasn't convinced that the *Black Lagoon* was the Eochair.

Mason reached out and touched the surface of the ship. It was smooth and sleek under his hand. Surprisingly, no plankton or other sea life had clung to the surface of the ship. Further, there was no sign of aging or water deterioration on the craft.

"What do you see?" Vedrik asked Mr. Wikk.

Mason's dad rubbed his hand across the edge of the docking port. He placed his ear against the door. He knocked. Next, he pressed both hands against it.

"It's thick," he said.

"Well, aren't you observant," Vedrik sneered.

"How long until the *Black Lagoon* repairs are complete?" asked Mr. Wikk. Mason was sure that the question was meant to irk Vedrik for his sarcasm. It struck him that they were deep underwater and having a normal conversation as if they were standing on the beach.

"Still no update on its status," Vedrik said with a glance at the device on his wrist.

"Then we might as well go back and wait at the *Skull*," Mr. Wikk said.

"Sir," Lieutenant Jaxon interrupted. "We could use the archeologist's expertise to review the symbols etched on the twelve cradle arms."

"Right. Let's start at the front of the ship," Vedrik said, and the lieutenant led them deeper through the sea.

The symbol *II* was etched into the cradle before them; Mason recognized it immediately. Tiffany had called these *roman numerals*. Mason tried to recall his and his sister's con-

416 | SEA GRASS

versation. *I* stood for one and *V* for five. So *II* was two ones, or eleven. No. That wasn't right. The symbols each represented a unit of measurement.

"Two," Mason said.

"Nice work, Mason," his dad said.

Pride swept over Mason. The team swam toward the next cradle base. It didn't take long for Mr. Wikk to hypothesize that each cradle arm was simply labeled with a number from one to—he suspected—twelve.

"Nothing more than numbers to mark each cradle, sir," Jaxon said. "I'm sorry for concerning you."

The lieutenant's apology was interesting. It didn't have the sound of the forced respect that Mason had heard thus far from Übel soldiers, but instead one of actual respect.

"No, Jaxon, I don't think that's all," Vedrik said. He laughed. "Elliot, don't tell me I've gotten to this conclusion before you. There are—"

Before Vedrik had finished his sentence, the answer hit Mason: twelve crosses, twelve cradles.

"—twelve crosses. Each one will unlock one of these arms to release the ship," Vedrik finished.

Mason's guess was right. At least, it matched Vedrik's.

"Indeed," Mr. Wikk said. "However, we're still missing a few crosses."

"We will take back the crosses from the pirates," Vedrik assured them. "Lieutenant Jaxon, have your teams stop searching for other entrances. They are to scour the area near the cradle arms for keyholes."

"Captain, if you recall, each of the crosses had a silver circle inset in the bottom," Mr. Wikk said. "The shape surrounding it was twelve-sided. That may be the shape of the keyhole we're looking for."

Mason listened with interest.

"Further, I believe that we should search the islands above," Mason's dad said. "I believe we are to use the Washed Stones maps to locate where each cross is to be placed. The maps and crosses had corresponding symbols."

"An excellent suggestion," Captain Vedrik said. "Connect to Dr. Chase."

A second passed.

"Dr. Chase speaking," said the scientist through the Audiox.

"Upload the recovered Washed Stones maps for review," Captain Vedrik said.

"Yes, sir. I'll have them in five minutes."

"We'll examine this area until we have the maps. We're more protected here than on the surface," Vedrik said. "Come with me."

Mason pointed out an odd-shaped formation in the reef toward the front of the *Ark*. The three swam out to it. There were odd markings on the reef's surface as if another structure had once existed there.

Mason and his dad floated about three hundred feet out from the nose of the massive ship. Its huge wings curved and flowed from the top like two waves rolling out from its fuselage.

"Corsairs inbound," came a sudden warning over the earpiece.

Mason's dad turned and swam next to him. "Son, stay close."

Mason looked toward the surface of the water. He couldn't see anything. The threat probably hadn't even crossed into YelNik Eisle's atmosphere.

"Take positions. Defend the *Ark!*" Vedrik ordered his men.

4.61

Basin Hamlet

T he ridge encompassed a densely forested basin. Looking down, Oliver saw no sign that someone lived there, just high trees and a long, narrow lake fed by a waterfall on the north end.

"Are you sure he's here?" Oliver asked.

"What is real can't always be seen," Brother Sam said.

Oliver recalled the words from before. *This is what faith is: believing without seeing.*

"Would you lead the way?" Brother Sam asked.

Before him a ledge slanted down into the valley. Several ledges connected by narrow pathways, with a few jumps here or there, formed a visible way to the ground.

When Oliver stepped toward the ledge, his leg suddenly disappeared. He yanked his foot back. It reappeared. Brother Sam smiled.

Oliver stepped down again and moved until his waist disappeared.

"Cool." Austin jumped next to his brother. Before Oliver could, he ducked his head below the line of invisibility. "Whoa!"

Oliver dropped to a crouch, and the valley came to life. A series of platforms extended out across several large trees at the far north of the valley; bridges led from one platform to the next, and rope ladders fell to the ground. It was a massive tree house. A waterwheel spun at the base of the waterfall; a bridge arched over the stream from the falls to the lake. Small canals crisscrossed through a checkerboard of gardens. Two dozen windmills and domed stone buildings dotted the valley, and slat fences stretched across the land, penning cows, pigs, chickens, horses, and oxen. Oliver recoiled as he saw several panthers roaming freely. A few lay resting in a pen, but its gate was open. Had they eaten the poor animals inside?

"He'll know we're here," Brother Sam said. "Probably has for a while."

Oliver looked up; he could see Brother Sam just fine. There was some sort of one-directional cloaking dome over the valley. He stood, and his feet, Austin, and the valley again disappeared. He waved his hand through the line of invisibility. "A cloak field?"

"Cloak projection, we call it. Rudimentary in comparison to the cloaking we use on the *Phoenix*."

"Those panther things are down there, and it looks like they've already helped themselves to a meal of animals," Oliver said.

"Maybe they got Brother Noah," Austin said.

Brother Sam scratched his chin. "They may be tame. The Veritas Nachfolger once trained and groomed creatures of the night to stand guard and patrol their settlements. They were called the Midnight Protectors."

"So you think those things are on our side?" Oliver asked.

"If they are, they don't know it," Ashley pointed out.

"It'd be nice if someone let them know," Austin said. "Want to take that one, Ashley?"

"No, thanks."

"I don't believe that all of them are tame," Brother Sam said. "The ones on Evad had clearly gone wild, and probably so have the ones we met outside this valley. Though they could have just been patrolling. As I understand it, they can be trained as loyal pets."

"That'll make Tiffany happy," Austin said. "Though I'm not sure Mom and Dad will let her keep a pet of that size."

"Ashley, try stepping through the cloak," Oliver said. "It's weird to see your legs disappear."

Oliver held out his hand, and Ashley took it as she stepped onto the ridge. Oliver filled with happiness. His desire to be around Ashley had been growing since he'd rescued her from the escape pod on Cixot. Now even the simple act of taking her hand made him want to protect her.

"Thanks."

They ducked beneath the cloak. Austin was missing. Oliver looked a short way down the path. His brother was bounding down it. Apparently he wasn't worried about the panthers anymore.

"Wait for us," Oliver called. He and Ashley started after Austin as Brother Sam stepped below the cloak projection.

"Kids, wait at the bottom," he warned. "It's best that I introduce us to Brother Noah first and give the pass phrase."

Oliver heard the instructions, but it was clear that Austin had not, because he continued to jump down the path from ledge to ledge.

"Austin!" Oliver called, but his little brother didn't look back.

This was it: the final stop on their journey before Ursprung. Living in this awesome tree house was the *Ark*'s Guardian. The basin was protected by the Veritas Nachfolger, and Austin felt safe and secure.

Oliver, Ashley, and Brother Sam were coming behind him. With a few more steps, Austin reached the bottom of the ridge.

The grass was highly manicured: soft, green, and trimmed. Several flat, white stones stretched across the grass like a path, so he ran toward them. Going left would lead him to the tree house and the waterfall, where Brother Noah probably was.

Austin started off at a sprint, his excitement to meet Brother Noah taking over. Frost jumped from his shoulder and flew into the air.

Austin quickly lost sight of the rest of his party. His feet echoed on the white stones as he ran. When he paused for breath, Frost landed on a nearby tree and let off a high-pitched series of tweets.

"It's okay. Come back to my shoulder; I won't run again," Austin promised. He started to whistle the tune Brother Sam had taught him. Before he could finish, he heard someone approaching.

Austin looked behind him, expecting to see his brother. Instead, a young man in a red cloak swung a wide stick toward Austin, striking him in the chest and sending him to the ground.

Austin coughed. A sharp pain rang through his stomach and side.

The man held the stick high, ready to strike again. "Who are you? Why are you here?"

Austin fought to catch his breath; the wind had been knocked clean out of him. "Aus . . . Austin. I'm Austin. I'm here to . . . to find you. I'm with Brother Sam."

The man scowled. "I know no Brother Sam. What is the activation code?"

"I . . . I don't know about a phrase. You're part of the Veritas Nachfolger; you guard the Truth, the *Ark*."

Brother Noah lowered the stick and scratched his spiked dark-brown hair. "How did you find me?"

Austin started to push himself up, but Brother Noah raised the stick again.

"Don't move," he warned.

Austin raised his hands. "Okay."

"What is the Truth?"

Austin stared at the man. This was a challenge. "The Truth is not a 'what' but a 'who.'"

Brother Noah considered the answer, then lowered his stick. "You know. Do you believe?"

Austin nodded.

"Say it," Brother Noah said.

"I believe in the Truth."

Brother Noah lowered a hand and pulled Austin to his feet. "You are quite young," he said.

Austin recoiled. Four large panthers stood at a distance. "Uh, sir, are those dangerous?" he asked.

Brother Noah turned, then softly laughed. He whistled, and the three panthers broke into a sprint. The one in the lead leaped past Brother Noah.

Austin shrieked, but it was too late. The beast's heavy black paws knocked him backward onto the soft grass.

"Ahhhhhhhh!" screamed Austin.

4.62

Total Assault

As the *Phoenix* flew out over the sea, *Deep Blue* sat before Tiffany like a dark memory of the dream she'd had just hours before.

A voice came over the speakers. "We're over the location for the *Ark*."

Sister Dorothy unstrapped, and Tiffany followed suit. They walked to the control console that Tiffany would use to monitor Sister Dorothy's progress.

"I'll board the submersible and use this to release it." Dorothy showed Tiffany a small silver circle with a glowing blue button. "Once I'm released, I'll need you to prepare this harness." She pointed to a set of four hooks and rings. "If something happens, we'll use this to retrieve *Deep Blue* if we can. If not, I'll grab on to the line and you'll hoist me up. The controls are on the panel over there."

Tiffany had seen Oliver use the hoist with the sky scooter, and she'd been ready to use it with Ashley and Oliver on Yl Revaw.

The pilot's voice shouted over the speaker, "Inbound! Inbound!"

Sister Dorothy brought up four video feeds of the area around the ship. One showed maybe fifty winged soldiers diving through the air. Tiffany and Oliver had circled down to Re Lyt with the Corsairs using the same technique.

Sister Dorothy readjusted the screens. The three feeds showing the inbound Corsairs were replaced by close-ups and other feeds. One showed the beach and the large Übel cruiser, the *Skull.* Zips of green fired from the spaceship's many turrets and weapons. Purple streaks rained down from above.

Sister Dorothy adjusted the screens again. There, high in the sky, was the *Vulture* and swarms of other Corsairs ships— fighters, shuttles, and bombers. There was no sign of the *Black Ranger.* It had been heavily damaged; perhaps it wasn't ready to enter the fight yet. Was Mr. O'Farrell on the *Vulture?* Was he diving down with the winged soldiers? Was Drex?

The *Phoenix* jerked, and Tiffany grabbed the console to steady herself.

Sister Dorothy raised her wrist. "Sister Rose, take us back to our landing site. We don't want to be in the middle of this. The Übel's progress will be halted until the Corsair attack is over."

Schoop! Schoop! Schoop!

A barrage of green light zipped up from the skiffs hovering across the sea. The Corsair wing-gliders were sitting targets. The men wove and turned, but the Übel turrets were too fast. The Corsairs' wings were torn to shreds, causing the soldiers to plummet toward the sea. The surface of the water would feel like stone if hit from this height.

To Tiffany's relief, parachutes began to open. The falling Corsairs floated down toward the water.

Schoop! Schoop! Schoop!

Green shots ripped apart the parachutes' canopies, and the soldiers began to free-fall again. The Übel were relentless. Ruthless.

The *Phoenix* bucked. Sister Dorothy fell backward with a shriek. "I'm fine," she said with a grimace, cradling her arm.

"No, you're not." Tiffany started for her when the ship twisted to the right. She fell to the ground; *Deep Blue* swung wildly in its cradle.

Tiffany's mTalk beeped. She looked down at the screen: *Help!*

The simple phrase was followed by a name: Lt. Drex.

4.63

Rain Down

The water erupted as something splashed into its surface. It took a moment for Mason to realize that it was Corsair soldiers.

"Base, secure the royal family and the McGregors. Put the McGregors in a shuttle on launch standby. Notify Zebra Xavier, and escort Mrs. Wikk to his office." Vedrik motioned to the lieutenant. "Jaxon, take the boy back to base. Personally make sure that he reaches his mother. Elliot stays with me."

Jaxon and two Übel soldiers swam toward Mason. One pointed toward the distant surface. The other trained his weapon on him. Mason looked at his dad, who nodded. "It'll be okay."

Mason grabbed his Aqua-Zip and let it pull him forward. He followed Lieutenant Jaxon to a skiff directly overhead.

Purple streaks began to zip toward the *Ark*; some of the Corsairs who were in the water were beginning their assault. Others were struggling to get free of parachutes and winged suits.

They were nearly to the skiff, and none of the Corsairs had taken aim at them yet. Mason was worried for his dad, who remained deeper with Vedrik. Where would they go? Mason hadn't seen any shelter or protective enclosure, but Vedrik must have had some sort of plan for keeping Mr. Wikk out of the Corsairs' grasp.

The sky was ablaze with zooming fighters. Purple streaks rained down, and green streaks shot up. Mason popped his head above the surface. It was difficult to see whether anyone was winning yet.

Jaxon directed Mason to the skiff. A soldier shoved him onto the bench. "Sit!"

The deluxe scooter shot forward. It hadn't gotten far when a Corsair fighter swooped down from the sky and laid down a hail of shots. Two Übel soldiers dove from the skiff; Mason hit the deck and curled himself into a ball. Lieutenant Jaxon took to the turret and returned fire.

Mason peeked out from his position. The Corsair ship twisted and came back in for another strike. An explosion at the front of the skiff caused it to drop a few feet. Water splashed up into the skiff and swirled around Mason. He pushed himself up. The skiff sat dead in the water.

Green streaks sparked across the fighter craft as Lieutenant Jaxon tracked it. It twisted, then dove and splashed into the sea several hundred feet away.

"Damage?" Lieutenant Jaxon shouted.

"Engines gone!" yelled the skiff pilot.

The lieutenant climbed out of the turret. One of the two soldiers who'd dived from the skiff was starting back up the ladder. Jaxon walked over and shoved him back off with his foot. "No, you'll swim back!"

"Sir, there's—"

"You chose the water over protecting the craft," Lieutenant Jaxon yelled. He pulled a small pistol from a holster at his side. Mason hadn't noticed the weapon before.

The offending soldier turned and began swimming toward the nearest small island—the elephant-shaped rock.

Mason felt a sharp twinge in his right leg. He peeled off his dive suit and took off his flippers. A narrow gash crossed his calf. In his attempt to not get hit by the attacking ship, he'd struck something on his quick drop to the floor of the skiff.

To Save a Life

Tiffany's heart sank. She read the message again; it was in the feed meant for all Corsairs. Drex was sending a desperate rescue call to the others. He must have been one of the wing-gliders soaring toward the sea.

Tiffany dashed toward *Deep Blue*.

"What are you doing?" Sister Dorothy called.

"Drex needs help," she said as she jumped into the open canopy and took the pilot seat.

"The Corsair?"

"Yes."

Sister Dorothy nodded. "Go! I will pray."

Tiffany activated *Deep Blue*'s controls and closed the canopy, sealing herself inside the ship that had been a coffin in her nightmare.

She waved to Sister Dorothy, who dashed to the control console.

The ship dove, and *Deep Blue* swung forward. Tiffany caught herself with her hands before her head slammed into the dash before her. Light entered the cargo bay from below—the belly bay doors were open. *Just a moment . . .*

She felt weightless. Her stomach seemed to rise into her chest. *Deep Blue* had been released, and she was free-falling toward the surface of the sea. Water filled the entire view of the canopy as the submersible dove nose first to make a smooth entrance into the surface. Seconds later, Tiffany saw the bottom of the sea through crystal-clear water.

Tiffany wasted no time but took the controls and activated the generator and propellers. She activated the robotic arms that extended from the nose of the submarine.

Many Corsair soldiers were already engaging the Übel, but nearly as many were trying to detangle from parachutes and wings. A Corsair struggled, panicking, in the water directly before her, tangled in his glide wings, chute, and cords. He wore an Oxyverter, so he wasn't necessarily in danger of drowning. Obviously the soldiers had been equipped for an underwater assault.

She maneuvered the submersible closer, extended the robotic arms, and activated the laser cutter. Like a doctor using an ion-scalpel, she cut through the cords of the chute, avoiding the soldier's flailing limbs. A second later, he was free, charging for the surface of the sea. It hadn't been Drex. Still, she knew he was down there somewhere.

She piloted the submersible toward another struggling soldier, deeper in the water. Long, green plants had twisted around him and his gear. The remnants of his parachute added color to the jumble.

The water boiled with movement. Streaks of green and purple zipped around her.

BWOOOF! *Deep Blue* flipped to its side. Tiffany's shoulder slammed against the canopy. She groaned, then caught a glimpse of a sweeping, silver-finned tail passing over her. She followed it with her gaze. Twisting to come back for her again was a large hammerhead shark.

A warning flashed on the screen: *External Fuselage Damage.*

The shark's large fin whipped back and forth as it rushed toward Tiffany at full speed, its mouth open wide. It crashed against the sub, and an eerie screech rang out through the cabin as the shark's teeth dragged across *Deep Blue*'s canopy. Tiffany covered her ears. The shark flung the submersible down toward the thick green plants.

Tiffany grabbed the controls and brought the ship level. But before she could slow its movement, *Deep Blue* entered the green forest. She quickly shut off *Deep Blue*'s propellers. She'd learned about sea grass from her mom. The plant was most dangerous when it got caught in propellers or wrapped around a person's limbs and body.

Tiffany looked for the soldier she'd been trying to rescue. He was just twenty feet away, still struggling in the sea grass. And where was the shark? Had it given up on her? She spotted the hammerhead and a half dozen more of its kind circling above.

The creatures must have seen the submersible as large prey, because more were joining to feast on *Deep Blue*. Though the ship wouldn't be an appetizing meal, the sharks would significantly damage the ship as they discovered that.

Thus far the damage to *Deep Blue* was minimal. Only the external alert flashed. She silenced the warning. She was in the sea grass, but the plants weren't a guarantee against the sharks if they thought that *Deep Blue* was a worthy meal.

She needed to get out, but she wanted to save the soldier in the tangle of sea grass. The problem was how to get the ship through the sea grass to rescue him without getting the submersible tangled. Using the robotic arms and laser cutter seemed like her only option to clear a path. It would take patience and a bit of work, but she had to try.

As the long strands of green grass fell around her, she looked up at the circling sharks. They hesitated, even though she had created a gap in the seaweed jungle that gave them a nearly clean shot at the ship.

Tiffany neared the struggling soldier. He was still working to free himself, bubbles spurting from his Oxyverter. He looked up at *Deep Blue*.

Tiffany gasped. It was Drex. She'd found him, and he was in trouble. It wasn't exactly like her dream, but for that she was thankful. "Thank you, Rescuer," she whispered.

Drex stared toward her. She couldn't tell if he was relieved to see her or if he was contemplating how to capture her.

He motioned toward a thick cord wrapped around his leg. It extended into the darkness below, attached to something like an anchor. Apparently, his knife hadn't been sharp enough to cut through the cord.

Tiffany maneuvered the submersible closer, then extended the cutting arm. The laser burned right through the cord. Drex's leg was free. He motioned toward the surface. He was weaponless with the exception of his knife. Was he requesting an escort through the sharks?

For the moment they were safer in the sea grass. *Deep Blue* wasn't armed and hadn't exactly performed well against the sharks thus far. If only they had a way to communicate with each other.

Of course—her mTalk was attached to the Corsairs' communication system. Tiffany tapped out a quick, short message and sent it. The message posted to the Corsair feed, which could have consequences, but as they were in the midst of a battle, Tiffany wasn't too concerned.

She looked at Drex to see whether he'd received the message. He was swimming away from her—not up, but into the green sea grass. She looked toward the surface. The sharks had gone.

Tiffany shook her head. Why had she thought for a moment that she and Drex might work together?

Thunk! Schloop! Squick!

Tiffany looked around. What had just hit the ship? Suddenly *Deep Blue* jerked downward. She strained to see outside.

Had her propellers caught in the sea grass? If so, it would pull her toward the plant's roots.

No, that wasn't it. It was something worse. A massive, blue-purple tentacle slapped across the canopy of *Deep Blue* with a loud *squick*.

The submersible rolled over to its belly. Tiffany found herself staring down into the gaping mouth of some sort of squid. The sea creature pulled her deeper into the grass, deeper into the water.

Tiffany wasn't sure what to do. More tentacles had wrapped around *Deep Blue*; her descent toward the squid's fanged mouth was quickening. She looked at the console. Several warnings flashed on the screen about the submersible's fuselage integrity.

The *Phoenix* was still overhead—at least, she hoped it was. She searched the screen for the link to call the ship. Where was it? Time was running out. She hit the Emergency Rescue Signal icon and began to pray.

Meeting Noah

Oliver heard the scream. He ran forward, Zinger lifted.

"Wait, Oliver!" shouted Ashley, but he couldn't stop; his brother was in trouble.

Ahead, three panthers were circling a man in a red cloak, but there was no sign of his brother. Was he too late?

The panthers weren't attacking the cloaked man. He turned to face Oliver as he approached, raised his hand, and gave an odd call. The three beasts sat at his feet. A fourth stood over a crumpled Austin.

Oliver raised his weapon.

The man in the red cloak whistled. The three panthers leaped to their feet and ran to flank Oliver.

Oliver slowed.

"I'd stop, young man. Lower your weapon," the man in the red cloak warned. "They'll be on you before you can blink."

Oliver obeyed. Ashley and Brother Sam weren't far behind.

The cloaked man whistled again. A panther pounced from the branches above Oliver. The large creature padded to a tree trunk and lay down. A second paced behind Oliver with a low growl.

440 | MEETING NOAH

"What have you done to my brother?" Oliver yelled.

The man in the red cloak turned, and Oliver heard a laugh: Austin's laugh. The man reached down and pulled Austin to his feet. The large panther that had hovered over him rolled to its back, exposing its belly. Austin stroked its fur.

"These are my sentinels," the man said. "My name is Brother Noah. Who are you?"

Oliver stared at his brother and the cat. "I'm Oliver."

"Brother Noah, I am Brother Sam," a voice said from behind him. "And with me is Ashley. We've been looking for you."

Oliver thought it odd that the men had to introduce themselves. Weren't they all working together as part of the Veritas Nachfolger?

"You have come to release the *Ark*," Brother Noah said.

"We have," Brother Sam said. He reached into a pocket in his cloak and pulled out a ruby amulet surrounded by clear stones. Oliver remembered the amulet; the man in the video in the chess chamber on Evad had worn the same kind.

Brother Noah revealed a matching amulet that had been hanging on a chain around his neck. He pressed the backs of the amulets together. The red jewels glowed.

"I have waited more than two thousand years for this day," Brother Noah said as he handed Brother Sam's amulet back to him.

Oliver's mouth dropped open. Thousands of years? How was that possible?

"It is finally time for the journey to Ursprung," Brother Sam said. "These kids have discovered the Truth. The revival has begun."

"Then we have no time to waste." Brother Noah turned and started down the white stone path. "Follow me."

Brother Sam leaned toward the kids. "'The revival has begun' is the activation code. Things are about to get really exciting."

Hadn't they already been?

Austin walked directly behind Brother Noah, a large panther on either side. Brother Sam followed next, then Ashley. Oliver came last.

"Ashley," he whispered.

She glanced over her shoulder. "What?"

"Isn't this odd?" Oliver said. "This place is perfect—too perfect, don't you think?"

Ashley nodded. "It's a bit much. Are you worried?"

"A little," Oliver said. "We shouldn't let our guard down yet."

They approached a wide tree with massive branches. Several wooden room-sized pods sat among the branches. They looked like birds' nests, but with windows. A rope ladder led to the first landing, where several walkways stretched out to the pods.

"Welcome to my home," Brother Noah said as they stepped onto the first landing. Two panthers leaped up onto a nearby branch and stalked toward them. "My guest pod is this way."

"Brother Noah, we won't be staying," Brother Sam said. "Our mission to Ursprung must begin immediately. The soldiers of darkness are here as well."

"I have been monitoring their arrival," said Brother Noah. "The command pod is this way."

They walked across a rope and wood-slat bridge to a larger pod. While the pod's exterior had branches, sticks, and wood beams like a thrown-together fort, the inside was sleek and modern. A large screen consumed one entire wall. Separate applications and video feeds ran across it. Oliver saw the outline of what he assumed was the *Ark*—a massive ship settled on the bottom of the seabed. Some sort of battle seemed to be occurring.

"What's happening?" Oliver asked.

Everyone gathered close, and Brother Noah expanded the image feed.

"The Übel and Corsairs are fighting," Brother Sam said. "We're running out of time."

"Time for what?" asked Ashley.

"We must coordinate the launch of the *Ark*, or the soldiers could inadvertently flood the *Ark* while trying to get access," Brother Sam explained.

"Brother Sam." Sister Dorothy's voice came over his mTalk. "What is it?"

It had to be urgent. They were supposed to maintain communication silence.

"It's Tiffany—"

Oliver's heart sank into his stomach. Ashley gasped.

"She's taken *Deep Blue* into the sea to rescue Drex."

Oliver looked at Brother Sam. The old man was smiling. "Then she has done what she was supposed to do," he said.

"What?" cried Ashley. "No, she was terrified. Her dream . . ."

"What dream?" asked Oliver and Austin.

Brother Sam held up his hand. "Your sister is in the hands of Helper. She is following the path that was set before her by Creator."

"No!" Oliver said. "She's in danger. We have to go save her."

Brother Sam put his hand on Oliver's shoulder, but he shrugged it off. "I'm sorry, but this is too dangerous."

Then Ashley reached out and put an arm around him.

"Oliver, this caught us off guard. I know it sounds dire, but"—she paused—"I think we need to trust Brother Sam. He hasn't steered us wrong yet."

"No, we need to trust Rescuer. *He* hasn't steered us wrong yet," Austin countered. He put a hand on Oliver's other shoulder, his bright green eyes drilling into Oliver's. "Trust Him. Tiffany is."

Ashley nodded.

Oliver took a deep breath. "Can we find her?" he asked.

Brother Noah turned to the screen and swiped with astonishing speed, zipping through nearly fifty video feeds. "I'm sorry, but I do not know what she looks like."

"She has long brown hair like mine," Ashley said. "She has brown eyes, and she's about my height too."

Brother Noah stared at Ashley.

"She's the only teenage girl in a submarine!" Austin shouted.

Brother Noah nodded and went back to his search.

"Oliver, she's going to be okay," Ashley promised, squeezing his hand. There was comforting warmth in her grasp. "She's strong and smart."

"I know, but she's my sister," Oliver said. "My little sister."

Never had he been so worried for her. Maybe it was because all their enemies were converging at the same time. Maybe it was because the *Ark* lay before him and his family felt even more severed than it had before. Whatever it was, the anxiousness in his heart wanted to get beyond his newfound trust in Rescuer and consume him.

He silently prayed, "Rescuer, please provide comfort and peace. Give me the reassurance I need that my sister will be okay."

4.66

Mason's Moment

A few moments ago, a Corsair soldier had surfaced near Mason's skiff. Two Übel soldiers had captured him. He now sat unconscious on the floor of the skiff, his hands bound, while the pilot and copilot tried to fix the skiff's engine.

Several sharks had circled the ship, their dorsal fins breaching the surface. Mason was thankful not to be in the water. He wondered what was happening with his dad down below. Who was winning the fight? His aqua-oculus showed him a green target labeled *Elliot Wikk, 700 feet*, as well as red targets that he assumed were Corsairs.

Suddenly an alert rang out across the control console speakers. "Alert! Submersible *Deep Blue* requesting assistance. Alert! Submersible *Deep Blue* requesting assistance."

Mason froze. He ran to the other side of the ship. A new icon had appeared in his aqua-oculus. Orange and flashing, it marked the location of the distress call. Who was in his family's sub?

He glanced around the skiff. Two SwirlZaps hung ready for use. The pilot and Lieutenant Jaxon were busy at the console. The copilot was still at the front of the skiff, messing with the engine.

445

Mason slipped on his flippers. He took his Oxyverter from the bench and strapped his knife to his leg. He grabbed a Swirl-Zap, dashed to the edge of the skiff, and leaped into the water. Water surged around him as he kicked downward. No green streaks pursued him. He looked back and forth; there was no sign of sharks. He angled toward the orange icon on his aqua-oculus.

Two splashes came behind him. Lieutenant Jaxon and the pilot were swimming toward him. They weren't going to let him get away. What would Vedrik do to them if he escaped? What would Zebra Xavier do to Vedrik?

Mason fired at them with the SwirlZap. The pilot went limp as he hit him square in the chest. Lieutenant Jaxon hesitated. Then he swam for his comrade and pulled him to the surface.

A silver shark swam quickly toward the soldiers. Mason fired at the hammerhead and stopped it before it reached the lieutenant and his unconscious comrade. Three more sharks approached from a distance; Mason was their target.

He looked down. Sea grass swirled below. The water bubbled and boiled. *Deep Blue* was down there. Perhaps the sharks wouldn't follow him.

As Mason approached the grass, he recalled his dad's words of caution. If he went quickly, he risked getting caught in the plants. If he took his time, he might come to the rescue too late. He slipped his knife from its holster and sliced at the sea grass as he went. The slimy green plants slipped across his bare skin like slithering snakes.

BwaBoom! A purple flash of light exploded somewhere ahead. Had the submersible exploded? Panic struck Mason. He forgot about cutting the sea grass and swam all out. The bubbles thinned and cleared. *Deep Blue* was floating in one piece, and a giant squid was retracting its tentacles and sinking into the sea grass. The explosion had halted the squid's attack.

Tiffany's head appeared in the windshield canopy. But she wasn't looking at Mason.

Mason followed her gaze. A Corsair soldier swam out from the sea grass, holding a weapon. Mason prepared to fire, but the Corsair swam below the submersible to look for the squid. Satisfied, he swam back up to the front of *Deep Blue* and motioned to Tiffany. She raised her wrist. They were communicating by mTalk.

What had happened while he'd been prisoner? Were Mason's siblings working with the Corsairs? Had Mr. O'Farrell really been good?

Tiffany and the Corsair seemed to be communicating about the surface, because both pointed or looked up several times. The soldier swam toward the propellers. He grabbed the tail fin, then kicked the propeller casing with the heel of his flippered foot. Something was jammed.

Mason was ready to reunite with his sister. Even though the Corsair appeared to be helping, Mason didn't trust him. He pushed back the sea grass and moved into the area that had been cleared by the squid's thrashing tentacles.

The Corsair lifted his weapon and took aim. Mason put his hands up, but kept holding his weapons. He shook his head. *No.*

The Corsair lowered his weapon. Mason slipped his knife into its holster, then swam forward. He held his SwirlZap at the ready, just in case.

As he drew nearer, he realized that the Corsair was Drex. He stopped. Drex was trying to recapture his sister. Mason lifted the SwirlZap and took aim. Drex instantly drew his weapon. The two aimed at each other and waited.

Then Drex lowered his weapon and motioned for Mason to lower his.

Could Mason trust Drex? Was this a trap? Mason looked at his sister. She too was motioning for him to lower his weapon. If Tiffany trusted him, he would also.

Mason lowered the SwirlZap and swam past Drex to the sub. Tiffany smiled and pressed a hand against the windshield; Mason did the same. He was so glad to see his sister again.

Sure, she was in an inoperable submersible, but she didn't look injured. She held up her mTalk to display a communication transponder code. He typed it in and immediately received a communication from her: *Mason! You're here!*

He tapped back a message. *You too. I've missed you.*

Are you okay?

Mason nodded. *We'll get you out of here.*

He swam toward Drex, who had the engine compartment open and was looking at the propeller. He had set his weapon down on the submersible. Drex tapped out a message. *Nebulas bearing jammed.*

Mason nodded. He swam to the far side of the craft, set his weapon atop *Deep Blue*'s side fin, and opened another compartment. It had a multitude of small parts, with bearings among them.

A long, bluish-purple tentacle shot out of the sea grass below and wrapped itself around Drex, then retracted, pulling the Corsair down. A second tentacle shot toward Mason but missed and hit *Deep Blue*, rolling it. A third tentacle swept toward him. Mason kicked hard as the tentacle swept past. He reached for his SwirlZap, but the squid's strike on *Deep Blue* had knocked both his and Drex's weapons into the water.

Mason reached for his knife as the squid's tentacle encircled his left leg. Its suckers latched on to his bare skin. He swept his knife down as a second tentacle coiled around his other leg. He slit the top layer of the squid's skin, but the tentacle's grip did not loosen. Mason drove the blade deeper. A jagged gash appeared, and dark blue liquid poured out.

Mason kicked his leg, freeing himself of the injured tentacle. He looked for Drex.

The Corsair's upper body was wrapped tightly in a tentacle, and Drex had been pulled within feet of the squid's gaping mouth.

Mason dove toward the squid, his blade at the ready. A long tentacle smacked him across his bare back. It stung like a rug burn. Another tentacle caught Mason under his knife-wielding arm, jerking the blade from his grasp. Three seconds later, the squid had him tightly in its tentacle. His arms were bound. His legs were bound. The tip of the tentacle squiggled across his face, nudging the Oxyverter in his mouth. Without it, his oxygen would be cut off.

Mason was trapped. Claustrophobia entangled his thoughts. He couldn't move; soon he wouldn't be able to breathe.

"Rescuer," he cried in his mind. "Helper, where are You? Free me from this trap! Save me!"

Drex was still struggling to keep himself from the jaws of the squid.

A terrible thought replaced the terror of claustrophobia. Drex did not know Rescuer. He was about to die. What would happen to him? From what Obbin and Brother Sam had said, he wouldn't get eternal life if he didn't believe.

Mason squirmed. The tips of the squid's tentacle gripped the Oxyverter. Mason jerked his head, and the tentacle lost hold.

BwaBoom! BwaBoom! BwaBoom!

Purple light filled the water. Mason shut his eyes.

BwaBoom! BwaBoom! BwaBoom!

The squid's grip on him loosened. The tentacle slithered from Mason's body. He opened his eyes and looked down. Drex too was free. He was kicking upward, clearly worn out, but still putting as much space between him and the squid as possible.

Mason looked for *Deep Blue*. The submersible's canopy was open. Tiffany was twenty feet away, fully dressed. She breathed through an Oxyverter and held Drex's weapon in her hand. Beneath her, the squid appeared lifeless, its tentacles swishing back and forth in the water.

Mason stared up at the water's surface. The hammerhead sharks were circling, swarming above them. They looked hungry.

Mason scanned the nearby reef. The elephant rock was somewhere near. The cowering Übel soldier had swum to it earlier, when Jaxon hadn't let him back on the skiff. Mason just needed to figure out the direction of the island.

The disabled Übel skiff he'd escaped appeared as a green dot in his oculus. Mason looked around and found the marker for the *Ark*. Facing away from the *Ark*, Elephant Rock had been on the right side.

He tapped a message to Tiffany and Drex. *This way.*

4.67

Enemy Rescued

Wait.

Tiffany swam to the disabled submersible and retrieved a survival kit from the back. Swimming was difficult without diving clothes or flippers. As she returned to Mason and Drex, she saw a dozen hammerhead sharks diving toward them. She fired several shots, but the sharks continued past her toward the clearing in the sea grass.

Tiffany realized why they'd been so hesitant to enter the sea grass before. The squid had been larger and more powerful, but now it lay immobile on the seabed. The large silver sharks were swimming in to attack it.

A new message from Mason told her that there was an island not far away. The three swam until they reached a wall of underwater rock.

Drex messaged them. *I'll scout the area.* He swam up.

As Tiffany and Mason waited, she stared at her little brother. He'd come to her rescue, but he was also working alongside their prior enemy, Drex.

The Corsair messaged them. *Come up. All clear.*

Tiffany noticed Mason's hesitation. She saw bubbles exhale from his Oxyverter and knew he'd taken a deep breath. She understood why he was hesitant. She was too, yet after her dream she knew that this was the right path. She'd already saved Drex once, but her mission wouldn't be over until she'd shared the Truth with him.

She handed her weapon to Mason, hoping that it would make him feel safer. He nodded and followed her to the island.

The sun had dropped lower in the sky. Was night falling? She pulled off her Oxyverter. "Drex?"

He pulled her up onto a ledge. "It appears clear," he said, his voice unemotional.

It was obvious that he was uncomfortable, unsure where he stood with her and Mason. They'd been enemies only hours before.

"I'm glad you're safe," Tiffany said.

Mason popped above the surface. "Dwer wz a—" He stopped trying to talk and removed his Oxyverter. "There was an Übel skiff not far from here."

Drex pointed. "I saw something that way, but this recess in the rock is blocking their view of us."

Mason climbed out of the water and gave Tiffany a hug. "Sis, I'm glad to see you."

"I missed you," Tiffany said. It felt good to have her little brother with her again.

Mason looked around. "We should get farther inland. Be careful, though. I saw an Übel soldier swim here." He checked the Corsair weapon.

"Be careful with that," Drex said. "Why don't you give it back to me?"

Mason shifted, putting the weapon farther from Drex. "No, I don't think so."

Drex scowled. "I've been trained to use it. You haven't."

"I'm not worried about your training, I'm worried about your intentions," Mason said. "Besides, I've fired plenty of weapons, and you're one of the reasons why."

Drex balled his fists.

"We need to work together," Tiffany said, stepping in. "I arrived with the Veritas Nachfolger; the *Phoenix* should be nearby. I can get us rescued."

"I'm not going to be a prisoner," Drex said.

Mason aimed his weapon. "You already are."

Tiffany raised her hands, standing squarely between Drex and Mason. She motioned for her brother to lower his weapon.

"Stop. He's not our prisoner," she said. "Drex, the Veritas don't want to harm or imprison you. They want to help you." She tried another tactic. "I saw how your aunt treated you."

Drex looked at Tiffany, but Mason shook his head. "You met his family?"

"Yes and no," Tiffany said. "She's not family as we know it."

Drex grunted. "Don't judge DarkStone."

Tiffany paused. "Sorry."

The three stood silent for a moment.

Mason cleared his throat. "Look, Tiffany and I aren't going to fall prisoner to the Corsairs again. Though my parents are with the Übel, I don't want to go back there either. Drex, Tiffany is right. Our best move is to call the *Phoenix*."

Drex took a deep breath. "You both saved me when I was in trouble. Why?"

Tiffany smiled. This was her chance, the opportunity Creator had planned. "Because I believe in the Truth and I follow His way."

"The Truth? You believe that fanta—"

Tiffany raised her hand. "Stop. He's not a fantasy. He's real."

"Our belief in the Truth saved you," Mason said. "Trust me, I'd have left you to that squid a week ago."

Tiffany hoped that wasn't true, but it did drive home the point.

"The Truth's name is Rescuer," she said. "He came to this world to save us from ourselves, from death."

"Yes, I know the line. 'And I give unto them eternal life.'"

"That's our Creator speaking," Mason said.

"We can't make you believe, and we won't try," Tiffany said. "But at least trust us enough to come with us and not go back to the Corsairs."

"We did save you," Mason added.

"You've made that plenty clear," Drex said.

It was going to be difficult to convince Drex that he wouldn't be a prisoner. "When I call the Veritas Nachfolger, I won't mention you," Tiffany said. "You can hide while we're extracted, or you can come with us. It's your choice."

Drex eyed her, then looked toward the sky. "Okay. But before you do, let's at least get to the top of this rock so I can see what else is going on. That Übel solider—was he armed?"

"I don't think so," Mason said. "He left the skiff pretty quickly when it was attacked."

"Good. That'll make it easier," Drex said.

4.68

Dino Weapons

"What's that?" Ashley pointed to a screen that had previously shown only the *Skull*. A second black ship had just flattened a large section of jungle to the right of the Übel battle cruiser.

"The Übel have two battle cruisers?" Austin asked.

"They have several," Brother Sam said. "That one is the battle destroyer *Bones*."

Reinforcements charged out of the ship, though the Übel already controlled the entire beach. They began to construct a fence along the left side of the *Bones*, cutting the beach in half.

"There's so many," Ashley said.

"More than I knew," Oliver said. "But it doesn't matter. We're still going to rescue our parents, my brother, and the Blauwe Mensen."

She turned to him. "And Tiffany?"

They still had no visual on her.

"Her too," Oliver promised. He awkwardly put his arm around Ashley and gave her a side hug. Austin smirked.

A large tyrannosaurus rex stomped out of the newly arrived black cruiser. A sleek, black pod was harnessed to its back with turrets mounted on either side. The dinosaur wore a black helmet that covered its eyes but left its gaping mouth free to chomp down on its enemies. A second and third rex stomped forth, similarly armed.

"Battle dinosaurs?" asked Austin.

"Tiffany said she saw one of those at the Hatchery," Oliver said.

"All those dinosaurs were meant to be weapons," Austin said.

"Indeed, RepFuse's genetics testing on reptiles to improve medical treatments was a cover for the Übel's cloning and genetics test lab. A byproduct was powerful creatures they could harness as weapons," Brother Sam said. "Don't worry. We'll keep clear of them. And my companions are equipped to deal with the dinosaurs, should we cross paths." He turned to Brother Noah. "Now, in order to unlock the *Ark*, we will need to activate the thermal generator plant. Only you know its location, Brother Noah."

Brother Noah brought up a new map. "A shaft here will take you to the plant. I must warn you, this path will take you toward the planet core. There are rivers of lava and geysers within."

"We will take all precautions," Brother Sam said.

"Can you transfer the map to my device?" Ashley asked.

Brother Noah swept his finger across the screen toward Ashley.

She smiled. "Got it."

"Thank you for your help, Brother Noah," Brother Sam said. "We will return once we've completed our mission."

"Of course. I will be here," Brother Noah said.

Brother Noah led them out of the tree house and directed them toward the waterfall. "The entrance you seek is through there."

Ashley led, Oliver at her side. Brother Sam and Austin came a few steps behind.

"Brother Sam, sir . . ." Austin hesitated, and Frost flitted up to land on his shoulder. "Brother Noah said he had waited some two thousand years." Austin paused again. He wanted to know the truth, but he worried that he was going to find out that the Veritas Nachfolger were into the same life-extending practices as the Übel and Corsairs. "How is that possible?"

Brother Sam stopped. *Here it comes*, thought Austin.

"Brother Noah is not human," Brother Sam said. "He was placed here by the original colonists from Ursprung. He is an android."

"Android?" asked Austin.

"A robot programmed to think and act like a human. He has artificial intelligence, but he is not alive," Brother Sam explained. "After the Thankless Rebellion, the Empire banned the production and design of robots that looked like humans. Brother Noah had been built long before, and was hidden far out of reach."

"How is Brother Noah still operating?" Austin asked.

Brother Sam laughed lightly. "Good question. Brother Noah was programmed to duplicate himself. His duplicates receive direct real-time memory transfers. When the current Brother Noah ceases to operate and send updates, the next duplicate activates, locates the deactivated Brother Noah, repairs it, and places it in storage. There are at least two dozen Brother Noah androids ready to serve."

Austin was intrigued. He really wanted to see those extras. And he wanted to interact with Brother Noah more to see how he—it—worked.

"Perhaps we'll be able to bring Brother Noah along on our journey," Brother Sam said. "Once we launch the *Ark*, his mission here will be complete."

"That would be really cool," Austin said.

"This way," Ashley called. "The entrance is back here."

Ashley and Oliver were standing before a solid stone wall.

"The arrow is pointing right here," Ashley said.

Oliver was looking over the sides of the wall. "There has to be an indent."

Austin joined him. "Look." To the side, a series of white stones formed a cross. He touched each one, and they glowed green.

The wall slid open. Cold, dank air swept over them.

"On to the planet core!" Austin said.

4.69

The Odd Calm Before

Mason was first atop the rock. They hadn't spotted the Übel soldier, but that didn't mean that he wasn't hidden somewhere. He remained low and looked out from the island. The Übel skiff he'd escaped wasn't on the water any longer, and overhead there were no spacecraft to be seen.

Where had the ships gone? Had the two forces destroyed each other? Mason was hopeful, but the answer to the second question was clearly no. The *Skull* still sat intact on the beach, another ship next to it. Two large Übel ships meant even more soldiers.

Tiffany climbed next to him, lifting her mTalk to tap on the screen. "I guess I should call the *Phoenix*." She tapped the mTalk screen again, and her smile disappeared. "I can't relink with it."

"Try Oliver or Austin," Mason suggested.

She tried. "I can't."

"They've blocked you," Drex said. "When you switched off their frequency and connected with me, they assumed your device had been compromised."

"What now?" Mason asked.

Drex looked toward the sinking sun. It had become a deep red as it dropped below the horizon. Was he going to suggest contacting the Corsairs? If he did, Mason wouldn't go along with it.

"We should stay here tonight," Drex suggested.

"What do you think, Mason?" asked Tiffany.

He shrugged. "For the first time, I have to agree with the Corsair."

Mason couldn't think of another option. Any attempt to signal would be seen by their enemies as much as by the Veritas Nachfolger. Trying to swim across the dark waters at night would only turn them into shark food.

"Then I'm glad I grabbed this." Tiffany opened the survival kit. Inside were two emergency beacons, a folded tent, a couple of blankets, a dozen fireballs, two H2O converter siphons, and twenty-four instant-meal tubes.

"We've got enough to last us eight days if we ration," Mason said. That was only one meal a day, but it was survivable.

"I don't plan to be out here for eight days," Tiffany said.

"We won't be," Drex said. "I'll get us off this island tomorrow. But first let's get you dry."

Mason caught a tone he'd never heard from Drex before: kindness.

Drex set the tent next to a large rise in the island. He pulled a tab, and the domed tent expanded immediately. "I don't think this will be seen if it's close to the rock face, but we should take it down before sunrise."

Mason nodded.

The sun had nearly set; a bright green moon shone in the twilight sky. Mason stretched his arms and rolled his neck. His body ached, but his mind wasn't tired.

Mason climbed into the dome. His sister followed him. Drex remained outside.

Tiffany grabbed Mason's hand. "Thank you for being kind. For giving him a chance."

Mason looked into her hopeful brown eyes. "Tell me why."

Tiffany smiled. "I will. Tomorrow."

Drex ducked in and sealed the tent flap. The interior was dark. Mason lay next to his sister; Drex lay on his other side. They had no sleep sacks or pillows, just two blankets and the floor canvas against hard rock.

"I'm actually not tired," Mason said. "I slept on the *Skull*."

"I'm not tired either," Tiffany said. "I rested on the *Phoenix*. Drex?"

Drex gave a half-laugh. "I'm exhausted. I haven't slept since you escaped."

There was an awkward silence.

"Get some rest," Tiffany said. "Mason and I will listen for any danger."

Drex turned to his side. "Wake me if anything happens."

"Good night," Mason said.

"Good night," repeated Tiffany.

"Night," Drex said. "And thank you both."

Mason and Tiffany spoke briefly about the squid and the current situation, but they hesitated to discuss their separate experiences until Drex began snoring.

"Do you think he's really asleep?" Mason asked.

Tiffany raised herself up and looked at the Corsair. She shrugged. "I think."

"Let's go outside the tent just in case. I want to tell you what I learned about the Übel and the Blauwe Mensen," Mason said.

"And I want to tell you what we learned about the Veritas Nachfolger and Corsairs," Tiffany said.

The two slipped out of the tent and found a couple of rocks to sit on. Night had fully fallen over the sea and the jungle.

"Zebra Xavier is Mr. Thule," Mason said.

"The man you met in Cobalt Gorge?"

Mason nodded. "That's why the Übel attacked. Mr. Thule wasn't just a spy, but also the leader of the Übel."

"Well, Mr. O'Farrell is more than a hundred years old," Tiffany said, providing an equally surprising fact.

"What? How?" Mason asked.

"That's why the Corsairs are so interested in cybornotics, biotronics, and genetics," Tiffany explained. "As the leader, he's had more done than any of them."

For the next hour or so, Tiffany and Mason discussed the histories and goals of each of the three groups, comparing and contrasting them. Mason took comfort in being with his sister again. He'd really missed his siblings.

A stone clattered behind them, and Mason spun around. He reached for his weapon, but he'd left it in the tent.

A dark form stood behind them.

A sick feeling came over Mason. He'd let down his guard and left the weapon for Drex to take.

Now the truth about the Corsair would be revealed.

Visual Glossary

Academy, Federal Star Fleet: The Academy provides top-of-the-line education while creating future leaders for the Federal Fleet.

Advanced Nano-Helix Genetics: A class at Bewaldeter that teaches genetics technology and theory.

Aqua-Oculus: Small lenses that fit over the eyes and allow the wearer to see underwater.

Aqua-Zip: An oval-shaped device with a propeller on one end and two arching handles on the other, used to pull a diver through the water quickly.

Archeos Alliance: An organization that exists to unlock the past.

Ark: A ship suspected to have traveled from Ursprung. Some believe the ship holds the coordinates for Ursprung and may possibly provide transport to the planet. An image of the ship appeared on the mural in the Cathedral of the Star on Enaid.

Atmospheric Transfer Chamber (ATC): The chamber allows movement from a stable environment, such as the inside of a spacecraft, to an unstable environment, such as a planet with a nonbreathable or corrosive atmosphere.

Audiox: A communication earpiece that can be used underwater.

Bewaldeter: A private boarding school and premier K–12 establishment.

Biotronics: The replacement of limbs and organs with mechanical devices. Banned in the Federation.

Black Lagoon: A large ship believed to have been designed to lead to the *Ark*.

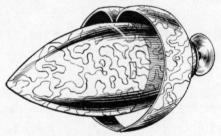

Black Ranger: The flagship of the Corsairs.

Blauwe Mensen (*Blue People*): A mysterious group from the planet Jahr des Eises. Their home was Cobalt Gorge.

Cao: A sparsely populated desert planet with minimal Federation presence. The Valley of Shadows is located on Cao. Mr. and Mrs. Wikk visited the planet in their effort to locate clues and artifacts related to their search for Ursprung.

Cavern Haven: An underground city, built as the Blauwe Mensen's sanctuary in times of danger.

Celtyx: A creature created from synthesizing the DNA of a lexovisaurus into the genes of an attack dog.

Cixot: A moon with a thick corrosive atmosphere. It orbits the molten planet Ledram.

Cloak Projection: A basic cloaking device that provides a reflective holographic image to mask an area or object.

Corsairs: Also known as pirates, corsairs plague trade routes in the far reaches of the Federation and are a constant burden to federal forces.

Corsair Swords: Weapons with black handles and blades that glow silver with energy. Strikes can either stun someone or give a warning shock.

Cryostore: A refrigeration and freezing appliance.

Cybornotics: The actual integration of information into a human's brain or nervous system. Banned in the Federation.

Deep Blue: A two-man submarine belonging to the Wikks. It has a test depth of approximately eight hundred feet and can reach speeds of twenty-five knots.

DNA-Helix NanoVault: A unit designed to store and protect synthesized DNA.

e-Journal: An electronic notebook in which Mr. and Mrs. Wikk stored all their archeological notes.

e-Papyrus: A single-screen tablet for drawing or writing.

Eagle: A sister ship to the *Phoenix*, previously piloted by Brother Samuel.

Empire: The government preceding the Federation.

Enaid: This planet was the site of the beginning of the Empire and is somewhat centrally located in the current boundaries of the Federation.

Energen: The boys' favorite drink.

Enviro-Stabilizer: A silver orb supported by three glowing green columns. Often deployed in smaller spaces, the device is used to create a localized atmosphere conducive to human life, creating a comfortable environment for its user.

Eochair: Brother Sam states that this is needed to unlock the *Ark*.

Evad: The only habitable planet in the Rel Krev system. It is covered in lush green tropical plants, some of which can be deadly. The Wikks encountered Brother Sam and the Übel among its ziggurats and cross-shaped pool.

Federal Destroyer: A primary combat platform of the Federation. Destroyers are used to patrol trade routes and guard federal planets. Their armament is light in comparison to larger federal ships.

Federation: The Federation consists of 1,983 planets, asteroids, or stations. Governed by a president and senate, the Federation is currently enjoying a time of great wealth and expansion.

GenTexic: A genetics company funded by many organizations but controlled by the Übel.

Gläubigen: A group of people believed to hold clues to finding Ursprung. The Blauwe Mensen have been confirmed as their descendants.

GlobeX Glowmap: A disc that generates a detailed map of a planet, asteroid, moon, or other orbital location when the user speaks the name of the place he or she wants to see.

Griffin: The sister ship of the *Phoenix*, built as an identical twin. It was given to Rand and Jenn McGregor to use on the quest for Ursprung.

Hatchery: The primary laboratory for GenTexic, where lifetime-enhancing genetics research is carried out.

Hyper Flight: Space-flight navigation at extreme speeds, considered very dangerous for inexperienced pilots.

Jahr des Eises: A small forest planet, discovered and initially settled by the Blauwe Mensen.

Kugel: A sport consisting of hover balls, hover boards, and three teams, with fifteen players per team.

Ledram: A planet covered in molten lava. Occasionally explosions on the surface send chunks of burning earth out of the atmosphere. It has a moon called Cixot.

LibrixCaptex: A scanner created by Archeos that instantly scans the contents of a book.

LuminOrb: A small orb that glows when squeezed.

Magnilox: A tool that uses magnetism to seal and unseal things.

mTalk: Worn on the wrist like a watch, the mTalk has many useful features, including a built-in video call feature, flashlight, and navigation.

Nano-injectors: Small robots designed to look for ailments in the body such as muscle tears or bone fractures.

Ontdekking: The space ship that brought the Blauwe Mensen to Cobalt Gorge.

Orbstrobes: Sensors that survey the exterior of a ship or building to locate access points.

Oxyverter: A small mouthpiece that separates oxygen directly from water.

Para-Orbs: Emergency floatation devices that can be deployed in an atmosphere where the craft is unable to create or gain lift.

Phaser-Beam Enclosures: Specialized cages to restrain prisoners or creatures.

Phoenix: A spaceship donated to the Wikks to facilitate their research.

Portable Atmospheric Transfer Bubble: A unit that functions similarly to the Atmospheric Transfer Chamber but is primarily used in emergency situations and can only be used a few times.

Raven: The fastest shuttle in the Übel fleet, the *Raven* is used primarily by Zebra Xavier and Captain Vedrik. Its armament and propulsion systems are classified to all but Zebra Xavier's elite squadron.

Re Lyt: A planet of deep blue earth, pocketed with millions of lava fissures and pools.

RepFuse: A subsidiary of GenTexic.

Saharvics: A once-nomadic band, these people began to occupy the Valley of Shadows several decades ago. The Federation has not granted them official rights to the territory, as it is considered an archeological site that cannot be owned.

Sand Rover: A vehicle with large tracks capable of maneuvering across sand dunes at high speeds. It is able to carry large loads of cargo and equipment and is preferred over sky scooters for long expeditions and sandy environments.

Shock-Locks: Wrist restraints. They are clear in color when undone, but glow red when they are fastened.

Skull (Übel cruiser): One of the primary craft in the Übel's small fleet.

Sky Scooter: This small craft seats two and has multiple storage compartments. It can hover up to twenty feet above the ground and can reach speeds of one hundred miles per hour.

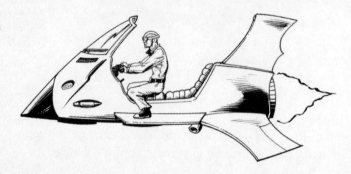

Slimme Degenen (*The Smart Ones*): Crown Prince Voltran's inner circle.

Storm Unit: A room on board a spacecraft designed to quickly deploy soldiers onto the ground.

Tragiws: The planet the Wikks call home.

Turning Leaf: An Archeos transport used by the Wikks prior to the *Phoenix*. It was used on the expedition to the Valley of Shadows.

Übel: A secret order/society composed of renegade forces.

Ultra-Wear: Highly durable, temperature-controlled clothing invented by the Wikk children's grandfather and made of titanium-flex fabric.

Ursprung: A fabled planet believed to be the birthplace of mankind.

Ursprung Verification Keys: Vials containing earth from Ursprung. Their use is currently unknown.

Valley of Shadows: An archeological site believed to have been home to the Gläubigen until they were chased off. The site consists of an immense network of underground tunnels, canals, and chambers and is believed to contain many artifacts and clues. Sections of the valley are currently inhabited by a formerly nomadic group, the Saharvics.

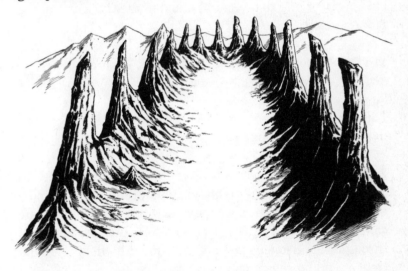

Veritas Nachfolger: A group of people who are guardians of the Truth. They have been seen wearing red cloaks and understand the Übel to be the forces of darkness.

Vortex Progression: Technology used to increase a ship's speed exponentially. It has been successfully used in general takeoff and flight but has yet to have an official successful trial in hyper flight.

Vulture: A Corsair ship used for select missions. The *Vulture* is under the command and supervision of Commander DarkStone. Its large bay allows for storage of captured cargo and ships. It has recently been outfitted to utilize vortex progression technology.

Wartock: Lizards the size of full-grown men, created by RepFuse.

YelNik Eisle: The planet where the *Ark* appears to have been hidden, according to the mural found in the Cathedral of the Star in Enaid.

Yth Orod: The city that the Veritas Nachfolger inhabited while on Evad.

Zapp-It: A small defense device that uses an electric shock to either deter or stun an assailant.

Zapp-Tap: A nano-electron with a unique identifier used to control prisoners. A guard can selectively send a shock to specific prisoners who have been tagged with a Zapp-Tap and are causing a disturbance. The electron sends a debilitating shock through the prisoner's nervous system with effects ranging from a tickling sensation to unconsciousness.

Zazzer Blasters: Multibarrel cannons that can lay down a rapid-fire barrage of stuns.

Zinger: A larger version of the Zapp-It that has the ability to shoot small projectiles at a target. Once connected, the projectiles give off a series of disabling shocks.

Wikk Family Recipe for Baked Apple Almond Oatmeal

Thanks to Ashley Eastman for sharing this recipe with our fans.

Ingredients
2 cups oats
1 cup chopped almonds
½ cup maple syrup
1 teaspoon baking powder
1 teaspoon cinnamon
¼ teaspoon salt
2 ¼ cups milk
1 teaspoon vanilla
1 egg
3 tablespoons coconut oil
1 finely chopped apple

Directions
1. Mix all ingredients in a large mixing bowl.
2. Pour ingredients into a 9x13 glass dish.
3. Bake at 375 degrees Fahrenheit for 35 minutes.
4. Serve warm.

Prayer for God's Help

In The Quest for Truth series, I use other words to name Jesus, God the Father, and the Holy Spirit. My characters come from a different time and different cultures and have different words to refer to God, just like Christians in other cultures today have names for God in their own languages. The Truth/Rescuer is Jesus Christ, Creator is God the Father, and Helper is the Holy Spirit.

The Bible says that God delivers and rescues (Daniel 6:27). He is our helper (Hebrews 13:6). If you've ever felt afraid, why don't you pray for help like Oliver, Tiffany, Mason, and Austin do in *Tangle*?

Dear Father in heaven, I am frightened right now, and I need Your help. Please save me out of this situation, but while I am in it, please be with me and give me Your peace. Amen.

If you have prayed this prayer, please let us know. We want to pray for you too. Contact us at info@BrockEastman.com.

Brock Eastman lives in Colorado with his wife, four kids, two cats, and leopard gecko. Brock is the author of The Quest for Truth series, the Sages of Darkness series, *Showdown with the Shepherd* in the Imagination Station series, and the novella *Wasted Wood*. He writes articles for *FamilyFiction* digital magazine and *Clubhouse* magazine. You may have seen him on the official *Adventures in Odyssey* podcast and on its Social Shout-Out. He was the first producer of the Odyssey Adventure Club. Brock currently works for Compassion International, whose mission is to release kids from poverty worldwide.

Brock enjoys getting letters and artwork from fans. You can keep track of what he is working on and connect with him at

Website: http://brockeastman.wordpress.com
Twitter: @bdeastman
Facebook: http://www.facebook.com/eastmanbrock
YouTube: http://www.youtube.com/user/FictionforAll/videos
Pinterest: http://www.pinterest.com/brockeastman/

MORE FROM BROCK EASTMAN!

BOOK ONE   **THE QUEST FOR TRUTH**

> "Taken is a riveting tale of just how far mankind is willing to go . . . for the ultimate prize."
> —**Wayne Thomas Batson,** Bestselling Author of *The Door Within* Trilogy, *The Berinfell Prophecies*, and *The Dark Sea Annals*

THE QUEST FOR TRUTH series follows the four Wikk kids in their desperate race to find the mysterious planet Ursprung and stop the Übel renegades from misusing its long-lost secrets. Ancient cities, treacherous villains, high-tech gadgets, The Phoenix—encounter all of these and more on this futuristic, interplanetary adventure!

BUY *TAKEN* WHEREVER BOOKS ARE SOLD.

WWW.BROCKEASTMAN.COM   WWW.PRPBOOKS.COM